A Popular History of the Art of Music
From the Earliest Times Until the Present

W. S. B. Mathews

Alpha Editions

This edition published in 2024

ISBN 9789361474781

Design and Setting By

Alpha Editions

www.alphaedis.com

Email - info@alphaedis.com

Contents

PREFACE.

I HAVE here endeavored to provide a readable account of the entire history of the art of music, within the compass of a single small volume, and to treat the luxuriant and many-sided later development with the particularity proportionate to its importance, and the greater interest appertaining to it from its proximity to the times of the reader.

The range of the work can be most easily estimated from the Table of Contents (pages 5-10). It will be seen that I have attempted to cover the same extent of history, in treating of which the standard musical histories of Naumann, Ambros, Fétis and others have employed from three times to ten times as much space. In the nature of the case there will be differences of opinion among competent judges concerning my success in this difficult undertaking. Upon this point I can only plead absolute sincerity of purpose, and a certain familiarity with the ground to be covered, due to having treated it in my lectures in the Chicago Musical College for five years, to the extent of about thirty-five lectures yearly. I have made free use of all the standard histories—those of Fétis, Ambros, Naumann, Brendel, Gevaert, Hawkins, Burney, the writings of Dr. Hugo Riemann, Dr. Ritter, Prof. Fillmore, and the dictionaries of Grove and Mendel, as well as many monographs in all the leading modern languages.

I have divided the entire history into books, placing at the beginning of each book a general chapter defining the central idea and salient features of the step in development therein recounted. The student who will attentively peruse these chapters in succession will have in them a fairly complete account of the entire progress.

W. S. B. MATHEWS.

Chicago, May 5, 1891.

CHRONOLOGY OF THE GREATEST COMPOSERS.

(Copyright.)

EXPLANATION.—The heavy vertical lines are century lines. Light vertical, twenty-year lines. Horizontal lines, the life of the composer.

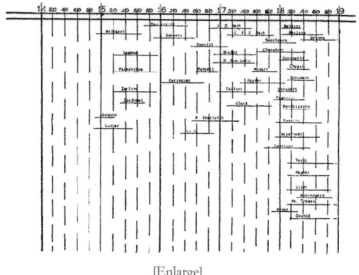

[Enlarge]

CHRONOLOGY OF PRINCIPAL ITALIAN COMPOSERS.

(Copyright.)

From Palestrina to Present Time. (See explanation, page 11.)

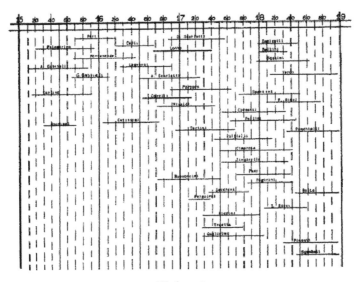

[Enlarge]

CHRONOLOGICAL CHART OF THE MORE IMPORTANT
GERMAN COMPOSERS.

(Copyright.)

From Orlando Lassus to the Present Time. (See page 11.)

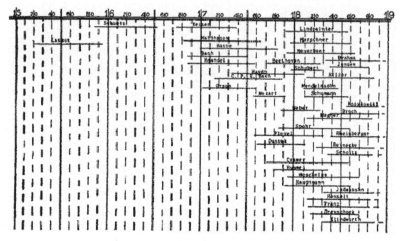

[Enlarge]

CHRONOLOGICAL SUCCESSION OF PIANISTS AND COMPOSERS FOR THE PIANOFORTE.

(Copyright.)

From 1660 to the Present Time (1891).

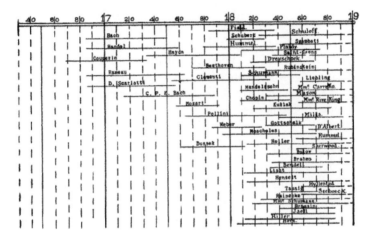

[Enlarge]

INTRODUCTION

I.

THE name "music" contains two ideas, both of them important in our modern use of the term: The general meaning is that of "a pleasing modulation of sounds." In this sense the term is used constantly by poets, novelists and even in conversation—as when we speak of the "music of the forest," the "music of the brook" or the "music of nature." There is also a reminiscence of the etymological derivation of the term, as something derived from the "Muses," the fabled retinue of the Greek god Apollo, who presided over all the higher operations of the mind and imagination. Thus the name "music," when applied to an art, contains a suggestion of an inspiration, a something derived from a special inner light, or from a higher source outside the composer, as all true imagination seems to be to those who exercise it.

2. Music has to do with tones, sounds selected on account of their musical quality and relations. These tones, again, before becoming music in the artistic sense, must be so joined together, set in order, controlled by the human imagination, that they express sentiment. Every manifestation of musical art has in it these two elements: *The fit selection* of tones; and, second, the *use of them for expressing sentiment and feeling.* Hence the practical art of music, like every other fine art, has in it two elements, an *outer,* or technical, where trained intelligence rules, and teaching and study are the principal means of progress; and an *inner,* the imagination and musical feeling, which can indeed be strengthened by judicious experience in hearing, but which when wanting cannot be supplied by the teacher, or the laws of their action reduced to satisfactory statement.

3. There is no fine art which reflects the activity of spirit more perfectly than that of music. There is something in the nature of this form of art which renders it particularly acceptable to quick and sensitive minds. If evidence of this statement were needed beyond the intuitive assent which every musical reader will immediately give, it could easily be furnished in the correspondence between the activity of mind in general and in the art of music in particular, every great period of mental strength having been accompanied by a corresponding term of activity in music. Furthermore, the development of the art of music has kept pace with the deepening of mental activity in general, so that in these later times when the general movement of mind is so much greater than in ancient times, and the

operations of intellect so much more diffused throughout all classes, the art of music has come to a period of unprecedented richness and strength.

II.

4. The earlier forms of music were very simple; the range of tones employed was narrow, and the habits of mind in the people employing them apparently calm and almost inactive. As time passed on more and more tones were added to the musical scales, and more and more complicated relations recognized between them, and the music thereby became more diversified in its tonal effects, and therein better adapted for the expression of a more energetic or more sensitive action of mind and feeling. This has been the general course of the progress, from the earliest times in which there was an art of music until now.

The two-fold progress of an education in tone perception, and an increasing ability to employ elaborate combinations for the expression of feelings too high-strung for the older forms of expression, is observable in almost all stages of musical history, and in our own days has received a striking illustration in the progress made in appreciating the works of the latest of the great musical geniuses, Richard Wagner, whose music twenty-five years ago was regarded by the public generally as unmusical and atrocious; whereas now it is heard with pleasure, and takes hold of the more advanced musical minds with a firmness beyond that of any other musical production. The explanation is to be found in the development of finer tone perceptions—the ability to co-ordinate tonal combinations so distantly related that to the musical ears of a generation ago their relation was not recognized, therefore to those ears they were not music. Wagner felt these strange combinations as music. The deeper relations between tones and chords apparently remote, he felt, and employed them for the expression of his imagination. Other ears now feel them as he did. An education has taken place.

5. It is altogether likely that the education will still go on until many new combinations which to our ears would be meaningless will become a part of the ordinary vernacular of the art. Indeed, a writer quite recently (Julius Klauser, in "The Septonnate") points out a vast amount of musical material already contained within our tonal systems which as yet is entirely unused. The new chords and relations thus suggested are quite in line with the additions made by Wagner to the vocabulary of his day.

III.

6. There are certain conditions which must be met before a fine art will be developed. These it is worth while to consider briefly:

The state of art, in any community or nation, at any period of its history, depends upon a fortunate correspondence between two elements which we might call the internal and the external. By the former is meant the inner movement of mind or spirit, which must be of such depth and force as to leave a surplusage after the material needs of existence have been met. In every community where there is a certain degree of wealth, leisure and a vigorous movement of mind, this surplus force, remaining over after the necessary wheels of common life have been set in motion, will expend itself in some form of art or literature. The nature of the form selected as the expression of this surplus force will depend upon the fashion, the prevalent activity of the life of the day, or, in other words, the environment. Illustrating this principle, reference might be made to the condition of Greek art in the flowering time of its history, when the wealth of Athens was so great as to leave resources unemployed in the material uses of life, and when the intellectual movement was so splendid as to leave it until now a brilliant tradition of history. Only one form of art was pre-eminently successful here; it was sculpture, which at that time reached its fullest development—to such a degree that modern sculpture is only a weak repetition of ancient works in this line. So also the brilliant period of Italian painting, when the mental movement represented by Leonardo da Vinci, Michael Angelo, Lorenzo de Medici, and the pleasure-loving existence, the brilliant fêtes, in which noble men and beautifully appareled women performed all sorts of allegorical representations, and the colors, groupings, etc., afforded the painter an endless variety of material and suggestion. When Rubens flourished in the Netherlands, a century later, similar conditions accompanied his appearance and the prolific manifestations of his genius. In the same way, music depends upon peculiar conditions of its own. They are three: The vigor of the mental movement in general, its strength upon the imaginative and sentimental side, and the suggestion from the environment in the way of musical instruments of adequate tonal powers. Such instruments never existed in the history of the art until about the sixteenth and seventeenth centuries. The organ, the violin and the predecessor of the pianoforte, the spinet, came to practical form at nearly the same time. At the same time the instruments of plucked strings—the guitars, lutes and other instruments which until then had occupied the exclusive attention of musicians—began to go out. Moreover, musical science had been worked out, and the arts of counterpoint, canonic imitation, fugue, harmony, etc., had all reached a high degree of perfection when Bach and Händel appeared.

7. The entire history of music is merely an illustration of these principles. Wherever there has been vigorous movement of mind and material prosperity (and they have always been associated) there has been an art of music, the richness of which, however, has always been limited by the state of the musical ears of the people or generation, and the perfection of their musical instruments. The instruments are an indispensable ingredient in musical progress, since it is only by means of instruments that tonal combinations can be exactly repeated, the voice mastering the more difficult relations of tones only when the ear has become quick to perceive tonal relations, and tenacious to retain them—in other words, educated. Hence in the pages following, the instruments peculiar to each epoch will receive the attention their importance deserves, which is considerably more than that usually allotted them in concise accounts of the history of this art.

8. The conditions of a satisfactory Art Form are three: Unity, the expression of a single ruling idea; variety, the relief of the monotony due to the over-ascendency of unity (or contrast, an exact and definite form of variety); and symmetry, or the due proportion of the different parts of the work as a whole. These principles, universally recognized as governing in the other fine arts, are equally valid in music. As will be seen later, all musical progress has been toward their more complete attainment and their due co-ordination into a single satisfactory whole. Every musical form that has ever been created is an effort to solve this problem; and analysis shows which one of the leading principles has been most considered, and the manner in which it has been carried out. Ancient music was very weak in all respects, and never fully attained the first of these qualities. Modern music has mastered all three to a very respectable degree.

9. The art of music appears to have been earliest of all the fine arts in the order of time; but it has been longer than any of the others in reaching its maturity, most of the master works now current having been created within the last two centuries, and the greater proportion of them within the last century. Sculpture came to its perfection in Greece about 500 B.C.; architecture about 1200 to 1300 A.D., when the great European cathedrals were built; painting about 1500 to 1600 A.D. Poetry, like music, representing the continual life of soul, has never been completed, new works of highest quality remaining possible as long as hearts can feel and minds can conceive; but the productions of Shakespeare, about 1650, are believed to represent a point of perfection not likely to be surpassed. Music, on the other hand, has been continually progressive, at least until the

appearance of Beethoven, about the beginning of the present century, and the romantic composers between 1830 and the present time.

IV.

10. The history of music may be divided into two great periods—*Ancient* and *Modern*—the Christian era forming a dividing line between them. Each of these periods, again, may be subdivided into two other periods, one long, the other quite short—an Apprentice Period, when types of instruments were being found out, melodic or harmonic forms mastered; in other words, the tonal sense undergoing its primary education. The other, a Master Period, when an art of music suddenly blossoms out, complete and satisfactory according to the principles recognized by the musicians of the time. In the natural course of things such an art, having once found its heart, ought to go on to perfection; but this has not generally been the case. After a period of vigorous growth and the production of master works suitable to the time, a decline has ensued, and at length musical productivity has entirely ceased. Occasionally a cessation in art progress of this kind may have been dependent upon the failure of one or other of the primary conditions of successful art mentioned above, especially the failure of material prosperity. This had something to do with the cessation of progress in ancient Egypt, very likely; but more often the stoppage of progress has been due to the exhaustion of the suggestive powers of the musical instruments in use. The composers of the music of ancient Greece had for instruments only lyres of six or eight strings, with little vibrative power. After ten centuries of use every suggestion in the compass of these instruments to furnish, had been carried out. If other and richer instruments could have been introduced, no doubt Greek music would have taken a new lease of life, *i.e.*, supposing that the material prosperity had remained constant.

The apprentice periods of ancient history extend back to the earliest traces of music which we have, beginning perhaps with the early Aryans in central Asia, whom Max Müller represents as circling around the family altar at sunrise and sunset, and with clasped hands repeating in musical tones a hymn, perhaps one of the earliest of those in the Vedas, or a still older one. From this early association of music with religious worship we derive something of our heredity of reverence for the art, a sentiment which in all ages has associated music with religious ritual and worship, and out of which has come much of the tender regard we have for it as the expression of home and love in the higher aspects.

All the leading types of instruments were discovered in the early periods of human history, but the full powers of the best have been reached only in recent times.

11. The art of music was highly esteemed in antiquity, and every great nation had a form of its own. But it was only in three or four countries that an art was developed of such beauty and depth of principle as to have interest for us. The countries where this was done were Egypt, Greece and India.

12. Modern music differs from ancient in two radical points: Tonality, or the dependence of all tones in the series upon a single leading tone called the Key; and Harmony, or the satisfactory use of combined sounds. This part of music was not possible to the ancients, for want of correctly tuned scales, and the selection of the proper tone as key. The only form of combined sounds which they used was the octave, and rarely the fifth or fourth. The idea of using other combined sounds than the octave seems to have been suggested by Aristotle, about 300 B.C. The period from the Christian era until about 1400 A.D. was devoted to apprentice work in this department of art, the central concept wanted being a *principle of unity*. After the beginning of the schools of the Netherlands, about 1400, progress was very rapid. The blossoming time of the modern art of music, however, cannot be considered to have begun before about 1600, when opera was commenced; or 1700, when instrumental music began to receive its full development. Upon the whole, the former of these dates is regarded as the more just, and it will be so used in the present work.

KING DAVID, PLAYING ON THE THREE-STRINGED CRWTH.

[From a manuscript of the eleventh century now in the National Library, Paris.]

Book First.

THE

Music of the Ancient World.

PRIMITIVE TYPES OF INSTRUMENTS, AND AN ARTISTIC MONODY, WITHOUT REAL TONALITY.

CHAPTER I.
MUSIC AMONG THE ANCIENT EGYPTIANS.

BY a curious fortune we are able to form an approximately accurate idea of the musical instruments in use in Egypt as long ago as about 4000 B.C. The earliest advanced civilization of which any coherent traces have come down to us was developed along the Nile, where the equable climate and the periodic inundations of the river raised the pursuit of the husbandman above the uncertainties incident to less favorable climates, while at the same time the mild climate reduced to a minimum the demands upon his productive powers for the supply of the necessaries of life. This interesting people had the curious custom of depositing the mummies of their dead in tombs elaborately hewn out of the rock, or excavated in more yielding ground, in the hills which border the narrow valley of the Nile. Many of these excavations are of very considerable extent, reaching sometimes to the number of twenty rooms, and a linear distance of 600 feet from the entrance. The walls of these underground apartments are generally decorated in outline intaglio if the rock be hard; or in color if the walls be plaster, as is often the case. The subjects of the decorations embrace the entire range of the domestic and public life of the people, among them being many of a musical character. One of the first discoveries of this kind was made toward the close of the preceding century, when Bruce, an English traveler, found in a tomb at Biban-El-Moulouk representations of two magnificently decorated harps played by priests. These have since generally been called "Bruce's Harpers." The instruments have been represented in many ways by different writers, the most curious perversion of the facts being found in Burney's "History of Music," where they have the form of the modern harp.

Harps, pipe, and flute, from an ancient tomb near the Pyramids.

[Enlarge]

Fig. 1.

EXPLANATION OF FIG. 1.—(1) Harper, with harp, bent, of seven cords; over him is inscribed in hieroglyphs sqa em bents (*a*), "player [literally "scraper"] on the harp." (2) Singer, seated; above him, hes t (*b*) "singer." (3, 4) Similar harper and singer, and same inscriptions (*c*, *d*). (5, 6) Singer and player on the direct flute or pipe; before the former, hes (*h*) "singer"; before the latter, mem t (*g*) "pipe." (7, 8) Singer and player on the oblique flute, seba (*e*); before the former, hes (*f*) "singer."

Several large works have been devoted to plates of the pictorial discoveries in these ancient tombs, but not until the colossal work of Lepsius, issued under the auspices of the German government, were we in possession of data for the study of this civilization from the standpoint of a progressive development.

The oldest of the musical representations are found in tombs near Thebes, and already we find the art in an advanced state. The preceding cut shows one of these pictures. A musical group is represented, consisting of eight figures. Their occupations are designated by the hieroglyphics above them. The harper is designated as "harp scraper."

It is not possible to make out in the present state of these drawings the exact number of strings upon the harps, but explorers agree that it must have been either five or seven. From the length of the strings and the structure of the instrument without a "pillar" in front for resisting the pull of the strings, the tones must have been within the register of the male voice. The long flute played by the figure bearing the number 8 must also have produced low tones. It is not plain whether these players are supposed to be all playing at the same time, or whether their ministrations may have taken place separately. Most likely, however, they all played and sang together.

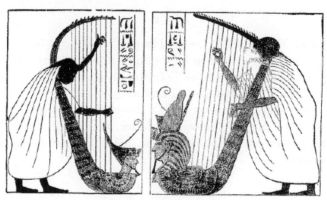

Fig. 2.

BRUCE'S HARPERS.

The most advanced harps found in Egypt were the elegantly colored and ornamented priestly instruments which Bruce found in what was afterward discovered to be the tomb of Rameses III, at Biban-El-Moulouk. The black and white cuts give but a poor idea of the elaborate structure and rich ornamentation of these fine instruments (Fig. 2). The instruments are not playing together; each harper plays before his own particular divinity. They occupy opposite sides in the same hall. The players, by their white robes and positions, evidently belonged to the highest order of the priesthood. The harp upon the right is represented by some writers as having had twenty-one strings; whereas the one upon the left has only eleven. This would be an interesting fact if it were well founded. But, unfortunately, the truth is that the painting was somewhat defaced after Bruce saw it, and it was only within later years that a clever explorer discovered that by passing a wet sponge over it the original lines could be made out. According to Lepsius it has thirteen strings.

In the XXth dynasty, about 1300 B.C., there were harps having twenty-one strings, of which a good example is shown in Fig. 3. This instrument, also, is elaborately colored and ornamented in gold and carving. The strings are shorter than those of Bruce's harpers, and the pitch was most likely within the treble register. The second figure clapping hands is marking time. The one upon the right is playing upon a sort of banjo, of which mention will be made presently.

Fig. 3.

Some time before the period of the Hyksos, the "Shepherd Kings" of the Exodus, there is a scene of a procession of foreigners presenting tribute to one of the sovereigns of Egypt. Among the figures is one playing upon a sort of lyre. Later this instrument became the established instrument of the higher classes, as it was afterward in Greece and Rome. Several complete instruments have been found, which, although dating most likely from a period near the Christian era, are nevertheless sufficiently like the representations of ten centuries earlier to make them instructive as well as interesting. Figs. 4 and 5 are from Fétis. One of these lyres had originally six strings, as is shown by the notches in the cross-piece at the top. They were tuned approximately by making the cord tense and then sliding the loop over its notch. From the clever construction of the resonance cases these instruments should have had a very good quality of tone. In some of the later representations there are lyres of twenty strings.

Fig. 4.

LYRE AT BERLIN.

Fig. 5.

FROM THE LEYDEN MUSEUM.

Fig. 6.

A GROUP OF STREET MUSICIANS.

(1) Woman with tall light harp, of fourteen strings. (2) Cithara. (3) Te-bouni, or banjo. (4) Double flute. (5) Shoulder harp. (6) Singer, clapping hands.

It will be observed that up to this point all the musicians represented are men. In later representations women are more common. Fig. 6 represents the entire musical culture of the later empire, this particular representation belonging apparently to an epoch not more than a few centuries before the Christian era. The harp in this case is of a different construction, and lighter than those in the former examples. It would seem to have been played while the player walked, for we find it in what seems to be moving processions. The lyre occupies here the post of honor next the harp. The banjo and double flute come next, and then a curious instrument of three or four strings, played while carried upon the shoulder. Several of these instruments have been found in a very respectable state of preservation. Their construction is better shown in the illustrations following:

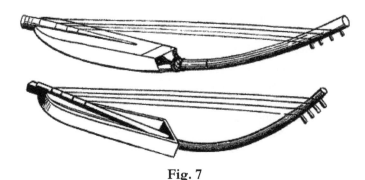

Fig. 7

The tonal relation of these instruments to the larger harps is difficult to conceive. Wilkinson gives the dimensions of the most perfect one in the British Museum as forty-one inches long, the neck occupying twenty-two inches, and the body being four inches wide.

The instrument with the long neck and the short body, seen in Figs. 3 and 6, belongs to the banjo family. Its resonance body consisted of a sort of hoop, or a hollowed out piece of sycamore, the sounding board being a piece of parchment or rawhide. Some of these have two strings, others one; three are occasionally met with. The name of this instrument was te-bouni, and it was of Assyrian origin. It was afterward known as the "monochord," and by its means all the ancients demonstrated the ratios of the octave, fourth and fifth, as we will later see.

We have no knowledge whatever of the tonal sound of the music which so interested these ancient players and singers. There is, however, an ancient poem, called "The Song of the Harper" found in a papyrus dating from about 1500 B.C., which gives an idea of the sentiments the music was intended to convey. Here it is, from Rawlinson's "History of Ancient Egypt," p. 48:

"THE SONG OF THE HARPER."

[From a papyrus of the XVIIIth Dynasty.]

The great one has gone to his rest
Ended his task and his race;
Thus men are aye passing away,
And youths are aye taking their place.
As Ra rises up every morn,
And Tum every evening doth set.
So women conceive and bring forth,
And men without ceasing beget.
Each soul in its turn draweth breath,
Each man born of woman sees death.

Take thy pleasure to-day,
Father! Holy one! See,
Spices and fragrant oils,
Father, we bring to thee.
On thy sister's bosom and arms
Wreaths of lotus we place;
On thy sister, dear to thy heart,
Aye sitting before thy face.
Sing the song, let music be played,

And let cares behind thee be laid.

Take thy pleasure to-day;
Mind thee of joy and delight!
Soon life's pilgrimage ends,
And we pass to silence and night.
Patriarch, perfect and pure,
Neferhotep, blessed one! Thou
Didst finish thy course upon earth,
And art with the blessed ones now.
Men pass to the silent shore,
And their place shall know them no more.

They are as they never had been
Since the sun went forth upon high;
They sit on the banks of the stream
That floweth in stillness by.
Thy soul is among them; thou
Dost drink of the sacred tide,
Having the wish of thy heart,
At peace ever since thou hast died.
Give bread to the man who is poor,
And thy name shall be blest evermore.

All princely households appear to have had their regular staff of musicians, at the head being the "Overest of Musicians," whose tombs still furnish some of the most instructive information upon this part of the ancient life. People of lower social grade had to be content with the temporary services of the street musicians, such as those represented in Fig. 6. They played and sang and danced for weddings and festivities, and undertook the entire contract of mourning for the dead, the measure being the production of a small vial full of tears, under the immediate inspection of the relative of the deceased whose grief might happen to need this official assistance.

For warlike purposes the Egyptians had a short trumpet of bronze, and a long trumpet, not unlike a straight trombone. They had drums of many kinds, but as none of these instruments have reference to the development of the higher art of music, we do not delay to describe them.

One thing which might surprise us in casting an eye over the foregoing representations as a whole is the small progress made considering the immensely long period covered by the glimpses we have of the music of this far-away race. From the days of the harpers in our earliest illustrations to those of the last is more than 2,000 years, in fact considerably longer than from the beginning of the Christian era until now. The explanation is easy to find. In the first place, the incitations upon the side of sense perception were comparatively meager. Neither in sonority nor in delicacy of tonal resource were the Egyptian instruments a tenth part as stimulating as those of to-day. Moreover, we have here to deal with childlike intelligences, slow perceptions, and limited opportunities of comparison. Hence if these were all the discouraging elements there would be but little cause for wonder at the slow progress. But there was another element deeper and more powerful. The Egyptian mind was conservative to reaction. Plato in his "Laws," says: "Long ago the Egyptians appear to have recognized the very principle of which we are now speaking—that their young citizens must be habituated to the forms and strains of virtue. These they fixed, and exhibited the patterns of them in their temples, and no painter or artist is allowed to innovate upon them, or to leave the traditional forms or invent new ones. To this day no alteration is allowed in these arts nor in music at all. And you will find that their works of art are painted or modeled in the same forms that they were 10,000 years ago. This is literally true, and no exaggeration—their ancient paintings and sculptures are not a whit better or worse than those of to-day, but are with just the same skill." This, which Dr. Draper calls the "protective idea," was undoubtedly the cause of their little progress.

In another place Plato gives a very interesting glimpse of the Egyptian method of education, and describes something having in it much the spirit of the modern kindergarten. He says ("Laws," Jowett's translation, p. 815): "In that country systems of calculation have been actually invented for the use of children, which they learn as a pleasure and amusement. They have to distribute apples and garlands, adapting the same number to either a larger or less number of persons; and they distribute to pugilists and wrestlers, or they follow one another, or pair together by lot. Another mode of amusing them is by taking vessels of gold, and brass, and silver, and the like, and mingling them, or distributing them without mingling. As I was saying, they adapt to their amusement the numbers in common use, and in this way make more intelligible to their pupils the arrangements and movements of armies and expeditions, and in the management of a household they make people more useful to themselves, and wide-awake." This, together with the well known expectation of the Egyptians to be judged after death according to the "deeds done in the body," as our sacred writings have it, affords a high idea of their serious and lofty turn of mind, as well as of the great advance they had made toward a true notion of the means of education.

CHAPTER II.
MUSIC AMONG THE HEBREWS AND
ASSYRIANS.

SECOND in point of antiquity, but first in modern association, comes the music of the Hebrews, and of the other allied nations of Assyria and Babylon, from whom they learned a part of their art of music. The place of music in the cult of the Hebrews was very large and important, yet in spite of this fact they never elevated their music into an art, strictly so called. There are no evidences of a progressive development of instruments and a tonal sense among this people. As they were when first we meet them, so they continued until they pass out of the view of history as a nation, when the sacrificial fires went out in the great temple at Jerusalem on the 11th of July, A.D. 70, and the heathen Roman defiled the altars of God. In the beginning Genesis tells us of one Jubal, who was the father of such as handle the harp and the organ (kinnor and ugabh—the little triangular harp of Assyria, and the shepherd's pipe, which here stands for all sorts of wind instruments). In the course of the centuries the harp changed its form somewhat, and perhaps had an increased number of strings; the flute was multiplied into several sub-varieties, and the horn was added. From Egypt they had the timbrel, a tambourine, to which Miriam, the sister of Moses, intoned the sublime canticle, "The horse and his rider hath He thrown into the sea." There were also the sistra, those metallic instruments serving in the temple service the same purpose that the bells serve in the mass at the present day—that, namely, of letting the distant worshipers know when the solemn moment has arrived.

Vast numbers of musicians were employed in the greater temple service, 4,000 being mentioned in I Chronicles xxiii, 5, as praising God with the kinds of instruments appointed by David. According to Josephus, this great number was vastly increased in still later times, the numbers given being 200,000 trumpeters and 40,000 harpers and players upon stringed instruments. Even if we take the figures as greatly exaggerated, they show nevertheless that the art of music had a great place among this people.

The instruments known were few in number, and their type underwent little change from the earliest days. The principal instrument of the older time was the *Kinnor*, or little triangular harp, which we find in the record of the primeval Jubal, and which more than 1,000 years later was played before Saul to defend him from the evil spirit. This also was the instrument most prominent in the temple service, and this again was hung upon the willows of Babylon. The name kinnor is said to have been Phœnician, a fact which points to this as the source of its derivation. It is not easy to see how this could well be, unless we regard the name as having been applied to the invention of Jubal at a later time, for Jubal lived many years anterior to the founding of the great metropolis of the Mediterranean. The kinnor was a small harp having from ten to twenty strings. The usual forms are shown in the accompanying illustration. The strings were fastened upon a metal rod lying along the face of the sounding board. The type of construction is totally unlike that of the Egyptian harps, and its musical powers were apparently considerably inferior. Its form was the following:

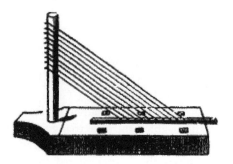

Fig. 8.

Another instrument often mentioned in the English version of the Bible is the psaltery, of which the form is somewhat uncertain, but is thought to have been four-sided. Various ancient representations have been supposed to be this instrument, but none of them satisfactorily, at least not authoritatively. It was probably a variety of harp. The nebel is also said to have been a psaltery, but its etymology points to the Phœnician nabel, a triangular harp like a Greek delta. The forms of the psaltery were four-sided or triangular. It was probably the predecessor of the Arab canon, which again is much the same as the santir. (See Fig. 25.)

There were two kinds of flute, both of them reed pipes, the smaller being merely a shepherd's pipe. They were used for lamentations and for certain festivals, as in Isaiah xxx, 29: "Ye shall have a song as in the night when a holy solemnity is kept; and gladness of heart as when one goeth with a pipe to come into the mountain of the Lord, the Holy One of Israel."

Many of the different names of musical instruments in the common version of the Scriptures are merely blunders of the Septuagint translators, who rendered the word kinnor by about six different terms, where no distinction had been originally intended by the sacred writers.

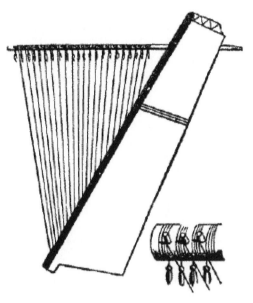

Fig. 9.

Among the Hebrews we find the same progression from men alone as musicians to women almost exclusively, and it is likely that the Hebrews gained the idea from Egypt. Jubal was the discoverer of the harp, according to the tradition in Genesis, and David manifested no loss of manliness while playing before the Lord. Nevertheless when he sang and danced before the ark his wife despised him in her heart. Miriam, the sister of Moses, may well have been a professional musician, one of the singing and dancing women, such as are represented over and over again in the monuments. In the time of Moses, and for some time later, women had no status in the public service; but in the later days of the second temple the women singers are an important element of the display. Ezra and Nehemiah speak of them, and the son of Sirach, in the Apocrypha, recommends the reader to "beware of female singers, that they entice thee not with their charms."

According to the views of many writers, the Hebrews had a larger harp than the small one represented in Fig. 8. It may have been something like one which was found in Egypt, but the form is clearly Assyrian, belonging to the same type as the small harps already given. It certainly is not Egyptian. (See Fig. 9.)

The liturgy of the temple must have been singularly noble and imposing. Never had a church so grand a body of poetry as this of the Hebrews, which they heard in the very sonorous words of David, Moses, Isaiah and Ezekiel, with all the subtle suggestion of a vernacular as employed by minds of the first poetic order. The Hebrew parallelism afforded exactly the kind of formula in which one congregation could most effectively respond to another.

"The earth is the Lord's, and the fullness thereof;
The world and they that dwell therein;
For He hath founded it upon the seas,
And established it upon the floods.
Who shall ascend into the hill of the Lord?
And who shall stand in His holy place?"

When the priests had intoned one line, we may suppose that the whole choir of Levites made answer in the second line, completing the parallelism.

There are other psalms in which the people have a refrain which comes in periodically, as, for instance, in the one: "O give thanks unto the Lord; [refrain] for His mercy endureth forever." (Ps. cxxxvi.)

Fig. 10.

The voice of these masses stood to the Hebrews' mind as the feeble type of the great song which should go up from the entire Israel of God when the scattered members of the cult were gathered in their time of fullness and glory. For us also the same image stands. And while the art of this venerable and singularly gifted people did not attain a place of commanding influence upon the tonal side of music, it nevertheless has borne no small part in affording a vantage ground for later art in the line of noble conceptions, inspiring motives and brilliant suggestions. It has been, and still is, one of the most potent influences in the art-music of the world. Nor is it without interest that the scattered representatives of this race have been and continue to be ministers of art in all the lands into which they have come. The race of Israel has made a proud record in modern music, no less than that of the ancient temple.

II.

The Assyrians held music in honor, and employed it for liturgical purposes, as well as those of social and private life. Among the discoveries at Nineveh and Babylon are many of a musical character. Strong bearded men are playing upon harps which are of a triangular form, but of a different structure to any which we have thus far given. (See Fig. 10.)

The one upon the left is a eunuch. In the following figure we have the banjo-like instrument so constantly seen in the Egyptian representations.

Fig. 11.

There are several instances of some sort of an instrument, apparently consisting of metallic plates or rods, played by means of a hammer. Many have considered these to have been the original type of the modern instruments of percussion, where metal plates are vibrated by means of hammers or mallets. The following is one of this kind.

Fig. 12.

The general appearance of these processions indicates that the Assyrians were in the habit of massing a large number of players upon important occasions. We have no idea what the effect of this music can have been, but upon the tonal side it cannot have had any great resonance or power. Enough if it satisfied the ears of the dignified players and those who employed their services as a part of the pageant of their great festivals.

CHAPTER III.
MUSIC AMONG THE ANCIENT GREEKS.

UPON several accounts the development of the art of music among the ancient Greeks is both important and interesting. Our word "music" is theirs; it carries within its etymology the derivation from the Muses, the nine agreeable divinities who presided over the more becoming and nobler activities of the Greek mind. By music the Greeks meant much more than merely the tonal art itself. Under this term they included pretty much all that they had of a liberal education; grammar, history, rhetoric, mathematics, poetry and song—all were included in this one elastic and comprehensive term. Music itself, the art of tone-sequence, they called harmony.

Our information concerning the general course of the development of music among this people is pretty accurate through a period of about 1300 years. The entire course of the Greek history of music may be divided into four great divisions, each of which was principally devoted to a certain part of the art. These divisions begin at a date which we might take approximately at about 1000 B.C., when the Homeric poems began to be chanted or sung by traveling minstrels called Rhapsodists. The schools of rhapsodies lasted for about 250 years, when choral and patriotic song began to be developed. In connection with this part of the history, there was in the later portion of it a more ornamental and fanciful development of the smaller and social uses of song, represented by Sappho, Anacreon and others. This period endured for about two centuries and a half, and by insensible degrees passed into the Attic drama, which came to its maturity at the hands of Æschylus, Sophocles and Euripides about 450 B.C.

Here was the culmination of Greek musical art upon the purely artistic and æsthetic side. Then followed a period of philosophizing, theory and mathematical deduction, which extended to the end of the Alexandrian schools, about 300 A.D. The limits of the present work do not permit tracing this course of progress with the amplitude which its relation to liberal education would otherwise warrant, or even to the extent which its bearing upon the present ideals of the tonal art would justify, were not the range of subjects indispensable to even a summarized treatment of musical history so wide as it has now become. But the general features of the different steps in the Greek music are the following:

As already noticed, the earliest traces of music are those in the Homeric poems, which are thought to have been composed about 1000 B.C. In these we find the minstrel everywhere a central figure, an honored guest, ready at call to entertain the company with some ballad of the ancient times, or to improvise a new one appropriate to the case in hand. The heroes themselves were not loth to take part in these exercises. Ulysses, the Odyssey tells us, occasionally took the lyre in his own hand and sang a rhapsody of his own adventures. Several centuries later, Solon, one of the famed seven wise men of Greece, composed the rhapsody of "Salamis, or the Lost Island," and sang it in a public assembly of the Athenians with so much effect that an expedition was organized, with Solon at its head, for its recovery, which presently followed triumphantly.

Many passages in the Odyssey will occur to the classical reader in illustration of the position of the minstrel in Argos in the earlier times. For example (Odyssey I, 400, Bryant's translation):

"Silent all
They sat and listened to the illustrious bard
Who sang of the calamitous return
Of the Greek host from Troy, at the command
Of Pallas. From her chamber o'er the hall
The daughter of Icarius, the sage queen
Penelope, had heard the heavenly strain,
And knew its theme. Down by the lofty stairs
She came, but not alone; there followed her
Two maidens. When the glorious lady reached
The threshold of the strong-built hall, where sat
The suitors, holding up a delicate veil
Before her face, and with a gush of tears,
The queen bespake the sacred minstrel thus:
'Phemius, thou knowest many a pleasing theme—
The deeds of gods and heroes, such as bards
Are wont to celebrate. Take, then, thy place,
And sing of one of these, and let the guests
In silence drink the wine; but cease this strain;
It is too sad. It cuts me to the heart,
And wakes a sorrow without bounds—such grief
I bear for him, my lord, of whom I think
Continually; whose glory is abroad
Through Hellas and through Argos, everywhere.'

"And then Telemachus, the prudent, spake—

Why, O my mother! canst thou not endure
That thus the well graced poet should delight
His hearers with a theme to which his mind
Is inly moved? The bards deserve no blame;
Jove is the cause, for he at will inspires
The lay that each must sing.'"

Later than the Homeric rhapsodists, the Hesiodic poems were composed
and sung similarly by wandering minstrels, who, although wandering, were
not on that account lowly esteemed. There were regular schools, or more
properly guilds, of rhapsodists, into which only those were admitted as
masters who were able to treat the current topics with the light and
inspiring touch of real poetry, and only those taken as apprentices who
evinced proper talent and promise. The training of these schools was long,
partly spent in acquiring technique of treating subjects and the mastery of
the lyre, and partly in memorizing the Homeric and Hesiodic hymns. It is
supposed that these poems were transmitted for more than three centuries
orally in this way, before having been reduced to writing.

In Hesiod's poem of "The Shield of Hercules" (Bank's translation, 365), the
general idea of the Greek festive processions is illustrated:

"There men in dances and in festive joys
Held revelry. Some on the smooth-wheeled car
A virgin bride conducted; then burst forth
Aloud the marriage song; and far and wide
Long splendors flash'd from many a quivering torch
Borne in the hands of slaves. Gay blooming girls
Preceded, and the dancers followed blithe:
These, with shrill pipe indenting the soft lip,
Breath'd melody, while broken echoes thrill'd
Around them; to the lyre with flying touch
Those led the love-enkindled dance. A group
Of youths was elsewhere imaged, to the flute
Disporting; some in dances, and in song;
In laughter others. To the minstrel's flute
So pass'd they on; and the whole city seem'd
As fill'd with pomps, with dances, and with feasts."

So again in the same poem (274) there is a scene of a minstrel contest among the immortal gods themselves, described by the poet from one of the scenes upon the shield of Hercules.

"And the tuneful choir appear'd
Of heaven's immortals; in the midst, the son
Of Jove and of Latona sweetly rang
Upon his golden harp; th' Olympian mount,
Dwelling of gods, thrill'd back the broken sound.
And there were seen th' assembly of the gods
Listening; encircled with beatitude;
And in sweet contest with Apollo there
The virgins of Pieria raised the strain
Preluding; and they seemed as though they sang
With clear, sonorous voices."

As early as 750 B.C. we find the famous rhapsodist, Terpander, summoned to Sparta to sing patriotic songs, in the hope of preventing a secession of this rather unruly state. He accomplished his mission, a circumstance creditable alike to the talent of the poet-minstrel and the high estimation in which the class was held.

The application of music to patriotic purposes was no novelty. Plutarch, in his "Life of Lycurgus," says that "Thales was famed for his wisdom and his political abilities; he was withal a lyric poet who, under cover of exercising his art, performed as great things as the most excellent lawgivers. For his odes were so many persuasions to obedience and unanimity, and as by means of numbers they had great grace and power, they softened insensibly the manners of the audience, drew them off from the animosities which then prevailed, and united them in zeal for excellence and virtue." Again, of the subject matter of the Spartan songs, he says: "Their songs had a spirit which could arouse the soul and impel to an enthusiastic action. The language was plain and manly; the subject serious and moral. For they consisted chiefly of praises of heroes who had died for Sparta, or else of expressions of detestation for such wretches as had declined the glorious privilege."

About this time the art of choral song began to be much cultivated in Greece, particularly in connection with the cult of certain divinities, especially Dionysos and Apollo. By the term choral song we are not to understand anything resembling our singing of a chorus in parts. There was no part-singing in Greece, but merely a singing, or rather chanting, of national and patriotic songs in unison, accompanied by the cithara, the national instrument.

Plato speaks of the imitative and semi-dramatic character of the choral dance ("Laws," II, 655): "Choric movements are imitations of manners occurring in various actions, chances, characters—each particular is imitated, and those to whom the words, the song or the dances are suited, either by nature or habit, or both, cannot help feeling pleasure in them and calling them beautiful."

About 500 B.C. a room was rented upon the market place for the practice of the chorus. Every town had its body of singers, who sang and performed the evolutions of the representative dance appropriate to the service of the particular divinity to whom they were devoted. Presently competitive singing came into vogue, in connection with the famous games, and the art of the poet was taxed, as well as the musical and more purely vocal arts of the singers themselves, striving in honorable competition for the glory of their native towns.

In some of the festival occasions the proceedings of the choral songs were varied by the leader, who improvised rhapsodies upon topics connected with the life of the divinity or upon national stories. At proper points the chorus came in with the refrain, which remained a fixed quantity, being put in, apparently, at whatever points the inspiration or breath of the leader needed a point of repose. None of these compositions have come down to us, but the allusions to them in ancient writings give, perhaps, a sufficiently accurate idea of their nature.

The added interest incident to the fresh improvisations of the leader in this form of choral song presently opened toward a lyric drama. Thespis is credited with having been the first to place the leader upon a centrally located stage where he could be plainly seen and heard by all concerned. Now the recitations became more dramatic, the choruses more varied. The speaker illustrated by gestures the acts which he described; he varied his style of delivery according to the feeling appropriate to the incidents represented. The chorus meanwhile was not upon the stage, but in a central location below, and during their strophes they circled around the platform of the leader in a sort of mystic dance, each man accompanying himself upon his cithara. From this to adding a second speaker to the one already upon the stage was but a short step. It was taken, and the result was a drama with a chorus in connection. In the earlier plays the speakers represented as many characters as necessary for carrying out the action. Later they changed costume to some extent, the chorus meanwhile occupying the time with their own songs, which generally had the character of a comment upon the action as developed at the moment. The changes of costume were extremely slight, merely a different head dress, a mantle or some slight modification of appearance more or less symbolical in character. All the dialogue was delivered in a musical voice, and, it is thought, all accompanied by the cithara, which every player carried in his hand. The instrument was sometimes played all the time, in the same notes as those of the song or chant; at other, times the speaker employed it for ritournelles, for affording breathing time or points of emphasis. Once in a great while, it is thought, the instrument had a note different from that of the song in connection with it. Upon this point great uncertainty prevails.

At length, about 470 B.C., Æschylus, the great tragedian, made his début as actor and author, and placed three speakers upon the stage. Besides the three principals, each man had a suite, if his station demanded such an appendage according to the ideas or customs of the times. These, however, had the rank of supernumeraries, merely following the speaker around, but never taking part in the dialogue. The principals each represented more than one character, effecting some slight change of costume for indicating the transformation. The stage was simply an open platform, with three doors in the rear. The actor entering by one door represented a prince at home; from another a prince abroad; by another door he represented a common person. The chorus occupied the central place in front of the stage, much in the same location as the parquet is now. In the center of this space was an altar, originally dedicated to Dionysos, and an offering was probably placed upon it. Later the Choreagos, or leader of the chorus, sat upon it and directed the movements of the singers, much as the operatic director does now. The theaters were very large, being vast amphitheaters, open to the sky, but with an awning available over the more expensive seats. The seats were of stone, arranged exactly like those in a modern circus. The theater in Athens is said to have held 25,000 persons. At first admission was free, the theater being conducted by the state. The plays were mounted very expensively at times, although with the absence of scenery or properties of an elaborate character it is not easy to imagine what was the use made of the vast sums reported to have been expended in different productions. There was a rivalry of leading citizens, each taking upon himself the expense of mounting a new play, and striving to outdo the last before him upon the list.

There were three great dramatic authors whose names have come down to us as the Shakespeares of the Athenian drama. They were Æschylus, Sophocles and Euripides. All were great poets, the first perhaps the greatest. Sophocles was a fine musician and an elegant poet, and for many years he remained the popular idol. All these men wrote not only the words of the plays, but the music as well, every phrase of every character having been noted for musical utterance, and all the choral effects carefully planned. Besides this he composed what was then called the "Orchestic," whence we have our word orchestra. By orchestic they meant an apparatus of mystical dancing or posturing and marching and certain gestures. We do not know precisely what this famous orchestic was, for no example of it has come down to us in intelligible form. But from the descriptions of it by contemporary writers, it seems to have formed the pantomimic complement of the acting, with a certain added grace of art in grouping and posturing, suited to attract and satisfy the eye of a public accustomed to national games, and the beautiful conceptions of Phidias upon the Parthenon frieze. Thus, as will be readily seen, this drama was essentially opera. For reasons to be hereafter detailed, the music is thought to have been of slight tonal value. This is inferred from the compass of the instruments and the general deficiency of the Greeks upon this side, although popular report assigns them a place entirely different. This mystical drama, leaving so much to the imagination, and supplementing its actual representation by the help of chorus and a sort of sanctity derived from music, lasted but a few years. Other causes were at work destined to bring it to a close.

Almost immediately after Euripides, appeared the great comedy writer, Aristophanes, about 420 B.C. This great artist was not simply a dramatist, but also a patriot and a philosopher. In several of his plays he satirizes the classical dramas effectively, parodies their effects, and in general pokes fun at them. He was, however, a well accomplished musician, who might, if he had chosen, have gone on in the steps of his predecessors. But the times were not favorable to this. Previous to the time of Socrates, orators in addressing popular assemblies, lawyers in pleading cases, and all public speakers, appear to have made use of the cithara as a sort of accompaniment, if for no other purpose than to assure themselves of securing a proper pitch of the voice. But Socrates drew attention to verbal distinctions, made words the image of exact concepts, and in general set in operation an era of scientific classification and purely intellectual development, into which music could not enter, especially in a form so poor upon the tonal side as Greek art then was, and always remained. Then came the great orators, of whom Demosthenes was the greatest, who seems to have been the first to speak without musical aids; and Plato, with his philosophy; and after him the great Aristotle, the father of scientific classification and orderly knowledge.

To a disciple of Aristotle, Aristoxenus, we are indebted for the first really musical work which has come down to us. It is true that the so-called Problems of Aristotle contain many of a musical character, showing that this great master observed tonal effects in a purely musical spirit, but he did not make a scientific treatise upon the art. In his Politics he has much admirable matter relating to music, and its influence upon the feelings and its office in life has hardly been better explained than by him. But music upon the practical side remained a sealed book.

Among the lucid musical questions of Aristotle's Problems (which, if not by Aristotle himself, are at least the product of his time or the succeeding century) he refers to the phenomena of sympathetic resonance; he asks further, why it is that when *mese* (the keynote of the lyre) is out of tune everything is out of tune; yet when any other string is out of tune it affects only the particular string which is not correctly adjusted. One of his most instructive, but also, as it turned out, most misleading questions was why they did not magadize (sing in) fourths and fifths as well as in octaves, since the consonances of the fourth and the fifth are almost as well sounding as those of the octave. This question appears to have led to the practice of what Hucbald called "diaphony." This question, it may be remarked incidentally, is conclusive that they did *not* use the third as a consonance in Aristotle's time, nor sing together in fourths, fifths, or any other intervals than the octave.

In spite of the talk about music by the Greek writers, musical theory, in an exact form, occupies but a small place in the volume of their works. The earliest theorist of whom we have any account was Pythagoras, who lived about 580 B.C. He was one of the first of the Greek wise men to avail himself of the opening of Egypt to foreigners, which took place by Psammeticus I in the year 600 B.C. Pythagoras lived there twenty years in connection with one of the temples, where he seems to have gained the confidence of the priesthood and learned much of his philosophy and so-called musical science. He defined the mathematical relation of the octave as produced by half of a given string, the fifth produced by two-thirds and the fourth by three-fourths. He also found the ratio of the major step by subtracting the fourth from the fifth. This was the ratio 9:8. With this as a measure he attempted to place the tones of the tetrachord, or Greek scale of four tones, which was the unit of their tonal system. This gave him two major steps, and a half step somewhat too small, being equal to the ratio of 256:243.

The most important part of Pythagoras' influence upon the art of music was of a sentimental character. From Egypt he acquired many ideas of a musical nature, such as that certain tones represented the planets, and that time was the essence of all things. It was one of the laws of his religion that before retiring at night his disciples should sing a hymn in order to compose their spirits and prepare them for rest. The verses selected for this use were probably of a devotional character, like what are now known as the Orphic hymns, of which the lines upon the next page may be taken as a specimen. Ambros well remarks that such hymns could only have been sung appropriately to melodies of a choral-like character.

"Thou ruler of the sea, the sky, and vast abyss,

Thou who shatterest the heavens with Thy thunder peals;
Thou before whom spirits fall in awe, and gods do tremble;
Thou to whom fates belong, so wise, so unrelenting Thou;
Draw near and shine in us."

Various musicians and theorists later are credited with having made additions to the musical resources of the Greeks, and it was a proverb, said of any smart man, that he "added a new string to the lyre." This was said of Terpander especially; but it is pretty certain that the lyre had six or seven strings some time before Terpander, and that the form of expression was purely symbolical, as if they had said of him "he set the river on fire." The first real contributions to musical science after the Problems of Aristotle, already cited, are the two works of his pupil Aristoxenus—one on harmony, the other on rhythm. These give a full account of the Greek musical systems, and are the source of the greater part of our information upon the subject. From them it appears that the basis of their scale was the tetrachord of four tones, placed at an interval of two steps and a half step. The outside tones of the tetrachord remained fixed upon the lyre, but the two middle ones were varied for the purpose of modulation. The Dorian tetrachord corresponded to our succession mi, fa, sol, la; the Phrygian re, mi, fa, sol; the Lydian from do. Besides these modes, the Greeks had what they called genera, of which there were three—the diatonic, to which the examples already given belong; the chromatic, in which the tetrachord had the form of mi, fa, fi, la, the interval between the two upper tones being equal to a step and a half; and the enharmonic, in which the first two intervals were one-quarter of a step and the upper one a major third. We are entirely ignorant of the practical use made of these different forms of scale. Whether the quarter tones were used habitually, or were glided like appoggiaturas, or passing tones, has been vigorously maintained on both sides by different writers. The evidence seems to point to the enharmonic as having been the most ancient, and the chromatic and diatonic gradually superseding it. In Plato, Aristotle and many of the Greek writers, especially in Athenæus, much is said about the characteristic expression of the different modes, but as they are mutually contradictory, one saying of a given mode that it is bold and manly, while another calls it feeble and enervating, we may leave this for the antiquarians to settle for themselves.

After Aristotle, there were several Greek theorists who devoted themselves to mathematical computations, the favorite problem seeming to be to find as many ways as possible of dividing the major fourth, or the ratio 4:3, into what they called super-particular ratios—that is to say, a series of fractions in which each numerator differed from the denominator by unity. They had observed that all the ratios discovered by Pythagoras had this character,

1/2, 2/3, 3/4, 8/9, and they attributed magical properties to the fact, and sought to demonstrate the entire theory of music by the production of similar combinations. The latest writer of the Greek school was Claudius Ptolemy, who lived at Alexandria about 150 A.D. In his work upon harmony he gives a very large number of tables of fractions of this kind— his own and those of all previous Greek theorists, and it is to his book that we principally owe all the exact knowledge of Greek musical theory which we possess. Among other computations, Ptolemy gives the precise formula of the first four notes of the scale as we now have it, but as this occurred only as one among many of a similar character, and is in no way distinguished from any of the others by any adjective implying greater confidence in it, we can only count it as a lucky accident. The eminence that has been awarded to Ptolemy as the original discoverer of the correct ratio of the major scale, therefore, does not properly belong to him.

This will more clearly appear from the entire table of the various determinations of the diatonic mode made by Ptolemy, taken from his work. (Edition by John Wallis, Oxford, 1682, pp. 88 and 172.) He gives no less than five of his own forms of diatonic genus, as follows: (The fractions give vibration ratios.)

Soft diatonic, $8/7 \times 10/9 \times 21/20 = 4/3$.
Medium diatonic, $9/8 \times 8/7 \times 28/27 = 4/3$.
Intense diatonic, $10/9 \times 9/8 \times 16/15 = 4/3$.
Equable diatonic, $10/9 \times 11/10 \times 12/11 = 4/3$.
Diatonic diatonic, $9/8 \times 9/8 \times 256/243 = 4/3$.

Among these there is no one that is correct or rational. The proper ratios are given in the diatonic intense, but the large and small steps stand in the wrong order. It is in Ptolemy's record of the determinations of Didymus (born at Alexandria, 63 B.C.) that the true tuning of the first four tones of the scale occurs. This is it:

Diatonic (Didymus), $9/8 \times 10/9 \times 16/15 = 4/3$.

Thus it appears that it was Didymus, and not Ptolemy, who proposed the tuning of the tetrachord which is now accepted as correct. It is very evident from the entire course of the discussion as conducted by Ptolemy that his calculations were purely abstract. He is to be reckoned among the Pythagoreans, who held that in time and number all things consist. It was not until some centuries later that the happy thought of Didymus came to recognition as the true statement of the mathematical relation of the first four tones of the scale, and then only through the ears of a race of musicians following the great thesis of Aristoxenos, that in music it is always the ear which must be the arbiter, and not abstract reasoning or calculation. The ratios of the major and minor third also occur among the calculations of Didymus; but here, again, they count for nothing in the history of art, because these intervals derive their value and expressive quality from their harmonic relation, while Didymus and all the Greeks employed them as melodic skips only, and reckoned them in with a multitude of other skips and progressions, without distinguishing them in any way.

The one characteristic instrument of Greek music from the earliest to the latest days was the lyre. In the oldest times, those of Homer and Hesiod, it was called phorminx, which is believed to have been the form so often represented on Greek vases of a turtle shell with side pieces like horns, an instrument having but little effective resonance. The later form was the so-called cithara, the most common shape of which is that made familiar to all by the pedal piece of the square pianoforte. This instrument rarely had more than six strings, and as it had no finger board it could have had no more notes than strings. Chappell, the English historian, attempts to demonstrate that certain ones of these instruments had a bridge dividing the string into two parts, thus largely increasing the compass, but the evidence supporting this hypothesis is not satisfactory. Plato speaks of instruments of many strings imported from Asia, which seem to have been the fashion or fad in his day. He disapproved of them very heartily, but the terms in which he speaks of them show that he cannot have been very familiar with their appearance, for it is impossible to make out what he is driving at.

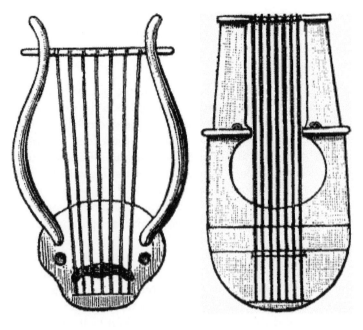

| Fig. 13. | Fig. 14. |
| LYRE. | CITHARA. |

There is considerable doubt as to the extent to which the larger instruments of Asiatic origin penetrated the general musical practice of Greece. Athenæus, in his "Banquets of the Learned" (B. xvi, C), quotes Anakreon as saying:

"I hold my magadis, and sing,
Striking loud the twentieth string,
Leucaspis at the rapid hour
Leads you to youth and beauty's bower."

Most certainly the lyre of Terpander had no twenty strings.

The so-called Greek flute was a very reedy oboe or clarinet, a pipe played with a reed, the pitch determined by holes stopped by the fingers. These instruments were so hard to blow that the players wore bands over their cheeks because there were cases on record where, in the contests, they broke their cheeks by the wind pressure. The flute or aulos does not seem to have been used in connection with the cithara at all, and the Greeks had nothing corresponding to what we call an orchestra. The aulos was appropriate to certain religious services and to certain festivals, and it had a moderate status in the various contests of the national games, but the great instrument of Greek music, the universal dependence for all occasions, public and private, was the lyre.

In spite of the meager resources of Greek music upon its tonal side, this development of art has had a very important bearing upon the progress of music, even down to our own times. Opera was re-discovered about 1600 in the effort to re-create the Greek musical drama, and the ideal proposed to himself by Richard Wagner was nothing else than that of a new music drama in which the severe and lofty conceptions of the old Greek poets should be embodied in musical forms the most advanced that the modern mind has been able to conceive. Upon the æsthetic side musical theory is entirely indebted to the Greek. Nothing more suitable or appropriate can be said concerning musical taste and cultivation than what was said by Aristotle 300 years before Christ. For example, he has the following (Politics, viii, C. Jowett's translation, p. 245): "The customary branches of education are in number four. They are: (1) reading and writing, (2) gymnastic exercises, (3) music, to which is somewhat added (4) drawing. Of these, reading, writing and drawing are regarded as useful to the purposes of life in a variety of ways." He recommends the study of music as part of the preparation of the fit occupation of leisure. "There remains, then, the use of music for the intellectual enjoyment of leisure; which appears to have been the reason of its introduction, this being one of the ways in which it is thought that a freeman should pass his leisure; as Homer says:

'How good it is to invite men to the pleasant feast,'

and afterward he speaks of others whom he describes as inviting

'The bard who would delight them all' (Od. xvii, 385);

and in another place he says that there is no better way of passing life than when

'Men's hearts are merry, and the banqueters in the hall
Sitting in order hear the voice of the minstrel.'"

Plato is particular that only the noble harmonies shall be permitted in his state. He says, "Of the harmonies I want to have one warlike, which will sound the word or note which a brave man utters in the hour of danger or stern resolve, or when his cause is failing and he is going to wounds or death, or is overtaken by some other evil, and in every such crisis meets fortune with calmness and endurance; and another which may be used by him in times of peace and freedom of action, when there is no pressure of necessity—expressive of entreaty or persuasion or prayer to God, or of instruction to man, or again willingness to listen to persuasion or entreaty or advice. These two harmonies I ask you to leave; the strain of necessity and the strain of freedom, the strain of the unfortunate and the strain of the fortunate, the strain of courage and the strain of temperance; these, I say, leave." These he explains will be only the Dorian and the Phrygian harmonies. In another place Plato shows himself a disciple of the Egyptian ideas of conservatism, already mentioned. "And therefore when one of these clever and multiform gentlemen who can imitate anything comes to our state, and proposes to exhibit himself and his poetry, we will fall down and worship him as a sweet and holy and wonderful being; but we must also inform him that there is no place for such as he is in our state—the law will not allow him. And so when we have anointed him with myrrh and set a garland of wool upon his head, we shall send him away to another city." (Republic, Jowett, iii, 398.)

In fact, upon the subject of music, Plato is one of the least satisfactory of writers. He has many noble sentiments which might well be printed in letters of gold and hung upon the walls of educational institutions to-day, as ("Laws," Jowett's translation, 668): "Those who seek for the best kind of song and music, ought not to seek for that which is pleasant, but for that which is true." In another place, however, he speaks of music as a kind of imitation. He says that music without words is very difficult to understand. ("Laws," *ibid.*, 668.) All these inconsistencies disappear, however, as soon as we recognize the limitations of the music which Plato knew, upon its tonal side. All the richness of sense incitation, and all the definiteness of expression which come into our modern music through the magic of "tones in key," were wholly outside the range of Plato's knowledge.

The musical notation of the Greeks consisted of letters of the alphabet placed over the syllables to which the tones indicated were to be sung. The letters represented absolute pitch, and as, owing to the variety of genera, modes and chroa, the total number of tones was very large, parts of older forms of the alphabet were also employed, the whole number of characters thus demanded being upwards of seventy. There was little or no classification of tones, and the entire twenty-four letters were applied in regular order to the diatonic series of the Dorian mode. Tones in the chromatic or enharmonic modes were named by other letters, and the system was extremely complicated. The notes of the instrumental accompaniment were still different from those of the vocal part. No genuine example of this music has come down to us in reliable form, and curiously enough, no classical writer gives any idea of the notation of music. All that we know of this notation we derive from Alypius, who lived about 150 A.D. Athanasius Kircher, a Jesuit of a monastery in Sicily, published in the last century the text of what purported to be a fragment of the first Pythic Ode of Pindar. (See <u>page 69</u>.) In the original the musical characters stood in immediate proximity to the words of the text. At the middle of the third line begins the chorus of Citharodists. As all the musical characters of the Greeks indicated absolute pitch, the student will discover the difference between the vocal and instrumental notation by comparing the notes in the early part of the ode with those of the same pitches noted for instruments later.

Three other pieces of similar apocryphal character have come down to us. It is likely that these melodies, if not really genuine, as related to the composition of Pindar, nevertheless belong to a period a little anterior to the Christian era.

FRAGMENT OF THE FIRST PYTHIC ODE OF PINDAR,

According to the musical notation given by Athanasius Kircher, (F.A. Gevaert's *"La Musique dans l'Antiquité."*)

[Listen]

¹ KIRCHER, *Musurgia universalis*, I, p. 541.

² Le savant jésuite, ne connaissant que les notes du ton lydien, aura probablement changé ⊃ (si♭₂) en ∪ (si♭₂), signe inusité dans le trope phrygien.

[Transliteration of Greek lyrics]

NOTE.—The amateur unfamiliar with the C clef, will obtain the true tonal effect of the above fragment from Pindar, by considering the clef to be G, and the signature five flats. This will transpose the piece one degree lower than above written, but the melody will be preserved. In other words, read it exactly like the treble part of any piano piece, only considering the signature to be five flats.

CHAPTER IV.
MUSIC IN INDIA, CHINA AND JAPAN.
I.

VERY important developments of the art of music took place in India from a remote period, but dates are entirely uncertain. When the hymns of the Rig-Veda were collected into their present form, which appears to have been about 1500 B.C., music was highly esteemed. It was in India that the art of inciting vibrations of a string by means of a bow was discovered; and our violin had its origin there, but the date is entirely unknown. The primitive violin was the ravanastron, which the Ceylonese claim to have been invented by one of their kings, who reigned about 5000 B.C. The form of this instrument is given in Fig. 16. It must have been some time before the Mohammedan invasion, for they brought a rude violin back to Arabia, from whence it came into Europe after the crusades. They had many forms of guitar, instruments of percussion, and the varieties of viol, as well as trumpets and the like. The national instrument was the vina. This was a sort of guitar, its body made of a strip of bamboo about eight inches wide and four feet long. Near each end a large gourd was fixed, for reinforcing the resonance. In playing, it was held obliquely in front of the player, like a guitar, one gourd resting upon the left shoulder, the other under the right arm. It was strung with six strings of silk and wire, and had a very elaborate apparatus of frets, much higher than those of a guitar, many of them movable, in order to permit modulation into any of the twenty-four Hindoo "modes." The instrument had a light, thin tone, not unpleasing. A fine specimen is figured in "Hipkins' Plates of Rare Instruments" in the South Kensington Museum, a copy of which may be seen in the Newberry Library.

Fig. 15.

JIWAN CHAH.

[Portrait of Jiwan Chah, one of the latest masters of the vina. He died about 1790.]

The Hindoos carried the theory of music to an extremely fine point, having many curious scales, some of them with twenty-four divisions in an octave. Twenty-two was the usual number. The pitch of each note in every mode was accurately calculated mathematically, and the frets of the vina located thereby, according to very old theoretical works by one Soma, written in Sanskrit at least as early as 1500 B.C. When this work first became known to Europeans, its elaboration led it to be regarded as a purely theoretical fancy piece, and it was thought to be impossible that practical musicians could have been governed by theories apparently so fine-drawn. A study of the structure of the vina, however, perfectly adapted to these theories, set all doubts at rest. None of the intervals of the Hindoo scale exactly correspond to our own. Harmony they never conceived. Well sounding chords are impossible in their scales. All their music was monodic—one-voiced.

Fig. 16.

There was a curious development of the musical drama in India about 300 B.C., having certain of the traits of modern opera. Several of these ancient pieces have come down to us, but without the musical notes. They are long, consisting of as many as eleven acts, part of them sung, part spoken. Curiously enough, the different acts are not all in the same dialect. The musical acts are in Sanskrit, which had then ceased to be a spoken language for at least 500 years; the spoken acts were in Pakrit, a dialect of Sanskrit, which likewise had ceased to be spoken for several centuries. A fuller account of the Hindoo drama is given in Wilson's "Theater of the Hindoos." The curious circumstance of the drama of the Hindoos of this epoch is that it was contemporaneous with another very celebrated development of musical drama in Greece.

Besides the primitive form of the bowed instrument, the ravanastron (Fig. 16), many forms more advanced are figured among the instruments from India in European museums, but as they are all of absurd and impossible acoustical conception, besides being most likely of comparatively modern origin, we do not present them at this point. Later, in the history of the violin, one or two of the most curious will be given.

II.

China has had an art of music from extremely remote periods, and singularly sagacious ideas concerning the art were advanced there very long ago, at a time when Europe and most other parts of the world were still in the darkness of barbarism. For example: There is a saying of the Emperor Tschun, about 2300 B.C., "Teach the children of the great; thereby reached through thy care they will become mild and reasonable, and the unmanageable ones able to receive dignities without arrogance or assumption. This teaching must thou embody in poems, and sing them therewith to suitable melodies and with the play of instrumental accompaniment. The music must follow the sense of the words; if they are simple and natural then also must the music be easy, unforced and without pretension. Music is the expression of soul-feeling. If now the soul of the musician be virtuous, so also will his music become noble and full of virtuous expression, and will set the souls of men in union with those of the spirits in heaven." (Quoted by Ambros.)

Fig. 17.

The principal instruments of Chinese music are the Kin and the Ke. The former is a sort of guitar, of which no illustration has come to hand. The main instrument of their culture-music is the ke, a stringed instrument entirely unlike any other of which we have accounts, saving the Japanese ko-ko, which was most likely derived from it. The ke is strung with fifty strings of silk. Originally it had but twenty-five, but in the reign of Hoang-Ti, about 2637 B.C., it is said to have been enlarged to its present dimensions and compass. The appearance of the ke and the arrangement of its bridges are shown in Fig. 17. The strings were plucked with the fingers.

In the earlier times the Chinese had the pentatonic scale, approximately the same as that of the black keys of the piano. Later it was enlarged to seven notes in the octave, and it is claimed by some that long before the Christian era they had a complete chromatic scale of twelve tones in the octave. The evidence upon this point, however, is insufficient. And even if they had this musical resource at so early a period the fact counts very little to their credit, since at best the chromatic scale is only an impure harmonic compromise, which they have never learned to use understandingly. Chinese music has always been monodic, and they use a great variety of melodic shadings composed of intervals of small fractions of a step. These they call lu. There are movable bridges which can be placed in such way as to divide the strings of the ke at proper proportions of its length for producing the lu. The places for the fingers upon the finger board are marked by small brass points. Besides the intonations due to stopping the strings, the players upon the ke are in the habit of adding expression in a manner analogous to that of the *tremolo* of the modern violinist. With the left hand he touches the string beyond the bridge and pulls it slightly, thus imparting to the tone a sliding intonation upward or downward, familiar to all who have experimented with strings. This habit the Japanese still have in playing their ko-ko, and the results are said to be not unpleasing. The volume of tone in the ke is very light, but the quality is sweet.

As a natural consequence of the long existence of this nation and their commercial relations to the other parts of the world, which with all their care they have never been able wholly to avoid, the Chinese have many other varieties of instruments, including many trumpets; an unexampled wealth of instruments of percussion, and a few of the ruder types of the violin kind, which seem to have come in from India or Thibet by the way of the Buddhist monks. The ravanastron is a common instrument with the mendicant friars of this order. The characteristic instrument of the Chinese, however, the one which stands as the representative of all their higher musical culture, is the ke.

In common with all other nations of antiquity, and with some of the present day, the Chinese have always held strong conservative opinions. The principle has been held among them from the earliest times that the pattern of a good thing, whether a religion, an art or a mechanism, having once been found satisfactory, should be made official and never afterward changed. This principle, taken in connection with the limited powers of their chief instrument, accounts for the small progress they have made in music within the past 2000 years. It must be remembered, however, that our knowledge of the music of this country is still far from perfect, the travelers and missionaries from whom it has reached us not having been practical musicians, nor having had sufficiently long opportunities for mastering musical systems so different from what they had previously known, and so contrary to all their inherited percepts of tone.

Fig. 18.

The Japanese are a very musical people in their way. The chief instrument of their culture is the ko-ko. (See Fig. 18.)

In structure it much resembles the Chinese ke. They have also many other instruments, especially various kinds of imperfect guitars, a few rude violins, and the usual outfit of trumpets, reed pipes and instruments of percussion. Like all the other barbarous nations, they have never had harmony until since they began to learn it from the Europeans.

Book Second.

THE

Apprentice Period of Modern Music.

THE DEVELOPMENT OF HARMONY, TONALITY, CANONIC IMITATION AND POLYPHONY.

THE GENERAL POPULARIZATION
OF THE ART OF MUSIC IN
EVERY DIRECTION.

CHAPTER V.
THE NATURE OF THE TRANSFORMATION,
AND
THE AGENCIES EFFECTING IT.

ACCORDING to the division of the subject in the beginning of this work, the period from the Christian era to that of Palestrina, A.D. 1600, is one of apprentice work, in which the details of art were being mastered, but in which no music, according to our acceptation of the term, was produced. The history of this period is somewhat obscure, the writers who throw light on it averaging scarcely more than one to a century, scattered about in different parts of Europe. Nevertheless, the most important changes in the history of music took place during this period. The monody and empyrical tonality of the ancients gave place to polyphony and harmonized melodies resting upon the relations of tones in key. New instruments came in, and the entire practice of the art of music was deepened, ennobled and immeasurably enlarged in every direction. There were four causes co-operating in this transformation of the art, and it is not easy to say of any one of them that this one was the chief. First of these, in the Roman empire, or in the south of Europe more particularly, for about 800 years the Greek principles remained more or less in force. The Church is here the foremost influence, and its part in the transformation already noted will be considered presently. In the north of Europe the Goths, Celts and Scandinavians built mighty empires and impressed their enthusiastic and idealistic natures upon the whole form of modern art. The Saracens conquered a foot-hold in the south of France about 819, and remained there for twenty years. Their influence was very important in the development of music, and became still more active after the crusades, where the armies of the west came again in contact with this peculiar civilization. Besides these three sources measurably unprofessional and outside of music, or amateur, as we say now, there was the work of the professional musicians strictly so-called, who, from about 1100 in the old French school, commenced the development of what is now known as polyphony, which culminated in the hands of the Netherlanders, about 1580, Palestrina himself being one of the latest products of this school. These influences reacted upon each other, and all have entered into modern art, and have imparted to it their most essential elements.

All modern music differs from the ancient in two important particulars—*Harmony and Tonality.* Harmony is the use of combined sounds. These may be either dissonant, inharmonious in relation to each other, or harmonious, agreeable. All points of repose in a harmonized piece of music must be consonant; or, to say it differently, the combined sound (chord) standing at the beginning or end of a musical phrase must be harmonious. All the elements in it must bear consonant relations to all the others. Between the points of repose the combined sounds may or may not be consonant. Under certain conditions dissonances make an effect even better than consonance—better because more appealing. The law of the introduction of dissonances is that every dissonance must arise out of a consonance, and subside into a consonance. When this law is observed there is hardly any combination possible in the range of music which may not be employed with good effect. Here already we have a progress in perception of tones, in the ability to discriminate between those which harmonize and those which dissonate. All consonance and dissonance are purely relative. There is no such thing as a dissonant tone in music, by itself considered; a tone becomes dissonant by being brought into juxtaposition with some other tone with which it does not agree. This part of the development of a tonal sense had its beginnings in Greece, but only reached the point where the most elementary relations were regarded as agreeable. The octave, the fourth and the fifth, were the only consonances which they knew, and of these they used in the combined sounds of their music only the octave. The third, which with us is the most agreeable part of a pure harmony, because it adds so many elements of agreement to the combined sound into which it enters, was not only regarded as a dissonance by them, but actually *was* a dissonance as they tuned their scale.

The entire course of harmonic perception in modern music may be roughly divided into three steps: First, the recognition of consonance, especially of the most fruitful consonance of all—that of the thirds, and the differentiation between consonance and dissonance. A second step involved the recognition of dissonance as an element in musical expression, on account of the motion it imparts to a harmonic movement. Third, the establishment of these materials of music in the mind in such depth and fullness that their æsthetic implications became realized as elements of expression, so that when a composer had a certain feeling to express, the proper combination of consonance and dissonance immediately presented itself to his mind. The first of these steps was taken by the minstrels of the north, somewhere between the Christian era and the tenth century. The second was the particular work of the old French school, the Netherlanders, and of all who composed music between about 1100 A.D. and the epoch of Palestrina, about 1600. The third, the spontaneous application of musical material to the expression of feeling, had in it another element, that of tonality, concerning which it is proper to say something at this point.

By "tonality" is meant the dependence or interdependence of all the tones in a key upon some one principal tone called the Key-tone. The tonality of the music of the ancients was wholly artificial and unreal. A mode and a point of repose for the melody were chosen arbitrarily; the beginning was here made, and still more the ending was conducted to this point of repose. Between the beginning and the ending the same tones were employed, whether the melody proposed to repose upon re, upon fa or do. The usual points of repose in Greek music were mi, fa and re; never upon do, the real key tone, and rarely upon la, the natural tonic of the minor mode.

One of the chief elements of modern musical expression, particularly in the expression of melody, is the unconscious perception of the "relation of tones in key." With every tone sung the singer conceives not only that tone, its predecessor and its follower, but all other tones in the entire course of the melody; and the expression of every tone in the series rests upon its place in rhythm, and still more upon its "place in key." Change a single tone in a melody, as, for instance, to make fa a half step sharp, and the expression of the entire melody is thereby changed, until such time as the hearer has forgotten the change of key effected by the introduction of the foreign tone. It is not at all unlikely that what little of melodic expression the music of the Greeks had, may have rested to some extent upon an unconscious perception of these relations, which, although foreign to their musical theory, may nevertheless have made their way into the ears of these acute minstrels. The discovery of simple tonality seems to have been due to the northern minstrels, for it is here that we find the earliest melodies purely tonalized. But the natural bounds of a melodic tonality as established by these northern harpers have been very much exceeded in modern times, so that now there is hardly a chord possible which might not be introduced in the course of a composition in any key whatever, without effecting a digression into the new key suggested by the strange chord. Not only all the natural or diatonic notes are regarded as belonging to a key, but also all the chromatics, the sharps and flats, and the double sharps and double flats.

All this implies a growth of tonal perception on the part of the hearers, and especially of the ability to co-ordinate tonal impressions over a wide and constantly increasing range. For the hearer has in mind not only the particular tone which at the moment occupies his ear, and the others which preceded it, and a sort of inner feeling of the tone which will follow the present one, but also all the other tones over which the singer would pass in going from one tone to another. And unless he has this he cannot realize the true place of the melody tone in key, and therefore rests unconscious of its real expression. It is, indeed, possible for him to make a mistake in regard to the tones which he unconsciously associates with the tones actually heard—as, for example, when one hears an E followed by a C higher, and one thinks of the four white keys of the piano between them, while the melody may be thinking of the black keys between them. In the one case the melody would be in the key of C, in the other of C sharp minor. And the expression of the melodic skip would be enormously changed thereby. This larger education of the faculties of tonal perception and tonal co-ordination has been the work mainly of the last century and a half, and more particularly of the present century itself. During this period the progress has been more rapid than within any other in the entire course of the history of our art, and it is to the successive steps preparing for this that we now address ourselves.

CHAPTER VI.
THE MINSTRELS OF THE NORTH.

UPON many accounts the development of minstrelsy by the Celtic singers and harpers was one of the most important of all the forces operative in the transformation of the art from the monody of the ancients to the expressive melody and rich harmony of modern music. As it is to a considerable extent one side of the direct course of this history, which hitherto has dealt largely with the south of Europe, the present is the most convenient time for giving it the consideration its importance deserves. I do this more readily because English influence upon the development of music has generally been underrated by continental writers, the erudite Fétis alone excepted; while their own national writers, even, have not shown themselves generally conscious of the splendid record which was made by their fathers.

The Celts appear upon the field of history several centuries before the Christian era. Cæsar's account of them leaves no doubt of the place which music held in their religion, education and national life. The minstrel was a prominent figure, ready at a moment's notice to perform the service of religion, patriotism or entertainment. There is a tradition of one King Blegywied ap Scifyllt, who reigned in Brittany about 160 B.C., who was a good musician and a player upon the harp. While we have no precise knowledge of the music they sang in the oldest times, it was very likely something like the following old Breton air, which is supposed to have come down from the Druids. It is full of a rude energy, making it impressive even to modern ears. By successive migrations of Angles, Danes and Northmen, the Celts were crowded into Wales, where they still remain. The harp has always been their principal instrument, and for many centuries a rude kind of violin called the crwth, of which there will be occasion to speak in connection with the violin, at a later period in this work.

OLD BRETON SONG.

[Listen]

According to the best authorities the bards were divided into three great classes. The first class was composed of the historians and antiquaries, who piqued themselves a little upon their sorcery, and who, upon occasion, took up the rôles of diviners and prophets. The second class was composed of domestic bards, living in private houses, quite after the custom of ancient Greece. These we may suppose were chiefly devoted to the annals and glories of their wealthy patrons. The third class, the heraldic bards, was the most influential of all. They wrote the national annals. All these classes were poet-bards as well as musicians.

The musical bards were divided into three classes. In the first were the players upon the harp; they were called doctors of music. To be admitted into this class it was necessary that they should perform successfully the three Mwchwl—that is, the three most difficult pieces in the bardic repertory. The second class of musical bards was composed of the players upon the crwth, of six strings. The third class were the singers. From the wording of the requirement it would seem that these must have had the same qualification as the first class, and therefore have been true doctors of music. For, in addition to being able to accord the harp or the crwth, and play different themes with their variations, two preludes and other pieces "with their sharps and their flats," they had to know the "three styles of expression," and accent them with the voice in different styles of song. They had also to know the twenty-four meters of poetry as well as the "twenty-four measures of music." Finally, they must be able to compose songs in many of these meters, to read Welsh correctly, to write exactly, and to correct an ancient poem corrupted by the copyists.

The classification of new bards was made at an Eisteddfod once in three years. It was a public contest, after the custom of the Greeks. The degrees were three, conferred at intervals of three years respectively. The organization of the bards existed until the sixteenth century; it was suppressed under Queen Elizabeth. The Eisteddfod has been maintained until the present time. The learned musical historian, J.J. Fétis, attended one in 1829, of which he has left an interesting account. The performances of the blind minstrel of Caernarvon, Richard Robinson, excited his admiration beyond anything else that he mentions. He says: "His skill was something extraordinary. The modern harp of Wales has no pedals for the semitones in modulations. It is supplied with three ranks of strings, of which the left and right give diatonic notes, those in the middle the half-tones. Nothing more inconvenient could be imagined; in spite of his blindness, this minstrel, in the most difficult passages, seized the strings of the middle ranks with most marvelous address. The innate skill of this musician of nature, the calm and goodness painted upon his visage, rendered him an object of general interest."

Independently of the minstrels of this high class, they had also wandering minstrels who played the crwth of three strings, and who made themselves useful in the customary dances and songs of the peasants and the common people.

There exists an old manuscript, supposed to have been begun in the third or fourth century, *Y Trioeddy nys Prydain* ("The Triads of the Isle of Britain"). It contains the traditions from the ancient times until the seventh century. Among the famous triads of this book are: The three bards who bore the cloth of gold, Merlin Ambrosius, Merlin, son of Morvryn, and Taleisin, chief of the bards. There were three principles of song: Composition of poetry, execution upon the harp, and erudition. In the sixth century we see the bards playing the harp and singing their stirring songs with inspiring effect in animating the hearts of their compatriots again in their successful combats against the Saxons. Edward Jones, bard of the Prince of Wales in the last part of the eighteenth century, preserved the names of twenty-three bards who lived in the sixth century. The principal were Taleisin pen Beirrd, Aneurin Gwawrydd, Gildas ab Caw, Gildas Badonius. Taleisin was bard of Prince Elphin, then of King Maelgwin, and in the last place of Prince Urien Reged. He lived about 550; a number of his poems remain, but no fragment of his melody. Aneurin was author of "Gododn," one of the best Welsh poems that has come down to us.

In the British Museum there is a manuscript supposed to have been begun in the eleventh century, containing much music for the harp. Among it are exercises in the curious notation of the Welsh, in which chords are freely used, and in positions suggesting the immediate occasion of their introduction—that, namely of supplementing the small power of the instrument by sounding several tones together, which, as octaves were impossible outside the middle range or pitch, were necessarily chords. Among the songs given are several which betray the transition period of tonality, when chords had come into legitimate use, but the true feeling for a tonic had not yet been acquired. The preceding, for instance, proceeds regularly in the key of G in all respects but the very ending of each strain, which takes place in the key of C. Or to speak tonically, the melody and accompaniment after being written nearly all the way in the key of Do, suddenly diverge to the key of Fa, and there close.

DADLE DAU—THE TWO LOVERS.

[Listen]

This old song was a great favorite with Henry V, while he was yet Prince of Wales, and with his jolly companions he used to shout it vigorously at the Bear's Head tavern, about 1410. (Edward Jones' "Relics of the Welsh Bards," p. 176)

Another (p. 94) is quite modern in spirit and treatment. It is a vigorous love song, and there is a boisterous chorus of bards which comes in with the refrain. A curious feature of this melody is the full-measure rest, immediately following the strong chorus of the bards. During the rests we seem to hear the chorus repeated.

OLD WELSH SONG, IN PRAISE OF LOVE.

[Listen]

In the eleventh century, Gerald Barry, an entertaining writer, made a tour of Britain, and his account of the people in different parts of the country is still extant and full of interest. Of the Welsh he says: "Those who arrive in the morning are entertained until evening with the conversation of young women, and the music of the harp, for each house has its young women and harps allotted to this purpose. In each family the art of playing the harp is held preferable to any other learning."

He adds (chapter XIII, "Of their Symphonies and Songs"): "In their musical concerts they do not sing in unison, like the inhabitants of other countries, but in many different parts, so that in a company of singers, which one very frequently meets with in Wales, you will hear as many different parts and voices as there are performers, while all at length unite with organic melody in one consonance, and in the soft sweetness of B-flat. In the north district of Britain, beyond the Humber and on the borders of Yorkshire, the inhabitants make use of the same kind of symphonious harmony, but with less variety, singing in only two parts, one murmuring in the bass, the other warbling in the acute or treble. Neither of the two nations has acquired this peculiarity by art, but by long habit, which has rendered it natural and familiar; and the practice is now so firmly rooted in them that it is unusual to hear a single and simple melody well sung, and what is still more wonderful, the children, even from their infancy, sing in the same manner. As the English in general do not adopt this mode of singing, but only those to the north of the countries, I believe it was from the Danes and Norwegians, by whom these parts of the island were more frequently invaded, and held longer under their dominion, that the natives contracted this method of singing." In further token of the universality of music among these people, Gerald mentions the story of Richard de Clare, who a short time after the death of Richard I, passed from England into Wales, accompanied by certain other lords and attendants. At the passage of Coed Grono, at the entrance into the woods, he dismissed his attendants and pursued his journey undefended, preceded by a minstrel and a singer, the one accompanying the other on the fiddle. ["*Tibicinem præviens habens et precentorem cantilenæ notulis alternatim in fidiculare respondentem.*"]

Similar devotion to music he found in Ireland. He says: "The only thing to which I find this people to apply commendable industry is playing upon musical instruments, in which they are incomparably more skillful than any other that I have seen. For their modulation on these instruments, unlike that of the Britons, to which I am accustomed, is not slow and harsh, but lively and rapid, while the harmony is both sweet and gay. It is astonishing that in so complex and rapid a movement of the fingers the musical proportions can be preserved, and that throughout the difficult modulations on their various instruments the harmony is completed with so sweet a velocity, so unequal an equality, so discordant a concord, as if the chords sounded together fourths and fifths. They enter into a movement and conclude it in so delicate a manner, and play the little notes so sportively under the blunter sounds of the bass strings, enlivening with wanton levity, or communicating a deeper internal sense of pleasure, so that the perfection of their art appears in the concealment of it. From this cause those very strains afford an unspeakable mental delight to those who have skillfully penetrated into the mysteries of the art; fatigue rather than gratify the ears of others, who seeing do not perceive, and hearing do not understand, and by whom the finest music is esteemed no better than a confused and disorderly noise, to be heard with unwillingness and disgust. Ireland only uses and delights in two instruments—the harp and tabor. Scotland has three—the harp, the tabor and the crowth or crowd. Wales, the harp, the pipes and the crowd. The Irish also used strings of brass instead of catgut."

The brilliant time of Ireland was the reign of Sir Brian Boirohen, in the tenth century. After his victory over the Danes, and their expulsion from the island, he opened schools and colleges for indigent students, founded libraries, and encouraged learning heartily. He was one of the best harpers of his kingdom. His harp is preserved in the library of Trinity College, Dublin, and a well made instrument it is, albeit now somewhat out of repair. It is about thirty inches high; the wood is oak and arms of brass. There are twenty-eight strings fixed in the sounding table by silver buttons in copper-lined holes. The present appearance of the instrument is this:

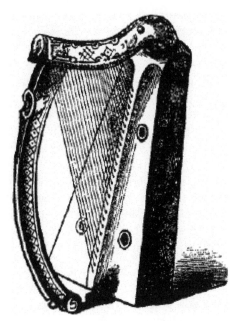

Fig. 19.

The Anglo-Saxons also were great amateurs of music. Up to the sixth century they remained pagan. Gregory the Great sent missionaries to them, and more than 10,000 were baptized in a single day. The Venerable Bede represents St. Benoit as establishing the music of the new church, substituting the plain song of Rome for the Gallic songs previously used.

While few remains of the literature of the early English have come down to us, we have enough from the period of the Venerable Bede and the generation immediately following to give an idea of the vigor and depth of the national consciousness here brought to expression. From the seventh to the tenth centuries there was in England a movement more vigorous, more productive and consequently more modern, than anything like it in any other part of Europe for three centuries later. The Saxon poets Cædmon, the Venerable Bede, Alcuin, the friend, teacher and adviser of that mighty genius Charlemagne, were minds of the first order.

King Arthur the Great was an enthusiastic and talented minstrel. It is told of him that in this disguise he made his way successfully into the Danish camp, and was able to spy out the plans of his invading enemies. The incident has also a light upon the other side, since it shows the estimation in which the wandering minstrel was held by the Danes themselves. King Alfred also established a professorship of music at Oxford, where, indeed, the university, properly so-called, did not yet exist, but a school of considerable vigor had been founded. All the remains of Anglo-Saxon poetry are full of allusions to the bards, the gleemen and the minstrels; and the poems themselves, most likely, were the production of poet-musicians classed under these different names. Many additional reasons might be given for believing that the art of music was more carefully cultivated in England at this time than in any other European country. For instance, at Winchester, in the year 900, a large organ was built in the cathedral—larger than had ever been built before. It had 400 pipes, whereas most of the organs previously in use had no more than forty or fifty pipes. There is reason to believe that among the other musical devices here practiced that of "round" singing was brought to a high degree of popular skill. Apparently also they had something like what was afterward called a burden, a refrain which, instead of coming in at the end of the melody, was sung by a part of the singers continually with it.

Nor was musical cultivation confined to England. In the eighth and ninth centuries the Scandinavians had a civilization of considerable vigor. The minstrels were called Scalds, polishers or smoothers of language. Fétis well says: "As eminently poets and singers as they were barbarians, they put into their songs a strength of ideas, an energy of sentiment, a richness of imagination with which we are struck even in translations, admittedly inferior to the originals. Not less valiant than inspired, their scalds by turns played the harp, raising their voices in praise of heroes, and precipitated themselves into the combat with sword and lance, meeting the enemy in fiercest conflict. Most that remains from these poet-minstrels is contained in the great national collections called Eddas, of which the oldest received their present form early in the eleventh century. The sagas contained in the Eddas form but a mere fragment of this ancient literature. More than 200 scalds are known by name as authors of sagas. These warriors, so pitiless and ferocious in battle, show themselves full of devotion to their families. They were good sons, tender husbands and kind fathers. The Eddas contain pieces of singular delicacy of sentiment." Their songs, when compared with those of other races, are more musical, the sentiment is richer and more profound, and the rhythms have more variety. The melodic intervals, also, indicate a more delicate sense of harmony than we find in other parts of Europe at so early a date. Their instrument was the harp. Iceland was the foremost musical center of the civilized world in the ninth century, and it is said that kings in other parts of Europe sent there for capable minstrels to lead the music in the courts.

A very highly finished English composition, a round with strict canon for four voices, with a burden of the kind already mentioned, repeated over and over by two other voices has been discovered. It is the famous "Summer is Coming In," composed, apparently, some time before the year 1240.

On page 101 is given a reduced *fac simile*. It is written on a staff of six lines, in the square notes of the Franconian period. The clef is that of C. The asterisk at the end of the first phrase marks the proper place of entrance for the successive voices, each in turn commencing at the beginning when the previous one has arrived, at this point. Below is the *pes*, or burden, which is to be repeated over and over until the piece is finished. The complete solution is reproduced in miniature from Grove's Dictionary, on pages 102 and 103. The elaborateness of this piece of music led the original discoverers to place it much later than the date above given, but more careful examination of the manuscript justifies the conclusion that it was written some time before 1240. It is by far the most elaborate piece of ancient part music which has come down to us from times so remote. It indicates conclusively that early in the thirteenth century, when the composers of the old French school were struggling with the beginnings of canonic imitation, confining their work to ecclesiastical tonality, English musicians had arrived at a better art and a true feeling for the major scale and key. Following is the manuscript, the original size of the page being seven and seven-twelfths inches by five and five-twelfths inches. The reduced page before the reader represents the original upon a scale of about two-thirds. The Latin directions below the fourth staff indicate the manner of singing it.

FAC SIMILE OF MSS. OF "SUMER IS ICUMEN IN."

[Enlarge]

"SUMER IS ICUMEN IN."

[Listen]

[View modern transcription (PDF)]

This sign indicates the bar at which each successive Part is to make its entrance.
† Abbreviated form of Christicola.

[Enlarge]

Fig. 20.

SAXON HARP.

[From manuscript in the library of Cambridge University.]

The harp was the principal instrument of these people, and their songs and poems contain innumerable references to it. Sir Francis Palgrave says in his "History of the Anglo-Saxons": "They were great amateurs of rhythm and harmony. In their festivals the harp passed from hand to hand, and whoever could not show himself possessed of talent for music, was counted unworthy of being received in good society. Adhelm, bishop of Sherbourne, was not able to gain the attention of the citizens otherwise than by habilitating himself as a minstrel and taking his stand upon the bridge in the central part of the town and there singing the ballads he had composed." One of the earliest representations of the English harp that has come down to us is found in the Harleian manuscript in the British Museum. It is presumably of the tenth century.

Fig. 21.

KING DAVID.

[From Saxon Psalter of the tenth century.]

The harp was three or four feet in height. It had eleven strings. It was held between the knees, and was played with the right hand. In the thirteenth century it appears to have been played with both hands.

Two circumstances in this account may well surprise us; nor are there data available for resolving the questions to which they give rise. The presence of two such instruments as the harp and the crwth in this part of Europe is not to be explained by historical facts within our knowledge. The harp does not appear in musical history after its career in ancient Egypt until we find it in the hands of these bards, scalds and minstrels of northern Europe. The Aryans who crossed into India do not seem to have had it. Nor did the Greeks, nor the Romans. We find it for a while in Asia, but only in civilizations derived from that of Egypt, already in their decadence when they come under our observation. Inasmuch as there are no data existing whereby we can determine whether these people discovered the harp anew for themselves or derived it from some other nation, and greatly improved it, either supposition is allowable. Upon the whole, the probabilities appear to be that this instrument was among the primitive acquisitions of the Aryans. All of them were hunters, to whom the clang of the bow string must have been a familiar sound. As already suggested, it seems that the harp must have been the oldest type of stringed instrument of all. The Aryans who crossed the Himalayas into India may have lost it, in pursuit of some other type of instrument of plucked strings.

The crwth presents still more troublesome questions, which we must admit are still less hopeful of solution. (See Fig. 22.)

In this case we find an instrument played with a bow in northern Europe, far one side the course of Asiatic commerce, at a time when there was no such instrument elsewhere in the world but in India. Whence came the crwth? The rebec was not known in Arabia until nearly two centuries after we find the crwth mentioned by Venance Fortunatus. We have seen that the Sanskrit had four words meaning bow, a fact affording presumptive evidence of the knowledge of this mode of exciting vibrations, while the Sanskrit was still a spoken language. It is possible that the bow was a discovery of the Aryans in their early days, ere yet the family had begun to separate. The crwth may have been a survival of this primitive discovery, still cherished among a people not able to employ it intelligently, and not able to develop its powers. For while the crwth was in Europe two centuries before the violin, the improvement of this instrument was due to stimulation from quite another quarter. It was the Arab rebec that afforded the starting point for the modern violin, and this instrument was not known in Europe until it came in by way of the crusaders or the Spanish Arabs.

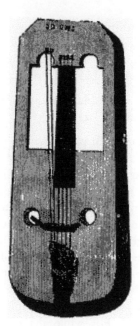

Fig. 22.

Another popular instrument of music in all parts of Britain from the earliest of modern times, was the bagpipe, a reed instrument generally of imperfect intonation, the melody pipe being accompanied by a faithful drone, consisting of the tonic and its octave, and occasionally the fifth. It was the witty Sidney Smith who described the effect as that of a "tune tied to a post." This instrument was common in all parts of Britain until driven out by better ones. It still survives in Scotland. Its influence is distinctly to be traced in the Scotch melodies founded upon the pentatonic scale, of which the following is a specimen:

SCOTCH MELODY
(IN THE PENTATONIC SCALE).

[Listen]

Lent.

The law - land lads think they are fine: But
O they're vain and wondrou, gawdy! How much unlike that
grace-fu' mien, And man-ly looks of no High-land Lad-die!
O my bon-ny, ben-ny High - land Lad-die,
O my hand-some High-land lad-die! when I was sick. and
like to die, he row'd me in his high - land plai-die.

CHAPTER VII.
THE ARABS OR SARACENS.

UPON many accounts the influence of the Arab civilization was important in this quarter of the musical world, and it may here well enough engage our attention, since its most important aspects are those in which it operates upon the European mind, awakening there ideas which but for this stimulus might have remained dormant centuries longer.

From the standpoint of the western world and the limited information concerning the followers of Mahomet which enters into our educational curricula, the Arab appears to us an inert figure, picturesque and imposing, upon the sandy carpet of northern Africa, but a force of little influence in the world of modern nineteenth-century thought.

Nevertheless, there was a time when this picturesque figure became seized with an activity which shook Europe and Christendom to its very center. The voice of the prophet Mahomet awakened the Arab from his slumber. He aroused himself to the duty of proselyting the world to the doctrine of the One God and the Great Prophet. With sword in hand and the rallying cry of his faith he went forth, with such result that a vast proportion of the inhabitants of the globe at this very hour profess the tenets of his religion. Once awakened into life, he penetrated the distant east, and brought back thence the foundation of our arithmetic, the predecessor of our greatest of musical instruments, the violin, and discovered for himself the productions of the greatest of the Greek minds, the works of the philosopher Aristotle. He established a new state in Spain, and for several centuries confronted Christendom with the alternative of the sword or his faith. One of the best characterizations of this people upon the musical-literary side is that of the eminent M. Ginguène, who in his "History of Italian Literature," remarks as follows, concerning the points under immediate consideration:

"In the most ancient times the Arabs had a particular taste for poetry, which among almost all people had opened a way to the most elevated and abstract studies. Their language, rich, flexible and abundant, favored their fertile imagination; their spirit lively and sententious; their eloquence natural and artless, they declaimed with energy the pieces they had composed, or they sang, accompanied with instruments, in a very expressive chorus. These poems make upon the simple and sensitive auditors a prodigious effect. The young poets receive the praises of the tribe, and all celebrate their genius and merit. They prepare a solemn festival. The women, dressed in their most beautiful habits, sing a chorus before their sons and husbands upon the happiness of their tribe. During the annual fair, where tribes from a distance are gathered for thirty days, a large part of the time is spent in a contest of poetry and eloquence. The works which gain praise are deposited in the archives of the princess or emirs. The best ones are painted or embroidered with letters of gold upon silk cloth, and suspended in the temple at Mecca. Seven of these poems had obtained this honor in the time of Mahomet, and they say that Mahomet himself was flattered to see one of the chapters of the Koran compared with these seven poems and judged worthy to be hung up with them. Almansor, the second of the Abassides, loved poetry and letters, and was very well learned in laws, philosophy and astronomy. They say that in building the famous town of Bagdad he took the suggestions from the astronomers for placing the principal building. The university at Bagdad was honored and very celebrated. Copious translations from the Greek were made, and many original treatises produced in other parts of Arabia, but the most brilliant development of Arabic letters was in Spain. Cordova, Grenada, Valencia were distinguished for their schools, colleges and academies. Spain possessed seventy libraries, open to the public in different towns, when the rest of Europe, without books, without letters, without culture, was sunk in the most shameful ignorance. A crowd of celebrated writers enriched the Spanish-Arabic literature in all its parts. The influence of the Arab upon science and literature extended into all Europe; to him are owed many useful inventions. The famous tower at Seville was built for the observatory. It is to be noticed, however, that the Arabs, while taking much from the Greeks, did not take any of their literature, properly so-called—neither Sophocles, Euripides, Sappho, Anacreon, nor Demosthenes. The result is that their own literature preserved its original character; they preserved also in all purity the peculiarity of their music—an art in which they excelled and in which the theory was very complicated. Their works are full of the praises of music and its marvelous effect. They attributed very powerful effects not alone to music sung, but to the sound of certain instruments and to certain instrumental strings and to certain inflections of the voice."

Fig. 23.

THE ARAB REBEC.

The modern world is indebted to the Arab for at least three of its most important instruments of music. The ravanastron he brought home with him from India, and under the name Rebec it found its way into Europe, where in an appreciative soil it grew and expanded into that miracle of sonority and expression, the modern violin. The instrument of the south of Europe during the latter part of the Middle Ages was the lute, which had its origin in the Arab Eoud. (See Fig. 24.)

Fig. 24.

THE EOUD.

Still more familiar to domestic eyes is that descendant of the Arab santir, the modern pianoforte. This, under the name of psaltery, begins to figure in manuscript as early as the ninth century. The Arab canon, which is commonly taken as the immediate predecessor of the pianoforte, had the important difference of being strung with catgut strings. The essential foundation of the pianoforte was the metal strings, necessitating hammers for inciting the vibrations, and affording in the superior solidity incident to metal support a firmness and susceptibility to development. This is the santir. It has survived in Europe as the dulcimer, or the German hackbrett.

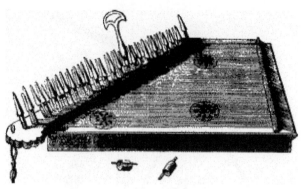

Fig. 25.

THE SANTIR.

Yet while the Arab wrote so abundantly upon the subject of music, and while it filled so prominent a part in his social and official life, and in spite of his sagacity in seizing perfectible types of instruments, there is very little in his treatment of the art which need delay us in the present work. His music belongs entirely to the ancient period of monody. He never had a harmony of combined sounds, nor a scale with intervals permitting combined sounds. He was sufficiently scientific to carry out the intonations of the Pythagorean theory, and when he went beyond this and formed a scale for himself he devised one which did not permit the association of sounds into chord masses; and, more fatal still, he not only invented such a scale, but carried it into execution so exactly that the ear of the race was hopelessly committed to monody, and has remained so until this very day. The scale of the Arabs in the latter times contained twenty-two divisions in the octave, of which only the fifth and fourth exactly correspond with the harmonic ratios. The place of the Arab in music, therefore, is that of an unintentional minister to a higher civilization and to the art of music.

CHAPTER VIII.
ORIGIN OF THE GREAT FRENCH EPICS.

ONE of the earliest developments of popular music on the continent was that of the *Chansons de Geste* ("Songs of Action"), which were, in effect, great national epics. The period of this activity was from about 800 to 1100 or 1200, and the greatest productions were the "Songs of Roland," the "Song of Antioch," etc., translations of which may be found in collections of mediæval romances. The social conditions out of which these songs grew have been well summarized by M. Léon Gautier, in his "*Les Épopées Françaises*": "If we transport ourselves in imagination into Gaul in the seventh century, and casting our eyes to the right, the left, and to all parts, we undertake to render to ourselves an exact account of the state in which we find the national poetry, the following will be the spectacle which will meet our gaze: Upon one hand in Amorican Brittany there are a group of popular poets who speak a Celtic dialect, and sing upon the harp certain legends, certain fables of Celtic origin. They form a league apart, and do not mix at all in the poetic movement of the great Gallo-Roman country. They are the popular singers of an abased race, of a conquered people. Toward the end of the twelfth century we see their legends emerge from their previous obscurity and conquer a sudden and astonishing popularity, which endured throughout all the remainder of the Middle Ages. But in the seventh century they had no profound influence in Gaul, and their voice had no echo except beyond the boundary straits among the harpers and singers of England, Wales and Ireland.

"Upon another side, that of the Moselle, the Meuse and the Rhine, in the country vaguely designated under the name of Austrasia, German invasions have left more indelible traces. The ideas, customs and even the language have taken on a Tudesque imprint. There they sing in a form purely Germanic the '*Antiquissima Carmina*' ["Most Ancient Songs"] which Charlemagne was one day to order his writers to compile and put in permanent form. Between these two extreme divisions there was a neutral territory where a new language was in process of forming—that of the 'Oc' and 'Oïl.' Here the songs were neither German nor Gallo-Roman, but Romance. And here were the germs of the future epics of France."

Out of this combination of contrasting spirits of race, the movement of awakened national life, arose, first, what were called Cantilenas—short songs of a ballad-like character. The language is a mixture of German, Latin and French, intermingled in a most curious manner. For example, consider the following verses from the cantilena of St. Eulalie, as given by M. Gautier, p. 65:

"Buona pulcella fût Eulalia;
Bel avret corps, bellezour anima.
Voldrent la vientre li Deo inimi,
Voldrent la faire diaule servir.
Elle n'out eskoltet les mal conselliers
Qu'elle Deo raniet chi maent sus en ciel."

Which being somewhat freely rendered into English, it says that:

"A good virgin was Eulalia;
She had a beautiful body, more beautiful spirit;
The enemies of God would conquer her,
Would make her serve the devil;
But never would she understand the evil ones who counsel
To deny God, who is above all in heaven."

And so the ballad goes on twenty-three verses more to narrate how she withstood the exhortations of the king of the pagans, that she would forsake the name of Christian; and when they threw her into the fire the fire would not burn her, for the fire was pure; and when the king drew his sword to cut off her head the *demoiselle* did not contradict him, for she wished to leave the world. She prayed to Christ, and under the form of a dove she flew away toward heaven. These charming verses of the ninth century were probably sung to music having little of the movement which we now associate with the term melody, but which was more of a chant-like character.

Of similar literary texture were a multitude of songs, of which many different ones related to the same hero. Hence in time there was a disposition on the part of the cleverer minstrels to combine them into a single narration, and to impart to the whole so composed something of an epic character. Thus arose the famous *Chansons de Geste* already mentioned, the origin and general character of which have been most happily elucidated in the work of M. Gautier, already referred to. He says:

"The great epics of the French had their origin in the romantic and commanding deeds of Charlemagne and the battles against Saracens in 792. The fate of civilization trembled in the balance at Ville Daigne and at Poitiers. It is the lot of Christianity, it is the lot of the world, which is at stake. The innumerable murders, the torrents of blood, these thousands of deaths have had their sure effect upon history. The world has been Christian in place of being Arab. It appertains to Jesus instead of Mahomet. This civilization, of which we are so proud, this beauty of the domestic circle, this independence of our spirit, this free character of our wives and children it is to Charles Martelle, and above all to William of Orange, that we owe them, after God. We possess only a limited number of these primitive epics, the *Chansons de Geste*, and are not certain that we have them in the second or even the third versions. At the head of the list we place the 'Song of Roland,' the Iliad of France. All the other songs of action, however beautiful and however ancient they may be, are far inferior. The text of the 'Song of Roland' as it has come down to us cannot have been written much before 1100. Besides this there is the '*Chanson de Nimes*,' '*Ogier le Danois*,' '*Jour de Blaibes*,' all of which were written in the languages of Oc and Oil. All these have something in common; the verse is ten syllables, the correspondences are assonances and not rhymes. In style these *Chansons de Geste* are rapid, military, but above all dramatic and popular. They are without shading, spontaneous, no labor, no false art, no study. Above all it is a style to which one can apply the words of Montaigne, and it is the same upon paper as in the mouth. Really these verses are made to be upon the living lip, and not upon the cold and dead parchment of the manuscript. The oldest manuscripts are small, in order that they may be carried in the pocket for use of traveling jongleurs and singers. They have Homeric epithets. The style is singularly grave. There is nothing to raise a laugh. The first epics were popular about the end of the eleventh century. The idea of woman is purer in the early poems. There is no description of the body; there is no gallantry. The beautiful Aude apprehends the death of Roland; she falls dead. In the second half of the twelfth century our poets would have been incapable of so simple and noble a conception. We find, even in '*Amis et Amelis*,' women who are still very German in physiognomy, and alluring, but they are Germans, so to say, of the second manner. They have a habit of throwing themselves into the arms of the first man who takes their fancy.

"Each one of the races which composed France or Gaul in the sixth or seventh century, contributed its share toward the future epics. The Celts furnished their character, the Romans their language, the Church its faith; but the Germans did more. For long centuries they had the habit of chanting in popular verse their origin, their victories and their heroes. Above all they penetrated the new poetry with their new spirit. All the German ideas upon war, royalty, family and government, upon woman and right, passed into the epic of the French.

"Our fathers had no epics, it is true, but they had popular chants, rapid, ardent and short, which are precisely what we have called cantilenas. A cantilena is at the same time a recitation and an ode. It is at times a complaint and more often a round. It is a hymn, above all religious and musical, which runs over the lips and which, thanks to its brevity, mainly, is easily graven upon the memory. The cantilenas were a power in society; they caused the most powerful to tremble. When a captain wished to nerve himself up against a bad action he said, 'They will make a bad song about me.'

"The heroes and the deeds which gave birth to French epics are those of the commencement of the eighth century to the end of the tenth. France is then more than a mere land; it is a country; a single religious faith fills all hearts and all intelligence. Toward the end of the tenth century we see the popular singers arresting crowds in all public places. They sing poems of 3,000 or 4,000 verses. These are the first of the *Chansons de Geste*. Out of the great number of cantilenas dedicated to a single hero it happened that some poet had the happy thought of combining them into a single poem. Thus came a suite of pieces about Roland or William, and from these, in time, an epic. The latest of the epic cycles was that concerning the crusades. The style is popular, rapid, easy to sing. It recalls the Homeric poetry. The constant epithets, the military enumerations, the discourses of the heroes before combat, and the idea of God, are simple, childlike, and superstition has no place. The supernatural exists in plenty, but no marvels."

CHAPTER IX.
THE TROUBADOURS, TROUVÈRES AND MINNESINGERS.

TO the full account of the origin of the *Chansons de Geste* in the foregoing chapter, it remains now to add a few notes concerning the *personnel* of the different classes of minstrels through whose efforts these great songs were created.

The first of these singers were the troubadours, who were traveling minstrels especially gifted in versification and in music. Their compositions appear to have been short, on the whole, and of various kinds, as will presently be seen. The earliest of the troubadours of whom we have definite account was Count Wilhelm of Poitiers, 1087-1127. Among the kind of songs cultivated by these singers were love songs, canzonets, chansons; serenade—that is, an evening song; auberde, or day song; servantes, written to extol the goodness of princes; tenzone, quarrelsome or contemptuous songs; and roundelays, terminated forever with the same refrain. There was also what was called the pastourelle, a make-believe shepherd's song.

The so-called chansonniers of the north, who flourished toward the end of the twelfth century, were also troubadours. Among them the name of Count Thibaut of Champagne, king of Navarre, stands celebrated—1201-1253. He composed both religious and secular songs. The following is one of his melodies unharmonized. Its date is about the same as that of "Summer is Coming In." Another celebrated name of these minstrels was Adam de la Halle, of Arras in Picardy—1240-1286. Upon many accounts the music of this author is of considerable interest to us. He was a good natural melodist, as the examples in Coussemaker's "Adam de la Halle" show. He is also the author of the earliest comic opera of which we have any account, the play of "Robin and Marion." We shall speak of this later, in connection with the development of opera in general.

[Listen]

L'autrier par la ma-ti-né-e, En-tre un bois et un ver-gier

U-ne pastoure ai trou-vé-e Chantant pour soi en-voi-sier,

Et di-soit un son pre-mier "Chi me tient li maus d'a-mor."

Tan-tost ce-le part m'entor, Ka je l'oi des rais-ner;

Si li dis sans de-la-ier. Bel-le Diex vous doint bon-jor.

Immediately following the troubadours came the trouvères, who were simply troubadours of nobler birth, and perhaps of finer imagination. There were so many of these singers that it is quite impossible here to give a list of their names. Among the more celebrated, forty-two names are given by Fétis, the most familiar among them being those of Blondel, the minstrel of Richard Cœur de Lion, and the Châtelaine de Coucy (died about 1192), from whom we have twenty-three chansons.

It was the trouvères who invented the *Chansons de Geste* already mentioned—songs of action; in other words, ballads. One of the most celebrated of these was the "Story of Antioch," a romance of the crusades, extending to more than 15,000 lines. This poem was not intended to be read, but was chanted by the minstrels during the crusades themselves. One Richard the Pilgrim was the author. The song is, in fact, a history of the crusade in which he took part, up to a short time before the battle in which he was killed. Another very celebrated piece of the same kind, the "Song of Roland," the history of a warrior in the suite of Charlemagne, is said to have been chanted before the battle of Hastings by the Jongleur Taillefer. Other pieces of the same kind were the "Legend of the Chevalier Cygne" ("Lohengrin") "Parsifal" and the "Holy Grail." Each one of these was sung to a short formula of melody, which was performed over and over incessantly, excepting variations of endings employed in the episodes. A very eminent author of pieces of this kind was the Chevalier de Coucy, who died 1192, in the crusade. There are twenty-four songs of his still in the Paris Library.

Fig. 26.

REINMAR, THE MINNESINGER.

[From a manuscript of the thirteenth century, in the National Library at Paris.]

A similar development of knightly music was had in Germany from the time of Frederick the Red—1152-1190. These were known as minnesingers. Among the most prominent were Heinrich of Beldeke, 1184-1228, an epic writer; Spervogel, 1150-1175; and Frauenlobe, middle of the twelfth century. The forms of the minne songs were the song (*lede*), lay (*lerch*), proverb (*spruch*). The song rarely exceeded one strophe; the lay frequently did. A little later we encounter certain names which have been recently celebrated in the poems of Wagner, such as Heinrich von Morungen, Reinmar von Hagenau, Wolfram von Eschenbach, Gottfried von Strassburg, Walther von der Vogelweide, Klingsor, Tannhäuser, etc. All of these were from the middle of the thirteenth century. A portrait of Reinmar, the minnesinger, has come down to us with a manuscript now contained in the National Library at Paris. The last of the minnesingers was Heinrich von Meissen, 1260-1318. His poems were always in the praise of woman, for which reason he was called Frauenlob ("Woman's Praise"). An old chronicle tells us that when he died the women of Mayence bore him to the tomb, moistened his grave with their tears, and poured out libations of the costliest wines of the Rhineland. The following illustration is supposed to be a representation of this minstrel, although the drawing is hardly up to the standard of the modern Academy.

Fig. 27.

MASTER HEINRICH FRAUENLOB.

[From a manuscript in the Manesse collection at Paris.]

The work of the minnesingers was succeeded in Germany by a class of humbler minstrels of the common people, known as the Mastersingers, the city of Nuremberg being their principal center. A few of these men were real geniuses—poets of the people. One of the most celebrated was Hans Sachs, since represented in Wagner's "Meistersingers." Sachs was a very prolific poet and composer, his pieces being of every kind, from the simpler songs of sentiment and home to quite elaborate plays. About nine volumes of his poems have been reprinted by the Stuttgart Literary Union.

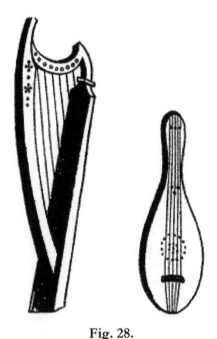

Fig. 28.

MINSTREL HARPS OF THE THIRTEENTH CENTURY.

The principal influence of these different classes of popular minstrel was temporary, in keeping alive a love for music and a certain appreciation of it. The most of their music was rather slow and labored, and it is impossible to discover in the later development of the art material traces of their influence upon it. In this respect they differ materially from the Celtic and English bards mentioned in the previous chapter. Although the productions of those minstrels have all passed away, they have left a distinct impress upon musical composition, even to our own day, in certain simple forms of diatonic melody of highly expressive character. The troubadours, trouvères and minnesingers, on the other hand, never acquired the art of spontaneous melody, and as for harmony, there is no evidence that they made any use of it. Their instrument of music was a small harp of ten or twelve strings, but no more—a much smaller and less effective instrument than the Irish harp of the eleventh century, or the Saxon of the tenth. (See Fig. 28.)

CHAPTER X.
THE INFLUENCE OF THE CHRISTIAN CHURCH.

IT is not easy to define the influence of the Christian Church in this transformation, for the reason that upon the technical side it was slight, although upon the æsthetic side it was of very great importance. From the circumstance that all the early theoretical writers from the sixth century to the thirteenth were monks or ecclesiastics of some degree, and from the very important part played by the large cathedrals in the development of polyphonic music, many historians have concluded that to the Church almost this entire transformation of the art of music is due. This, however, is wide of the truth. The Church as such had very little to do with developing an art of music through all the early centuries. The early Christians were humble people, for the most part, who had embraced a religion proscribed and at times persecuted. Their meetings were private, and attended by small numbers, as, for instance, in the Catacombs at Rome, where the little chapels in the dark passage ways under ground were incapable of holding more than twenty or thirty people at a time. Under these circumstances the singing cannot have been essentially of more musical importance than that of cottage prayer meetings of the present day. In another way the Church, indeed, exercised a certain amount of influence in this department as in all others, an influence which might be described as cosmopolitan. The early apostles and bishops traveled from one province to another, and it is likely that the congregation in each province made use of the melodies already in existence. The first Christian hymns and psalms were probably sung to temple melodies brought from Jerusalem by the apostles. As new hymns were written (something which happened very soon, under the inspiration of the new faith and hope), they were adapted to the best of these old melodies, just as has been done continually down to nearly our own time. Our knowledge of the early Church, in this side of its activity, is very limited. It is not until the time of St. Ambrose, who was bishop of Milan in the last part of the fourth century, that the Church began to have an official music. By this time the process of secularization had been carried so far that there was a great want of seriousness and nobility in the worship. St. Ambrose, accordingly, selected certain melodies as being suitable for the solemn hymns of the Church and the offices of the mass. He himself was a poet of some originality. He composed quite a number of hymns, of which the most famous is that noble piece of praise,

Te Deum Laudamus, a poem which has inspired a greater number of musical settings than any other outside the canon of the Scriptures. The melodies which St. Ambrose collected were probably from Palestine, and he selected four scales from the Greek system, within which, as he supposed, all future melodies should be composed. This was done, most likely, under the impression that each one of the Greek scales had a characteristic expression, and that the four which he chose would suffice for the varying needs of the hymns of the Church. In naming these scales a mistake was made, that upon re being called the Dorian, and all the other names being applied improperly. The series upon mi was called Phrygian, upon fa Lydian; upon sol Mixo-Lydian. The melodies of St. Ambrose were somewhat charged with ornament, a fact which indicates their Asiatic origin. It is probable that a part of the melodies of the Plain Song still in use are remains of the liturgies of St. Ambrose. The Church at Milan maintains the Ambrosian liturgy to the present date. In this action of St. Ambrose we have a characteristic representation of the influence which the Church has exerted upon music in all periods of its career. Upon the æsthetic and ethical sides the Church has awakened aspirations, hopes and faith, of essentially musical character, and in this respect it has been one of the most powerful sources of inspiration that musical art has experienced. But upon the technical side the action of the Church has been purely conservative and, not to say it disrespectfully, politic. The end sought in every modification of the existing music has been that of affording the congregation a musical setting for certain hymns—a setting not inconsistent with the spirit of the hymns themselves, but in melody agreeable to the congregation. The question which John Wesley is reported to have asked, "Why the devil should have all the good tunes," has been a favorite conundrum with the fathers of the Church.

Notwithstanding the firmness with which the Church at Milan maintained the Ambrosian liturgy, in other provinces this conservatism failed; and within the next two centuries very great abuses crept in through the adoption of local secular melodies not yet divested of their profane associations. St. Gregory the Great (540-595), who was elected pope about 590, set himself to restore church music to its purity, or rather to restrict the introduction of profane melodies, and to establish certain limits beyond which the music should not be allowed to pass. St. Gregory himself was not a musician. He therefore contented himself with restoring the Ambrosian chants as far as possible; but the musical scales established by Ambrose he somewhat enlarged, adding to them four other scales called plagal. These were the Hypo-Dorian, la to la; Hypo-Phrygian, si to si; Hypo-Lydian, do to do; Hypo-Æolian, mi to mi. I do not understand that the terminal notes of these plagal scales of St. Gregory were used as key notes, but only that melodies instead of being restricted between the tonic and its octave, were permitted to pass below and above the tonic, coming back to that as a center; for we must remember that in the ancient music the tonality was purely arbitrary, and, so to say, accidental. While all kinds of keys used the series of tones known by the names do, re, mi, fa, so, la, si, do, it was within the choice of the composer to bring his melodies to a close upon any one of these tones, which, being thus emphasized, was regarded as the tonic of the melody. Whatever of color one key had differing from another was due therefore to the preponderance of some one tone of the scale in the course of the melody. The Plain Song of the Roman Church, and of the English Church as well, has been called Gregorian, from St. Gregory, and the majority of ecclesiastical amateurs suppose that the square note notation upon four lines was invented by St. Gregory. This, however, is not the case. The melody, very likely, may have come down to us with few alterations. The notation, however, has undergone several very important changes, of which there will be more particular mention in chapter XV. The Gregorian notation of the sixth century was probably the Roman letters which we find in Hucbald, as will be seen farther on. Several of the tunes well known to Protestants have been arranged from the so-called Gregorian chants. They are "Boylston," "Olmutz" and "Hamburg." The eighth tone, from which "Olmutz" was arranged, has always been appropriated to the *Magnificat* ("My Soul doth Magnify the Lord").

The following are the ecclesiastical scales and names, as established by St. Gregory:

[Listen: Dorian Phrygian Lydian Mixo-Lydian]

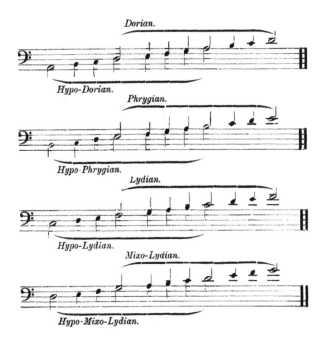

With the labors of St. Gregory the influence of the Church upon the course of musical development by no means ceased. At various epochs in its history synods, councils and popes have effected various reforms, every reform consisting in barring out a certain amount of novelty which had crept in, and in a supposed "restoration" of the service to its pristine purity. The restoration, however, has never been complete. Church music, like every other department of the art, has gone on in increasing complexity from the beginning until now. The main difference between the Church and the world in any century consists in drawing the line of the permissible at a different point. One of the latest reforms was that begun by Pope Marcellus and the Council of Trent, which ordered from Palestrina an example of church music as it should be.

Incidentally, in another direction, the Church has been of very great influence upon the course of musical development. The great cathedrals of the commercial centers of the world, in the effort to render their service worthy of the congregation, have afforded support to talented composers in all ages, and some of the most important movements in music have been made by ecclesiastics or officials deriving support from these sources. More extended particulars of this part of her influence will be given later. It may suffice to mention the cathedrals of Westminster and St. Paul in England, of Notre Dame in Paris, to which we owe the old French school and the beginning of polyphony; the cathedral at Strassburg, which supported important musicians; Cologne, where the celebrated Franco lived; St. Mark's, at Venice, where, from about 1350 to the end of the last century, an extremely brilliant succession of musical directors found a field for their activity.

CHAPTER XI.
THE DIDACTIC OF MUSIC FROM THE FIFTH CENTURY TO THE FOURTEENTH.

I.

THERE is very little in the Roman writers upon music that is of interest. Macrobus, an expert grammarian and encyclopedist living at Rome at the end of the fourth or beginning of the fifth century, wrote a commentary upon the song of Scipio, in which he quotes from Pythagoras concerning the music of the spheres: "What hear I? What is it which fills my ears with sounds so sweet and powerful? It is the harmony which, formed of unequal intervals, but according to just proportion, results from the impulse and movements of the spheres themselves, and of which the sharp sound tempered by the grave sound produces continually varied concerts." (Cicero, "*De Republica*," VI.) Commenting upon this passage, Macrobus says that Pythagoras was the first of the Greeks who divined that the planets and the sidereal universe must have harmonic properties such as Scipio spoke of, on account of their regular movements and proportions to each other. We find in the writings of Macrobus an advance upon the musical theories of Ptolemy. He shows that contrary to the doctrine of Aristoxenus there is not a true half tone, and that the relation 8:9 does not admit of being equally divided. In place of the three symphonies of the octave, fourth and fifth, mentioned by his predecessors, he makes five, including the octave and the double octave. "Such," he says, "is the number of symphonies that we ought to be astonished that the human ear can comprehend them."

Another of the Roman writers upon music was Martinus Capella. His work is called the "Nuptials of Philologus and Mercury" ("*De Nuptiis Philologiæ et Mercurii*"). The little upon music which the book contains was only an abridgment of the Greek treatise of Aristides Quintilianus.

The most important of the earliest treatises upon music, and by far the most famous, is that of Boethius, as it is also the most systematic. The following summary is from Fétis' "History of Music," Vol. IV:

"Born at Rome between 470 and 475, Boethius made at home classical studies, and went, they say, to Athens itself, where he studied philosophy with Proclus. He was of the age of about thirty-five when, in 510, he was made president of the senate. Theodoric, king of the Ostrogoths, called him to himself, on account of his reputation for wisdom and virtue; he confided to him an important position in the palace, and intrusted to him many important diplomatic negotiations. Boethius did nothing which was not to his credit, but this made him only the more hostile to the interests of the courtiers; he was therefore overthrown and cast into prison, where he composed his 'Consolations of Philosophy.' He was put to death 524 or 526."

Boethius' treatise on music is divided into five books. It is a vast repertory of the knowledge of the ancients relative to this art. Its doctrine is Pythagorean. The first book is divided into thirty-four chapters. In the first he develops the thought of Aristotle, that music is inherent in human nature. He there renders the text of a decree which the Ephori of Sparta rendered against Timotheus of Miletus, but which better critics have regarded as fictitious. The second chapter establishes that there are three sorts of music: the worldly, which is universal harmony; the human, which has its source in the intelligence, which reunites and co-ordinates the elements; finally, the third kind is artificial, made by instruments of different sorts. The chapters following treat of the voice as the source of music; of consonances and their proportions; of the division of the voice and its compass; of the perception of sounds by the ear; of the correspondence of the semitones; of the division of the octave; of tetrachords; of the three genera—enharmonic, chromatic and diatonic; of intervals of sounds compared to those of the stars; of the musical and different faculties.

All the second book, divided into thirty chapters, is speculative, and devotes itself to the different kinds and relations of intervals, according to the different systems of theoreticians. The third book, in seven chapters, is a continuation of the subject of the second. It is particularly employed in refuting the errors of Aristoxenus. The fourth book, in eighteen chapters, is entirely relative to the practice of the art, particularly to the notation. It is in this book that Boethius makes known the Latin notation of the first fifteen letters of the alphabet without preparation, without the slightest explanation, and as if he had done something which any one concerned with music at Rome would readily understand, as a matter of course. There is not one word to show that it was new, or that he claimed the invention. It was undoubtedly the usual notation.

The fifth book of this treatise has for its object the determination of intervals by the divisions of a monochord, and a refutation of the systems of Ptolemy and Archytas. We here find this proposition, remarkable if we recall the time when the author lived, that: "If the ear did not count the vibrations, and did not seize the inequalities of movement of two sounds resonating by percussion, the intelligence would not be able to render account of them by the science of numbers." After Boethius there is nothing in Roman literature concerning music. Notwithstanding that Italy fell under the dominion of the Goths and Lombards after 476, it preserved Greek traditions in music to the end of the sixth century.

Cassiodorus, who lived still in 562, aged almost 100 years, left a souvenir for music in the fifth chapter of his treatise on the "Discipline of Letters and Liberal Arts" (*De Artibus ac Disciplinis Litterarum*). He enumerates the fifteen modes of Alypius as not having been abandoned, and establishes them in their natural order, calling them tones. Here also we find the classification of six kinds of symphonies, about 300 years after this enumeration, first realized in notes by Hucbald. He gives a series of fourths and of fifths, occasionally for two voices, occasionally with the octave added. These are the most important of all the things concerning music to be found in that part of Cassiodorus' book dedicated to music.

In the seventh century the first, or perhaps the only author who wrote upon music was Bishop Isidore, of Seville. In his celebrated treatise on the etymologies or origins ("*Isidori Hispaniensis Episcopi Etymologiarum, Libri XX*") divided into twenty books, chapters XIV to XXII of the third book relate to music. These are the chapters published by the Abbé Gerbert, under the name of "*Sentences de Musique*," in the collection of ecclesiastical writers upon this art, after a manuscript in the imperial library at Vienna. While many of these chapters contain nothing more than generalities and pseudo historical anecdotes concerning the inventors of this art, this is not the case with the nineteenth chapter, the sixth in Gerbert's edition, for here he speaks "Of the First Division of Music, called Harmony." The definitions given by St. Isidore have a precision, a clearness not found in other writers of the Middle Ages. "Harmonic music," says he, "is at the same time modulation of the voice, and concordance of many simultaneous sounds. Symphony is the order established between concordant sounds, low and high, produced by the voice, the breath or by percussion. Concordant sounds, the highest and the lowest, agree in such way that if one of them happens to dissonate it offends the ear. The contrary is the case in diaphony, which is the union of dissonant sounds." Here we find St. Isidore employing the term diaphony in its original sense, as a Greek word, meaning dissonance—a sense exactly opposite to that of Jean de Muris.

The Venerable Bede was the light of the eighth century, and the glory of the Anglo-Saxons. His treatise upon music, however, deals in theories and generalities, throwing no light upon the music of his day. The elevation of his ideas may be seen in the following sentence, with which he introduces his subject: "It is to be remarked that all art is contained in reason; and so it is that music consists and develops itself in relations of numbers."

("Notandum est, quod omnis ars in ratione continetur. Musica quoque in ratione numerorum consistit atque versatur.")

Only two treatises upon music have come down to us from the ninth century. The first is by a monk, named Aurelian, in the abbey of Réomé or Montier-Saint-Jean, in the diocese of Langes, who appears to have lived about the year 850. His book, called *"Musicæ Disciplina,"* in twenty chapters, is a compilation of older anecdotes and theories, throwing no light upon the actual condition of the art in his day. The sole remaining work of this period was by Rémi, of Auxerre, who had opened the course of theology and music at Rheims in 893, and afterward at Paris in the earlier years of the tenth century. His book, like the preceding, is wholly devoted to the ideas of the ancients.

II.

This brings us to the first writer on music, during the Middle Ages, whose work throws any important light upon the actual practice of the art in the period when it was written, namely, Hucbald, a monk of the convent of St. Armand, in the diocese of Tournay, in French Flanders. Gerbert gives two treatises upon music, as having come down to us from this author. Nevertheless there is reason to doubt the genuineness of one of them—whereof presently. The first of these, the so-called "Treatise," from a manuscript in the library of the Franciscan convent at Strassburg, collated with another from Cesene, bears this title: "*Incipit Liber Ubaldi Peritissimi Musici de Harmonica Institutione.*" The other is called "*Hucbaldi Monachi Elonensis Musica Enchiriadis,*" or "Manual of Music, by the Monk Hucbald." The former work is of little interest, and if a genuine production of Hucbald's, probably belongs, as M. Fétis suggests, to his earlier period, when he was still teaching at Rheims, along with his former classmate, Rémi, of Auxerre.

The manual of Hucbald is not to be regarded as a complete treatise upon music. It has three principal subjects, namely: The formation of a new system of notation, the tonality of plain song, and symphony, or the singing of many voices at different intervals—in other words, harmony.

In treating the scale he divides it into tetrachords, precisely according to the Greek method, as far as known to him, and he nowhere appears to perceive the inapplicability of this division to the ecclesiastical modes. For representing the sounds of the scale, divided into four tetrachords, Hucbald proposed the Greek letters, which in effect, would have been a notation of absolute pitch, with the farther disadvantage of ignoring the harmonic principles of unity already discovered, and in fact involved in his own method of enlarging a two-voice passage by adding a third at the interval of an octave with the lowest.

He recognizes six kinds of symphony; in reality he employs only three, the others being reduplications. His symphonies are those of fourths, fifths and octaves. In all parts of his work but one he uses the term diaphony as synonymous with symphony; *there* he gives its ancient meaning of dissonance.

He proposed a sort of staff notation, upon which all the voices could be represented at once. The following illustration represents his staff and his diaphony, or harmony:

[Enlarge]

POLYPHONIC NOTATION OF HUCBALD.

The initial letters, T and S, at the beginning of the lines in the preceding staff indicate the place of the steps (tones) and half steps (semitones).

DECIPHERING OF ABOVE.

[Listen]

M. Fétis gives a two-voice parallelism in fifths, which is progressively enlarged to three voices by adding an octave to the lower voice; and then to four by doubling the original upper voice in the octave above. Thus:

[Listen]

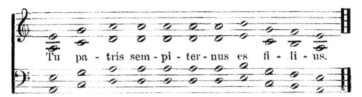

Tu pa-tris sem-pi-ter-nus es fi-li-us.

In addition to mechanical progressions of parallel motion in this way, Hucbald in another place gives an account of a so-called "roving" organum, in which, while parallel progressions of fourths and fifths still are found, there are also other intervals, while the beginning and the end must be in unison. This form of the harmony of simultaneous sounds has in it much of the character of counterpoint, especially in the restriction that the voices must begin and end in unison. This roving organum, or free organum, was also known as "profane" or "secular" organum, in contradistinction to the "sacred organum" already given, upon the sweetness of which Hucbald greatly prided himself.

Fétis has well said that Hucbald must be considered as one of those superior spirits who impress upon their epoch a movement in an art or science. Besides this, he merits particular mention in the history of music because his works are the first since those of Boethius—a period of four centuries—in which the art of music is treated systematically and without obscurity.

In the "*Epistola de Harmonica Institutione ad Rathbodum Episcopum Trevinesem*" ("Letter to Rathbodum, Bishop of Treves"), there is mention of the instruments of music during the seventh and eighth centuries. They are the cithara and harp as the stringed instruments; musetts, syrinx and organ among the wind instruments; cymbals and drums, instruments of percussion. In the tenth century there was a methodical treatise upon music in dialogue form, published by Odon, abbot of Cluny, who died in this monastery November 18, 942. This work, which was wrongfully attributed to Guido of Arezzo, contains a number of analyses of intervals showing an understanding of the exact dimensions of the various kinds of fourths, fifths, thirds and sixths. According to his doctrine, the intervals of the fourths, fifths and octaves are more natural for the voice than the others called thirds and sixths, because the former are invariable, while the latter may be larger or smaller by a half step. He makes a summary of ecclesiastical chant, mentioning the modes as established by St. Gregory, illustrating each of them by a selection from the "Plain Song." It is a fact significant of the unsettled condition of musical theory and the complete unconsciousness of musical amateurs that any essential change in the art was being undergone, that as late as 1000 or 1020 Adelbold, Bishop of Utrecht, published a treatise upon music in which the proportions of the tetrachords are calculated carefully according to the Greek theories, and demonstrated upon the monochord.

III.

The most important writer upon music in the eleventh century, and one of the most famous in the history of the art, was a monk named Guido, living at Arezzo, in Tuscany, a Benedictine in the abbey of Pontose. He was a remarkably skillful teacher of ecclesiastical singing, both in his own monastery and at Rome, and in the effort to systematize the elements of music he introduced a number of important reforms, and is credited by later writers with many others which he did not himself originate, but which grew out of some of his suggestions. He is generally credited with having invented the art of solmization, the introduction of the staff, the use of the hand for teaching intervals, and the introduction of notes. He was not the first who introduced the staff. Hucbald, as we have already seen, employed the spaces between the lines for designating pitch. Between his time and that of Guido, one or more lines were introduced in connection with the neumæ, as will be more particularly illustrated in chapter XV. Guido, however, employed both the lines and the spaces, but instead of notes he wrote the Roman letters upon the lines and spaces according to their pitch. The notes were invented shortly after his time. For determining the correct pitch of the notes of the scale he explains the manner of demonstrating them upon the monochord. He mentions organum and diaphony, and remarks that he finds the succession of fifths and fourths very tiresome. The last treatise of the thirteenth century was written by John Cotton, an English monk, whose entire theory of music is made up from the Greek works.

Fig. 29.

GUIDO OF AREZZO.

This summary of the didactic writers between Boethius and Franco at Cologne fully confirms the justice of the remark, in the chapter previous, concerning the influence of the Church upon music. At the very time when a well marked beginning was being made in counterpoint by the old French school at Paris, and when the English, Welsh and Scandinavian musicians were in possession of an art of expressive melody resting upon a simple harmonic foundation, these writers can find nothing to say but to repeat over and over again their tedious calculations concerning the intonations of *nete hypate* and the other Aristoxinean notes in the enharmonic and chromatic genera, which had been dead names in the art of music for more than ten centuries.

With the appearance of Franco at Cologne, there is something new in music. Late in the twelfth century he wrote a treatise upon measured music, the first one in all the history of the art, so far as we know, in which musical measure is treated independently of verse, and a notation given for representing it. He recognizes two kinds of measure—triple or perfect, and duple or imperfect. He gives four kinds of notes—the shortest being the *brevis*, an oblong note having twice the value of a whole note; a short stem affixed to this note doubled its value. It was then called the *longa*. A note head twice as long represented a still longer duration, called the *maxima* or longest. There was also a *semibreve*, a diamond-shaped note which was used when two or more tones were sung to one syllable. There were no bars for indicating the place of the strong pulse in the measure, but a bar was used to show the end of the musical phrase belonging to a line of verse. The notation was made still more uncertain by the license of the breve in triple time being equal to three semibreves, and so in general each long note in triple measure being equal to three of the next class shorter. In short, the time notation was of the most crude and imperfect description, but it was at least a beginning, and all the theoretical writers upon music for the next two centuries rest in the precepts of Franco of Cologne, as a sure stronghold, where no false doctrine can find admission. Franco remarks, concerning the dissonances, that the imperfect dissonances, the thirds and sixths, go very well between two consonances, showing that in his time the third and sixth were still regarded as licenses in harmony to be explained or excused. The general principle that any dissonance is admissible when smoothly placed between two consonances is a fundamental law of modern counterpoint.

There was another Franco whose work has often been confounded with that of the celebrated master at Cologne. Franco of Paris was connected with the Sorbonne or with Notre Dame, and his writing had mostly to do with harmonic music. He classifies the consonances as—complete, the unison and octave; the incomplete, the major and minor thirds; the middle, the fourth and fifth. This is the first instance in musical theory where the third has been recognized as a consonance. Among the dissonances he classes the major and minor sixth as incomplete, and says concerning these two only that immediately before a consonance any incomplete dissonance goes very well. From the superior celebrity of the Cologne Franco the work of the Parisian master was overlooked for many years, and it is only through the investigation of Coussemaker that his real standing and importance have been ascertained.

CHAPTER XII.
THE RISE OF POLYPHONY. OLD FRENCH AND
GALLO-BELGIC SCHOOLS.

I.

WE here enter upon one of the most interesting and important chapters in the history of music. The art of polyphony had its origin at the same period as the pointed arch and the great cathedrals of Europe, which our architects strive in vain to surpass. In the province of music it represents the same bounding movement of mind, filled with high ideality, which gave rise to the crusades, and poured out in their support such endless treasures of life and love. And in the same country, too, arose the Gothic arch, the beauties of the shrine of Notre Dame in Paris, and the involved and massive polyphony of music. *Polyphonic* is a term which relates itself to two others, as the leading types of all effort toward the expression of spirit through organized tones. They are *Monodic* and *Homophonic*. The musical art of the ancients was an art in which a single melodic formula was doubled in a lower or higher octave, but where no support of harmony was added, and where the only realization of variety could come through the province of rhythm alone; or, perhaps, to a very limited extent through changes in the mode or color of the scale from which the melody had been derived. Monodic art was an art of melody only, rhythm finding its explanation and source in the words, and so far as we understand the case, scarcely at all in the music. Our modern art of homophony is like that in having but a single melody at each moment of the piece; but it differs from the ancient in the important particular of a harmonic support for the melody tones composed of "chords in key." This harmonic accompaniment rules everything in modern music. It is within the power of the composer to confirm the obvious meaning of the melody tone by supporting it with the chord which would most readily suggest itself, within the narrowest limitations in the concept of key; or, second, it is within his reach to impart to any tone, apparently most commonplace, a deeper and a subtler meaning, by making it a peculiarly expressive tone of some related key. Instances of this use of harmonic accompaniment are numerous in Wagner's works, and form the most obvious peculiarity of his style, and the chief reason why the hearers to whom his works were first presented did not recognize the beauties and the novelties of poetic expression in them. Half way between these two types of musical art stands polyphony, which means etymologically "many sounds," but which in musical technique means "multiplicity of melodies." In a true polyphony not only has every tone of the leading voice a melodic character, but all the tones which sound together with it are themselves elements of other and independently moving melodies. Polyphony comprehends the most recondite elements of musical theory, but its essence consists of one leading concept—that of canonic imitation. The simplest form of this is furnished by that musical construction known as "round," in which one voice leads off with a phrase, and immediately a second voice begins with the same melodic idea at the same pitch, and follows after. At the proper interval a third voice enters and follows the procession at a corresponding distance behind. Thus, when there is only one voice singing we have monody; when the second voice enters we have combined sounds consisting of two elements; and when the third enters we have at each successive step chords of three tones. If there are four voices, as soon as the fourth enters, we have combined sounds of four elements. This form of musical construction was much practiced in England, as already noticed. A round, however, does not come to a close, but goes on in an endless sequence until arrested arbitrarily by the performers. Such a form is not proper to art, since it lacks the necessary element of completeness, for at whatever point it may have been arrested there was no innate reason why it might not have gone on indefinitely.

The polyphonic compositions of the schools in consideration in the present chapter go farther than this. While they consist of imitative treatment of a single subject carried through all the voices, or of several subjects which come together in such a way that the ear is not able to follow them as individuals, there is a conclusion, and the canonic imitation has a legitimate ending. Besides those compositions consisting of repetitions of the same subjects, these schools gave rise to other works in which several subjects are treated more or less in the same manner as a single subject would have been in a simpler composition. Nevertheless, in the earlier stages of the development, all the chords arose as incidents, and not as ends. The composer brought in his leading melodic idea at the interval prescribed or chosen. If crudities arose when all the voices were employed, he took no notice of them; the hearers, apparently, being too intent upon following the individual voices to notice the forbidden parallels of fifths or octaves, which inevitably arose until the composer had learned which intervals might be used without harmonic offense, and which not.

Before proceeding to the story of this chapter, the definition of a few terms may be advisable, in the interests of clearness. By "imitation," then, we mean the exact repetition of the melody of one part by another part, at the same or a different pitch. Such an imitation may be "strict," as when the intervals and progressions are exactly repeated; or "free," as when certain changes are made here and there in order to lead the imitation around better to the principal key. Canonic imitation is one in which the imitation is strict, the repeating voice exactly repeating the melody of the principal. By "counterpoint" we mean a second voice added to a melody already existing, the counterpoint having a strict relation to the leading melody, but a wholly independent movement. This conception had its origin in the art of extemporaneous descant, in which, while the choir and congregation repeated the melody of the plain song, a few talented singers performed variations to it, guided solely by ear and tradition, returning to the tone of the plain song at all the points of repose. We do not know when extemporaneous descant gave place to written composition, but it was probably early in the twelfth century. By "double counterpoint" is meant a counterpoint which, although written to be sung an octave lower than the principal song, can be transposed an octave and sung higher than the principal song without giving rise to forbidden progressions. This will be the case only when the original relations of the two voices have been restricted to certain prescribed intervals. By "fugue" is meant a form of composition in which every voice in turn enters with the leading melody of the piece, the same given out by the leading voice at first, called the "subject," responding alternately in tonic and dominant. This form comes later than the period we are now about to consider, but it grew out of the devices of polyphony, and accordingly is always to be kept in mind as the goal toward which all this progress was tending.

The art of polyphony is to be understood as an effort toward variety and unity combined. The unity consisted in all the voices following with the same melodic idea; variety, in the different combinations resulting in the course of the progress. The limitations of polyphony were reached when the true expression of melodic intervals was lost through their intermingling with so many incongruous elements.

II.

The beginnings of contrapuntal and polyphonic music have been traced to what is now known as the old French school, having its active period between about 1100 and 1370, or thereabouts. The principal masters known to us now by name, were all, or nearly all, connected with the cathedral of Notre Dame, Paris, and several of them with the university of the Sorbonne. Paris, during the earlier part of this period, in fact during the greater part of it, was the most advanced and active intellectual center of the entire civilized world. When the French school had ceased to advance, as happened some time before the close of the history in 1370, as above assigned, it found a successor in what is known as the Gallo-Belgic school, which was active between 1350 and 1432. This, in turn, was succeeded by the Netherland school, extending from about 1425 to 1625. The removal of the star of progress from one location to another, as here indicated in the succession of these great national schools, was probably influenced by corresponding or slightly antecedent changes in the commercial or political relations of the countries, rendering the old locality less favorable to art than the new one. For questions of this sort, however, there is not now time or space. To return to the old French school—the recognition of the importance of this school is due to a learned Belgian savant, M. Coussemaker, who happening to discover in the medical library at Montpelier, France, an old manuscript of music, analyzed it, and found that it represented masters previously unknown, and, for the most part, belonging to the period under present consideration. In several monographs upon the history of "Harmony in the Middle Ages," he traced the steps through which polyphony had arisen, and was able to show that, instead of dating from the fourteenth or fifteenth century, as previously supposed, it had its beginnings more than three centuries earlier, and that Paris was the first center of this form of musical effort.

For convenience of classification the entire duration of the old French school may be divided into four periods, of which the first may be taken to extend from 1100 to 1140, the great names being those of Léonin and Pérotin, both organists and deschanteurs at Notre Dame. The Montpelier manuscript contains several compositions by both these masters, and in them we find the germs of the most important devices of counterpoint.

Léonin was known to his contemporaries as "Optimus Organista," on account of his superior organ playing. He wrote a treatise upon the art, a manuscript copy of which appears to be in the British Museum, and its contents have been summarized by an anonymous observer, but never published in full. He is said to dwell mainly upon the proper manner of performing the antiphonary and the graduale. It is also stated that he noted his compositions according to a method invented by himself. If this work could be fully examined it might throw important light upon the point reached in the practice of church music in his day; his notation, also, would be a matter of interest and possibly of importance. Quite a number of compositions by Léonin have been discovered. The successor of Master Léonin, as director of the music at Notre Dame, was one Pérotin, who, besides being a capable deschanteur, was an even greater organist than his teacher, Léonin. He was also a very prolific composer, many of his compositions being still extant. He made additions to his predecessor's manual of the organ.

By descant in the foregoing account, reference is made to the practice of extemporaneous singing of an ornamental part to the plain song or a secular *cantus fermus*. This art had its origin one or two centuries earlier than the period now under consideration, in the secular organum of Hucbald (see p. 142), and all the more talented singers, who were also composers as well, were expert masters of it. Descant was the predecessor of counterpoint.

The chief forms of composition in vogue during this period were motette, rondo and conduit. The terms were rather inexactly applied, but in general the motette appears to have been a church composition, in which often the different voices had different texts, so that the words were wholly lost in performance. The rondo seems to have been a secular composition, and was sometimes written without words. The conduit was an organ piece, occasionally, if not generally, of a secular character. All of these forms were also distinguished as duplum, triplum and quadruplum, according to the number of voices. The harmonic treatment in them is still crude, occasional passages of parallel fifths occurring, after the manner of Hucbald, but in the works of Pérotin passages of this kind are softened somewhat by the device of contrary motion in the other parts. He made a beginning in canonic imitation, Coussemaker and Naumann, after him, giving examples from a composition of his called "*Posuit Adjutorium.*" In these works of Pérotin, and in many others of that day, traces are to be seen of an amelioration of the musical ear, and a preference for thirds and sixths, such as but a short time previously had been unknown to musical theory. This influence was probably due to what was called "*Faux Bourdon,*" a system of accompanying a melody by an extemporaneous second and third part in thirds or sixths.

This art, again, is clearly due to the influence of the round singing of the British isles. Thus we have already a beginning of at least three important elements of good music: The recognition of the triad, or, more properly, of the third and sixth, a beginning in imitation, and the contrapuntal concept of an independently moving melodic accompaniment to a second voice, which in turn had been the outcome of extemporaneous descant. The works of Pérotin were undoubtedly in advance of his time, having in them no small vitality, as is shown in their having formed a part of the repertory of Notre Dame for more than two centuries.

The second period of the old French school extended from about 1140 to 1170, and great improvements were made in the art of harmony meanwhile. The three great masters of this period were Robert of Sabillon, his successor in Notre Dame, Pierre de la Croix, and a theoretical writer named Jean de Garland. The first of these men was distinguished as a great deschanteur, in other words, a ready hand at extemporaneous counterpoint. Pierre de la Croix made certain improvements in notation, the nature of which, however, the musical historians fail to give us. Garland divided the consonances into perfect, imperfect and middle—a system which has remained in use, with slight alteration, to the present day. The thirds and sixths, however, still rank as dissonances. He also defines double counterpoint, and gives examples. The illustrations are crude, but the idea is correct.

The third period of the old French school is sometimes known as the Franconian period, from the two great names in it of Franco of Paris and Franco of Cologne, whose theories have already been noticed. (See page 146.)

Another celebrated name of this period was that of Jerome of Moravia, also a theoretical writer, whose treatise has been published along with the others in Coussemaker's "Mediæval Writers upon Music." He was a teacher and a Dominican monk at Paris. He was contemporaneous with Franco of Cologne.

The fourth period of the old French school extended from 1230 to 1370. The three great names were Phillippe de Vitry, Jean de Muris and Guillaume de Machaut. They were regarded by their contemporaries as exponents of the *ars nova*, in contradistinction to the Franconian teaching, which was called *ars antiqua*. One of these differences was the use of a number of signs permitting singers to introduce chromatics in order to carry out the imitations without destroying the tonality. Jean de Muris was born in Normandy. He was a doctor in the Sorbonne, and from 1330 a deacon and a canon. He died in 1370. He was a learned man of an active mind. He speaks of three kinds of tempo—lively, moderate and slow. He says that Pierre sometimes set against a breve four, six, seven and even nine semibreves—a license followed to this day in the small notes of the *fioratura*. This kind of license on the part of the deschanteurs had been carried to a great length, the melodic figures resulting being called "*fleurettes*" ("little flowers"). John Cotton compared the singers improvising the *fleurettes* of this kind to revelers, who, having at length reached home, cannot tell by what route they got there. Jean de Muris reproved them in turn, saying: "You throw tones by chance, like boys throwing stones, scarcely one in a hundred hitting the mark, and instead of giving pleasure you cause anger and ill-humor." Machaut was born in Rethel, a province in Champagne, in 1284. He was still living in 1369. He was a poet and musician who occupied important positions in the service of several princes, and wrote a mass for the coronation of Charles V. Naumann thinks that Machaut was the natural predecessor of the style of Lassus and Palestrina. He says that the use of double counterpoint slackened from this time, whereby the music of the Netherland composers—Dufay, Willaert and Palestrina—is simpler and less artificial than that of Odington and Jean de Garland. Chords were more regarded. This also had its source in the north.

III.

The Gallo-Belgic school occupies an intermediate place between the old French and Netherlandish. Its time was from 1360 to 1460, and Tournay the central point for most of the time. The first great name in this school was Dufay, 1350-1432. The compositions remained the same as formerly, triplum, quadruplum, etc. One of the masters of this school, Hans Zeelandia, who died about 1370, is to be noticed on account of his part writing being more euphonious than that of his predecessors. He uses the third more freely, and he gives the principal melody in his chansons to the treble, and not to the tenor, as do the others. This also is in line with the British influence. Dufay was regarded by his contemporaries as the greatest composer of his time. The open note notation succeeded the black notes about 1400, or, according to Ambros, as early as 1370. Coussemaker dates Dufay 1355 to 1435. The introduction of popular tunes as a *cantus fermus* in masses and other such compositions is due to him; there are a large number of such works still in the library of the Vatican. He was the first, so far as we know, who introduced "*L'Omme Armé*," and the same subject was treated by several other composers after him. Naumann thinks that the most noticeable peculiarity of the work of Dufay is the interrupted part writing, the imitation not running through the whole composition, but appearing here and there, according to the fancy of the composer. Dufay is also credited with having written pure canonic imitations without descending to the level of the rota, with its endless phrases. Quite a number of his compositions are preserved at the Vatican and the Royal Library at Brussels. The other great name of the first period of this school was that of Binchois, born in Hennegau, died about 1465. A few of his compositions are preserved, but they hardly present important differences from those of Dufay. There were several masters intervening between those just mentioned and Busnois, who closed the school, but at this lapse of time their work hardly retains sufficient individuality to warrant burdening the memory with them. Antoine de Busnois was born in Flanders in 1440, and died in 1482. During a great part of his active life he was *chapelain-chanteur* in the household of Charles the Bold, and that of his successor, Maria of Burgundy. His salary in this position was extremely meager, ranging between twelve and eighteen sous a day, or, in our currency, between about twenty-five cents and forty-eight cents a day, but as the position carried provision for all the real needs of a man in the matter of food and clothing, perhaps the salary was not so insufficient, considering the greater purchasing power of money, which must have been at least three or four times as great as at the present. Busnois appears to have been on cordial terms with the duke, accompanying him in his travels.

CHAPTER XIII.
THE SCHOOLS OF THE NETHERLANDS.

T HE wealth and commercial activity of the Low Countries, known as Flanders, Brabant and Hainault, had now become greater than that of any other part of Europe, Italy perhaps excepted. The organization of the Communes, which began, indeed, in France as early as the tenth century, naturally reached a greater extent during the crusades, when so many of the higher and more energetic nobility were absent in the Holy Land, since the defense and order of the people at home had to be maintained by those who were left behind. Under these circumstances, the power naturally drifted into the strongest hands available, which quite as naturally were those of the capable merchants and manufacturers of the burgher class. Hence the condition of society, while much hampered by the restrictions of the guilds requiring children to be brought up to the occupation of the parents, was nevertheless more favorable to the freedom of the individual than at any previous period. These social elements combining with the wealth aforesaid, and the public spirit which has always distinguished the mercantile classes engaged in foreign commerce upon a large scale, united to form an environment favorable to the development of art; and, as music was the form of art which happened to be most in demand at the time, the effects of the stimulating environment were immediately seen. It was perhaps partly in consequence of the burgher character of the classes most engaged in music in Flanders that the form music there developed should have been so exclusively vocal. All the work of this school, extending over two centuries, was either exclusively vocal, or written with main consideration for the voice, the instrumental additions, if any, having never taken on a descriptive or colorative character.

The schools of the Netherlands came into prominence about 1425, and endured, with little loss of prestige, for two centuries, or until 1625. During this period there was a succession of eminent names in music in these countries, and a great progress was made in polyphony, and a transition begun out of that into harmony (which was in part accidental, owing to their outdoing themselves, as we shall see). Moreover, in the later times, quite a number of eminent men emigrated to foreign countries, and there kindled the sacred fires of the art, and set new causes in operation, leading to the development of national schools of great vigor. The three most eminent names in the category last referred to were those of Tinctor, who founded the school of Naples shortly before 1500; Willaert, who founded that of Venice soon after 1500, and Orlando Lassus, who founded that of Munich a trifle later. The great Palestrina himself was an outcome of these schools of the Netherlands, and, aside from the independent musical life in Spain, there was no strong cultivation of music anywhere in Europe during this period, which did not have its source in these schools of the Netherlands. The entire relation of these schools is perhaps better shown in the following table taken from Naumann, than is possible in any other manner:

THE NETHERLAND SCHOOL. (1425-1625 A.D.)

BELGIAN SCHOOL.	DUTCH SCHOOL.
First Period—1425-1512.	*First Period—1430-1506.*
OKEGHEM, Compère, Petrus, Platenis, Tinctor.	Hobrecht.
Second Period—1455-1526.	*Second Period—1495-1570.*
JOSQUIN DES PRÈS, Agricola, Mouton.	ARKADELT, Holländer.
Third Period—1495-1572.	*Third Period—1440-1622.*
GOMBERT, WILLAERT, Goudimel, Clemens (*non papa*), Cyprian de Rore.	SCHWELINCK.
Fourth Period—1520-1625.	
ORLANDO LASSUS, Andreas Pavernage, Phillippus de Monte, Verdonck.	

The first composer of the Belgian branch of the Netherlandish school was Joannes Okeghem, who was a singer boy in the choir of the Antwerp cathedral in 1443, and is supposed to have been a pupil of Binchois. Directly after the date just mentioned he gave up his place at Antwerp, and entered the service of the king of France. For forty years he served three successive kings, having been in especial favor with Louis XI. He resigned his position at Tours soon after 1490, and lived in retirement until his death in 1513, at the age of nearly 100 years. Okeghem was a very ingenious and laborious composer, who carried the art of canonic imitation to a much finer point than had been reached before his time. He is generally credited with having composed a motette in thirty-six parts having almost all the devices later known as augmentation, diminution, inversion, retrograde, crab, etc. The thirty-six parts here mentioned, however, were not fully written out. Only six parts were written, the remainder being developed from these on the principle of a round, the successive choruses following each other at certain intervals, according to Latin directions printed with the music. The other composers belonging to this period were comparatively unimportant, with the exception of Johannes Tinctor, who was born about 1446 and died in 1511. Tinctor, after being educated to music in Belgium, emigrated to Naples. In early youth he studied law, and took the degree of doctor of jurisprudence, and afterward of theology; was admitted to the priesthood, and became a canon. He then entered the service of Ferdinand of Aragon, king of Naples, who appointed him chaplain and cantor. He founded a music school in Naples, and published a multitude of theoretical works of the nature of text books. He is entitled to the honorable distinction of having published the first musical dictionary of which we have any record. This book is without date, but is supposed to have been printed about 1475. None of the compositions of Tinctor have been printed, and his importance in music history ranks mainly upon the theoretical works which he composed, and his relation as founder of the Naples school.

The second period of the Belgian school has the great name of Josquin des Près, who was born about the middle of the fifteenth century, probably at St. Quentin, in Hainault. He was a pupil of Okeghem; was chapel master in his native town, and in 1471 was a musician at the papal court of Sixtus IV. This great master is to be remembered as the first of the Netherlandish school whose works still have vitality. He was a man of genius and of musical feeling. Martin Luther said of him that "Other composers make their music where their notes take them [referring to their canonic devices]; but Josquin takes his music where he wills." Baini, the biographer of Palestrina, speaks of him as having been the idol of Europe. He says: "They sing only Josquin in Italy; Josquin alone in France; only Josquin in Germany; in Flanders, in Hungary, in Bohemia, in Spain—only Josquin."

("*Si canta il solo Jusquino in Italia; il solo Jusquino in Francia; il solo Jusquino in Germania*," etc.) Josquin was a musician of ready wit, and many amusing stories are told of the skill with which he overcame obstacles. Among others it is told that while he was at the French court the courtier to whom he applied for promotion always put him off with the answer, "*Lascia fare mi*." Weary of waiting, Josquin composed a mass upon the subject la, sol, fa, re, mi, repeated over and over in mimicry of the oft repeated answer. The king was so much amused that he at once promised Josquin a position, but his memory not having proved faithful, Josquin appealed to him with a motette: "*Portio mea non est in terra viventium*" ("My portion is not in the land of the living"); and "*Memor esto verbi tui*" ("Remember thy words"). Another anecdote of similar readiness is that of the motette which the king, who was a very bad singer, asked Josquin to write, with a part in it for the royal voice. Josquin composed a very elaborate motette, full of all sorts of canonic devices, and in the center of the score one part with the same note repeated over and over, the one good note of the king's voice—the inscription being "*Vox regis*" ("voice of the king"). It will be too much to claim Josquin as a composer of expressive music. The mere fact of his having written motettes upon the genealogies in the first chapters of St. Matthew and St. Luke sufficiently defines the importance he attached to the words. Speaking of Josquin's treatment of effects, it is recorded of him that a single word is sometimes scattered through a whole page of notes, showing that he attached no importance to the words whatever. One of the most beautiful of his pieces was a dirge written upon the death of Okeghem. Owing to the good fortune of the invention of music printing from movable types, in 1498, when Josquin was at the height of his powers, a large number of his works have come down to modern times.

In the corresponding period of the Dutch school the name of Jacob Arkadelt is to be remembered, who, although not a composer of the first order, was nevertheless a man of decided power, and is known to us through a number of his works still existing in considerable freshness. Arkadelt was a singing master to the boys in St. Peter's in Rome in 1539, and was admitted to the college of papal singers in 1540. About 1555 he entered the service of Cardinal Charles of Lorraine, duke of Guise, and went to Paris, where probably he died. Besides a large number of motettes and masses, he was one of the most famous of the Venetian school of madrigal writers, a form of composition of which it will be in order to speak later. One of the most pleasing of Arkadelt's compositions is an *Ave Maria* which is often played and sung at the present day.

The third period of the Netherlandish school embraced four very eminent names—Gombert, Willaert, Goudimel and Cyprian de Rore. The three latter were successively chapel masters at the cathedral of St. Mark's in

Venice, and were eminent lights of the Venetian school. It is a significant indication of the commercial decadence of the Netherlands, which had now set in, that all the composers of this period distinguished themselves in foreign countries. Nicholas Gombert, a pupil of Josquin, became master of singers, and afterward directed the music at the royal chapel in Madrid from 1530. He was a prolific composer of masses, motettes, chansons and other works. Of the remaining members of this period mention will be made in connection with the account of the music in St. Mark's, where they all distinguished themselves.

The most gifted of all these Netherlandish masters was Orlando de Lassus, who was born in Belgium, educated at Antwerp, spent some time in Italy, and finally settled at Munich, where he lived for about forty years, as musical director and composer. The compositions of this great man fill many volumes. He distinguished himself in every province of music, being equally at home in secular madrigals—quite a number of which are heard even at the present day with satisfaction—masses and other heavy church compositions, and instrumental works. He was a cultivated man of the world who held an honored position at court and made a great mark in the community. He founded the school at Munich which, with rare good fortune, has occupied a distinguished position ever since, and has been, and still is, one of the most important musical centers in Europe, as all who are acquainted with the history of Richard Wagner, or the reputation of the present incumbent, the Master Rheinberger, will readily see. In Lassus we begin to have the spontaneity of the modern composer. The quaintness of the Middle Ages still lingers to some extent, and learning he had in plenty when it suited him to use it, but he was also capable of very simple and direct melodic expression and quaint and very fascinating harmony. While the tonality is still vague, like that of the church modes, the music itself is thoroughly chordal in character, and evidently planned with reference to the direct expression of the text. A large number of madrigals have come down to us from this great master; among them is the one called "Matona, Lovely Maiden," which is one of the most beautiful part songs in existence. The life of Lassus was full of dignity and honor. He was extremely popular in Munich and in all other parts of Europe. He is to be considered the first great genius in the art of music.

Fig. 30.

ORLANDO DE LASSUS.

[From a contemporary print by the French engraver Amelingue.]

CHAPTER XIV.
POLYPHONIC SCHOOLS OF ITALY.
PALESTRINA.

ITALY in the fifteenth century was in a highly prosperous condition. The great commercial cities had a profitable commerce with all parts of the then known world, and great public works had been under way for more than two centuries. The beginning of the Renaissance was marked by the great cathedrals, of which St. Mark's at Venice was a little earlier than Pisa, Siena, Florence and Milan. All these were built before 1300. Vast public works were undertaken in all parts of the country, such as the canal that supplied Milan with water, and irrigated a large part of the plain of Lombardy; the great sea wall of Genoa; roads, bridges, municipal buildings, fortresses and the like. By the beginning of the sixteenth century the art of painting had reached a very high eminence; the master Raphael was already at work, as was also that remarkable genius, Leonardo da Vinci—the most universally gifted artist who ever appeared. Michael Angelo was at work in the Sistine Chapel, and his plans for St. Peter's were partly being carried out. It was in this time that Johannes Tinctor, the Netherlandish composer, founded a music school at Naples. The school itself was short-lived, but it was presently succeeded by four others of a different kind which eventually produced a large number of eminent musicians, several of whom will occupy our attention later. Tinctor's music school appears to have been a private affair. Those which followed it were charitable institutions, taking poor boys from the streets, furnishing them with a living, the rudiments of an education, and musical training enough to make them available in the service of the Church. The founding of these schools took place some time later than the period under immediate discussion. *Santa Maria di Loreto* was founded in 1535, by a poor artisan of the name of Francisco, who received in his house orphans of both sexes, and caused them to be fed and clothed and instructed in music. He was assisted by donations from the rich, and presently a priest named Giovanni da Tappia undertook to raise a permanent endowment by begging alms from house to house. At the end of nine years he had accomplished his task. The building was called the Conservatorio, and in 1536 received certain government allowances. The pupils reached the number of 800, and among the illustrious musicians produced by this school were Alessandro Scarlatti, Durante, Porpora, Trajetta, Sacchini, Gugliemi and many more. The second school of this kind organized was that of *San Onofrio a Capuana*, in 1576. It received 120 orphans, who were instructed in religion and music. In 1797 the pupils of this school were transferred to *Santa Maria*. The third school of this kind was that of *De Poveri di Gesu Cristo*, established in 1589, for foundlings. In 1744 this conservatory was made into a diocesan seminary. The fourth of these schools was that of *Della Pieta di Turchini*, which originated about 1584. Quite a number of eminent composers were produced in this school. All of these conservatories were consolidated in 1808 as the *Reale Collegio di Musica* (Royal College of Music). The example of Naples was followed with more or less rapidity in the other principal Italian cities. The most important musical center of Italy during this time was Venice, where Adrian Willaert became musical director in the cathedral of St. Mark's, in 1527. Here he remained until 1562. The church of St. Mark's had already held a prominent position as a musical center at least two centuries of the four which it had been in existence. The recently published history of the music in St. Mark's extends back to 1380, from which time to the beginning of the present century there has been a succession of eminent musicians as organists and musical directors. There were two organs in this church, standing in galleries on opposite sides of the chancel. This circumstance had an important influence on the development of music in the cathedral, as will hereafter be seen. It was in this church, according to Italian tradition, that pedals were first applied to the organ. It is probable that these appliances were very rude at first, and few in number, but they served to supplement the resources of the hands of the organist, and enabled him to produce effects not otherwise obtainable. The existence of the two choirs and two organs, and no doubt the habit of antiphonal singing in the Plain Song of the Church, led Willaert to invent double choruses, and finally to divide his choir into three or more parts. Willaert is regarded by many as the founder of the madrigal, of which there is more to be said presently. He was also the teacher of two very eminent musicians who succeeded him in his position at St. Mark's—Zarlino and Cyprians de Rore. To go on with the story of St. Mark's from this point, the most important successor of Willaert was Gioseffo Zarlino, who spent his youth in studying for the Church, and was admitted to minor orders in 1539, and ordained deacon in 1541. He was a proficient scholar in Greek and Hebrew, in mathematics, astronomy and chemistry. After studying for some years with Willaert he was elected in 1555 first *Maestro di Capella* at St. Mark's. In this position his services were required not alone as director of music in the church, but also as a servant of the republic, and it was his duty to compose or arrange music for all of the public festivals. After the battle of Lepanto, October 7, 1571, Zarlino was appointed to celebrate the victory with appropriate music. When Henry III visited Venice, in 1574, he was greeted by music by Zarlino. This same composer is also credited with having composed a dramatic piece called *Orpheo*, which was performed with great splendor in the larger council chamber. Again, in 1577, Zarlino was commissioned to compose a mass for the commemoration of the terrible plague which devastated Italy and carried off Titian, among other great men. His ecclesiastical standing was so good that in 1583 he was elected bishop, but his accession to the see was so strongly opposed by the doge and the senate that he consented to retain the appointment of St. Mark's, where he remained until his death in 1590. Zarlino was very famous as a composer, in his own day, but few of his works have come down to us. He is best known by certain works of his on harmony and the theory of music, of which the most important was the *Institutioni Armoniche* (Venice, 1558), and his *Demonstrationi Armoniche* (Venice, 1571). Zarlino's distinction rests upon his having restored the true tuning of the tetrachord to that of 8:9, 9:10, 15:16, as opposed to the Pythagorean tuning of 9:8, 9:8, 256:243. He was the most important scientific authority in the music of the new epoch. His discoveries in harmony were afterward supplemented by those of Tartini, almost two centuries later. Among other strong points of Zarlino was his demonstration of equal temperament, which came into general use about 100 years later. Cypriano de Rore, whose name was mentioned above in connection with St. Mark's, held a position as master in that eminent cathedral only one year, his tenure of office falling between the death of Willaert and the appointment of Zarlino. He was a very prolific composer of motettes and madrigals, and after resigning his position at St. Mark's went to the Court of Parma, where he died at the age of forty-nine. The later eminent masters holding positions in this church will come into view in the next book, in connection with the opera, for Monteverde was director of the music here during the greater part of his career as a dramatic composer.

The most eminent development of the polyphonic school, and at the same time the dawn of a better era in church music, took place in Rome, where the influence of the Netherlandish composer is noticeable. Claude Goudimel, whose name appears in the table of the Netherlandish school in the preceding chapter, opened a music school in Rome in the early part of the sixteenth century, and among his pupils was the name of Palestrina. Goudimel's residence in Rome was not very long. He afterward returned to Paris, and in some way was connected with Calvin in preparing psalm books for the Calvinists. He was killed finally at Lyons in the massacre of St. Bartholomew, August 24, 1572.

The culmination of the contrapuntal school and the dawn of the new era in church music came about through the labors of the pupil of Goudimel, the great Palestrina. This master, whose name was Giovanni Pierluigi (English, John Peter Lewis), was born of humble parents at Palestrina, a small town in the vicinity of Rome. The date is uncertain, but it was probably about

1520. As early as 1540 he came to Rome to study music, where he made so good progress that in 1551 he was appointed musical director at the Julian chapel in the Vatican. He then commenced the publication of a series of remarkable musical works, the first of which were in the style prevalent in his day. There was much learning of every sort; all the devices of polyphony were freely and luxuriantly employed, but along with them were other passages of true expression. The dedication of some of these books to the pope secured for him certain small preferments, which, in his most profitable condition, aggregated about thirty *scudi* a month (perhaps equal to $20 of our money). On this miserable pittance he supported his wife and four children. In 1556 he was discharged from his place as a pontifical singer, on account of his marriage, a fact which had been ignored by the pope who appointed him. He then held the post of chapel master at the Lateran. In 1561 he was transferred to *Santa Maria Maggiore*, where he remained ten years at a monthly salary of sixteen *scudi*, until 1571, when he was once more elected to his old office of master at the Vatican. It would take us too long to speak of his various works in detail, although his numerous publications during this period demonstrate his claim to mastership of the first order. The best of his pieces had already been adopted in the apostolic chapel, and his reputation was now greater in Italy than that of any other musician. But the taste for elaboration in church music had reached a point where reform was imperatively demanded. Not content with having secular melodies employed as *canti fermi* in the music sung to the words of the mass, the words of these secular songs themselves were often written in and sung by a majority of the singers in the choir, only those in the front rows singing the solemn words of the ecclesiastical office. The Council of Trent (1545-1563) commented upon this state of things with great severity, and appointed a commission to inquire into the abuse and decide upon a remedy. It was contemplated to entirely do away with elaborate music in the Church, and sing only the Gregorian songs. A few of the music-loving cardinals succeeded in preventing so sweeping an order, and a commission was appointed to take the matter in hand. Two of the most active of these were Cardinals Borromeo and Vitellozzi. The former reported of the singing in the pontifical chapel, to the following effect: "These singers," said he, "count it for their principal glory that when one sings *sanctus*, another sings *Sabbaoth* and another *gloria tua*, and the whole effect of the music is little more than a confused whirring and snarling, more resembling the performance of cats in January than the beautiful flowers of May." At the same time Palestrina was desired to write a mass in a style suitable for the sacred office. Too modest to rest the case upon one work, he wrote three, which were performed with great care at the house of Cardinal Vitellozzi, and all were much admired, but the third, known as the mass *"Papæ Marcelli,"* in memory of the pope who had appointed Palestrina to one of his positions, was recognized as of transcendent excellence. It was copied in the collection of the Vatican, and the pope ordered a special performance of it in the Apostolic chapel. At the end of it he declared that it must have been some such music as this that the apostles of the Apocalypse heard sung by the triumphant hosts of angels in the New Jerusalem. Palestrina continued to write masses, motettes and other works during the remainder of his life, but during the entire time lived in the extremely limited condition already mentioned, and was subject to much enmity from jealous singers and composers. The most pleasing incident of his later life happened in 1575, when fifteen hundred singers from his native town came to Rome in two confraternities of the Crucifix and the Sacrament, making a solemn entry into the city, singing the music of their great townsman, who conducted at their head. The long and active life of this great master came to an end January 22, 1594. Among his greater works are ninety-three masses, a very large number of motettes, forty-five hymns for the whole year, sixty-eight offertories, and a large number of litanies, magnificats and madrigals.

It is not unlikely that reform in Catholic Church music had been very largely influenced by the Protestant music of Germany. Martin Luther (1483-1546) in arranging music for the Protestant Church, invented the chorale and added to the best melodies from the Plain Song some wonderfully fine ones of his own, such as "*Eine Feste Burg*," and caused many others to be written by the best composers of the Netherlandish school. The chorale was the exact opposite of the motette of the Netherlands. In the chorale all of the voices moved together. The same music was invariably sung to the same words, whereby an association was created, intensifying the effect of the music and the words respectively.

As examples of Palestrina's music are not common I have thought best to allow space for the following from his music for Holy Week. The pieces will produce a much better effect if sung by good voices than when played upon an instrument. They are written for the voice.

"TENEBRÆ FACTÆ SUNT," BY GIOVANNI PIERLUIGI DA PALESTRINA.

[Listen]

CHAPTER XV.
THE CHANGES IN MUSICAL NOTATION.

THE entire movement of musical thought since three or four tones began to be put together into scales, melodies and unities of various kinds, has been in the direction of classification. This is shown very conclusively in the history of musical notation, which, at the end of the period just now under consideration, had reached a form nearly the same as we now have it. The early notation regarded tones as individual, and wholly without classification of any kind. The first musical notation of which we have any authentic knowledge was that of the Greeks already noted in chapter III. Their scale consisted of two octaves and one note, their so-called "greater perfect system," and the tones were named by the first fifteen letters of the Greek alphabet. This, however, was only a beginning of their system, for the variety of pitches required in their enharmonic and chromatic scales, and in the various transposition scales was so great that they required sixty-seven characters for representing them. These characters were written above the words to which they applied, and they had additional marks for duration, especially in the later periods of Greek music. Besides this they had an entirely different set of characters for the same tones played upon the cithara, so that a word to be sung without accompaniment had one mark above it for the pitch of the note, while if accompanied even by the same tone upon the instrument, a second character was written for the instrumental part. The system was wholly without classification, except that the letters were applied from the lowest notes upward, the same as we now have them. There was nothing to assist the eye in forming an idea of the movement of the melody, and as the forms of the letters were very similar in some cases there is no doubt that mistakes of copyists were numerous. This, however, is a matter of little concern to us, since no authentic melodies of the classical period have come down to us. The example of Greek characters given on p. 69, in connection with the Ode of Pindar, sufficiently illustrates the nature of this notation, although the interposition of the staff between the musical notes and the words deprives the illustration of a part of its value.

The Romans had also a notation consisting of letters written above the words to which they applied; they made use of the first fifteen letters of the alphabet in the same manner as the Greeks, but we do not know whether they employed the same characters for the instruments and the voices, or had different ones. The only example we possess of the Roman notation from classical times, or in close tradition from classical times, is that in "Boethius' Consolations of Philosophy." From the fact of this being the only place where the Roman notation is illustrated, certain writers have concluded that Boethius invented it—a supposition which is utterly improbable. Boethius mentions the Roman notation, and employs it, as also does Hucbald in certain of his examples, but neither one of them explains it or gives any account of its origin. We have simply to take it for granted that the Romans transferred the letter notation of approximate pitch to their own characters instead of using Greek letters. The following example from Guido's book illustrates the appearance of the Roman notation as he uses it:

Fig. 31.

LETTER NOTATION OF GUIDO OF AREZZO, WITH DECIPHERING.

[Listen]

The most curious notation of which we have a record was that of the neumæ, or neumes, which were employed by the ecclesiastical writers mostly from about the sixth century to the twelfth. This writing, as will be seen from the examples hereafter given, very much resembled the curves and hooks of the modern shorthand. The learned Fétis thinks that the characters were derived from the Coptic notation, and these again from the hieratic notation of the ancient Egyptians. The neumes signified mostly intonations, upward or downward slides of the voice, and not absolute pitch.

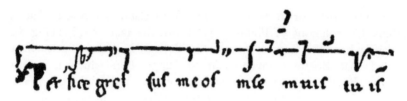

Fig. 32.

NEUME NOTATION OF THE TENTH CENTURY.

There are no clefs or other indications of the key, and it is little better than sheer guesswork to attempt to decipher one of them, for want of some one single base mark to reckon from. Accordingly, the various commentators have rendered the old pieces in a variety of ways. It is probable that the imperfections of this notation were helped out, when it was in current use, by tradition, which appropriated certain keys to each of the principal hymns of the Church; this being understood, the singer found himself able to make something intelligible out of a notation which, without the help of traditions, would have been meaningless. From about the eleventh century the supposed meanings of the various signs of the neumes are easily to be ascertained, because tables are given by a number of writers of that period; but the earlier examples are practically undecipherable. This notation came into use partly through ecclesiastical influence, and partly owing to its being easy to write, while at the same time it occupied little space upon the page. The earlier examples, as already said, were without clefs or any means of ascertaining the key note. After a while we find them with one line representing do or fa, and the signs arranged above, below, or upon the line, at intervals approximately representing the pitch intended. Still later we find a colored line for fa, a thumb nail line traced on the parchment, but not colored, for re, and a different one for la.

Fig. 33.

NEUME NOTATION OF THE ELEVENTH CENTURY, DECIPHERED BY MARTINI IN "GREGORIAN" NOTATION.

[Listen]

[View modern transcription]

Still later four lines were used. There were many varieties of forms of the neumes employed by the different copyists and by different nationalities, the heaviest marks of this kind being those of the Lombard-Gothic represented in Fig. 35. These marks were afterward written upon a four-line staff, and the note heads were derived from them.

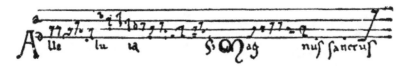

Fig. 34.

NEUME NOTATION OF GUIDO OF AREZZO.

There were no marks whatever for duration or measure in the neumes notation, and its persistence through so long a time signifies very plainly that it was not in the line of the musical life of the world, but was a special hieratic notation made to answer for ecclesiastical purposes by the help of carefully transmitted traditions.

Fig. 35.

DECIPHERED NEUME NOTATION OF THE LATEST PERIOD.

[Listen]

[View modern transcription]

One of the oldest forms of this notation is that of the lament for the death of Charlemagne, an extract from which is here presented, together with its translation as given by Naumann.

Incidentally this illustration gives a fair specimen of mediæval melody of the earlier period. It dates from the tenth century.

"LAMENT FOR CHARLEMAGNE."

[Listen]

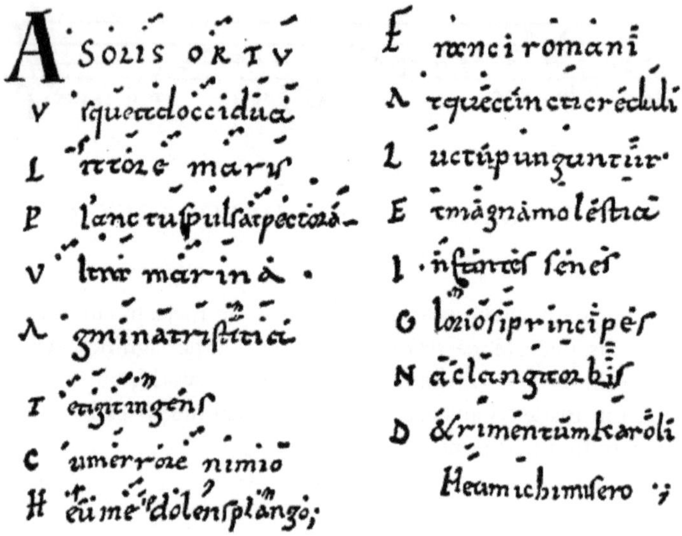

A solis ortu
v squecadoccidua
L ttore maris
P lancruspulsarpectora
v tenr marina
A gminatristitia
I engrtingens
C umerrore nimio
H eumedolensplango;

E ranci romani
A rquectinenncreduli
L uctupunguntur
E tmagnamolestia
I nfantes senes
O leriosiprincipes
N aclanguorbis
D &rimentumkaroli
Heumichimisero ;

The earliest suggestion of the staff that we have is that in the work of Hucbald already mentioned, in which he proposed to print the words in the spaces of the staff of eleven lines, placing each syllable according to its pitch (p. 141). The staff, in connection with neumes, as given above in Fig. 34, probably came into use about the same time as that when Hucbald's book was written, but it was not until the days of Guido of Arezzo that the staff was employed in anything like its modern form, nor is it certain that Guido had anything to do with introducing it. In one of the manuscripts of his book letters are written upon the lines and spaces, and in another the neumes are given. The note head was not invented until some little time after his death, probably about fifty years.

Fig. 36.

NOTATION OF THE FRENCH TROUVÈRES.

By the time of Franco of Cologne, the four-lined staff with square notes had come into use, the notes having the value already assigned them in the chapter upon Franco of Cologne. (See p. 145.) The place of fa was marked by a clef, and with some few exceptions all the musical notation from this time forward is susceptible of approximate translation. The term approximate is used above by reason of the fact that no sharps or flats were written until long after this period, but it is thought that they were occasionally interpolated by the singers quite a long time before it became customary to put them into the notation. In this way, for example, a piece of music beginning and ending on the degree appropriate to fa might be brought within the limits of the key of F by the singer changing B natural to B flat wherever it occurred. Our information in regard to this practice is extremely limited, and, in fact, rests upon two or three detached hints. The signature was not employed until some centuries later.

As already mentioned in chapter XI, there was no measure notation for a long time after Franco's death. The data are uncertain concerning the exact time when the bar began to be used to mark the measure. Its earliest use was that of marking the end of the music belonging to a line of poetry. This is the same use as now made of the double bar in vocal music. In fact, everything points to the progressive development of music in all respects, and the development of what we might call self-consciousness in musicians, whereby each succeeding generation sought to place upon record a greater number of particulars concerning their music, and to leave less and less to accident or tradition. This progress has gone on until the present time, when two particulars of our music are exactly recorded—the pitch and the rhythm. The exact relation of every tone to the key note is ascertainable from our musical notation, and the precise degree of rhythmic importance appertaining to each tone according to its place in measure and in the larger rhythms. We are still lame in the matter of expression, and in pianoforte music also in regard to the application of the pedals. Here our notation affords only a few detached suggestions. If the master works of the modern school could be noted for expression as completely as for pitch and rhythm, the labor of acquiring musical knowledge would be very greatly diminished.

The four-line staff has remained in use in the Catholic Church until the present time, and with it the square notes. It is generally called Gregorian, and by many is supposed to have been invented by Gregory the Great; but as a matter of fact, about six centuries elapsed after his death before this square-note notation came into use. The five-line staff came into use about 1500. Information is wanting as to the causes which led to its adoption in preference to the four-line notation so long in use. The clef for do (C clef) remained in use until very lately, and is still used by many strict theorists, being written upon the first line for the soprano, the fourth line for the tenor, the third line for the alto. The G clef, also, when first introduced, was often written upon the third or the first line; the F clef, moreover, was not definitely established on the fourth line until toward 1700. In the scores of Palestrina's work, now published in complete form, there are pieces written with the soprano in the G clef upon the first line, the alto in the C clef upon the second line, the tenor in the C clef upon the fourth line, and the bass in the F clef upon the third line. This, while affording the eye two familiar clefs, the treble and the bass, places them in such a way as to practically make it necessary for the modern reader to transpose every note of the composition in all the parts, and, in fact, to effect a transposition for each part upon principles peculiar to itself.

The progress of classification is distinctly seen in the use of seven letters instead of fifteen, affording a tacit recognition of the most essential underlying facts of harmony—*the equivalence of octaves*. The staff, however, affords the eye no assistance at this point, since the octaves of notes occupy relatively entirely different positions upon it, the octave of a space being invariably a line, and the octave of a line a space. Moreover, the octave of a bass line is always very differently located when it falls upon the treble staff, and, *vice versa*, the octave of a treble note falling in the bass is very differently placed. If a notation had to be made anew it would no doubt facilitate matters to make use of a staff so planned as to bring out the equivalence of octaves more perfectly. A recent American designer, Mrs. Wheeler, has proposed a double staff of six lines, divided into two groups of three, for the treble and bass, thus presenting for the piano score four groups of three lines each, separated by smaller or larger intervals. Upon such a staff every tone would fall in the same place upon the three lines in every octave, the octave of the first line of the lower three would be the first line of the second three, and so on.

This, however, is to anticipate. The smaller rhythmic divisions of the measure were very little used in the old music which, if not sung in slow time, was at least written in long notes, and the smaller varieties of notes are the invention of a period perhaps rather later than that at which we have now arrived. They belong to the elaborate rhythmic construction of the music of Händel, Bach, Scarlatti and Haydn.

CHAPTER XVI.
MUSICAL INSTRUMENTS. THE VIOLIN, ORGAN, ETC.

I.

DURING the entire period covered by the division of the story with which we have been now for some time dealing, the influences operating upon the tonal sense in the direction of harmonic perception had also been highly stimulative to the sense of melody. All the devices of counterpoint, with their two, three and four tones of the moving voice against one of the *cantus fermus*, were so many incitations in the direction of melodic cleverness. This influence was still further strengthened by the constant effort of the composer to impart to each voice as characteristic an individuality of movement as possible. Hence there is a distinct gain in smoothness of melody, and there are occasional appearances of truly expressive quality in this part of the music, even in the most elaborate of the contrapuntal compositions. Meanwhile the various forms of popular minstrelsy, whose general course we have already traced, were powerfully appealing to this part of the musical endowment of the hearers. But the great means of cultivating an ear for melody, both in players and hearers, was the violin, which, contemporaneously with the present point of our story, had reached its mature form and nearly all of its tonal powers. In fact, the tonal education of the mediæval musicians had been carried forward in several directions by the instruments in use. The harp and its influence upon the development of chord perceptions have already received attention, but there was another instrument which, during the period subsequent to about 1400, exerted even a more powerful influence—I mean the lute. The lute and the violin appear in crude forms at nearly the same time in Europe. The violin was the instrument of the north, the lute of the south. Later they move together geographically, sharing the popular suffrages. By the time of Palestrina the lute had come to its full powers and most complete form. Within twenty years after the death of Palestrina orchestral music started upon the career which has never since stopped, the violin at the head of the forces, thanks to the insight of the great musical genius, Monteverde.

The lute belongs to the same class of instruments as the guitar, differing from that, however, in important details of construction. It has a pear-shaped body, composed of narrow pieces of bent wood glued together; the sounding board is flat, and of fir. The neck is longer or shorter, according to the variety of lute. It was strung with from eight to eleven strings, which in the east were of silk, but in Europe were catgut down to the end of the seventeenth century, when spun strings were substituted for the bass. The finger board was marked by frets, indicating the places at which the strings should be stopped. There were four or more of the longest strings which were not upon the finger board, and were never stopped. They were used for basses. Melodically the instrument had little power, although its tone was gentle and sweet. Its influence, like that of the guitar of the present time, was in the direction of simple harmony, mainly restricted to the nearest chords of the key. The essential point in which the construction of the lute differed from that of the guitar, was in the back, which in the latter is flat, so that ribs are indispensable for preserving the rigidity of the body against the pull of the strings. The lute body is very solid, from the mode of its construction involving an application of the principle of the arch. The standard appearance of the lute was the following:

Fig. 37.

THE LUTE IN ITS STANDARD FORM.

[From Grove's Dictionary.]

The stringing and tuning varied much in different periods. According to Prætorius, the lute had four open strings tuned according to the scale in *a* below. Later, a G was added above and below, and the tuning was that at *b*.

[Listen]

Another authority—Baron—gives a tuning for an "eleven-course" lute, as follows:

[Listen]

The F below the bass staff had ten frets, G eleven, and each of the highest six strings twelve frets. The instrument thus had a compass of three octaves and a half from the C below the bass. All the strings were in pairs, two to each unison, excepting the upper two, which were single. The instrument was a very troublesome one to keep in order. Mattheson, who wrote in the latter part of the eighteenth century, when the lute was still cultivated, said that a lutist of eighty years must have spent nearly sixty in tuning his instrument. The pull of the strings broke down the sounding board or belly, which had therefore to be taken off and righted once in every two or three years. The lute was derived from an Arabian or Persian instrument, of which the Arab eoud, Fig. 24 (p. 113), was the latest representative.

The problem of locating the frets accurately upon the finger board was one of the causes which led to close investigation into the mathematical relation of the tones in the scale; and the directions given for placing them by various Arab and other writers afford precise and valuable information concerning their views of intonation. The lute was made in a great variety of sizes, the largest being what was called the arch lute, which was more than four feet long from bottom to the end of the neck. This was employed by Corelli for the basses of his violin sonatas, and Händel made similar use of it. A diminutive lute has come down to our own days under the name of

Mandolin. It is strung with metal strings, however, and played with a plectrum, whereas the mediæval lute was played with the fingers. Monteverde employed still another variety of the lute in his orchestra, called the Chitarrone, whence our word guitar. This was a very large lute, with many strings, which were wire, and played, therefore, with a plectrum. The chitarrone in the collection at South Kensington has twelve strings upon the finger board, and eight bass strings tuned by the pegs at the top of the long neck. It was used mainly for basses. The guitar, of which a figure is omitted on account of the familiarity of the instrument, was the Spanish form of the lute, or the Spanish form which the Moorish lute took in that country.

The essential feature of the violin is the incitation of the vibration by means of the bow. We do not know when or where this art was discovered, but it is supposed to have been in the remote east, at a very early period. The argument of Fétis, that since the Sanskrit has four terms for bow, according to the material of which it was made, therefore the art of the bow must have been known before the Sanskrit ceased to be a spoken language, has little weight. For while it is true that Sanskrit was not a spoken, or, more properly, a living, language in ordinary life after about 1500 B.C., it is true, on the other hand, that it remained in use as a language of religion and of the learned down to times very recent. In that case there would necessarily be additions made to it from time to time, as new concepts came up for expression, in the same manner as additions were made to Latin during the Middle Ages, and even in modern times. Still, all the nations around Hindostan have the tradition that the art of playing music by means of a bow is very old, the Ceylonese attributing the invention to one of their kings who reigned about 5000 B.C. Their ravanastron is very crude. (See page 72.) A similarly simple instrument is in use to the present day in many parts of the east. The Arab form of it, known as the rebec, is represented on p. 113, Fig. 23. It has two strings of silk, and is played with the point downward, like a 'cello. It is not possible after this lapse of time to determine which was the original form of the violin in Europe. Very early we find the crwth in the hands of the Celtic players, as noticed in chapter VI. The form given in Fig. 22 (p. 107) is rather late, most likely, and somewhat of a degradation, since many of the elements of the violin are wanting in it. The clumsy resonance body is of the same width all the way, preventing the depression of one end of the bow in order to avoid sounding adjacent strings. As the bridge of the crwth was nearly flat, the adjacent strings were octaves, or related in such a way that when sounding together chords were produced. Many have supposed that all the strings were sounded together at each drawing of the bow. This is not impossible, for in one of the sculptures on a capital in the old church at Boscherville in Normandy a stringed instrument is represented in which the tone is produced by a revolving bow, on the principle of the hurdy-gurdy, whereby chords must have been produced continually. (See p. 208.) The same carving has two stringed instruments of the violin family, one held like a violin (No. 6), the other bass downward, like a 'cello (No. 1). These two figures are fragments of the same carving. They are supposed to date from about the eleventh century. Many similar representations occur, such as the following from old manuscripts.

Fig. 38.

These oval instruments had the same deficiency as the crwth, in respect to indentations at the side of the instrument, for permitting the depression of the bow. The oldest type of this instrument in use appears to have been the form known as the rebec, the Arab form, which came into Europe in the time of the crusades. According to certain authorities this was the primitive type from which our violin was derived. The form is better shown in the cut on page 196, which is from an Italian painting of the thirteenth century.

The body of the rebec was pear-shaped. It was contemporaneous with many other forms partaking of the shape of the guitar. From this came the family of viols, which were very popular in England during the fifteenth and sixteenth centuries.

The viol differed from the violin family proper in having a flat back like a guitar, and rounded corners. The only individual of the viol family which attained to artistic development was the viol da Gamba, or bass viol, which was tuned like a lute, having six strings. This instrument was a favorite with many amateurs until late in the eighteenth century. (See p. 197.)

Fig. 39.

ANGEL PLAYING A REBEC.

[From an Italian painting of the thirteenth century.]

Still more curious was the form of viol known as the barytone, which, in addition to an outfit of six catgut strings upon the finger board, was furnished with twenty-four wire strings, stretched close under the sounding board, where they sounded by sympathetic vibration. This was the instrument which Prince Esterhazy, Haydn's patron, so much admired, and for which Haydn wrote more than 150 compositions. Its form is shown in Fig. 41.

Fig. 40.

VIOL DA GAMBA.

[From Reissman's "History of German Music."]

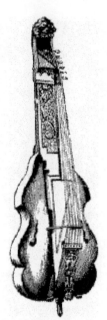

Fig. 41.

THE BARYTONE.

It is not easy within present limits to apportion the various steps by which the violin reached its present form. The first eminent master of violins, as distinguished from small viols, was the celebrated Gaspar da Salo, who lived and worked at Brescia during the latter part of the sixteenth century. The model varies, and the sound holes are straight and flat. His violins are small and weak of tone, but his tenors and basses are much sought for. His model was followed some time later by Guarnerius. The real mastership in violin making was attained at Cremona, in Lombardy, where were many religious houses with elaborate services, and a surrounding population of wealth and artistic instinct afforded the mechanic an appreciative public. It was here early in the sixteenth century that we first find the Amati family in the person of the oldest known violin maker, Andrea, from whom Fétis quotes two instruments dated 1546 and 1551. One of them is a rebec with three strings; the other is a small violin. They are a distinct advance over the violins of the western school, but they stop very far short of the modern instrument. The tone of his instruments is clear and silvery, but not very powerful. The most eminent of the Amatis was Nicolo, 1596-1684, a son of Geronimo and grandson of Andrea. The outline is more graceful, the varnish deeper and richer, and the proportions of his instruments better calculated. His instruments have greater power and intensity of tone, and his tenors and 'cellos are very famous. But the Cremona school came to a culmination in the works of the pupil of Nicolo Amati—Antonio Stradivari, 1649-1737. This great master of the violin pursued the principles of the Amati construction down to about 1700, having then been making violins for upwards of thirty-three years. After 1700 he changed his principles of construction somewhat, and developed the grand style distinguishing his later works. He marks the culminating point of the art of violin making. It was he who perfected the model of the violin and its fittings. The bridge in its present form, and the sound holes, are cut exactly as he planned them, and no artist has discovered a possibility of improving them. His main improvements consisted (1) in lowering the height of the model—that is, the arch of the belly; (2) in making the four corner blocks more massive, and in giving greater curvature to the middle ribs; (3) in altering the setting of the sound holes, giving them a decided inclination to each other at the top; (4) in making the scroll more massive and permanent. Every violin of Stradivari was a special study, modified in various details according to the nature of the wood which he happened to have, sometimes a trifle smaller, a trifle thicker in this place or the other, or some other slight change accounted for not by pre-established theory, but by adaptation to the peculiarities of the wood in hand. According to Fétis, his wood was always selected with reference to its tone-producing qualities— the fir of the belly always giving a certain note, and the maple of the back a certain other note. These peculiarities are not regarded as fully established. The tone of the Stradivarius violin is full, musical and high-spirited. The small number now in existence are held at extremely high prices. The usual pattern is that represented in the following figure.

Fig. 42.

THE STRADIVARIUS VIOLIN.

[From Grove.]

Stradivari established his own factory about 1680, and continued to make instruments up to 1730. The violin of 1708 weighs three-quarters of a pound. Besides making violins, this eminent artist also made guitars, lutes, 'cellos and tenors. It is wholly uncertain to what extent the peculiarities of the Stradivari instruments were matters of deduction and how far accidental. But there can be no question that the average excellence of his instruments, judging from the specimens still in existence, was much greater than that of any other violin maker.

Many other eminent artists made good violins in the century and a half from the time of Andrea Amati and Gaspar da Salo to Stradivari, among the most eminent being Maggini, of Brescia, whose violins are very highly esteemed. Still, inasmuch as the finishing touches were put to the instrument by Stradivarius, we need not linger to discuss the minor makers.

II.

Before 1600 the organ had attained its maturity, and had become furnished with its distinctive characteristics as we have it at the present time. As this instrument, from the nature of its tone qualities and its peculiar limitation to serious music of grave rhythm, is naturally suited to the service of the Church, it has remained till the present day in the province where it had already firmly established itself at the time now under consideration. The origin of the organ is very difficult to ascertain. There are traces of some sort of wind instrument before the Christian era. The so-called hydraulic organ was probably one in which water was used to perfect the air-holding qualities of the wind chest, in the same manner as now in gas holders. One of the earliest mediæval references to organs is to that sent King Pepin, of France, father of Charlemagne, in 742 by Constantine, emperor of Byzantium at that time. This instrument, says the old chronicler, had brass pipes, blown with bellows bags; it was struck with the hands and feet. It was the first of this kind seen in France.

Prætorius says that the organ which Vitellianus set in church 300 years before Pepin, must have been the small instrument of fifteen pipes, for which the wind was collected in twelve bellows bags.

According to Julianus, a Spanish bishop who flourished in 450, the organ was in common use in churches at that time. In 822 an organ was sent to Charlemagne by the Caliph Haroun Alraschid, made by an Arabian maker. This instrument was placed in a church at Aix-la-Chapelle. There were good organ builders in Venice as early as 822, and before 900 there was an organ in the cathedral at Munich. In the ninth century organs had become common in England, and in the tenth the English prelate, St. Dunstan, erected one in Malmesbury Abbey, of which the pipes were of brass. The instruments of that time were extremely crude.

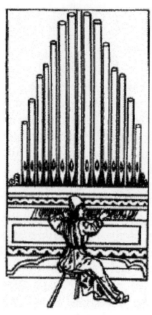

Fig. 43.

[From Franchinus Gaffurius, "*Theorica Musica,*" Milan, 1492.]

From this time on there are many authentic remains in the way of treatises on organ building and description of organs. The essential elements of this instrument consist of pipes for producing sound, of which a complete set, one pipe for each key of the keyboard, is called a stop; bellows and wind chest for holding the wind, sliders or valves for admitting it to the pipes, and keys for controlling the valves.

In his studies for a history of musical notation, Dr. Hugo Riemann quotes an extract from an anonymous manuscript of the tenth century, in which the author gives directions for a set of organ pipes. "Take first," he says, "ten pipes of a proper dimension and of equal length and size. Divide the first pipe into nine parts; eight of these will be the length of the second. Dividing the length of this again into nine parts, eight of these will be the proper length of the third; dividing the first pipe into four parts, three of them will be the length of the fourth; taking the first pipe as three parts, two of them will be the length of the fifth; eight-ninths of this again will give the proper length of the sixth; eight-ninths of this, the length of the seventh; one-half the first, the length of the eighth, or octave." This gives a major scale, with the Pythagorean third, consisting of two great steps, which was too sharp to be consonant. The semitone between the third and the fourth is too small, as is also that between the seventh and eighth. The modern way of making the pipes of smaller diameter as they become shorter, had evidently not been thought of. Nevertheless, these directions are very important, since they throw positive light upon the tuning of the various intervals, the pipe lengths and proportions affording accurate determinations of the musical relations intended.

Fig. 44.

PORTABLE ORGAN FROM THE PROCESSION IN HONOR OF MAXIMILIAN I.

[From Prætorius' "*Syntagma Musica*," about 1500 A.D.]

The early organs were furnished with slides which the organist pulled out when he wished to make a pipe speak, and pushed back to check its utterance. The date of the invention of the valve is uncertain, but it must have been about as soon as the power of the instrument was increased by the addition of the second or third stop. Before this, however, and perhaps for some little time after, there were many organs in use, which were committed to the diaphony of Hucbald, having in place of the diapason three ranks of pipes, speaking an octave and the fifth between. Each of these combined sounds was treated in the same way as simple ones are on other instruments, and if chords were attempted upon them the effect must have been hideous indeed; but it is probable that at this time the notes were played singly, and not in chords, or at most in octaves. We do not know the date at which this style of organ building ceased, but it is probably before the thirteenth century. There is a manuscript of the fourteenth century in the Royal Library at Madrid, stating that the clavier at that epoch comprised as many as thirty-one keys, and that the larger pipes were placed on one side, and small pipes in the center, the same as now. The earliest chromatic keyboards known are those in the organ erected at Halberstadt cathedral in 1361. This instrument had twenty-two keys, fourteen diatonics and eight chromatics, extending from B natural up to A; and twenty bellows blown by ten men. Its larger pipe B stood in front, and was thirty-one Brunswick feet in length and three and a half feet in circumference. This note would now be marked as a semitone below the C of thirty-two feet. In this organ for the first time a provision was made for using the soft stop independently of the loud one. This result was obtained by means of three keyboards. The keys were very wide, those of the upper and middle keyboards measuring four inches from center to center. The sharps and flats were about two and a half inches above the diatonic keys, and had a fall of about one and a quarter inches. The mechanical features of the organ were very greatly improved during the next century, but it was not until the old organ in the Church of St. Ægidien in Brunswick that the sharps and naturals were combined in one keyboard in the same manner as at present. The keys were still very large, the naturals of the great manual being about one and three-quarters inches in width. It was to the organ at Halberstadt that pedals were added in 1495, but no pipes were assigned to them. They merely pulled down the lower keys of the manual.

Fig. 45.

BELLOWS BAGS IN THE ORGAN AT HALBERSTADT, AND METHOD OF BLOWING.

[Prætorius.]

Some time before the beginning of the seventeenth century the organ had acquired nearly the entire variety of tone that it has ever had. The mechanism was rude, no doubt, and the voicing perhaps imperfect. The tuning was by the unequal system, throwing the discords into remote keys as much as possible. In Michael Prætorius' "*Syntagma Musica*," the great source of information upon this part of the history (published at Wolfenbüttel, 1618), he describes a number of large organs. Among them he mentions the organ in the Church of St. Mary at Danzig, built in 1585, having three manuals and pedal; there were fifty-five stops. The balance must have been very bad, since there were in the great organ three stops of sixteen feet, and only three of eight feet. There was a mixture having twenty-four pipes to each key, besides a "zimbel" in the same manual, having three ranks.

Prætorius also gives many other specifications of large organs of three manuals, some with dates, some without. They belong mostly to the beginning of the seventeenth century, and the number indicates unmistakably the interest awakened in this part of the musical furnishing of the large churches. Many points in these organs were imperfect, but the foundation had been laid, and the general character of the subsequent building settled. There was also a beginning of virtuosity upon the organ, but this will come up for consideration at a later point in the narrative.

Fig. 46.

SCULPTURED HEAD OF COLUMN, FOUND IN THE RUINS OF THE ABBEY OF ST. GEORGE, AT BOSCHERVILLE, IN NORMANDY.
ELEVENTH CENTURY.

(1) Three-stringed viol or rebec. (2) Two persons playing the organistrum, a stringed instrument vibrated by means of a circular bow or wheel, like the hurdy-gurdy. (3) Pandean pipes. (4) Apparently a small harp. (5) Psaltery. (6) Rotta or crwth. (7) Acrobat. (8) Harp. (9), (10) Instruments of percussion, perhaps bells.

Book Third.

THE

Dawn of Modern Music.

THE BEGINNING OF FREE EXPRESSION IN SONG, OPERA, ORATORIO AND FREE INSTRUMENTAL MUSIC.

CHAPTER XVII.
CONDITION OF MUSIC AT THE BEGINNING
OF THE SEVENTEENTH CENTURY.

IN justification of the name "apprentice period" for that part of the history of music ending with Palestrina as the representative of the finished art of the Netherlands (helped out, we may well enough admit, with no small measure of the original insight and genius of his own), a general view of the condition of music in all European countries at the beginning of the seventeenth century may well be taken. The fullness with which the details have already been treated renders it unnecessary to repeat them here, but it will be enough to recapitulate the principal features of the art thus far attained, adding thereto a number of incidents omitted. Upon the side of musical phraseology, then, we find in the north the attainment of a simple and expressive form of melody almost or quite up to the standard of modern taste. In the direction of the musically elaborative element we have the schools of the Netherlands and of Italy, in which absolutely everything of this kind was realized which modern art can show, saving perhaps the fugue, which involved questions of tonality belonging to a grade of taste and harmonic perception more advanced and refined than that as yet attained. It took nearly another century before the ecclesiastical keys were thoroughly disenchanted in the estimation of classical musicians. It was Bach who finally made true tonality the rule rather than the exception.

In the line of instruments the harp had had its day, its never ending tuning having been one of the most operative forces in the development of the ear. Its successor, the lute, equally weak in tenacity of intonation, but with greater artistic resources, had been fully tested in every direction. The organ had attained a very respectable size, even when measured according to modern ideas, and its influence in the direction of harmonic education had been well begun. The keyed instrument, of which our pianoforte is the living representative, had found its keyboard and a practical method of eliciting tones, which, whatever their weakness, were at least better than those of the lute, the chitarrone, the psaltery or harp. Best of all, the violin had found master hands able to shape it into a model graceful to the eye, and sonorous beyond anything else which the art of music can show. True, it was not until about sixty years later that the powers of this instrument in the direction of solos were fully recognized, or, indeed, brought before the public. This was the work of Corelli, whose sonatas were published in the third quarter of the century with which we are now dealing. The viol, the weaker predecessor of the violin, had made great headway, and Monteverde put himself on record in 1607, much to his credit, by placing it at the head of his orchestra.

Moreover, not only were the instruments of music in a condition creditable even in the light of modern ideas, but the popular taste for music was more lively and far-reaching than ever before. Everywhere in the civilized world the practice of music was the universal attribute of a gentleman. In Italy we shall find a circle composed of some of the best minds of the nation engaged in the regular study of classical learning, and in discussions having for their object the re-discovery of the art of ancient music, which the seekers wrongfully imagined to have been as far superior to the music then in vogue as the sculpture of the ancients had been superior to that of mediæval Italy. In no country was the art of music more highly esteemed, or, we may add, in a more advanced state than in England.

Richard Braithwaite, a writer of the reign of Elizabeth, formulated certain rules for the government of the house of an earl, in which the earl was "to keep five musicians, skillful in that commendable sweet science"; and they were required to teach "the earl's children to sing and to play upon the bass viol, the virginals, the lute, the bandour or cittern." When he gave great feasts, the musicians were "to play whilst the service was going to the table, upon sackbuts, cornets, shawms and such other instruments going with wind, and upon viols, violins or other broken music during repast." In barber shops they had lutes and virginals wherewith the gentlemen might amuse themselves while awaiting their turn. It was the same in reception rooms; musical instruments were provided as the surest method of enabling waiting guests to amuse themselves.

If it be asked why it was that in spite of this high esteem for music so little came out of its cultivation in England that was creditable upon the highest plane, according to the scales in which we are accustomed to weigh the music of Italy and Germany, the answer is not hard to find. It was in consequence of the little attention paid to musical learning in the highest sense, as compared with the learning and training in musicianship on the continent. English music died out, or grew small, for want of depth of earth. High ideals and thorough training in the technique are two prime conditions of a successful development of an art. Besides, the art of music suffered irreparable damage in England at the hands of the Puritans. The protectorate lasted long enough to put the art under an eclipse from which it did not fully emerge until nearly our own time.

A similar fondness for this form of art pervaded all European countries. In Italy music was the delight of the common people and the favorite pursuit of the great. In Germany the Reformation and the influence of Luther had set the people singing. The organ had attained an advanced state there, and other instruments of every sort were cultivated. It was the same in France. The love for music was universal. Hence the times were ripe for a great advance in art. There was concentrated upon music an attention which it has rarely enjoyed at any other period of its history, and the advances now to be mentioned were correspondingly abundant and striking.

The contrapuntal schools had done more to educate harmonic perception than is commonly supposed. All the devices of counterpoint, as we have them to-day, were invented by the various schools of this period, and brought to a high degree of perfection. But the learning had somewhat overshot its mark. The multiplicity of parts in the compositions of Willaert, and the other masters of the polyphonic schools, served for the cultivation of chord perception just as surely as if they had intentionally written chord successions without troubling themselves with imitative canon in any degree. For, when there were so many voice parts as ten, fifteen or twenty within the limits of the compass of the human organ, that is to say, mainly within the limits of two octaves and a half, the parts had no recourse but to cross continually, and since there was no aid afforded the ear by differences in tone color between one voice part and another, it necessarily followed that they fell upon the ear with the effect not of voice parts, in which the melody of each could be followed independently of the others, but rather as chord masses, in which here and there a prominent melodic phrase occasionally emerged, only to be lost the next moment by the prominence of a bit of the melody of some other voice. The effect of a composition of this kind was no other than that of a succession of chords, and the ear was as thoroughly educated to chord perception by this class of music as if the composer had intended only to write successions of chords. Still the training of these schools, while incidentally affording education to the ear upon the harmonic side, was thoroughly contrapuntal, and the study of every composer was to make something more elaborate than anything that had been written by his predecessors.

Nevertheless there was an influence in another direction. An art form was invented, which by the end of this period had established itself as the type of a musical form whenever the composer would arrive at something more spontaneous than could conveniently be attained by the way of a motette or conduit. That form was the madrigal. The meaning of the name is unknown. Some have derived it from Mary, and point to the sacred madrigals, many of which were composed by all the contrapuntal writers. Others have assigned a different origin for it, and it is not possible now to decide which is the true one. Enough if we find this form emerging from obscurity by the middle of the fifteenth century. The first writer of compositions under this title whose name is known to us was Busnois, and in the same collection are compositions of the same class by many other composers of the Netherlandish schools. A madrigal was a secular composition, generally devoted to love, but in polyphonic style, and in one of the ecclesiastical modes. They were always vocal down to the seventeenth century, but from that time forward they were generally marked for voices and instruments. One of the best composers of madrigals was Arkadelt, of the Netherlandish school. The success of the great Orlando Lassus in this school has already been mentioned, together with the name of one of the best known of his compositions in this line (p. 167).

The strange modulations, like that from F to E flat in one of Arkadelt's madrigals, are current incidents of the ecclesiastical mode in which they are written. Many of the secular works of this class are hardly to be distinguished from those intended for the Church, and some are to be met with, having two sets of words, one secular, occasionally almost profane; the other sacred, some hymn or other from the offices of divine service.

In England this school had a great currency, and the madrigals of the British writers of the seventeenth century are every whit as free and melodious as the best of those of the Italian school. The number of writers of this class of works was innumerable, so much so that we might well class it as the ruling art form of the century, just as the dramatic song was in the eighteenth century, the fugue in the last half of it, and the sonata in the beginning of the nineteenth. Everybody wrote madrigals who ever wrote music at all. According to the dates of collections published, the English followed the Italian composers. The earliest Italian compositions of this class are contained in three collections printed by Ottaviano di Petrucci, the inventor of the process of printing music from movable type. These collections were published in Venice, 1501-1503, and copies are still retained in the library at Bologna and at Vienna. The English cultivation of this form of composition became general toward the last of this century, and in the first part of the next ensuing, and it is but just to say that the English composers finally surpassed the continental in this school, and developed out of it a beautiful art genre of their own, the glee. Toward the latter part of the sixteenth century certain attempts were made in Italy at something resembling our opera, but in place of solo pieces by any of the performers there were madrigals. When Juliet, for example, would soliloquize upon the balcony, she did so in a madrigal, the remaining four parts being carried by chambermaids inside. When Romeo climbed the balcony and breathed his sweet vows to Juliet, one or two of his friends around the corner carried the missing melodies in which he sought to improvise his warm affection. The absurdity of the proceeding was manifest, but it needed yet another point of emphasis. There was a grand wedding in Venice in 1595, at which the music consisted of madrigals, all in slow time and minor key. The contradiction between the doleful music and the festive occasion was too plain to be ignored, and led, presently, to the invention of a totally different style of song of which later there is much to say.

The seventeenth century was one of the most memorable in the history of music, not so much, however, for what it fully accomplished as for the new ideas brought out and in part developed. The specific part of the general development of music which this century accomplished was *the development of free melodic expression*. While, as already noticed, the musical productions of the preceding centuries had manifested an increasing melodic force and propriety, the secret of genuine melodic expression had yet to be found. In the madrigal and motette the conditions were wholly unsuited to the development of this part of music. Instead of one prominent voice, in which the main interest of the production centered itself, the composer of that period had a certain number of equally important voice parts, all taking part in the development of the one leading idea of his piece. Melodically speaking, the standpoint was wrong and the situation false. Melody means individuality, individualism; the free representation of a personality in its own self-determined motion. At the point of the year 1600, speaking with sufficient exactness for ordinary purposes, the ruling standpoint of musical production changed, in the effort to rediscover the lost vocal forms of the Greek drama. The new problem was that of finding, for every moment and every speech of the drama, a form of utterance suitable to the sentiment and the occasion. Thus entered into music, through the ministry of self-forgetfulness, the most important principle which has actuated its later progress, the principle namely, of dramatic expression—in other words, the *representative* principle, the effort to represent in music something which until now had been outside of music. Out of this principle, co-operating with that other idea of two centuries later, the inherent interest of the individual, has grown the richness and manifold luxuriance of modern romantic music, together with the entire province of opera and oratorio. We have now to trace the steps which led to this great transformation in the art of music; and to illustrate the application of the new principles to the province of instrumental music, which had no beginning of genuine art value before this period. When examined with reference to the matured productions of the century next ensuing, those of the seventeenth appear quite as much like apprentice efforts as those of the latter part of the period covered in the preceding book of our story; but they have in them, however, the seeds of the later development, and stand to us, therefore, in the character of first fruits. To state it still more unmistakably, we have to trace in the operations of the seventeenth century the *origin of dramatic song*, the beginnings of *free instrumental music*, the discovery of the *art of voice training* and the formation of what is called the "old Italian school of singing," and the operation of the representative element in music, together with the new forms created through its entrance into art.

The musical movement of this century in its entirety was a part of the general operation of mind, which was now of great amplitude and spontaneity. The fervor of the Renaissance indeed had passed, having resulted in the creation of masterpieces of architecture, sculpture, painting and poetry during the previous two centuries. Music came to expression last of the forms of art, and when mental movement was less intense. For this reason the Italian mind failed to rule in it after the early beginnings in the new direction had been made. The representative element entered the art of music in Italy; but the mastery of its application, and the development of new forms fully completing the representation, were carried on by other nationalities where the mental movement still retained the pristine vigor of new impulses and rich vitality.

The city of Florence was the center where the drama and song-like melody found its beginning. Almost immediately, however, Venice became the home of music, and fostered the growth of dramatic song for more than half a century. At this time, as for a century previous, Venice was the most active intellectual center of Europe. Perhaps nothing gives so clear a realization of this supremacy as the statistics of books printed in the leading centers of Europe from 1470 to 1500. The largest centers were Strassburg, with 526; Basle, 320; Leipsic, 351; Nuremburg, 382; Cologne, 530; Paris, 751; Rome, 925; Bologna, 298; Milan, 625, while Venice heads the list with 2,835. Toward the end of the century, the appearance of the genius, Alexander Scarlatti, effected the transference of the musical supremacy of Italy to Naples.

CHAPTER XVIII.
FIRST CENTURY OF ITALIAN OPERA AND DRAMATIC SONG.

DURING the last decade of the sixteenth century a company of Florentine gentlemen were in the habit of meeting at the house of Count Bardi for the study of ancient literature. Their attention had concentrated itself upon the drama of the Greeks, and the one thing which they sought to discover was the music of ancient tragedy, the stately and measured intonation to which the great periods of Æschylus, Euripides and Sophocles had been uttered. The alleged fragments of Pindar's music since discovered by Athanasius Kircher (p. 69) were not yet known, and they had nothing whatever to guide their researches beyond the mathematical computations of Ptolemy and the other Greek writers. At length, one evening, Vincenzo Galilei, father of the astronomer Galileo, presented himself with a monody. Taking a scene from Dante's "*Purgatorio*" (the episode of Ugolini), he sang or chanted it to music of his own production, with the accompaniment of the viola played by himself. The assembly was in raptures. "Surely," they said, "*this* must have been the style of the music of the famous drama of Athens." Thereupon others set themselves to composing monodies, which, as yet, were not arias, but something between a recitative and an aria, having measure and a certain regularity of tune, but in general the freedom of the chant. Among the number at Count Bardi's was the poet Rinuccini, who prepared a drama called "Dafne." The music of this was composed in part by an amateur named Caccini, and in part by Jacopo Peri, all being members of this studious circle meeting at the house of Count Bardi. "Dafne" was performed in 1597 at the house of Count Corsi, with great success, but the music has been lost, and nothing more definite is known about it. This beginning of opera, for so it was, was also the beginning of opera in Germany, as we shall presently see, for about twenty years later a copy of "Dafne" was carried to Dresden for production there before the court, but when the libretto had been translated into German, it was found unsuited to the music of the Italian copy, whereupon the Dresden director, Heinrich Schütz, wrote new music for it, and thus became the composer of the first German opera ever written. In 1600 the marriage of Catherine de Medici with Henry IV of France was celebrated at Florence with great pomp, and Peri was commissioned to undertake a new opera, for which Rinuccini composed the text "Eurydice." The work was given with great *éclat*, and was shortly after printed. Only one copy of the first edition is now known to be in existence, and that, by a curious accident, is in the Newberry Library at Chicago. The British Museum has a copy of the second edition of 1608. The opera of "Eurydice" is short, the printed copy containing only fifty-eight pages, and the music is almost entirely recitative. There are two or three short choruses; there is one orchestral interlude for three flutes, extending to about twenty measures in all, but there is nothing like a finale or ensemble piece. Nevertheless, this is the beginning, out of which afterward grew the entire flower of Italian opera. On page 225 is an extract.

FLUTE TRIO AND SCENE.

[From the first opera, "Eurydice" (1600). Jacopo Peri.]

[Listen]

The new style thus invented was known to the Italians as *il stilo rappresentivo*, or the representative style, that is to say, the dramatic style, and there is some dispute as to the real author of the invention. About the same time with the production of "Eurydice," a Florentine musician, Emilio del Cavaliere, wrote the music to a sacred drama, of which the text had been composed for him by Laura Guidiccioni, the title being "*La Rappresentazione del Anima e del Corpo.*" The piece was an allegorical one, very elaborate in its structure, and written throughout in the representative style, of which

Cavaliere claimed to be the inventor. This oratorio, which was the first ever written, was produced at the oratory of St. Maria in Vallicella, in the month of February, ten months before the appearance of "Eurydice" at Florence. It is evident, therefore, that if the style had been in any manner derived from the Florentine experiments already noted, it must have been from the earlier opera "Dafne" and not from "Eurydice." The principal characters were "*Il Tempo*" (time), "*La Vita*" (life), "*Il Mondo*" (the world), etc. The orchestra consisted of one lira doppia, one clavicembalo, one chitarrone and two flutes. No part is written for violin. At one part of the performance there was a ballet. The whole was performed in church, as already noticed, as a part of religious service.

Seven years later we enter upon the second period of the opera, when, on the occasion of the marriage of Francesco Gongeaza with Margherita, Infanta of Savoy, Rinuccini prepared the libretti for two operas, entitled "Dafne" and "Arianna," the second of which was set to music by Claudio Monteverde, the ducal musical director, a man of extraordinary genius. The first of these operas has long since been forgotten, but Monteverde made a prodigious effect with his. The scene where Ariadne bewails the departure of her faithless lover affected the audience to tears. Monteverde was immediately commissioned to write another opera, for which he took the subject of "*Orfeo,*" and, being himself an accomplished violinist, he made an important addition to the orchestral appointments previously attempted in opera. The instruments used were the following:

2 Gravicembani.
2 Contrabassi de viola.
10 Viole da brazzo.
1 Arpa doppio.
2 Violini piccolo alla Francese.
2 Chitaroni.
2 Organi de Legno.
2 Bassa da Gamba.
4 Tromboni.
1 Regale.
2 Cornetti.
1 Flautino alla vigesima secunda.
1 Clarino, con 3 trombi sordine.

A very decided attempt is made in this work at orchestra coloring, each character being furnished with a combination of instruments appropriate to his place in the drama. These works were not given in public, but only in palaces for the great, and it was not for more than twenty years that a public opera house was erected in Venice. In 1624 Monteverde at the instance of Girolamo Mocenigo composed an intermezzo, "*Il Combatimento di Tancredi e Clorinda*," in which he introduced for the first time two important orchestral effects: The *pizzicati* (plucking the strings with the fingers) and the *tremolo*. These occur in the scene where Clorinda, disguised as a knight, fights a duel with her lover Tancredi, who, not knowing his opponent, gives her a fatal wound. The strokes of the sword are accompanied by the *pizzicati* of the violins, and the suspense when Clorinda falls is characterized by the tremolo—two devices universal in melodrama to the present day.

Monteverde had already for some time been a resident in Venice as director of the music at St. Mark's, where his salary had originally been established at 300 ducats per annum, and a house in the canon's close. In 1616 his salary was raised to 500 ducats, and he gave himself up entirely to the service of the republic. The first opera house was erected in 1637 and was followed within a few years by two other opera houses in Venice. In these places Monteverde's subsequent works were produced. The greater number of his manuscripts are hopelessly lost. We possess only eight books of madrigals, a volume of canzonettes, the complete edition of "Orpheus," and a quantity of church music.

The new path opened by this great composer was followed assiduously by a multitude of Italian musicians. Among these the more distinguished names are those of Cavalli, who wrote thirty-four operas for Venice alone, Legrenzi and Cesti. The latter wrote six operas, some of which were very successful. By 1699 there were eleven theaters in Venice at which operas were habitually given; at Rome there were three; in Bologna one; and in Naples one. It would take us too far to discuss in detail the successive steps in the history during this century, since in the nature of the case, an individual work like an opera can with difficulty rise above the popular musical phraseology of the day, the object being immediate success with a public largely uncultivated. Hence, popular operas for the most part are short-lived, rarely retaining their popularity more than thirty years.

The greatest genius in opera in this century after Monteverde was Alessandro Scarlatti, of Naples, the principal of the conservatory there, and, we might say, the inventor of the Italian art of singing—*bel canto*. For as there had been no monody, so there had been no solo singing, and as the operas of the first three-quarters of this century, in spite of the improvements of Monteverde, consisted mostly of recitative, there was still no singing in the modern acceptation of the term. Scarlatti introduced new forms. To the *recitativo secco*, or unaccompanied recitative, which until now had been the principal dependence for the movement of the drama, he added the *recitativo stromentato*, or accompanied recitative, in which the instruments afforded a dramatic coloring for the text of the singer. To these, again, he added a third element, the aria. The first he employed for the ordinary business of the stage; the second for the expression of deep pathos; the third for strongly individualized soliloquy. These three types of vocal delivery remain valid, and are still used by composers in the same way as by Scarlatti. His first opera was produced in Rome at the palace of Christina, ex-queen of Sweden, in 1680. This was followed by 108 others, the most of which were produced in Naples. The most celebrated of these were "*Pompei*" (Naples, 1684), "*La Theodora*" (Rome, 1693), "*Il Triompho de la Liberta*" (Venice, 1707) and, most celebrated of all, "*La Principessa Fidele.*" In addition to this he wrote a large number of cantatas, more or less dramatic in character. Scarlatti not only created the aria, calling for sustained and impassioned singing, but also invented or discovered methods of training singers to perform these numbers successfully. He was the founder of the Italian school of singing, and the external model upon which it was based undoubtedly was furnished by the violin which, having been perfected by the Amati, as already noted in the previous chapter, and its solo capacities having been brought out by Archangelo Corelli, whose first violin sonatas were published a few years before Scarlatti's first opera, had now established a standard of melodic phrasing and impassioned delivery superior to anything which had previously been known. It was a pupil of Scarlatti, Nicolo Porpora (1686-1766), who carried forward the work begun by his master. Porpora was even a greater teacher of singing than Scarlatti himself, and his pupils became the leading singers in Europe during the first quarter of the eighteenth century. The progress of vocal cultivation was remarkably helped by the fact that at this time women were not permitted to appear upon the stage, all the female parts being taken by male sopranos, *castrati*. These artificial sopranos, having no other career before them than that of operatic singing, devoted themselves vigorously to the technique of their art, and were efficient agents in awakening a taste for florid singing impossible for ordinary or untrained voices. Women did not appear upon the stage in opera until toward the middle of this century. Händel, in London, had male sopranos such as Farinelli, Senesimo, and the earlier of the female sopranos, of whom the vicious Cuzzoni was a shining example. The artistic merits of Porpora have been greatly exaggerated by certain writers, notably by Mme. George Sand in her "*Consuelo*," where he figures as one of the greatest and most devoted of artists. Her work, however, has the excellence of affording a very good representation of the artistic end proposed by the Italian masters of singing in their best moments. Porpora spent the early part of his life in Naples, but afterward he resided for some time in Dresden, Vienna, Rome and Venice, being principal of a conservatory in the latter place. In the latter years of his life (1736) he was invited to London to compose operas in competition with Händel, in which calling he but poorly succeeded. Porpora represents the ideal which has ruled Italian opera from his time to the present, the ideal, namely, of the pleasing, the well sounding, and the vocally agreeable. He is responsible for the fanciful roulades, the long arias and the many features of this part of dramatic music which please the unthinking, but mark such a wide departure from the severe and noble, if narrow, ideal of the original inventors of this form of art.

It is to be regretted that the limits of the present work do not permit the introduction of selections of music sufficiently extended for illustrating the finer modifications of style effected by the successive masters named in the text. The brief extracts following are taken from the excellent lectures of the late John Hullah upon "Transitional Periods in Musical History." The same valuable and suggestive work contains a number of more extended selections from these and other little known masters of the period, for which reason the book forms a useful addition to the library of teachers, schools, etc. Other illustrations will be found in Gevaert's "*Les Gloires d'Italie*" ("The Glories of Italy"). There are sixty arias in this collection, all well edited, and chosen for their effectiveness for public performance at the present day.

ARIA PARLANTE.—"LASCIATE MI MORIR."

[From the opera "Ariadne," 1607. Monteverde.]

[Listen]

EXTRACT FROM SONG, "VAGHE STELLE."

[From the opera "Erismena," 1655. Francesco Cavalli.]

[Listen]

ARIA.—"LASCIAMI PIANGERE."

[From a cantata. Alessandro Scarlatti.]

[Listen]

Lento non troppo.

CHAPTER XIX.
BEGINNINGS OF OPERA IN FRANCE AND GERMANY.

I.

FROM Florence the art of dramatic song spread to all other parts of the world, yet not so rapidly as would have been supposed. For it was not until nearly half of the century had already elapsed that opera made a beginning in France, the country where ruled the unfortunate princess for whose nuptials the first opera had been written. French opera grew out of the ballet. This term, which at present is restricted to entertainments in which dancing is the principal feature, and the story is entirely told in pantomime, had formerly a more extended signification. It was equivalent to the English term "Mask," a play in which dancing, songs and even dialogue found place. This light and sprightly form of drama has been favored in France from a remote period. As early as the first quarter of the seventeenth century Antoine Boesset (1585-1643) composed ballets for the entertainments of the king, Louis XIII. His son succeeded him at the court of Louis XIV. Some of the ballets of the elder Boesset were produced in 1635, and in these we must find the beginnings of French opera, if indeed we do not go back still farther, and find it in the play of "Robin and Marian," written by Adam de la Halle. In fact, dramatic entertainment has been indigenous in France from an early date, and it is by no means easy to say that at any particular moment the line was crossed where modern opera begins. The ballets of Boesset were, no doubt, slight upon the dramatic side, having even less of serious intention in the music than the lightest of comic opera of the present day.

The impulse to grand opera came from a different quarter. A sagacious cleric, the Abbé Perrin, heard, either at Florence or in Paris, from the company of Italian singers brought over in 1645, Peri's "Eurydice," which made a great impression upon him, and he suggested to a musician of his acquaintance, Robert Cambert, the production of another work in similar style. Several things in this account appear strange, but strangest of all, the total ignorance that prevailed in Paris of the vast development that had been made in Italian opera by Monteverde and the other Italians, during the forty years since Peri's experiment had been first composed. With the leisurely movement of the times, the new work of the French composers was produced in 1659. This was "*La Pastorale*," performed with the greatest applause at the chateau of Issy. This was followed by several other works in similar style, "Ariane," "Adonis" and the like, and in 1669 Perrin secured a patent giving him a monopoly of operatic performances in France for a period of years.

Meanwhile a certain ambitious and unscrupulous youngster was feeling his way to a position where he might make himself recognized. It was the youthful violinist, Jean Baptiste Lulli, the illegitimate son of a Florentine gentleman, his dates being about 1633-1687. Lulli had been taught the rudiments of knowledge, including that of the violin, by a kind-hearted priest of his native city, and, when yet a mere lad, made his way to Paris in the suite of the duke of Guise. Once in Paris his way was open. Gifted with a quick wit, a total absence of principle or honor, but of insatiable ambition, he made his way from one position to another, and at length had been so prominent as a composer of dance music, and leader of the king's violins, as to have opportunity to distinguish himself by composing the music for the ballet of "*Alcidiane*," and others, in which Louis XIV himself danced. Lulli's ambition was still farther stimulated and his style influenced by the study of the music of Cavalli, for several of whose operas he composed ballets, upon the occasion of their production in France.

Within thirteen years he produced no less than thirty ballets. In these he himself took part with considerable success as dancer and comic actor. The success of Cambert and Perrin's operas of "*Pomone*" and "The Pains and Pleasures of Love" (1671) awakened in him the desire of supplanting them in the regard of the king. After intrigues creditable neither to himself nor to the powers influenced by them, he succeeded in this same year in having the patent of Perrin set aside, and a new one issued, giving him the sole right of producing operas in France for a period of years. Then ensued a career of operatic productivity most creditable and influential from every point of view. In the space of fourteen years Lulli produced twenty operas, or *divertissements*, of which the best, perhaps, were "*Alceste*," 1674, "*Thesée*," 1675, "*Amadis de Gaule*," 1684, and "Roland," 1685. Lulli made certain improvements upon the Italian models, which he originally followed, making the recitative more stately, and employing the accompanying orchestra for purposes of dramatic coloration. He was a great master of the stage, and introduced his effects with consummate judgment. His declamation of the text was most excellent, and in this respect his operas have served as models in the traditions of the French stage from that time until now. As a musician, however, he was clever rather than deep, and the music is often monotonous and rather stilted. Nevertheless, his operas held the stage for many years after the death of their author, and occasional revivals have taken place at intervals, even after the advance in taste and musical knowledge had effectually quenched their ability to please a popular audience. His "Roland" was performed as an incident in the regular season at Paris as late as 1778, when Gluck's "Orpheus" had already been heard. The example of Lulli's music given on pages 240 and 241 is from this work. The melody is vigorous and appropriate.

The most commendable feature of this beginning of opera in France was the attention given to the musical treatment of the vernacular of the country. The principle once recognized, that opera not in the vernacular of the country can never have more than an incidental and adventitious importance, has always been maintained in France. The *Académie de Musique*, for which the patent was granted to Perrin, and transferred to Lulli, has been maintained with few interruptions ever since, and has been the home of a native French opera, constantly increasing in vigor, originality and interest. Italian opera has been fashionable in Paris for brief periods, and as the amusement of the fashionable world, but the native opera has nearly always held the place of honor in the affections of the people, and the foreign works produced there have been translated into the French language.

SONG.—"ROLAND, COUREZ AUX ARMES."

[From the opera "Roland," 1685. J.B. Lulli.]

[Listen]

Animato.

Ro - land, cou - rez aux ar - mes, aux
ar - mes, cou - rez aux ar - mes, Que la
gloi - re a de charm - es, Que la gloi - re a de charm - es; L'a-
mour de ses di - vins ap - pas, Fait vi - vre au de - là du tré-

pas, L'a - mour de ses di - vins ap - pas, Fait vi - vre au de-

là du tré - pas Ro - land, cou - rez aux ar - mes, -aux

ar mes, cou - rez aux ar - mes. Que la

gloi - re a de charm - es, Que la gloi - re a de charm - es.

II.

In Germany the contrary was the case for more than a century later. The first operatic performance, indeed, was given in the German language. A copy of Peri's "Dafne" was sent to Dresden and as a preparation for performance the text was translated, but it was found impossible to adapt the German words to the Italian recitative, owing to the different structure of the German sentences, bringing the emphasis in totally different places. In this stress the local master, Heinrich Schütz, was called upon to compose new music, which he did, and the work was given in 1627. This beginning of German opera, however, was totally accidental. All that was intended was the repetition of the famous Italian work. Nor did the persons concerned appear to recognize the importance and high significance of the act in which they had co-operated, for no other German operas were given there or elsewhere until much later. Schütz, moreover, did not pursue the career of an operatic composer, but turned his attention mainly to church music and oratorio, in which department he highly distinguished himself, as we will presently have occasion to examine farther.

It was not until the beginning of the century next ensuing, that German opera began to take root and grow. The beginning was made in the free city of Hamburg, which was at that time the richest and most independent city of Germany, and, being remote from the centers of political disturbance, it suffered less from the thirty years' war than most other parts of the country. The prime mover here was Reinhard Keiser (1673-1739), born at Weissenfels, near Leipsic, and educated at the Thomas School. His attention had been directed to dramatic music early, and at the age of nineteen he was commissioned to write a pastoral, "*Ismene*," for the court of Brunswick. The success of this gained him another libretto, "*Basilius*," also composed with success. He removed to Hamburg in 1694, and for forty years remained a favorite with the public, composing for that theater no less than 116 operas, of which the first, "Irene," was produced in 1697. In 1700 he opened a series of popular concerts, the prototypes of the star combinations of the present day. In these entertainments the greatest virtuosi were heard, the most popular and best singers, and the newest and best music. His direction of the opera did not begin until 1703; here also he proved himself a master. The place of this composer in the history of art is mainly an adventitious one, depending upon the chronological circumstance of his preceding others in the same field, rather than upon the more important reason of his having set a style, or established an ideal, for later masters. His operas subsided into farce, the serious element being almost wholly lacking, and, according to Riemann, the last of them shows no improvement over the first. Their only merit is that they are not imitations of the Italian nor upon mythological subjects, but from common life. In his later life he devoted himself to the composition of church music, in which department he accomplished notable, if somewhat conventional, success. The Hamburg theater furnished a field for another somewhat famous figure in musical history, that of Johann Mattheson, a singularly versatile and gifted man, a native of that city (1681-1764). After a liberal education, in which his musical taste and talent became distinguished at an early age, he appeared on the stage as singer, and in one of his own operas, after singing his rôle upon the stage, came back into the orchestra in order to conduct from the harpsichord the performance, until his rôle required him again upon the stage. Indeed, it was this eccentricity which occasioned a quarrel between him and Händel, who resented the implication that he himself was incapable of carrying on the performance. Mattheson composed a large number of works, including many church cantatas of the style made more celebrated in the works of Sebastian Bach, later, the intention of these works having been to render the church services more interesting by affording the congregation a practical place in the exercises. Mattheson is best known at the present time by his "Complete Orchestral Director," a compilation of musical knowledge and notions, intended for the instruction of those intending to act in this capacity.

CHAPTER XX.
THE PROGRESS OF ORATORIO.
I.

AS already noticed in the previous chapter, the oratorio had its origin at the same time as opera, both being phases of the *stilo rappresentativo*, or the effort to afford musical utterance to dramatic poetry—at first merely a solemn and impressive utterance, later, as the possibilities of the new phase of art unfolded themselves, a descriptive utterance, in which the music colored and emphasized the moods of the text and the situation. The idea of oratorio was not new. All through the Middle Ages they seem to have had miracle plays in the Church, as accessories of the less solemn services, and as means of instruction in biblical history. The mediæval plays had very plain music, which followed entirely the cadences of the plain song, and made no attempt at representing the dramatic situation or the feelings growing out of it. All that the music sought to do was to afford a decorous utterance, having in it, from association with the cadence of the music of the Church, something impressive, yet not in any manner growing out of the drama to which it was set. The Florentine music drama was something entirely different from this, or soon became so, and in oratorio this was just as apparent as in opera, although the opportunities of vocal display were not made so much of.

The modern oratorio exists in two types: The dramatic cantata, of which the form and general idea were established by Carissimi; and the church cantata, which differed from the Italian type chiefly in being of a more exclusively religious character, and of having occasional opportunities for the congregation to join in a chorale. The former of these types was established by Giacomo Carissimi (1604-1674), who was born near Rome, and held his first musical position as director at Assisi, but presently obtained the directorship at the Church of St. Apollinaris in Rome, where he served all the remainder of his long and active life. Without having been a genius of the first order, it was Carissimi's good fortune to exercise an important influence upon the course of musical progress, particularly in the direction of oratorio, in which all the more attractive elements came from his innovations. Carissimi was a prolific composer, having constant occasion for new and pleasing attractions for the musical service of the rich and important Jesuit church, where he held his appointment. These compositions are of every sort, but cantatas form the larger portion, consisting of passages of Scripture set in consecutive form, with due alternation of solo and chorus, in a style at once pleasing and dramatically appropriate. The majority of his compositions have been lost, many of them going to the waste paper baskets when the Jesuits were suppressed. Enough remain, however, to indicate the interest and importance of his work. Moreover, there, is another curious commentary upon the value of his music, in the fact that Händel took twelve measures well nigh bodily out of one of the choruses in Carissimi's "Jephthah," and incorporated them in "Hear Jacob's God" in his own "Samson." Mr. Hullah gives an excellent aria from this work, but it is too long for insertion here. The more important of Carissimi's innovations were in the direction of pleasing qualities in the accompaniments, and agreeable rhythms. He was teacher of several of the most important Italian musicians of the following generation, among them being Bassani, Cesti, Buononcini and Alessandro Scarlatti.

Fig. 47.

HEINRICH SCHÜTZ.

II.

The other type of oratorio received important assistance toward full realization in Germany, at the hands of Mattheson, as already noticed, and from those of Heinrich Schütz (1585-1672), who, after preliminary studies in Italy, where he acquired the Italian representative style from Gabrieli in Venice, in 1609, three years later returned to Germany, and in 1615 was appointed chapel master to the elector of Saxony, a position which he held with slight interruptions until his death, at the advanced age already indicated. Notice has already been taken in a <u>former chapter</u> of his appearance in the field of opera composition, in setting new music to Rinuccini's "Dafne," on account of the German words being incapable of adaptation to the music of Peri. But before this he had demonstrated his versatility and talent in the production of certain settings of the psalms of David, in the form of motettes for eight and more voices. In his second work, an oratorio upon the "Resurrection," he shows the same striving after a freer dramatic expression. His great work "*Symphoniæ Sacræ*," consists of cantatas for voices, with instrumental accompaniments, in which the instrumental part shows serious effort after dramatic coloration. The first of his works in this style was the "Last Seven Words" (1645), which contained the distinguishing marks of all the later Passion music. It consisted of a narrative, reflections, chorales, and the words of the Lord Himself. Many years later he produced his great Passions (1665-1666), and in these he accomplishes as much of the dramatic expression as possible by means of choruses, which are highly dramatic in style and very spirited. The voluminous works of this master have now been reprinted, and some of them possess a degree of interest warranting their occasional presentation. Schütz occupies an intermediate position between the masters of the old school, with whom the traditions of ecclesiastical modes governed everything, and those who have passed entirely beyond them and polyphony, into modern monody. The music of Schütz is always polyphonic, but there is much of dramatic feeling in it, nevertheless. He was one of those clear-headed, practical masters, who, without being geniuses in the intuitive sense, nevertheless contrive to impress themselves upon the subsequent activity in their province, chiefly through their sagacity in seizing new forms and bringing them into practicable perfection. Into the forms of the Passion, as Schütz created it, Bach poured the wealth of his devotion and his inspiration; so later Beethoven put into the symphony form, created to his hand by the somewhat mechanical Haydn, the amplitude of his musical imagination, which, but for this preparatory work of the lesser master, would have been driven to the creation of entirely new forms for his thoughts, not only hampering the composer, but—which would have been equally unfavorable to his success—depriving him of an audience prepared to appreciate the greatness of the new genius through their previous training in the same general style.

CHAPTER XXI.
BEGINNINGS OF INSTRUMENTAL MUSIC.

THE beginning of instrumental music, apart from vocal, is to be found in the latter part of the sixteenth century, but the main advances toward freedom of style and spontaneous expression were made during the seventeenth, and, as we might expect, originally in Italy, where the art of music was more prosperous, and incitations to advance were more numerous and diversified. Upon all accounts the honor of the first place in the account of this part of the development of modern music is to be given to Andreas Gabrieli (1510-1586), who from a singing boy in the choir of St. Mark's, under the direction of Adrian Willaert, succeeded in 1566 to the position of second organist, where his fame attracted many pupils. Among the numberless compositions emanating from his pen were masses, madrigals, and a considerable variety of pieces for organ alone, bearing the names of "*Canzone*," "*Ricerari*," "*Concerte*," and five-voiced *Sonatas*, the latter printed in 1586, being perhaps the earliest application of this now celebrated name to instrumental compositions. The pieces of Gabrieli were mostly imitations of compositions for the voice, fugal in style, and with never among them a melody fully carried out. Among the pupils of Andreas Gabrieli were Hans Leo Hassler, the celebrated Dresden composer, and Swelinck, the equally celebrated Netherlandish organist, of whom there is more to be said.

The beginning of organ composition, and the higher art of organ playing, made by Andreas Gabrieli, was carried much farther by his nephew and pupil, Giovanni Gabrieli (1557-1612), who, born and trained at Venice, early entered the service of its great cathedral, and in 1585 succeeded Claudio Merulo as first organist of the same. As a composer Giovanni Gabrieli continued the double-chorus effects which had been such a feature of the St. Mark's liturgy since the time of Willaert, but especially he distinguished himself in improving the style of organ playing, and in giving it a freedom and almost secular character somewhat surprising for the times. A large number of his compositions of all sorts are in print, very many "for voices or instruments." The alternative affords a good idea of the subordinate position still occupied by instrumental music, but a beginning had been made, which later was to lead to great things.

Fig. 48.

JEAN PIETERS SWELINCK.

The art of organ playing found its next great exponents in Holland and Germany, all of them having been pupils of the Venetian master. The most celebrated of these, considered purely as an organist, was Jean Pieters Swelinck (1560-1621), who was born at Deventer in Holland, and died at Amsterdam. He was more celebrated as a performer and improviser than for the instrumental pieces he published. Among his pupils was the celebrated Samuel Scheidt (1587-1654), organist at Halle, who is memorable as the first who made artistic use of the chorale. Scheidt is also famous as the author of a book upon organ tabulature, or the notation for organ, which in Germany at this period was different from that of the piano, and in fact much resembled the tabulature for the lute, from which it was derived. It consists of a combination of lines and signs, by the aid of which the organist was supposed to be capable of deciphering the intentions of the composer. No especial importance appears to have been attached to the difference of notation for instruments and voices in this period. And in fact, until our own times certain instruments, the viola, for example, have had their own notation, different from the voices, and different from that of other instruments. Another celebrated German organist of this period was Johann Hermann Schein, who, with Scheidt and Swelinck, constituted the three great German musical S's of the sixteenth century. Schein (1586-1630) was appointed cantor of the Leipsic St. Thomas school in 1615, and worked there as above. His numberless compositions are more free in style than the average of the century, and a number of them are distinctly secular. Nevertheless, in the development of instrumental music he had but small part, not being one of the highly gifted original geniuses who impress themselves upon following generations. The great German master of this period was Schütz, chapel master at Dresden, whose career forms part of the story of the oratorio, a form of music which he had so large a share in shaping into its present form.

Fig. 49.

SAMUEL SCHEIDT.

II.

In order to come once more into the path of musical empire, we must return again to Italy, where there was an organist at St. Peter's, who had in him the elements of greatness and originality. Girolamo Frescobaldi (1587-1640) was organist of St. Peter's at Rome from 1615. His education had been in part acquired in Italy, and in part in the Netherlands. As a virtuoso he attained an extraordinary success, and one of his recitals is reputed to have been attended by as many as 30,000 people. He distinguished himself as composer no less than as organist, and particularly by his compositions in free style. His Ricerari, Concertos and Canzones were all protests against the bondage of instrumental music to the fetters of vocal forms. It was the compositions of this master, together with those of Froberger, that Sebastian Bach desired to have, and which, in fact, he stole out of his brother's book case, and copied in the moonlight nights.

It would take us too far were we to enumerate all the composers who distinguished themselves in this century, no one of them succeeding in composing anything satisfactory to this later generation, but all contributing something toward the liberation of instrumental music, and all adding something to its too limited resources. Among these names were those of Johann Kasper Kerl, organist at St. Stephen's church in Vienna, who, after having served with distinction at Munich, returned later and died at Vienna in 1690. Another of these German masters, also one of those whose compositions Bach wished to study, was Johann Pachelbel, of Nuremberg (1635-1706). In 1674 he was assistant organist at Vienna, in 1677 organist at Eisenach, and soon back to Nuremberg a few years later. His multifarious works for organ, among which we find a variety of forms, were perhaps the chief model upon which Sebastian Bach formed his style. He especially excelled in improvising choral variations, and in fanciful and musicianly treatment of themes proposed by the hearer. Yet another name of this epoch, that of George Muffat, is now almost forgotten. He studied in France, and formed his style upon that of the French. A later master, also very influential in the style of Sebastian Bach, was Dietrich Buxtehude (1637-1707). For nearly forty years he was organist at the Church of St. Mary at Lübeck, where he was so celebrated that the young Sebastian Bach made a journey on foot there in order to hear and master the principles of his art. Buxtehude wrote a great number of pieces in free style for the organ, and, while his works have little value to modern ears, there is no doubt that this master was an important influence upon the enfranchisement of instrumental music. Among all these Netherlandish organists few are better known by name at the present day than Johann Adam Reinken (1623-1722), who was born at Deventer, Holland, and after the proper elementary and finishing studies, succeeded his master, Scheidemann, as organist at Hamburg. Here his fame was so great that the young Bach made two journeys there on foot, in order to hear him. He was a virtuoso of a high order, and his style exercised considerable influence over that of Bach.

Fig. 50.

JOHANN ADAM REINKEN.

III.

Return we now to Italy, where the violin led also to an important development of instrumental music, having in it the promise of the best that we have had since. In Fusignano, near Imola, was born in 1653 Archangelo Corelli, who became the first of violin virtuosi, and the first of composers for the instrument, and for violins in combination with other members of the same family, and so of our string quartette. He died in 1713 at Rome. Of his boyhood there is little known. About 1680 he appears in high favor at the court of Munich. In 1681 he was again in Rome, where he appears to have found a friend in Cardinal Ottoboni, in whose palace he died. His period of creative activity extended from 1683, when he began the publication of his forty-eight three-voiced sonatas, for two violins, in four numbers of twelve sonatas each. He also composed many other sonatas for the violin, for violin and piano, and for other instruments. These epoch-marking works are held in high esteem at the present time, and are in constant use for purposes of instruction.

Meanwhile the orchestra had been steadily enriched through the competition of successive operatic composers, each exerting himself to produce more effect than the preceding. In this way new combinations of tone color were contrived, and now and then introduced in a fortunate manner, and effects of greater sonority were attained through the greater number of instruments, and the more expert use of those they had. In the present state of knowledge it would be very difficult, if not impossible, to trace the successive steps of this progress, and to give proper credit to each composer for his own contribution to the general stock. At best, the orchestra at the end of this century was somewhat meager. The violin and the other members of its family had taken their places somewhat as we now have them, but the number of basses and tenors was much less than at present, their place being filled by the archlute and the harpsichord. The trumpet was occasionally employed, the flute, the oboe, and very rarely the trombone. The conductor at the harpsichord, playing from a figured bass, filled in chords according to his own judgment of the effect required. Nothing approaching the smoothness and discreet coloration of the orchestra of the present day, or even of the Haydn orchestra, existed at this time. The violin players were very cautious about using the second and third "positions," but played continually with their hands in the first position. This part of the music, therefore, wholly lacked the freedom which it now has, and the whole progress of this century was purely apprentice work in instrumental music, its value lying in its establishing the principle, first, that instrumental music might exist independently of vocal, and, second, that it might enhance the expressiveness of vocal music when associated with it. The groundwork of the two great forms of the period next ensuing, the fugue and the sonata, had been laid, and a certain amount of precedent established in favor of free composition in dance and fantasia form. Meanwhile the pianoforte of the day, the *clavicembalo*, as the Italians called it, had been considerably improved. The present scale of music had been demonstrated by Zarlino, and the ground prepared for the great geniuses whose coming made the eighteenth century forever memorable as the blossoming time of musical art.

Upon the whole, perhaps the most important part of the actual accomplishment of this century was in musical theory. While musicians for centuries had been employing the major and minor thirds, and the triads as we now have them, the fact had remained unacknowledged in musical theory, and the supposed authority of the Greeks still remained binding upon all. Zarlino, however, made a new departure. He not only assigned the true intervals of the major scale, according to perfect intonation, but argued strongly for equal temperament, and demonstrated the impossibility of chromatic music upon any other basis. Purists may still continue to doubt whether this was an absolute advantage to the art of music, since it carries with it the necessity of having all harmonic relations something short of perfection; but the immediate benefit to musical progress was unquestionable, and according to all appearance the art of music is irrevocably committed to the tempered scale of twelve tones in the octave.

Book Fourth.

THE

Flowering Time of Modern Music.

BACH, HÄNDEL, HAYDN, MOZART, BEETHOVEN.

THE FUGUE AND THE SONATA.

CHAPTER XXII.
GENERAL VIEW OF MUSIC IN THE EIGHTEENTH CENTURY.

IT is not easy to characterize simply and clearly the nature of the musical development which took place during the eighteenth century. The blossoming of music was so manifold, so diversified, so irrepressible in every direction, that there was not one single province of it, wherein new and masterly creations were not brought out. The central figures of this period were those of the two Colossi, Bach and Händel; after them Haydn, the master of genial proportion and taste; Mozart, the melodist of ineffable sweetness, and finally at the end of the century, the great master, Beethoven. In opera we have the entire work of that great reformer, the Chevalier Gluck, and a succession of Italian composers who enlarged the boundaries of the Italian music-drama in every direction, but especially in the direction of the impassioned and sensational. Add to these influences, already sufficiently diversified, that of a succession of brilliant virtuosi upon the leading instruments, whereby the resources of all the effective musical apparatuses were more fully explored and illustrated, with the final result of affording the poetic composer additional means of bringing his ideas to a more effective expression—and we have the general features of a period in music so luxuriant that in it we might easily lose ourselves; nor can we easily form a clear idea of the entire movement as the expression of a single underlying spiritual impulse. Yet such in its inner apprehension it most assuredly was.

Upon the whole, all the improvements of the time arrange themselves into two categories, namely: The better proportion, contrast, and more agreeable succession of moments in art works; and, second, the more ample means for intense expression. In the department of form, indeed, there was a very important transition made between the first half of the century and the last. The typical form of the first part of this division was the fugue, which came to a perfection under the hands of Bach and Händel, far beyond anything to be found in the form previously. The fugue was the creation of this epoch, and while based upon the general idea of canonic imitation, after the Netherlandish ideal, it differed from their productions in several highly significant respects. While all of a fugue is contained within the original subject, and the counter-subject, which accompanies it at every repetition, it has an element of tonality in it which places it upon an immensely higher plane of musical art than any form known, or possible, before the obsolescence of the ecclesiastical modes. Moreover, the fugue has opportunities for episode, which enable it to acquire variety to a degree impossible for any form developed earlier; and which, when these opportunities were fresh, afforded composers a field for the display of fancy which was practically free. This, one may still realize by comparing the different fugues in Bach's "Well Tempered Clavier" with each other, and with those of any other collection. It is impossible to detect anywhere the point where the inspiration of the composer felt itself bound by the restrictions of this form. It was for Bach and Händel practically a free form. And the few other contemporaneous geniuses of a high order either experienced the same freedom in it, or found ways of evading its strictness by the production of various styles of fancy pieces, which, while conforming to the fugue form in their main features, were nevertheless free enough to be received by the musical public of that day with substantially the same satisfaction as a fantasia would have been received a century later. Roughly speaking, Bach and Händel exhausted the fugue. While Bach displayed his mental activity in almost every province of music, and like some one since, of whom it has been much less truthfully said, "touched nothing which he did not adorn," he was all his life a writer of fugues. His preludes are not fugues, and their number almost equals that of the fugues; but the operative principles were not essentially different—merely the applications of thematic development were different. Yet strange as it may seem, within thirty years from his death it became impossible to write fugues, and at the same time be free. Why was this?

A new element came into music, incompatible with fugue, requiring a different form of expression, and incapable of combination with fugue. That element was the people's song, with its symmetrical cadences and its universal intelligibility. Let the reader take any one of the Mozart sonatas, and play the first melody he finds—he will immediately see that here is something for which no place could have been found in a fugue, nor yet in its complement, the prelude of Bach's days. The same is true of many similar passages in the sonatas of Haydn. Music had now found the missing half of its dual nature. For we must know that in the same manner as the thematic or fugal element in music represents the play of musical fantasy, turning over musical ideas intellectually or seriously; so there is a spontaneous melody, into which no thought of developing an idea enters. The melody flows or soars like the song of a bird, because it is the free expression, not of musical fantasy, as such (the unconscious play of tonal fancy), but the flow of *melody*, *song*, the soaring of spirit in some one particular direction, floating upon buoyant pinions, and in directions well conceived and sure. The symmetry of the people's song follows as a natural part of the progress. The spontaneous element of the music of the northern harpers now found its way into the musical productions of the highest geniuses. Henceforth the fugue subsides from its pre-eminence, and remains possible only as a highly specialized department of the general art of musical composition, useful and necessary at times, but nevermore the expression of the unfettered fancy of the musical mind.

The discovery of the secret of musical contrast, in the types of development, the *thematic* and the *lyric*, led to the creation of a new form, in which they mutually contrast with and help each other. That form was the Sonata, which having been begun earlier, was developed further by the sons of Bach, but which received its characteristic touches from the hands of Haydn and Mozart. This was the crowning glory of the eighteenth century—the sonata. A form had been created, into which the greatest of masters was even then beginning to breathe his mighty soul, producing thereby a succession of master works, which stand without parallel in the realm of music.

CHAPTER XXIII.
JOHN SEBASTIAN BACH.

ALL things considered, the most remarkable figure of this period was that of the great John Sebastian Bach, who was born at Eisenach, in Prussia, in 1685, and died at Leipsic in 1750. It is scarcely too much to say that this great man has exercised more influence upon the development of music than any other composer who has ever lived. In his own day he led a quiet, uneventful life, at first as student, then as court musician at Weimar, where he played the violin; later as organist at Arnstadt, a small village near Weimar, and still later as director of music in the St. Thomas church and school at Leipsic. In the sixty-five years of his life, Bach produced an enormous number of compositions, of which about half were in fugue form, a form which was at its prime at the beginning of this century and which Bach carried to the farthest point in the direction of freedom and spontaneity which it ever reached.

Fig. 51.

JOHN SEBASTIAN BACH.

It is the remarkable glory of Bach to have rendered his compositions indispensable to thorough mastery in three different provinces of musical effort. The modern art of violin playing rests upon two works, the six sonatas of Bach for violin solo, and the Caprices of Paganini. The former contain everything that belongs to the classical, the latter everything that belongs to the sensational. In organ playing the foundation is Bach, and Bach alone. Nine-tenths of organ playing is comprised in the Bach works. Upon the piano his influence has been little less. While it is true that at least four works are necessary for making a pianist of the modern school, viz., the "Well Tempered Clavier," of Bach; the "*Gradus ad Parnassum*," of Clementi; the "Studies," of Chopin, and the Rhapsodies, of Liszt, the works of Bach form, on the whole, considerably more than one-third of this preparation. Nor has the influence of Bach been confined to the province of technical instruction alone. On the contrary, all composers since his time have felt the stimulus of his great tone poems, and Mendelssohn, Schumann, Chopin and Wagner found him the most productive of great masters.

The life of Bach need not long detain us. A musician of the tenth generation, member of a family which occupies a liberal space in German encyclopedias of music, art and literature, Sebastian Bach led the life of a teacher, productive artist and virtuoso, mainly within the limits of the comparatively unimportant provincial city of Leipsic. His three wives in succession and his twenty-one children were the domestic incidents which bound him to his home. Here he trained his choir, taught his pupils, composed those master works which modern musicians try in vain to equal, and the even tenor of his life was broken in upon by very few incidents of a sensational kind. We do not understand that Bach was a virtuoso upon the violin, although no other master has required more of that greatest of musical instruments. Upon the piano and organ the case is different. Bach's piano was the clavier, upon which he was the greatest virtuoso of his time. His touch was clear and liquid, his technique unbounded, and his musical fantasy absolutely without limit. Hence in improvisation or in the performance of previously arranged numbers he never failed to delight his audience. It was the same upon the organ. The art of obligato pedal playing he brought to a point which it had never before reached and scarcely afterward surpassed. He comprehended the full extent of organ technique, and with the exception of a few tricks of quasi-orchestral imitation, made possible in modern organs, he covered the entire ground of organ playing in a manner at once solid and brilliant. Many stories are told of his capacity in this direction, but the general characterization already given is sufficient. He was a master of the first order. The common impression that he played habitually upon the full organ is undoubtedly erroneous. He made ample use of registration to the fullest extent practicable on the organs of his day.

The most remarkable feature of the career of Bach is his productivity in the line of choral works. As leader of the music in the St. Thomas church, he had under his control two organs, two choirs, the children of the school and an orchestra. For these resources he composed a succession of cantatas, every feast day in the ecclesiastical year being represented by from one to five separate works. The total number of these cantatas reaches more than 230. Some of them are short, ten or fifteen minutes long, but most of them are from thirty to forty minutes, and some of them reach an hour. Their treasures have been but imperfectly explored, although most of them are now in print. In the course of his ministrations at Leipsic he produced five great Passion oratorios for Good Friday in Holy Week. The greatest of these was the Passion of St. Matthew, so named from the source of its text. This work occupies about two hours in performance. It is in two parts, and the sermon was supposed to intervene. It consists of recitative, arias and choruses, some of which are extremely elaborate and highly dramatic. The other Passions are less fortunate. Nevertheless they contain many beautiful and highly dramatic moments. Bach's oratorios belong to the category of church works, as distinguished from those intended for concert purposes. This is seen especially in the treatment of the chorale, in which he expects the congregation to co-operate. In one direction Bach was subject to serious limitation. His knowledge of the voice, and his consideration for its convenience, were far below the standard of composers of the same time educated in Italy. In his works, while many passages are very impressive, and while the melody and harmony are always appropriate to the matter in hand, the intervals and especially the convenience of the different registers of the voice are very imperfectly considered, for which reason his works have not been performed to anything like the extent to which their musical interest would otherwise have carried them. This is especially true of the greatest of all, the Passion according to St. Matthew. It was first performed on Good Friday, 1729, in the St. Thomas church at Leipsic, and it does not appear to have been given again until 1829, when Mendelssohn brought it out. Since that time it has been given almost every year in Leipsic, and more or less frequently in all the musical centers of the world, but its elaboration is very great and its vocal treatment unsatisfactory to solo voices, for which reason it succeeds only under the inspiration of an artistic and enthusiastic leader. In fact, all the great works of Bach are more or less in the category of classics, which are well spoken of and seldom consulted. While, in Beethoven's time, the whole of the "Well Tempered Clavier" was not thought too much for an ambitious youngster, at the present time there are few pianists who play half a dozen of these pieces. The easier inventions for two parts, some of the suites, several gavottes, modernized from his violin and chamber music, and a very few of his other pieces for the clavier, are habitually played.

It would be unjust to close the account of this great artist without mentioning what we might call the prophetic element in his works. The great bulk of Bach's compositions are in two forms, the Prelude and the Fugue. The fugue came to perfection in his hands. It was an application of the Netherlandish art of canonic imitation, combined with modern tonality. In a fugue the first voice gives the subject in the tonic, the second voice answers in the dominant, the third voice comes again in the tonic, and the fourth voice, if there be one, again in the dominant. Then ensues a digression into some key upon what theorists call the dominant side, when one or two voices give out the subject and answer it again, always in the tonic and dominant of the new key. Then more or less modulating matter, thematically developed out of some leading motive of the subject, and again the principal material of the theme, with one or more answers. The final close is preceded by a more or less elaborate pedal point upon the dominant of the principal key, after which the subject comes in. With very few exceptions the fugues of Bach are in modern tonality, the major key or the modern minor, with their usual relatives.

The prelude is a less closely organized composition. Sometimes it is purely harmonic in its interest, like the first of the "Well Tempered Clavier." At other times it is highly melodic, like the preludes in C sharp major and minor of the first book of the Clavier, and, as a rule, the prelude either treats its motives in a somewhat lyric manner or dispenses with the melodic material altogether. Thus the prelude and fugue mutually complete each other. But it is a great mistake to regard Bach as a writer of fugues alone. He was also very free in fantasies, and one of his pianoforte works, concerning the origin of which nothing whatever is known, the "Chromatic Fantasia and Fugue," is one of the four or five greatest compositions that exist for this instrument. The remarkable thing about this fantasia is the freedom of its treatment and the facility with which it lends itself to virtuoso handling, as distinguished from the rather limited treatment of the piano usual in Bach's works. The second part of the fantasia is occupied by a succession of recitatives of an extremely graphic and poetic character. Melodically and harmonically these recitatives are thoroughly modern and dramatic, the latter element being very forcibly represented by the succession of diminished sevenths on which the phrases of the recitative end. The fugue following is long, highly diversified and extremely climactic in its interest. In other parts of his work Bach has left fantasies of a more descriptive character. He has, for instance, a hunting scene with various incidents of a realistic character, and in general he shows himself in his piano works a man of wide range of mind and extremely vigorous musical fantasy.

In the department of concertos for solo instruments and orchestra, his works are very rich. There are a large number for piano, quite a number for organ, several for two and three pianos, with orchestra, and various other combinations of instruments, such as two violins and 'cellos, and so on. In these each solo player has an equal chance with the other, and solos and accompaniment work together understandingly for mutual ends. The most noticeable feature of his elaborate works is the rhythm, which is vigorous, highly organized and extremely effective. In the department of harmony, it is believed by almost all close observers that no combination of tones since made by any writer is without a precedent in the works of Bach; the strange chords of Schumann and Wagner find their prototypes in the works of this great Leipsic master. Melodically considered, Bach was a genius of the highest order. Not only did he make this impression upon his own time and upon the great masters of the next two generations, but many of his airs have attained genuine popularity within the present generation, and are played with more real satisfaction than most other works that we have. This is the more remarkable because from the time of his first residence in Leipsic when he was only twenty-four years old he went out of that city but a few times, and heard very little music but his own. He was three times married, and had twenty-one children, many of whom were musical. Three of his sons became eminent, and the principal episode of his later life was his visit to Potsdam, where his son, Carl Phillip Emanuel, was musician to Frederick the Great. Here he was received with the utmost informality by the king and made to play and improvise upon all the pianos and organs in the palace and the adjacent churches. As a reminiscence of this visit he produced a fugue upon a subject given by Frederick himself, written for six real parts. This work was called the "Musical Offering," and was dedicated to Frederick the Great. In his later years Bach became blind from having over-exerted his eyes in childhood and in later life. He died on Good Friday in 1750.

CHAPTER XXIV.
GEO. FREDERICK HÄNDEL.

THE companion figure to Bach, in this epoch, was that of George Frederick Händel, who was born at the little town of Halle in the same year as Bach, 1685, and died in London in 1759. Händel's father was a physician, and although the boy showed considerable aptitude for music his father did not think favorably of his pursuing it as a vocation; but the fates were too strong for him. When George Frederick was about eight years old, he managed to go with his father to the court of the duke of Saxe Weissenfels, some distance away, where an older brother was in service. Here he obtained access to the organ in the chapel, and was overheard by the duke, who recognized the boy's talent, and, with the authority inherent in princely rank, admonished the father that on no account was he to thwart so gifted an inclination. Accordingly the youngster had lessons in music upon the clavier, the organ and the violin, the three standard instruments of the time. The older Händel died, and before he was nineteen George Frederick made his way to Hamburg, which was then one of the musical centers of Germany. Here he obtained an engagement in the theater orchestra as *ripieno* violin, a sort of fifth wheel in the orchestral chariot, its duty being that of filling in missing parts. The boy was then rather more than six feet high, heavy and awkward. He was an indifferent violinist, and the other players were disposed to make a butt of him, although he was known to be an accomplished harpsichordist. It happened presently, however, that the leader of the orchestra, who presided at the harpsichord, fell sick, and Händel, being at the same time the best harpsichordist and the poorest violinist of all, was placed at the head. He carried the rehearsals and the performances through with such spirit that it resulted in his being made assistant director, and two works of his were presently performed— "Almira" and "Nero." The first made a great hit and was retained in performance for several weeks. The Italian ambassador immediately recognized the talent of the young man, and offered to take him to Italy in his suite, but Händel declined, preferring to go with his own money, which, after the production of "Nero," and its successful run of several weeks, he was able to do.

Fig. 52.

GEORGE FREDERICK HÄNDEL.

1685-1759.

Accordingly we find him in Italy, in 1710, first at Naples, where he made the acquaintance of the greatest harpsichord player of that time, Domenico Scarlatti. The style of the young German was so charming, and so different from that of the great Italian player, that he immediately became a favorite, and was called *Il Caro Sassone* ("The dear Saxon"). He produced an opera in Naples with good success. Afterward he produced others at Rome and Venice. In a few years he was back at Hanover, where he was made musical director to the Elector George, who afterward became George I of England. Here, presently, he took a vacation in order to visit London, where he found things so much to his liking that he remained, having good employment under Queen Anne, and a public anxious to hear his Italian operas. Presently Queen Anne died and George the First came over to reign as king. This was altogether a different matter, for Händel had his unsettled account with the elector of Hanover, upon whom he had so cavalierly turned his back. The peace was finally made, however, by a set of compositions very celebrated in England under the name of "The Water Music." When King George was going from Whitehall to Westminster in his barge, Händel followed with a company of musicians, playing a succession of pieces, which the king knew well enough for a production of his truant capellmeister. Accordingly he received him once more into favor, and Händel went on with his work.

For upwards of twenty years, Händel pursued his course in London as a composer of Italian operas, of which the number reached about forty. During the greater part of his time he had his own theater, and employed the singers from Italy and elsewhere, producing his works in the best manner of his time. His operas were somewhat conventional in their treatment, but every one of them contained good points. Here and there a chorus, occasionally a recitative, now and then an aria—always something to repay a careful hearing, and occasionally a master effect, such as only genius of the first order could produce. His education during this period was exactly opposite to that of Bach. Bach lived in Leipsic all his life, and, being in a position from which only a decided fault of his own could discharge him, he consulted no one's taste but his own, writing his music from within, and adapting it to his forces in hand, or not adapting it, as it pleased him. Händel, on the other hand, had always the public. He commenced as an operatic composer. As an operatic composer he succeeded in Hamburg, and as an operatic composer he succeeded in Italy. The same career held him in London. There was always an audience to be moved, to be affected, to be pleased, and there were always singers of high talents to carry out his conceptions. Hence his whole training was in the direction of smoothness, facility, pleasing quality. Nevertheless, there came an end to the popularity of Händel. A most shabby *pasticcio* called the "Beggar's Opera," was the immediate cause of his downfall. This queer compilation was made up of old ballad tunes, with hastily improvised words, and the merest thread of a story, and included some tunes of Händel's own. This being produced at an opposition house, took the town. The result was that Händel was bankrupted for the second time, owing more than £75,000.

Some time before this he had held the position of private musical director to the earl of Chandos, who had a chapel in connection with his palace, a short distance out of London, as it then was. In this place Händel had already produced a number of elaborate anthems and one oratorio— "Esther." In the stress of his present circumstances, after a few weeks, he remembered the oratorio of "Esther," and immediately brought it out in an enlarged form. The effect was enormous. Whatever the English taste might be for opera, for oratorio their recognition was irrepressible. "Esther" brought him a great deal of money, and he presently wrote other oratorios with such good effect that in a very few years he had completely paid up the enormous indebtedness of his operatic ventures. At length, in 1741, he composed his master work—the "Messiah." This epoch-marking composition was improvised in less than a fortnight, a rate of speed calling for about three numbers per day. The work was produced in Dublin for charitable purposes. It had the advantage of a text containing the most beautiful and impressive passages of Scripture relating to the Messiah, a circumstance which no doubt inspired the beauty of the music, and added to the early popularity of the work. In later times it is perhaps not too much to say that the music has been equally useful to the text, in keeping its place in the consciousness of successive generations of Christians. In this beautiful master work we have the result of the whole of Händel's training. The work is very cleverly arranged in a succession of recitatives, arias and choruses, following each other in a highly dramatic and effective manner. There are certain passages in the "Messiah" which have never been surpassed for tender and poetic expression. Among these are the "Behold and See if There Be Any Sorrow Like His Sorrow," "Come unto Him," and "He was Despised." In the direction of sublimity nothing grander can be found than the "Hallelujah," "Worthy is the Lamb," "Lift up Your Heads," nor anything more dramatically impressive than the splendid burst at the words, "Wonderful," "Counsellor." The work, as a whole, while containing mannerisms in the roulades of such choruses as "He shall Purify," and "For unto Us," marks the highest point reached in the direction of oratorio; for, while Händel himself surpassed its sublimity in "Israel in Egypt," and Bach its dramatic qualities in the thunder and lightning chorus in the St. Matthew Passion; and Mendelssohn its melodiousness in his "Elijah"; for a balance of good qualities, and for even and sustained inspiration throughout, the "Messiah" is justly entitled to the rank which, by common consent, it holds as the most complete master work which oratorio can show.

In the "Israel in Egypt" Händel illustrates a different phase of his talent. This curious work is composed almost entirely of choruses, the most of which are for two choirs, very elaborately treated. Among them all, the two which perhaps stand out pre-eminent are "The Horse and His Rider" and the "Hailstone," two colossal works, as dramatic as they are imposing. The masterly effect of the Händelian chorus rests upon the combination of good qualities such as no other master has accomplished to the same extent. They are extremely well written for the voice, with an accurate appreciation of the effect of different registers and masses, the melodic ideas are smooth and vigorous, and the harmonic treatment as forcible as possible, without ever controlling the composer further than it suited his artistic purpose to go. Bach very often commences a fugue which he feels obliged to finish, losing thereby the opportunity of a dramatic effect. Händel perfects his fugue only when the dramatic effect will be improved by so doing, and in this respect he makes a distinct gain over his great contemporary at Leipsic. The total list of the Händel works comprises the following: Two Italian oratorios; nineteen English oratorios; five Te Deums; six psalms; twenty anthems; three German operas; one English opera; thirty-nine Italian operas; two Italian serenatas, two English serenatas; one Italian intermezzo, "Terpsichore"; four odes; twenty-four chamber duets; ninety-four cantatas; seven French songs; thirty-three concertos; nineteen English songs; sixteen Italian airs; twenty-four sonatas.

Händel was never married; nor, so far as we know, ever in love. He had among his friends some of the most eminent writers of his day, such as Addison, Pope, Dean Swift and others. His later years were so successful that when he died his fortune of above £50,000 was left for charitable purposes. This was after he had paid all of the indebtedness incurred in his earlier bankruptcy. It would be a mistake to dismiss this great master without some notice of his harpsichord and organ playing. As a teacher of the princesses of the royal family, he produced many suites and lessons for the harpsichord, in one of which, as an unnoticed incident, occur the air and variations since so universally popular under the name of "The Harmonious Blacksmith." It is not known to whom the composer was indebted for the name generally applied to this extremely broad air, and clever variations. Very likely some music publisher was the unknown poet. As an organist Händel was both great and popular. In the middle of his oratorios he used to play an organ concerto with orchestra. Of these compositions he wrote a very large number. They are always fresh and hearty in style, well written for organ, and with a very flowing pedal part. Händel appears to have played the pedals upon a somewhat different plan from that of Bach. Bach is generally supposed to have used his toes for the most part, employing the heel only for an occasional note where the toes were insufficient. Händel seems to have used toe and heel habitually in almost equal proportion.

It is a curious feature of the later part of Händel's career that he brought out his oratorios in costume. Several of the original bills are extant, in which an oratorio is promised "with new cloathes." "Esther" is said to have been given with complete stage appointment at Chandos, like an opera; but the Lord Chamberlain prohibited future representations of the kind on account of the supposed sacredness of the subject. Afterward the characters were costumed, and the stage set, but there was no action. While Händel was German by birth, his long residence in England and his habitual writing for the last ten or fifteen years of his life oratorios in the English language, made him, to all intents and purposes, an English composer. For nearly a century he stood to the English school as a model of everything that was good and great, to such an extent that very little of original value was accomplished in that country, and when, by lapse of time and a deeper self-consciousness on the part of English musicians, this influence had begun to wane, a new German composer came in the person of Felix Mendelssohn Bartholdy, who, in turn, became a popular idol, and for many years a barrier to original effort.

The influence of Händel upon the later course of music is by no means so marked as that of Bach. Nevertheless, he was one of the great tone poets of all times, and his works form an indispensable part of the literature of music. It was his good fortune to embody certain types of melody and harmony with a clearness and effectiveness that no other composer has equaled. The oratorio, in particular, not only fulfilled itself in Händel, but we might almost say *completed* itself there, for very little of decided originality has been produced in this department since. The Händelian operas have been mostly forgotten for many years, but they contain gems of melody in the solo and chorus parts which have still a future. His first opera, "Almira," was revived at Hamburg a few years ago with remarkable effect, and it is not at all unlikely that extracts from many of the other works will eventually find their way into the current repertory of the singer, as many of the arias already have.

CHAPTER XXV.
EMANUEL BACH; HAYDN; THE SONATA.
I.

NONE of the sons of Bach inherited the commanding genius of their father, although four of them showed talent above the average of musicians of their day, and one of them distinguished himself and exercised an important influence upon the subsequent course of pianoforte music. The most gifted of Bach's sons was Wilhelm Friedmann, the eldest (1710-1784), who was especially educated by his father for a musician. He turned out badly, however, his enormous talents not being able to save him from the natural consequences of a dissolute life. He died in Berlin in the greatest degradation and want. This Bach wrote comparatively few compositions, owing to his invincible repugnance to the labor of putting them upon paper; he was famous as an improviser, and certain pieces of his in the Berlin library are considered to manifest musical gifts of a high order. Johann Christian (1735-1782), the eleventh son, known as the Milanese or London Bach, devoted himself to the lighter forms of music, and after having served some years as organist of the cathedral at Milan, and having distinguished himself by certain operas successfully produced in Italy, he removed to London, where he led an easy and enjoyable life. He was an elegant and fluent writer for the pianoforte. The one son of Bach who is commonly regarded as having left a mark upon the later course of music was Carl Philip Emanuel (1714-1788), the third son, commonly known as the Berlin or Hamburg Bach. His father intended him for a philosopher, and had him educated accordingly in the Leipsic and Frankfort universities, but his love for music and the thorough grounding in it he had at home eventually determined him in this direction. While in the Frankfort University he conducted a singing society, which naturally led to his exercising himself in composition. Presently he gave up law for music, and going to Berlin he obtained an appointment as "Kammer-musiker" to Frederick the Great, his especial business being that of accompanying the king in his flute concertos. The seven years' war having put an end to these duties, he migrated to Hamburg, where he held honorable appointments as organist and conductor until his death. He wrote in a tasteful and free, but somewhat superficial, style; and while his compositions bear favorable comparison with those of other musicians of his time, they are by no means of a commanding nature like those of his father. There were, however, two reasons for this, wholly aside from the question of less ability in the younger composer. One of these is to be found in the free form which

Emanuel Bach began to develop. Sebastian Bach had the advantage of writing his greatest works in a form which had been prepared for him, without having been exhausted. The technique of fugue had been created before his time, but its possibilities in the direction of freedom and spontaneity had never been illustrated. Bach proceeded to do this for the fugue form, and, it may be added, did it with such amplitude that no composer has been able to write a free and original fugue since. The son recognizing both that the fugue had been exhausted as a free art-form, and feeling no doubt that something more intuitively intelligible than fugue was possible, addressed himself to composition in the free style, in which the means of producing effects had not yet been mastered. The thematic use of material had been acquired, or was easily inferable from the fugue, but the proper manner of contrasting that material with other, calculated to relieve the attention and at the same time intensify the interest, remained for later explorers. The missing contrast was the lyric element, but it was not until the next generation of composers that it came into pianoforte music in satisfactory form. Accordingly the sonatas of Emanuel Bach sound dry and superficial, and while they are interesting as the remote models upon which Beethoven occasionally built, they do not repay study for the purposes of public performance. There is little heart in them. As a literary musician Bach deserves to be remembered for his work upon "The True Art of Playing the Piano." This was the first systematic instruction book for the instrument of which we have a record, and it still is the main dependence for information concerning the method of Bach's playing, and the way in which he intended the embellishments in his works to be performed.

II.

In the little village of Rohrau, in Austria, was born to a master wheelwright's wife, in 1732, a little son, dark-skinned, not large of frame, nor handsome, but gifted with that most imperishable of endowments, a genius for melody and tonal symmetry. The baby was named Francis Joseph, and he grew to the age of about six in the family of his parents, in a little house which although twice somewhat rebuilt, still stands in its original form. Hither people come from many lands in order to see the birthplace of the great composer Haydn, the indefatigable and simple-hearted tone poet of many symphonies, sonatas, and the two favorite cantatas or oratorios, the "Creation" and the "Seasons." In his earliest childhood the boy showed a talent for music, which, as his parents both sang and played a little, he had often an opportunity of hearing. Before he was quite six years old he was able to stand up in the choir of the village church and lead in solos, with his sweet and true, if not strong, voice. This was his delight. At length George Reutter, the director of the music in the cathedral of St. Stephen at Vienna, heard him, and offered the boy a place in his choir. Now indeed his fortune seemed made, and he embraced the offer with gratitude. As a choir boy he ought to have been taught music in a thorough manner, but as Reutter was rather a careless man this did not happen in Haydn's case, but the boy grew up in his own devices. He composed constantly, without having had the slightest regular training. One day Reutter saw one of his pieces, a mass movement for twelve parts. He offered the passing advice, that the composer would have done better to have taken two voices, and that the best exercise for him would be to write "divisions" (variations) upon the airs he sang in the service—but no instruction. At length the boy's voice began to break, and at the age of fourteen or fifteen, he was turned out to shift for himself. He found an asylum in the house of a wig maker, Keller, with whom he lived for several years, earning small sums by lessons, playing the organ at one of the churches, the violin at another, singing at another and so on, in all managing to place himself upon the road to fortune—that of industry and sobriety. This part of his career lasted from 1748, when he left the choir of the cathedral, to 1752, when he became accompanist to the Italian master, Porpora, who was then living in Vienna in the house of an Italian lady, whose daughter's education he was superintending. With Porpora he learned the art of singing, and the proper manner of accompanying the voice. He also got many hints in regard to the correct manner of composing. He had already produced a number of works in various styles. In 1759 he was appointed conductor of the music at the palace of Count

Morzin, where he had a small number of musicians under his direction, only sixteen in all. Here he began his life work. Two years later he was invited to assume the assistant directorship of the private orchestra and choir of Prince Esterhazy, who lived in magnificent style, and for many years had maintained a private musical chapel. Very soon the old prince died, and his son reigned in his place. The new master was the one named "The Magnificent," and greatly enlarged the musical appointment of his predecessor. He built a great palace at Esterhaz, where there was a theater, in which opera was given, and a smaller one where there was a marionette company, the machinery of which had been brought to great perfection. There were frequent concerts. The prince was a great amateur of the peculiar viol called the barytone, and it was one of Haydn's duties to provide new compositions for this instrument. Here for thirty years he continued in service, with few interruptions, and always on the very best of terms with his prince, and with the men under him. The players called Haydn "Papa."

Fig. 53.

Owing to its situation, remote from town, and to the prince's constantly increasing aversion to living in Vienna, Haydn scarcely left the vicinity for years together. Here, wholly from within his own resources, he evolved a succession of works in every style, and for almost every possible combination of instruments, from operas for the large theater, to marionette music for the small place, orchestral compositions, among which the 175 symphonies form a not inconsiderable portion; there are also concertos for many kinds of instruments, and songs, masses, *divertissements* and the like. In short, there is scarcely any form of music which Haydn did not have to make at some time or other in his long service in the Esterhazy establishment. Being his own orchestral director, he had the opportunity of trying and experimenting and of realizing what would be effective and what would not. The motive mainly operative in his work, necessarily, was that of pleasing and amusing. Nobler intentions were not wanting, but the pleasing element had to be considered in most that he did. Thus he developed a style of his own, original, becoming, with a certain taste and symmetry, and with a melodious element which never loses its charm. Withal he became very clever in his treatment of themes. It was a saying of his that the "idea" did not matter at all; "treatment is everything." From this standpoint it is impossible to deny Haydn the credit of having accomplished his ideal.

He commenced his musical career as a violinist and a singer. His orchestral symphonies were for violins (for strings), with occasional seasoning from the brass and wood wind. The constant study of the violin led to modifications in his style, and evolved first, the string quartette in the form which has always remained standard. The symphonies are only larger string quartettes, for, in the order of the themes, the general manner of treating them and the principles of contrast or relief which actuated them, the quartettes are sonatas, as also are the symphonies. Haydn gave the sonata form its present shape. The insertion of a second theme in the first movement, and the principle of contrasting this second theme with the first in such a way that the second theme is generally lyric in style, or at least tending in that direction, was Haydn's. He also developed the middle part of the sonata into what is known as the "elaboration," "*Durchführungssatz*". The cantabile slow movement, modeled somewhat after the Italian cantilena, was his. Mozart and Beethoven did wonders with it later, but the suggestion was Haydn's. The endless productivity, the constant succession of new pieces demanded, led to a somewhat systematic proceeding in their production, and so the form and the method of the sonata became stereotyped. All the instrumental movements of this time, whenever there was any serious intention, assumed the form of sonatas; *i.e.*, of the instrumental sonatas—the symphony and the quartette.

At length Haydn's master died, and he accepted an invitation from Salamon, the publisher, to London, where he produced several new symphonies, conducted many concerts and returned to Vienna richer by about $6,000 than when he had left his home a few months before. He had become a great master, known all over the world, without himself knowing it. If any man ever woke up and found himself famous, Haydn was that man, although he had been in the way of having his compositions played and sung before most of the important personages in Europe for years, Prince Esterhazy being a royal entertainer. It was for Madrid that Haydn composed his first Passion oratorio, "The Last Seven Words." This work, by a curious chance, he made over into an instrumental piece for his London concerts, the prejudice against "popery" preventing its being given there in its original form. In 1794 he was again in London. Upon the first visit to London he took the journey down the Rhine, and at Bonn, in going or coming, the young Beethoven showed him a new cantata. In 1794 he was again in London, where the same success attended him as before. He produced many new works, and was royally entertained. Again he went home richer by many thousands of dollars than when he set out. With his savings he purchased a house in the suburbs of Vienna, where he lived the remainder of his life, dying in 1809. It was during these last years that he wrote his two oratorios already mentioned. That by which he is best known is the "Creation," which is a master work indeed, if only we do not look in it for too much of the distinctly religious or sublime. It belongs to the pleasing in art, and certain of its numbers are worthy of Italian opera, so sweetly melodious are they, yet ever refined and beautiful. Of this kind are the solo arias, "On Mighty Pens," the famous "With Verdure Clad," the lovely trio, "Most Beautiful Appear." Several choruses in this work are really splendid. At the head of the list I would place the two choruses, "Achieved Is the Glorious Work," with the beautiful trio between, "On Thee Each Living Soul Awaits." The development of the fugue in the second chorus is masterly and effective indeed. Everybody knows "The Heavens are Telling," which, however, has rather more reputation than it deserves. The English have made much of Haydn's descriptive music in the accompanied recitatives. This part of his work, however, was but clever when first written, and now, through the enormous development which this part of musical composition has since reached, is little more than childish. Withal, the "Creation" is not difficult. It can be rendered effectively with moderate resources. This fact, added to its many charming and engaging qualities, has insured its popularity in all parts of the musical world. It bids fair to remain for amateur societies for many years yet.

As a tone poet Haydn belonged by no means to the first rank—at least in so far as the inherent weight and range of his ideas is concerned. His one claim to musical fame rests upon his graceful manner of treating a musical idea, and upon the readiness of his invention in contrasting his themes, to which may be added the sweet and genial flavor of his music, which in every line shows a pure and childlike spirit, simple, unaffected, yet deep and true. It was his good fortune to stand to Mozart and Beethoven in the rôle of master. Both were in many ways his superiors, yet both revered him, the one until his own life went out in the freshness of his youth; the other until when an old man, having stood upon the very Pisgah tops of the tone world, full of honors, he spoke of the old master, Haydn, with affection, in his very last days. Higher testimony than this it would be impossible to quote. For, in the nature of the case, the composer, Haydn, can never be judged again by musicians and poets who know so well his aims and the value of what he accomplished as the two Vienna masters, Mozart and Beethoven, who were younger than he, yet not too young to understand the condition of the musical world into which Haydn had been born, and the musical world as it had become from his living in it.

CHAPTER XXVI.
MOZART AND HIS GENIUS.

ONE of the most engaging personalities, and at the same time one of the most highly gifted, versatile and richly endowed geniuses who ever adorned the art of music, was that of Wolfgang Amadeus Mozart (1756-1791). He was a son of the violin player and musician, Leopold Mozart, living at Salzburg. At an extremely early age he showed his love for music by listening to the lessons of his sister. By the time he was four, his father commenced to give him lessons, and when he was less than five years old he was discovered one day making marks upon music paper, which he stoutly maintained belonged to a concerto. The statement was received with incredulity, but upon carefully examining the manuscript it was found correctly written, and sensible; but so difficult as to be impossible to play. Upon the boy's attention being called to this, he replied, "I call it a concerto because it *is* so difficult; they should practice it until they *can* play it." In childhood, and indeed all through life, his ear was very sensitive. He could not bear to hear the sound of a trumpet, and upon his father seeking to overcome his nervousness by having a trumpet blown in the room, it threw him into convulsions. The boy was of a most active mind, interested in everything that went on about him, and eager to learn in every direction. Nothing came amiss, arithmetic, grammar and language—he was immediately at home in any subject which he took up. Music was intuitive to him. So remarkable was his progress, that when he was yet but six years old his father began to travel with him. Their first journey was to Munich, where the elector received them kindly. The programmes consisted of improvisations by the youthful Mozart upon themes assigned by the audience; pieces for violin and piano, the father taking the violin part, and the sister in turn played piano pieces. The father was a good violinist and the author of an excellent school for that instrument. He also composed many ambitious works, which rise above the capellmeister average. Highly gratified with their reception at Munich, they went on to Vienna, where again they were cordially received, the emperor especially being highly delighted with the "little magician," as he called the promising boy. Even at this early age Mozart had a distinct idea of his own authority in music, although no one could be freer than he from the charge of self-conceit. In Vienna, he asked expressly for Wagenseil, the court composer, that he might be sure of having a real connoisseur among his hearers. "I am playing a concerto of yours," he said, "you must turn over for me." The ladies of the aristocracy went wild over the fascinating young fellow, but presently he had an attack of scarlet fever, which brought the tour to an end. After the return to Salzburg, the practice went on every day, and regular lessons in books, as they had during the journey; and, when he was still less than nine years of age, the family undertook a longer tour to Paris, playing at all the important towns on the way. In several of the cities, Wolfgang played the violin, and also the organ in the churches. At Paris they had a remarkable success, playing before the court at Versailles, and in many of the houses of the nobility. Here the father had four of the boy's sonatas for piano and violin engraved and published. The stay at Paris lasted five months, until November 10, 1764, when they departed for London. Here they met a favorable reception at court, the king, George III, taking a great interest in the wonderful young master. He put before him pieces of Bach, Wagenseil and Händel, which he played at sight. On the fifth of June they gave a concert in Spring Gardens, where their receipts were as much as 100 guineas. His next appearance was as an organist for the benefit of a charity. The father having taken cold, was ill for some time, during which time, as the boy was unable to play on the piano, he wrote his first symphony, and the year following three others. Before leaving London they visited the British Museum, and in memory of his visit Wolfgang composed a four-part quartette, and presented the autograph to the museum.

Fig. 54.

**CONCERT BY THE MOZART FAMILY. THE LITTLE
WOLFGANG AT THE PIANO.**

[From a painting by Carmontil, 1763.]

Without pausing to trace the concert career of the young virtuoso it must
suffice to say, that by the time he was twelve years old, he had become
favorably known in every court of southern Europe. His talent had been
illustrated in many different ways, and tested by the most severe masters.
One of the most celebrated cases of this kind happened at Bologna, where

the Philharmonic Academy received him as a member, after his passing the usual severe test, over which the famous master, Padre Martini, presided. The conditions of membership required the candidate to write an elaborate motette in six parts, founded upon a melody assigned from the Roman Antiphonarium, the work to conform to the strictest rules, with double counterpoint and fugue. In consequence of the nervous feeling due to the limit of time allowed, candidates very often failed. Mozart, however, took his paper in the cheerful frame of mind which everywhere distinguished him, and was duly locked up. In less than three-quarters of an hour he rapped at his door and asked to be let out. The authorities sent him word not to be discouraged, but to keep on trying, as he had yet three hours, and might accomplish it. They were greatly astonished on finding that he had already finished, having produced a complete master work, abundantly up to all requirements, the whole written in his peculiarly neat and accurate manner.

His compositions had already reached the number of eighty, including a number of symphonies. It was now late in the year 1771, and at Milan Wolfgang set seriously to work upon his opera, which was produced December 26 and repeated to full houses twenty times, the author himself conducting it. This was "*Mitridate, Re di Ponto.*" The year following he composed two other operas for Italy, and several symphonies, so that when his new opera of "*Lucio Silla*" was performed in Milan October 24, 1772, the number of his works had reached 135. From 1773 to 1777 Mozart remained at Salzburg, with occasional journeys to Vienna and other cities, always pursuing a life of unflagging industry. The number of his works had increased by the end of this period to upwards of 250, including an immense variety of pieces of chamber music, symphonies, two or three operas, a number of masses, and the like. He was now twenty-one years old, and since the age of fourteen he had been assistant conductor at Salzburg in the service of the prince archbishop, who was a small-souled man, wholly unworthy the service which Mozart rendered him. There is at least a small satisfaction in remembering that the archbishop himself had a distinct impression of the dis-esteem in which he was held by his talented young musical conductor.

With the attainment of his majority the second period in the life of this great genius began. Unable to obtain permission from the shabby prelate for father and son to go together upon an artistic tour, the father at length decided to send the young man out with his mother, and in September, 1777, the two started for Paris, traveling in their own carriage with post horses. Their plan was to give a concert at every promising town, taking whatever time might be necessary for working it up in due form. In this way their journey was considerably prolonged by delays at Munich,

Mannheim and Augsburg. At Mannheim, especially, the incidents of the tour were varied by Mozart's falling in love with the charming daughter of the theatrical prompter and copyist, a promising singer, who afterward married happily in quite a different quarter. At Paris things did not turn out quite so favorably as the father had anticipated. Most afflicting of all, the mother fell sick there, and died, so that the son left Paris in September for home with a far heavier heart than when he entered it. During the most of 1779 and 1780 he remained at Salzburg, fulfilling his duties as assistant conductor. Then came his first opera in Germany, "*Idomeneo, Re di Creta*," produced at Munich January 29, 1781. The success of this work was so decided that it determined Mozart's career as an operatic composer. A few months later he quarreled with the archbishop, and the unpleasant connection came to an end. His second opera, "*Die Entführung aus dem Serail*" ("The Elopement from the Seraglio"), was produced at Vienna July 16, 1782. This was his first opera in German. In August of this year he was married to Constance Weber, younger sister of her who had first enchanted him. The marriage was congenial in many ways, but as the wife was incapable in money matters and administration, and Mozart himself careless as a business man, and in receipt of a small and irregular income, they soon found themselves in a sea of little troubles, from which the struggling artist was nevermore free. Only at the last moment, when indeed his life was all but extinct, did the clouds disappear, and a prospect open before him, which if he had lived to enjoy it, would have placed his remaining days in easy circumstances. In 1785 the father visited his son in Vienna, and upon one of the first days of his stay, there was a little dinner party at Mozart's house, with Haydn and the two Barons Todi. In his letter home, Leopold Mozart says that Haydn said to him: "I declare to you, before God, as a man of honor, that your son is the greatest composer that I know, either personally or by reputation; he has taste, and beyond that the most consummate knowledge of composition." In return for this compliment Mozart dedicated to Haydn six string quartettes, with a laudatory preface, in which he says that it was "but his due, for from Haydn I first learned to compose a quartette." Mozart was an enthusiastic Freemason, and through his influence his father, who had always previously opposed the order, became a member, during this visit at Vienna. Soon afterward the father died. For the lodge Mozart wrote much music, both of a liturgical character and for concerts, and special entertainments, and in the "Magic Flute" there are many reminiscences of the order.

A year later he made the acquaintance of the celebrated librettist, Lorenzo da Ponte, who proposed to adapt Beaumarchais' comedy, "The Marriage of Figaro," which after some difficulty in obtaining the consent of the emperor, on account of the objectionable character of the story, was done, and the work produced at Vienna, May 1, 1786. The theater was crowded, and many airs were repeated, until at later performances the emperor prohibited encores. A pleasing scene took place at the last dress rehearsal. Kelly, who took the parts of Don Basilio and of Don Curzio, writes: "Never was anything more complete than the triumph of Mozart and his 'Marriage of Figaro,' to which numerous overflowing audiences bore witness. Even at the first full band rehearsal, all present were roused to enthusiasm, and when Benucci came to the fine passage '*Cherubino Alla Vittoria, Alla Gloria Militar*,' which he gave with stentorian lungs, the effect was electric, for the whole of the performers on the stage, and those in the orchestra, as if actuated by one feeling of delight, vociferated '*Bravo, Bravo, Maestro. Viva, Viva, grande Mozart*.' Those in the orchestra I thought would never have ceased applauding, by beating the bows of their violins against their music desks. And Mozart, I never shall forget his little animated countenance. When lighted up with the glowing rays of genius, it is as impossible to describe it as it would be to paint sunbeams." Yet the success did not improve his position in money affairs. Soon afterward, however, he was invited to Prague, to see the success his beautiful work was making there. He was entertained handsomely, and found the town wild with delight, at the novelty, the spontaneity and charming quality of his music. He also gave two concerts there, which were brilliantly successful, and having been many times recalled he sat down at the piano and improvised for half an hour, the audience resisting every effort he made to stop. After returning to Vienna he obtained another libretto from Da Ponte, that of "*Don Giovanni*," which was produced at Prague, October 29, 1787. It is told, as a characteristic incident of Mozart's method of working, that the overture of this opera had not been written until the night before the performance. At every suggestion Mozart answered, tapping his forehead, "I have it all here." But not a line had been written. Late at night he set about writing it. His wife made him some punch, of which he was very fond, and sat with him telling him fairy stories, in order to keep him awake. Early in the morning the overture was finished, and after being copied it was played *prima vista* at night, with grand success. In response to repeated appeals for court recognition, Mozart was made chamber composer, with a salary of about $400, which he pronounced, "Too much for what I produce; too little for what I might produce." "*Don Giovanni*" was not given in Vienna until May, 1788.

Fig. 55.

MOZART, AT THE AGE OF THIRTY-THREE.

[From a drawing by Dora Stock, a friend of Schiller, 1789. (Grove.)]

His pecuniary circumstances continued desperate but there were certain incidents of an artistic kind which afforded the struggling genius a meager consolation. One Van Swieten, director of the royal library, who was a great amateur of classical chamber music, held meetings every Sunday for the rehearsal of works of this class. Mozart sat at the piano. For these occasions he arranged several of the fugues of Bach's "Well Tempered Clavier," for string quartette. The year following the practices took on larger proportions, a subscription having been made to provide for giving oratorios with chorus and orchestra. Mozart conducted, and Weigl took the pianoforte. It was for performances of this club, that Mozart added the wind parts to certain works of Händel. They gave "Acis and Galatea" (November, 1778), the "Messiah" (March, 1779), "Ode to St. Cæcilia's Day" and "Alexander's Feast" (July, 1790). Space forbids our following his later career beyond mentioning the chief incidents in a life where sadness had larger and larger place, when nevertheless the great master was pouring out his most noble and beautiful strains of melody and tonal delight. A visit to Berlin resulted in receptions at court, at Potsdam, where the truthful composer replied to the king's question, how he liked his band, that: "It contains great virtuosi, but if the gentlemen would play together they would make a better effect"—a remark which has been appropriate to many later orchestras. The king apparently laid the remark to heart, and offered Mozart the post of director, with a salary of 3,000 thalers, almost equal to the same number of our dollars. It would have been well for Mozart if he had accepted this liberal offer; but his answer was, "How can I abandon my good emperor?"—certainly an affection most misplaced.

Fig. 56.

MOZART.

[From the Lange painting.]

The list of the Mozart operas was closed with the "Magic Flute," produced September 30, 1783, which at first was not so successful as most of his previous works, but which continued to improve upon hearing, until at length it reached the estimation which it has ever since held, as one of the most characteristic and interesting of all his works. He had already begun upon his "Requiem," which had been mysteriously ordered of him by a messenger, who declined to state the object for which the work was intended. It is now ascertained that the unknown patron was a Count Walsegg, an amateur desirous of being thought a great composer. It was his intention to have performed the work as his own. Mozart was now in low spirits, worn out with work, late hours and financial worry. The mystery of the "Requiem" preyed on his imagination none the less that he felt that in it he was writing some of his noblest and best thoughts. He said: "I am sure that this will be my own requiem." Nothing could dissuade him from the idea. It returned again and again. At length he fell ill, poisoned, as he thought, by some envious rival. No one knows whether there was anything in the notion that actual poison had been administered, although there were rivals who had been heard to wish that he were out of the way. Without having quite finished the "Requiem" he breathed his last December 5, 1791. His premonition proved correct. The "Requiem" was given at his own funeral.

This account of the life of Mozart has hardly the merit of an outline, for within the short thirty-five years of his earthly existence this great master produced a variety of works in every province of music, greater than that produced by any other of the great masters, scarcely excepting the indefatigable and long-lived Händel.

It is extremely difficult to assign Mozart a definite place in the musical Pantheon without praising him too highly on the one hand, or going to the other extreme and belittling his genius by pointing out the evident fact that noble, beautiful, sprightly, sweet and charming as were his compositions, he has not left so large an influence upon the later course of music as quite a number of artists apparently his inferiors. His influence in music was largely temporary, but none the less indispensable to musical progress. To the neat and symmetrical periods of the Haydn symphony and sonata, with their fresh, thematic treatment, Mozart added a tender grace and sweetness like the conceptions of a Raphael in painting. He was the apostle of melody. If he had never written, the art of music would have remained something quite different from what we know it. And wherever there are lovers of refined, noble melody, there will the music of Mozart be loved. Moreover, in his best symphonies, such as the one in G minor, and the "Jupiter" in C, there is a boldness and freedom of flight which Beethoven scarcely surpassed. He was at his best as a composer of operas. He was one of the fathers of the artistic song, with music for every stanza differing according to the sentiment of the words; and while the dramatic coloration is not forgotten in his operas, they are a constant flow of charming, inexhaustible melody, which sings most divinely. In short, taking his works through and through, Mozart was what, in the words of Mr. Matthew Arnold, we might call the composer of "sweetness and light." His music glows with the radiance of immortal beauty.

CHAPTER XXVII.
BEETHOVEN AND HIS WORKS.

THE labors of Haydn and Mozart in the rich field of instrumental music were followed immediately by those of Ludwig van Beethoven, who was born at the little town of Bonn, on the Rhine, about twenty miles above Cologne, in 1770. He died at Vienna, 1827. The years between these dates were filled with labor and inspiration, beyond those of any other master. Beethoven's place in music is at the head. Whether he or Bach ought to be reckoned the very greatest of all the great geniuses who have appeared in music, is a question which might be discussed eternally without ever being settled. Considered merely as an artist capable of transforming musical material in an endless variety of ways, he would perhaps be placed somewhat lower than Bach; but considered as a tone poet gifted with the faculty of making hearers feel as he felt, and see as he saw (with the inner eyes of tonal sense), no master ought to be placed above him. This is the general opinion now, of all the world. Taine, the French critic, in his work on art, names four great souls belonging to the highest order of genius— Dante, Shakespeare, Michael Angelo and Beethoven. The company is a good one, and Beethoven rightfully belongs in it. His early life was wholly different from that of the gifted Mozart. He was the son of a dissipated tenor singer, and his mother was rather an incapable person. When the boy was about eleven years old he began to play the viola in the orchestra. He was already a good pianist, and it was said of him that he was able to play nearly the whole of the "Well Tempered Clavier" by heart, and at the age of eleven and a half he was left in charge during Neefe's absence, as deputy organist. His improvisations had already attracted attention, and when he was a little past twelve he was made assistant musical conductor (cembalist), having to prepare the operas, adapt them to the orchestra and the players of the theater, and sometimes to train the whole company for several months together, while Neefe, the director, was away. All this without salary. In this practical school of adversity the boy grew up, arranging continually, training the orchestra, adapting music and composing—for he began this very soon; in fact, we have certain sonatinas of his, composed while he was but ten years old.

He was direct in his speech, almost to rudeness, not, like Mozart, attractive in his personal appearance, and rather awkward in society, where he was continually breaking things, upsetting the water, the ink, or whatever liquid was in his way. Nevertheless, there must have been something attractive about this young man of independent manners, for very early in life, and all the way through it, he made friends with the aristocracy. Count Waldstein, a few years his senior, to whom he afterward dedicated the so-called "Waldstein" sonata, Opus 53, in C, early became interested in him, hired a piano for him and sent it to his room, that he might have opportunity to practice. There was a family of Von Breunings in Bonn, consisting of the mother, three boys and a daughter, where the young Beethoven often stayed for several days together. This was one of the most refined families in town, and it was here that the unfortunate young Beethoven got his first glimpses of a true home life, and his first realization of the refining influence of woman's society. He learned English in order that he might be able to read Shakespeare in the original. He also learned a little Italian and French. In short, the boy appears at good advantage from every point of view, except from that of mere appearance. This life of labor and responsibility was broken in upon when he was about seventeen (in 1787). He was sent to Vienna, and there is a tradition that he played there before Mozart, who is reported to have prophesied favorably concerning him. There is very little left us concerning his first visit to the great Austrian capital, then, as ever since, the home of music. He was soon back again in Bonn, and there for yet another year and a half he went on with his work. His mother dying, he had no longer any responsibility to retain him there, so when he was about twenty-one he set out again for Vienna, where all the remainder of his life was spent. At Vienna he immediately began to give concerts, in which his piano playing was the main feature, and his improvising upon themes presented by the audience. This art always remained one of his great distinctions—the surest proof of genius, the possession of musical fantasy, in which every thought immediately suggests something else. He devoted himself to serious study of counterpoint and composition under the instruction of Haydn at first, but later with Albrechtsberger. His two great elements of power at this period were his playing and his improvising. Czerny says: "His improvisation was most brilliant and striking; in whatever company he might chance to be, he knew how to produce such an effect upon every hearer that frequently not an eye remained dry, while many would break out into loud sobs; for there was something wonderful about his expression, in addition to the beauty and originality of his ideas, and his spirited manner of rendering them."

The limits of the present work do not admit of following the career of this great master in the detail which would otherwise be desirable. It must suffice to mention the more salient features. Contrary to the precedent established by Mozart, Beethoven was in no hurry to appear as a composer of ambitious pieces. After the early practical experiences above described, and the further advantage of studies in Vienna under the best teachers at that time living, it was not until 1795 that he appeared as composer of his first concerto for pianoforte and orchestra, a Mozart-like work, but with an *Adagio* of true Beethovenish flavor. A year later he published his first three sonatas for pianoforte, dedicated to Haydn. These three works are in styles totally unlike each other, and there is little or no doubt that each one of them was modeled after some existing work, which at that time was highly esteemed in Vienna. The first in F minor, is plainly after one by Emanuel Bach in the same key. The *Adagio* of this is especially interesting, not only because it shows a freedom and a pure lyric quality totally foreign to Emanuel Bach, and beyond Mozart even, but because it was taken out of a quartette which he had written when he was fifteen years old. This shows that even at that early age Beethoven had arrived at the conception of his peculiar style of slow movements, which differed from those of Mozart in having a more song-like quality, and a deeper and more serious expression. The impression of a deep soul is very marked in the *Largo* of the first concerto, and there are few of his later works which carry it more plainly. In all, some sixty works precede this Opus 2, which is the modest mark affixed to these three sonatas. The third, in C, is still different from the other two, and was fashioned apparently after some composition of Clementi or Dussek. The *Adagio* takes a direction which must have been regarded as not entirely successful, for nowhere else does the composer follow it out. Then followed a succession of pieces of every sort, not rapidly, like Mozart's compositions, as if they represented the overflowing of an inexhaustible spring, but deliberately, as if the world were not ready for them too rapidly, one after another, each in succession carrying the treatment of the pianoforte to a finer point, and each different from its predecessor, whether of contemporaneous publication or of a former year, until by the end of the century he had reached the "*Sonata Pathetique*," a work which marked a prodigious advance in expression and boldness over anything that can be shown from any other master of the period. Mention having been made of the slow movements in these works, in which point they were perhaps more strikingly differentiated from those of the composers previous—the *Largo* of the sonata in D major, Opus 10, may be mentioned as an example of a peculiarly broad and dramatic, almost *speaking* rhapsody, or reverie, for piano, which not only calls for true feeling in the interpreter, but also for technical qualities of touch and breadth of tone, such as must have been distinctly in advance of the instruments of the day. Meanwhile a variety of chamber pieces had been composed, many of them of decided merit. This was a great period of activity with the young composer. He had found his voice. Within two years from the "*Sonata Pathetique*," he had composed all the sonatas up to the two numbered Opus 27, in which the so-called "Moonlight" stands second, and between these a variety of variations, and several important chamber pieces, not forgetting the oratorio, "Christ on the Mount of Olives"—a work which although not fully successful, nevertheless contained many beautiful ideas, and one chorus which must be ranked among the best which the repertory of oratorio can show—"Hallelujah to the Father." The year 1800 also saw the first performance of the beautiful and romantic third concerto for pianoforte and orchestra. The first symphony had been performed in 1800, and by 1804 we have the great heroic symphony, the "*Kreutzer Sonata*," and the "*Appassionata*" with all that lie between. Never did tone poet give out great inspirations like these so freely. Each is an advance upon the previous, distancing all works of similar composers, and each one surpassing his own previous efforts. This activity continued with little or no interruption until 1812, after which there is quite a break, Beethoven occupying himself with pot-boilers for the English market, in the way of arrangements of songs for instrumental accompaniment. Of these there are many, Scotch and other, besides masses, canons for voices and the like. In 1814 we have the lovely sonata in E minor for piano, Opus 90, and in 1818 the great sonata for hammer klavier, Opus 106. Then in 1821 and 1822 the last of the sonatas, which carry this form of pianoforte writing to a point which it had never previously reached, if since; and then the "*Messe Solennelle*," and the ninth symphony, the latter having been composed in 1822-1823. After this came the last quartettes for strings, compositions which have been much written about, but which time has shown to be among the most beautiful and understandable of all that great master produced.

Fig. 57.

BEETHOVEN.

Meanwhile, as a man Beethoven had been subject to his vicissitudes, but upon the whole, while no longer the popular composer of the day (his seriousness prevented that) he was in comfortable circumstances, but annoyed by the care of a nephew of irregular habits and reprehensible character. For many years now Beethoven had been getting deaf, and for the past ten or twelve he had been unable to hear ordinary conversation, so that communication had to be carried on with him by writing. Superficial observers inferred from this fact that the inability to hear his compositions must have reacted unfavorably upon them, and probably accounted for many passages which were unlike his early works, and unintelligible or unlovely to the critics aforesaid. It is true that between the early and the latest compositions of Beethoven there is a greater difference in intelligibility than between the early and the late compositions of any other master. But the difference is not one of judgment on his part, but purely one of different conception, different melodic structure and deeper effect. The ninth symphony, which the first players called impossible, has lived to be counted not simply the greatest of all of Beethoven's works, but the greatest of *all* instrumental music. It has been named as an impassable barrier beyond which no later composer might pass and compose an instrumental symphony. Nothing could be more unjust or mistaken. Every composition of Beethoven is a fantasia, which in his earlier work indeed has the form of the sonata, the accepted serious form of the day; but in the works of the middle period, the limits of the sonata form were crossed in many directions, and in the latest the sonata is forsaken entirely. But this is not to say that Beethoven had gone beyond the sonata form. Beethoven was an improviser in music, quite as surely as his wildest successor, Schumann, and he wrote as he felt at the time. He lost nothing in being deaf. His inner tonal sense was as acute as ever, and had been trained as the tonal sense of few composers ever was. In point of fact the compositions of the later period are as sweet as those of any former period whatever. The last sonata for the pianoforte is one of the most advanced compositions that exist for the instrument. It is a tone poem which will outlast most other things that Beethoven wrote for this instrument. In fact, the accuracy with which the capacity of the instrument is gauged is one of the most striking peculiarities of the last sonatas and other late works of this master. Meanwhile, piano technique has advanced to a point where these great works no longer present the insurmountable difficulties that they did when first composed. Their general acceptance has been delayed by the foolish notion that there was about them something sacred and secluded from the apprehension of ordinary readers. This is not the case. They are within reach, and repay study.

Beethoven's last days were not pleasant. He lived the life of a bachelor, and his nephew was a source of trouble. It is thought by many that the neglect of his nephew to order a physician in time, when requested to do so by his uncle, was the immediate occasion of the death of the great man. Beethoven died March 27, 1827, after a serious illness, in which dropsical symptoms were among the most troublesome. There was a grand funeral, in which impressive exercises were held, and the body was deposited in consecrated ground in the cemetery at Wahring, near Vienna.

The allusions to the compositions of this composer in the preceding pages are very fragmentary, and, in fact, are expected merely to direct attention to those mentioned. There are many others almost equally worthy of attention. But upon the whole, the reputation of Beethoven as a tone poet must rest first upon the nine symphonies; then upon the string quartettes and other chamber music; next upon the concertos, of which the third and fourth for pleasing beauty, and the fifth for deep poetical meaning, have never been equaled by those of any other composer. There remain the sonatas for pianoforte and for piano and violin, three large volumes, containing a multitude of exquisite strains, which the world would be poor indeed to lose.

Fig. 58.

BEETHOVEN AS HE APPEARED ON THE STREETS OF VIENNA.

[From a sketch by Lyser, to the accuracy of which Breuning testifies, excepting that the hat should be straight on the head, and not inclined to one side.]

In personal appearance Beethoven was rugged rather than pleasing. He was rather short, five feet five inches, but very wide across the shoulders, and strong. His ruddy face had high cheek bones, and was crowned by very thick hair, which originally was brown, but in later life perfectly white. His eyes were black and rather small, but very bright and piercing. His natural expression was grave, almost severe, but his smile was extremely winning, and he was jovial in humor. He was very fond of the country, walking in the fields, where under a tree he would lie for a half day together, humming the melodies which occurred to him, and making notes in the bits of blank paper which he always carried. These pocket note books have been preserved, and we find in them themes in crude form which he used for some important movement or other, often several years later. Among the works produced while this habit was strongest were the sixth and seventh symphonies, than which no works in music are more charming.

CHAPTER XXVIII.
HAYDN, MOZART AND BEETHOVEN COMPARED.

THE three masters, Haydn, Mozart and Beethoven, in relation to the symphony stand upon a plane of substantial equality, whether we estimate their merits according to the absolute worth of the compositions they produced in this form, or in the value of the additions which each in turn made to the ideal of his predecessor. Naturally, as the latest of the three, though so far contemporaneous with them as to form part of a single moment in the progress of art, the symphonies of Beethoven are greater in certain respects, and, as also was to have been expected from his general depth of mind and seriousness of purpose, they are perhaps somewhat more severe—or elevated—in style and sentiment. Nevertheless, the ideal of the three writers was but slightly different. All alike sought to weave tones into a succession of agreeable and beautiful combinations, related as representing a continued flight of spirit—a reverie of the beautiful. Haydn has the honor of having created the form. His fortunate innovation upon the traditions of his predecessors, by adding the second and contrasting theme, and his happy faculty of working out the middle part of the first movement thematically in a style of free fantasy based upon the various devices of counterpoint and canonic imitation, not only suggested to the later composers a way in which an endless variety of pleasing tone pictures might be created—but established, and demonstrated by the clearness with which he did it, and the ever fresh variety and charm of his works, that this was *the way* in which symphonic material must be put together. For further particulars relating to the sonata form, as such, the student is referred to my "Primer of Musical Forms" (Arthur P. Schmidt, Boston, 1891).

The form thus established by Haydn, Mozart accepted, and followed in all his symphonies, with few and unimportant variations. His additions to the general ideal of orchestral effect were in the direction of a sweeter *cantilena*, a vocal and song-like quality, which pervades every movement, and which in the slow movement rises to a height of refined and exquisite song never surpassed by any composer. Beethoven is often more impassioned; at times more forcible. But it is never possible to say of the pure spirit of Mozart, that this refined and gentle soul might not have broken mountains and shaken the hills if he had chosen to do so. His refinement is like that of a seraph, as we see it illustrated in the feminine-looking faces of the Greek

Apollos, and the St. Michaels and archangels of Guido Reni and Raphael. It is free from passion and toil; but no man dares set a limit to the strength therein concealed. In the slow movements of the pianoforte sonatas of Mozart we do not find this quality so plainly manifested. The instrument was still too imperfect, and did not invite it. Moreover, the greater portion of these compositions bear the appearance of having been written for the use of amateurs. But in the string quartette and the symphonies it is different. Here the spirit of Mozart has free course, and he goes from one beauty to another, with the sure instinct of a master before whom all tonal kingdoms are wide open. This can be seen even in the pianoforte arrangements of the greater symphonies. The melodies, apparently so simple and diatonic, are susceptible of being sung with heartfelt fervor under the fingers of the violinist, or by the voice of the great singer, and when so sung they become transfigured with beauty—luminous from within, like lovely angel faces, glowing with radiance from the higher realms of bliss. Without this idea of singing, and more than this, of a pure spirit singing, the Mozart adagios are open to the charge often made against them in these later days by the unthinking, who find in them only the external peculiarities of simplicity and diatonic quality, with the unsensationalism which technical reserve implies.

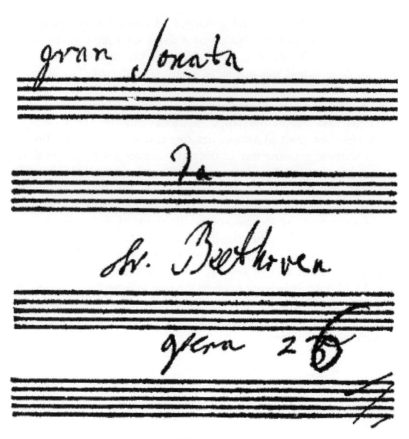

Fig. 59.

**REDUCED FACSIMILE OF THE TITLE PAGE OF
BEETHOVEN'S SONATA, OPUS 26, CONTAINING THE
CELEBRATED FUNERAL MARCH.**

Nor is it true that Beethoven is incapable of this elevated soaring in the higher realms of the merely beautiful in song. There is generally an undercurrent of deeper pathos in all his sustained slow movements, but in the earlier symphonies, especially in the second, there is a long slow movement of heavenly depth and quality. Indeed, without pausing to individualize we may say once for all that the slow movements of Beethoven are nearly as sweet and as forgetful, as rapturous, as those of Mozart. Even when he takes the lower key of the minor, with its implication of suffering and pain, there is still a sweetness, which once heard can never be forgotten. Think of the lovely *allegretto* of the seventh symphony, with its persistent motive of a quarter and two-eighths. Even in an arrangement for the pianoforte this is still impressive; upon the organ yet more so; but how much more so when given by the orchestra, with the lovely changing colors of Beethoven's instrumentation! The progress from Haydn's slow movement to that of Beethoven is in the direction of depth, self-forgetfulness, and elevated reverie, having in it a quality distinctly church-like, devotional, worshipful and reposeful in the heavenly sense. The finest example of this is in the slow movement of the ninth symphony of Beethoven, where the composer has one of those lofty moods, which even in his younger times Mrs. Von Breuning used to call his "*raptus*"— rapture of song.

In a technical point of view the handling of the themes becomes more masterly in Beethoven than even in Mozart—mainly perhaps because the symphonies of Beethoven represent a more mature point in his mental and artistic career than do those of Mozart. The third symphony of Beethoven was written in 1803, the composer being thirty-three years old; the fourth waited until he was thirty-five or six. Mozart died at the age of thirty-five, and whatever we have from his lofty pen came to the young Mozart, not yet having reached middle life. Observe also the rapidity with which these great works followed one another from the pen of Beethoven, when once he had found his voice. The fifth symphony was written in 1808. In the same year he wrote also the sixth; four years later, in 1812, the next two symphonies, the seventh and eight. Then a long pause, filled up with other works, and at length when the composer was fifty-three years of age, in 1823, the mighty ninth. If Mozart's life had been spared to enter into the more comfortable and dignified openings which his death prevented, what might we not have had from him!

In one sense there is a distinct difference between the symphonies of Mozart and those of Beethoven. The passionate ideal, the picture of a deep soul, tossed yet triumphant, is nearer to the latter. Whatever Mozart may have experienced in the way of "contradiction of sinners" (as St. Paul calls it), he never allows the fact to find entrance into his music, and especially into his symphonies. Whether he felt that these moments did not belong to a high ideal of orchestral pieces, or whether he was glad to find in the tone world forgetfulness of sorrows and troubles, we do not know. But Beethoven came nearer to the great time of the romantic. The inherent interest of whatever belongs to the human soul was an idea of his time, and unconsciously to himself, perhaps, it entered into and colored his work. The ninth symphony belongs to the period when Hegel was delivering his lectures upon the deepest questions of philosophy, and laying it down as a fundamental principle that it is the place of art to represent everything whatever, which sinks or swells in the human spirit; not alone all the noble and the lovely, but also the ignoble, the vicious, the unworthy, and particularly the tragic—to the end that the soul may learn to know itself, and awaken to a deeper and better self-consciousness. Beethoven felt the mental movement of his day. While his acquaintance with other prominent literary men of his time made little headway, owing in part to his deafness, and in part to his very strong self-consciousness, he read and thought, and felt himself akin with the whole human race. He was a socialist and a republican by instinct. "Man stands upon that which he really is," was a form of self-assertiveness, which, if not actually enunciated by him, at least represents his attitude toward the conventionalities and superficialities of the courts, the social orders, and the general movement of mind into which he entered. Moreover this was the time when the romantic poets of Germany had already set the world thinking their new ideas. Close by the great composer, in the same city in fact, worked a young man, worshiping almost the very ground upon which Beethoven walked, but for the most part unknown to him—Franz Schubert, who in the symphony was classic to the very highest degree, and a tone poet gifted lyrically not less than Mozart himself, a composer whose ideas have equal refinement and grace with those of Mozart, together with a certain charm peculiarly their own, and an instinct for musical coloration, which has never found its superior. This obscure young man, whose lofty genius was recognized only after his soul had taken its flight from earth, was the founder of the modern romantic school of music—the musical commentator upon the productions of all the best of German poets; a composer of such inexhaustible fertility and melodic inspiration that Schumann said of him, that if he had lived he would have set to music the whole German literature. Thus by the combined efforts of all these composers, of Schubert no less than of the three great masters of whom we are more particularly speaking, the symphony came to its full expression.

In their relation to the sonata, these three great masters do not stand in the same position of *quasi*-equality. Haydn is here the first, as already in the symphony. But in his sonatas he is always rather hampered, and never attains the flow of his slow melodies for the violin. Mozart, also, while a beautiful player upon the pianoforte of his day, did not possess the prescience of Beethoven, who was able to see over the pianoforte of his time and write as if he felt the assurance of the nobler and yet nobler instruments of these later times. Here he stands with Bach, who in his great Chromatic Fantasia and Fugue requires and confidently expects the breadth of tone and the power of the modern piano. It was Beethoven's fortune to live during the early days of the modern instrument. Just after his death the era of virtuoso piano playing began, the first appearances of Thalberg having been made as early as about 1830. He was himself a great pianist, as we see in the concertos which he wrote, always intending to play them at some concert or other in near prospect. Occasionally indeed he overshot his mark, as notably in the fifth, which, being finished just before his concert in 1809, he found too difficult for his fingers, whereupon he was obliged to fall back on the third. Moreover, the pianists Hummel and Dussek were already before the public, and Clementi had made his concert tours, and established the lines of the classical technique upon its brilliant side. All these influences find their illustration in the music of Beethoven, and especially find illustration in the last and greatest of his pianoforte sonatas. These beautiful tone poems were long regarded as impossible. But the genius of Schumann and Liszt came to their rescue by introducing a new style of touch and technique, which, when once found, proved to be the link missing for the proper interpretation of these till then obscure works.

Moreover, Beethoven occupied a different attitude toward the sonata form from that which he held to the symphony. He deviated from the sonata form in every direction, and this not alone in his later works, when we might suppose he had become wearied with the repetition of his ideas in the same order, but in his works of middle life, when as yet he might apparently have gone on writing sonatas indefinitely, so fresh, so novel and so varied were the tone pictures which he gave the world under this name. He seems to have regarded music as an improvisation, not to be held to some one fixed type of expression, but free to go wherever the fancy of the poet took him, to the end that the entire heavens of the tone world might in time be visited. He expects of his readers an element of the devotee. It is not for amateurs that he writes, still less for the votaries of fashionable society, with its emptiness and repeated insincerities. There is a suggestion of entering into the closet, and of shutting the door, as a prerequisite to the full enjoyment of these ineffable pictures and images which come from his revelation.

In the present full-grown faith in the doctrine of the capacity of man for a development continually progressive, it would be presumptuous to say that the three composers, Haydn, Mozart and Beethoven, have reached the limit of art, so far as instrumental music goes. In the nature of the case, there is not, nor can there be an *Ultima Thule* in art. Whatever the splendor of color, the nobility of conception, or the sincerity and loyalty of purpose, and however resplendent the works created by these exceptional talents, there is reason to hope that better works still may yet be in store. Stronger and yet stronger imaginations, more perfect technique of expression and finer inspiration, may yet be the lot of fortunate individuals of the twentieth century, inheriting the richly diversified musical experiences of the present time. But in one direction there is little doubt that these three great masters *did* carry the art of instrumental music to a pinnacle beyond which no one as yet has been able to soar. They represent the climax of classical art. In the nature of the case, the term classical itself is subject to an element of uncertainty. According to the philosopher Hegel, the classical is that art in which the *form* is beautiful and wholly satisfactory in symmetry, while the *content* exactly matches it in fullness and beauty. Or, in ordinary usage, the classical is the first-class, the superior, the highly finished, the standard. And since music is a matter of sense perception, and the impressions resulting from it are in some degree dependent upon the ability of the hearer to find the principles of unity (in other words, "the sense of it"), every generation extends the list of the classical, and includes much which the preceding one found imperfect and strained. So far as our knowledge and experience have yet gone, however, there is a sense in which the productions of these great masters are likely to remain long unmatched in beauty and worth.

Nothing has been done since that surpasses the sustained beauty of the Beethoven adagios, of which we find the most beautiful specimens naturally among the orchestral pieces and in the chamber music, where he could depend upon the long phrases and sustained tones of the violins. But in the sonatas for pianoforte he is equally at home. He seems to have foreseen the possibilities of the modern piano. In his latest sonatas there are passages which foresee the modern technique, and suggest effects which only the pianoforte of the past thirty years has been capable of attaining. This is the prophetic element in the writings of this great master.

The same difference in the sweep of mind shows itself in the lighter movements. In the minuets Haydn is playful, Mozart is occasionally tender and arch; Beethoven alone is vigorous and humoristic in the modern sense. And, in the finales of the sonatas there is a movement in those of Beethoven which we look for in vain in those of the older composers. It was not in Haydn, nor yet in Mozart, to play with tones in this masterly spirit.

Hence the true relation of these great masters might be summed up without intending to be disrespectful to either, as the following: Haydn provided the form, the order of keys and the general character of the contrasts between the two subjects. Mozart invented a myriad of tender *nuances* which illustrated the fine points of music, and imparted to the works a sweetness and pleasing quality which everybody recognized as irresistible. Beethoven added to these ingredients of popular music a depth, a soulful quality, an earnestness and a universal intelligibility to spirits of the necessary depth, which have stood to all the world ever since as models. Such, in general, are the points of relation and of contrast.

It is not to be overlooked, however, that the tendency of musical taste is to leave the works of Mozart behind. Haydn is gaining ground, relatively, through the admiration of musicians for the cleverness with which he treats themes. Beethoven holds his own by reason of his vigorous personality, which is to be felt in every page of his music. Mozart, however, appeals less to the taste of the present time, and his pianoforte works are now cultivated chiefly for technical purposes, in the earlier stages of study.

CHAPTER XXIX.
OPERA IN THE EIGHTEENTH CENTURY.
I.

UPON the musical side, and in one instance upon the dramatic side as well, there were three great forces in opera during this century. The first of these in order of time was Karl Heinrich Graun (1701-1759). A native of Dresden, he was educated there, and having early a beautiful voice became treble singer to the town council—a curious name for a position in the leading church. He profited by the instruction of the official directors of the choir and the church, Petzold and Schmidt, and very early he was an enthusiastic student of the compositions of the Hamburg director, Keiser, whose style influenced his own in his later work. Lotti, the Italian composer, who conducted a series of performances in Dresden with a picked company of Italian singers, was another force operative in his development. He early commenced to write cantatas and motettes for the seminary, of which he was a member, all of which show traces of the Italian influences. In particular his biographer speaks of a Passion cantata, in which an opening chorus, "*Lasset uns aufsehen auf Jesum*," is singularly forcible for the work of a boy of fifteen. His first entrance upon operatic work was as tenor, when he was scarcely twenty-four years of age. Being dissatisfied with the music of his part (written by one Schurmann, a local director), he substituted other airs of his own composition, which were so popular that he was commissioned to write an opera, and was appointed assistant director. His first opera, "*Polliodoro*," was successful, and he was commissioned to write five others, some in Italian, some in German. Besides these he composed several cantatas for church use, and several instrumental pieces. In 1735 he was invited to the residence of the crown prince of Prussia, afterward Frederick the Great. This powerful potentate remained Graun's friend and patron until his death. Here, among other works, he composed fifty Italian cantatas, usually consisting of two airs with recitative. In 1740 Frederick came to the throne, and gave Graun the post of musical director, with a salary of $2,000. Selecting his singers in Italy, where his singing was very highly appreciated, he returned to Berlin and assumed the duties of his position. Here he composed no less than twenty-seven operas, the last being in 1756, all in the Italian style, in so far as a German might master it, and all making the singer the prime person of consideration, and the listener next. The poet took whatever of opportunity these two might not have needed. His best talent both as singer and as composer lay in his power of expressing emotion in *adagios*. In this respect he had, no doubt, more influence upon the development of the lyric slow movement than he has generally been credited with. Later in his life he turned once more to church music, and in his cantatas, and especially in his oratorio, "*Der Tod Jesu*" ("The Death of Jesus"), a Passion oratorio, he made a distinct impression upon the practices of his successors. In Germany this work is held in nearly the same affection as the "Messiah," of Händel, in England. Graun's influence upon the later course of opera, besides the adagio aria already mentioned, lay principally in his accompaniments, which were often strong and highly dramatic.

Fig. 60.

The great operatic mind of this century, and one of the greatest of all time, was that of Christopher Willibald von Gluck (1714-1785). By the middle of the eighteenth century the influence of the Italian composers, helped out by the superficial German composers, such as Graun and Hasse, had reduced the Italian opera to a collection of mere showpieces of singing, the arias having indeed an excuse in the story, but the action of the drama had been lost entirely, owing to the long stretches of time needed for these elaborate arias and the recalls to which they inevitably gave rise. During these pauses the action ceased entirely, as we see at the present day in many Italian operas still current—as in the "mad scene" from "*Lucia*," for instance. In that scene where everything ought to be wild excitement, the chorus singers, representing the relatives and friends of poor Lucia, stand around while she sings long cadenzas with the flute, in such trying relationships as would test the vocal technique of a sane person. In the time of Gluck this abuse had reached about the same height, and to make the matter less bearable, the Italian composers had not yet attained the art of expressing sentiment simply and directly, but were intent upon sweet-sounding trivialities calculated to please the groundlings, but of little or no relation to the drama. Gluck sought to restore the ideal of the original inventors of opera, with such unconscious modification as had been made meanwhile. But before undertaking this he had to undergo the usual long and severe apprenticeship of reformers. In his time the rules for a composer had become well settled, every personage must have his or her aria immediately upon their first entrance. The character of the arias had been well settled. There was the *aria cantabile*, a flowing melody, very lightly accompanied, affording opportunity for embellishments; the *aria di portamento*, introducing long swelling notes, affording the singer opportunity for illustrating his length of breath and sustaining power. And so on with several other forms of aria. The part of hero, whether male or female, was assigned to a man, an artificial soprano, although it might be a hero—like Hercules, for example. The subject had to be classical, and the *dénouement* happy. There were invariably six principal characters, three men and three women. The first woman was always a high soprano; the second or third a contralto; the first man, always the hero of the piece, an artificial soprano. The second man might be an artificial soprano or a contralto. The third man might be a bass or tenor. But it was not at all unusual to confide all the male parts to artificial sopranos. Each principal character claimed the right to sing an aria in each of the three acts of the drama. Each scene ended with an aria of some one of the classes already mentioned, but no two arias of the same class were permitted to follow each other. Gluck was the reformer destined by the fates to rectify some of these artificial traditions. He was educated at the Jesuit seminary in Komotow, and later in Prague. He was engaged in the musical forces of Prince Melzi, who took him to Italy, where he became a pupil of the famous Italian composer and teacher, Sammartini. To this fact, no doubt, is due his early attachment to the Italian opera.

Here he wrote several operas, all more or less in the Italian style as he had been taught it, and as he heard it upon every hand. His first work,

"*Artaserse*," the book by Metastasio, was produced with such success in Milan, in 1741, that he presently wrote several others for other Italian theaters. For Venice in 1741, "*Demetrio,*" and "*Ipermestra*"; for Cremona, "*Artamene*" (1743); for Turin, "*Alessandro nelle Indie*" (1745); for Milan, "*Demofoonte,*" "*Siface*" and "*Fedra*" (1742-1744); in all, eight operas in five years. None of these works in their complete form are now in existence; fragments alone have been preserved. If any inference is justified from these extracts the style throughout was that of the Italian opera of the day.

The fame of Gluck had now extended to England, and in 1745 he was invited to London to compose operas for the Haymarket theater. He came and wrote the year following (1746) "*La Caduta de Giganti,*" after which he produced the Cremona opera. Händel assisted at the production of these two operas, and is reported to have said that the author knew no more of counterpoint than a pig. Naumann thinks that Gluck learned much from hearing Händel's oratorios in England, and that his subsequent deeper and nobler dramatic style was formed upon these great models. The two operas produced in London made but a moderate success, and Gluck was commissioned to write a "*pasticcio*" or medley of styles. He did so, imitating all styles according to the best of his ability, but it made no better effect than the works before it. This was the turning point in his career. The failure mortified him deeply, and led him to reflect concerning the nature of dramatic music. On his way back to Vienna he passed through Paris, where he heard certain operas of Rameau, which also influenced his style later. The declamation and the dramatic treatment of the recitative were the points upon which his attention principally dwelt. Upon reaching Vienna he wrote a number of instrumental pieces, bearing the name of symphonies, pieces which in no way differed from the conventional music of the day. The Haydn symphony had not yet been invented, and the form was wholly indeterminate. There was an opera in this year; also a love affair. Gluck was deeply in love with the beautiful and charming daughter of a rich merchant, who upon no account would consent to her marriage with a musician. So Gluck went back to Italy, and there he wrote another opera, rather better in quality than his previous ones. Early in 1750 the inexorable parent died, and late in the year Gluck married the woman of his choice, who made him a model wife, being educated above the average of her times, and entering into his ideals and aspirations with ever ready sympathy. Her wealth also placed the composer in an easy position as regarded the world, and permitted him to devote himself to study. For nearly ten years following Gluck produced occasionally an opera, but as yet the *man* had not arrived; all these were early and apprentice works. At length in 1762 was produced his first master work, "Orpheus and Eurydice," the libretto having been written by the imperial councillor Calzabigi. The novelty of this great work was not above the appreciation of the Viennese public of the day.

"Orpheus" made a decided success. Its principal innovations consisted in its more powerful instrumentation, the introduction of a chorus having an integral part in the movement of the piece, and in the highly dramatic treatment of the second act, where Orpheus descends into the lower world to seek his lost love. Nevertheless, the composer had not reached true self-consciousness. A retrogression followed. He went back to Metastasio, and in conjunction with him produced three or four small operas, all in his earlier style. But in 1767 he returned to Calzabigi, and upon a libretto of his wrote "*Alceste*" which was produced at the Vienna opera house in 1767 with vastly more success than "Orpheus." The story is that of the tragedy of Euripides, and the music is exclusively severe and tragic. The public was divided concerning the merit of the new work. Already the notion of a music of the future had been conceived, and the notion suggested that only in a more self-forgetful future would a work of such severity and of such lofty aim find acceptance.

In the dedicatory epistle to the duke of Tuscany, prefixed to the score, Gluck defines his intentions. He says: "I seek to put music to its true purpose; that is, to support the poem, and thus to strengthen the expression of the feelings and the interest of the situation, without interrupting the action. I have therefore refrained from interrupting the actor in the fervor of his dialogue by introducing the accustomed tedious *ritournelle*; nor have I broken his phrase at an opportune vowel that the flexibility of his voice might be exhibited in a lengthy flourish; nor have I written phrases for the orchestra to afford the singer opportunity to take a long breath preparatory to the accepted flourish; nor have I dared to hurry over the second part of an aria, when such contained the passion and the most important matter, to find myself in accord with the conventional repeat of the same phrase four times. As little have I permitted myself to close an aria where the sense was incomplete, solely to afford the singer an opportunity of introducing a cadenza. In short, I have striven to abolish all these bad habits, against which sound reasoning and true taste have been struggling now for so long in vain."

There were several numbers in "*Alceste*" which exercised an influence upon subsequent composers, among the more notable being the speech of the oracle, which Mozart must have had in mind in writing the commandatore's reply to Don Giovanni; and the sacrificial march, which probably influenced the priests' march in the "Magic Flute." Gluck was forty-eight when he wrote "Orpheus," and fifty-three when "*Alceste*" appeared.

Galled by the criticisms of his countrymen, and encouraged by the friendship of the French ambassador, Gluck now went to Paris, where his operas were presently brought out, but with the same varying favor as at home. Marie Antoinette, who had been his pupil, befriended him and granted him a pension of 6,000 francs. Thus supported, he brought out still another grand opera in the French language, "*Iphigenie en Aulide*," produced at Paris in 1774. In this work classical severity was scrupulously observed, and the opera is full of telling points of dramatic musical coloration. In "*Armide*," 1777, he endeavored to show that he was equally at home in richly conceived sensuous music, and succeeded so well that the famous controversy was precipitated with the Italian composer, Piccini, who had just arrived in Paris, preparatory to bringing out his opera of "Roland." Volumes were written in praise of Italian music, and in disparagement of the roughnesses of that of Gluck. On the other hand, the friends of Gluck stood up for him manfully, and the contest raged fiercely—with the usual result of thoroughly advertising the music of both. Gluck's last opera for Paris was "*Iphigenie en Tauride*," 1779, the same subject already having been treated by his rival Piccini. The superiority of Gluck's was incontestable. He died at Vienna, of apoplexy, November 15, 1787.

Gluck's place in art has been well summed up by Padre Martini, and the opinion is all the more worthy of attention from the general charge of Gluck's enemies that his music had overturned the traditions of pure Italian art. He says: "All the finest qualities of Italian, and many of those of French music, with the great beauties of the German orchestra, are united in his work." This is tantamount to crediting Gluck with having created a cosmopolitan music—which is precisely the position which posterity has assigned him. For the time when he wrote, his music is wonderfully fine. It still retains its vitality, as has been vividly shown in several revivals of his "Orpheus" within recent years, in two of which (in America and in Italy) the American prima donna, Mme. Helène Hastreiter, has nobly distinguished herself.

The third force alluded to at the outset of the chapter, as having been mainly influential in German opera during the eighteenth century (and until our own time, it might be added), was Mozart, whose works have already received attention in former pages of the narrative. It must suffice here to remind the reader of the successes and qualities of his operas, in order that he may be remembered in this connection; for, like Gluck, his art was cosmopolitan, having in it the sweetness of the Italian, the richness of the German, and occasional traces of the declamation of the French.

II.

After Lulli, the next great name in the history of French opera was that of Jean Philippe Rameau (1683-1765). This great master was one of the most versatile men of whom we have a record in music. He was a mathematician, physicist, a profound theorist, and a virtuoso upon the piano and harpsichord. He is one of the four great names in music of the period of Bach and Händel, the fourth being Scarlatti. His education in music began while he was very young, and it is said of him that such was his talent that he could improvise a fugue upon any theme assigned, when he was but fourteen years of age. His father wished him to be trained for the law, but music had greater charms for him, and the margins of his books were marked over with crotchets and quavers. Having become desperately in love with a fascinating young widow, whom his father was opposed to his marrying, he was sent at the age of seventeen to Italy, ostensibly to study. He came, therefore, to Milan about 1701, a few years before Händel came there. Italian music was little to his taste. The dignified declamation of the Lulli operas seemed to him better worthy the attention of men than the tunes of the Italians. Accordingly he took service as a violinist with a traveling operatic troupe, and in this capacity visited the south of France. In Paris he became a pupil of the court organist Marchand, of whom we hear again in connection with certain tests of proficiency with Händel. Marchand was at first delighted with his new pupil, but presently dropped him when he discovered how talented he was, and liable to prove a dangerous rival. Accordingly he left Paris and took service as organist at Lille, which post he exchanged afterward for one at Clermont. In this quiet town he devoted himself to the study of harmony, and to reflection upon the principles of music. He read here the works of Zarlino, and other Italian theorists, and in 1721 he returned to Paris and published his treatise on harmony, in which he propounded the theory of inversions. His second treatise on harmony, "New System of Musical Theory," was published in 1725. These works excited a great deal of attention and brought the author renown, but his soul yearned for recognition as composer, and in 1730 he obtained from Voltaire a libretto, "Samson." This work was declined at the national opera, on the ground that the public was not attracted by Biblical subjects. Three years later, however, he composed another, "*Hypolite et Arcie*," which was performed with moderate success. He had now reached the age of fifty, and entered upon the second stage of his artistic career, and the second period of the French opera. The admirers of Rameau invited appreciation of the new works upon the ground of their being better than those of Lulli, and all Paris was divided into two opposite camps. Rameau is entitled to having developed his operas more musically than those of Lulli, and the later ones became still richer upon the orchestral side.

The entire list of operas by Rameau numbers about thirty. That they did not preserve their popularity so long as those of Lulli is due to their deficiency upon the dramatic side, especially to the inherent inexpressiveness of the music itself. The treatment of the orchestra is clever in many places, showing a manifest improvement over that of Lulli, especially in the freedom of thematic work. He also ventures occasionally on enharmonic changes.

Contemporaneous with him was that remarkable genius, Jean Jacques Rousseau (1712-1778), the father of the kindergarten idea, and of many other humanitarian and educational novelties. Rousseau's importance in the history of music is not sufficient to justify an account of his early days. With a great fondness for music, he found it extremely difficult to read by note, as he was almost entirely self-taught. This led him to devise a simpler notation, which he did about 1740, publishing an account of it in 1743. His system was substantially that of the tonic sol fa, except that he used figures in place of letters. He presented a memorial to the Academy of Sciences upon this subject in 1742, but his plan was so vigorously opposed by Rameau that nothing came of it; nevertheless the idea was afterward worked out by M. Paris, in the present century, and has proven very useful among the *Orphéonistes*. In 1752 Rameau produced his first opera "*Le Devin du Village*," a very light affair, somewhat on the order of what Germans call a Singspiel. The most remarkable piece that he produced was his comedy "*Pygmalion*" in 1775. There is no song in this opera. The only music in it is that for orchestral interludes in the intervals between the phrases of declamation.

The continuation of French opera was due to Philidor, the celebrated chess player (1726-1795). He was very talented in many directions, and from the production of his first opera in 1759, to his last, *Bélisaire*, finished by his friend Berton, and produced in 1796, he enjoyed an uninterrupted popularity, having brought out in that time about twenty-one operas, some of them comic, one or two of them serious. His music is light and pleasing, and he is credited with having been the first to produce descriptive airs ("*Le Maréchal*") and the unaccompanied quartette ("Tom Jones," 1764). The great merit of his works was their clever construction for the stage. Contemporaneous with him was Pierre Alexander Monsigny (1729-1817). Not having been intended for the profession of music, he had a classical education, and upon the death of his father obtained a clerkship in Paris. He belonged to a noble family, and at first pursued music as a recreation. His first opera was produced after five months' tuition in harmony and theory, in 1759; this was followed by about thirty other works. His greatest skill was melody and ease of treatment. In 1812 he was appointed inspector of the Conservatory, and in 1813 he succeeded Grétry in the Institute, and in 1816 he received the cross of the Legion of Honor.

Fig. 61.

GRÉTRY.

Upon the appearance of André Ernest Modest Grétry, (1741-1813), we come to a real genius, although not of the first order. He was the son of a poor violinist of Liege, Belgium, and when about sixteen years of age he composed six small symphonies and a mass. The latter gained him the protection of the canon of the cathedral who sent him to Rome, where he pursued his studies with very little credit. After producing one small work in Rome, he made his way to Paris, and his first opera, "*Le Huron,*" was successfully produced in 1768. This was followed by more than fifty operas of all sorts, some of which still survive. Grétry was a very charming man, and wrote upon music and other subjects in a pleasing manner. His importance in the history of music is due more to the number of works by him, than to their striking musical qualities.

Another remarkable musician of this period in France was François Joseph Gossec (1733-1829), who also was a Belgian from Hainault. His early training was obtained in the cathedral at Antwerp. He came to Paris in 1751 and became a pupil of Rameau. He conceived the idea of writing orchestral symphonies, and produced some pieces of this kind in 1754, five years before the date of Haydn's first. In 1759 he published some quartettes. In 1760 he produced his best, "*Messe des Morts*," in which he made a sensation by writing the "*Tuba Mirum*" for two orchestras, one of wind instruments concealed outside. Berlioz probably derived an idea from this. He wrote twelve operas which were successfully produced, twenty-six symphonies and a variety of other works. He founded his amateur concerts in 1770, and his sacred concerts in 1773. In 1784 he organized his school of singing, out of which the Conservatory of Music was afterward developed. Upon the foundation of the conservatory, in 1795, he was appointed inspector with Cherubini and Méhul. His influence upon the general development of music is local to Paris, where he did more to enrich opera on the instrumental side than any other composer of the eighteenth century.

Étienne Henri Méhul (1763-1817) was another of these prolific composers of light operas. Son of a cook at Givet, he had passion for music, and soon became a good organist. At fourteen he was deputy organist, and in 1778 he arrived in Paris and at once commenced to study and teach. The next year he was so fortunate as to listen to Gluck's "*Iphigenie en Tauride*," which made a great impression upon him. He called upon Gluck himself in order to express his admiration, and, in consequence of the encouragement received from the eminent composer, he proceeded to write three operas, one after another, which are now lost. His fourth was accepted at the Academy, but not performed. Finally his "*Euphrosine et Coradin*" was produced at the Opéra Comique in 1790. The public immediately recognized a force, a sincerity of accent, a dramatic truth, and a gift of accurately expressing the meaning of words, which always remained the main characteristics of Méhul. Within the next seventeen years he produced twenty-four operas, besides a large number of cantatas and other works. Upon the whole, this sincere master must be regarded as one of the most eminent in the history of French opera.

Somewhat later in the operatic field was Jean François Lesueur (1763-1837). After serving as a boy chorister at Abbeville and Amiens, he came to Paris, where in 1786 he was appointed musical director at Notre Dame, and distinguished himself by giving magnificent performances of motettes and solemn masses, with a large orchestra in addition to the usual forces. His first opera, "*La Caverne*," was produced in 1793, after which he wrote four others, as well as three which were never performed. In the line of church music he was much more productive, and one might say, more at home. His music is marked by grand simplicity. As a teacher in later life he was very celebrated, among his pupils being the greatest of French masters, Berlioz.

Fig. 62.

BOIELDIEU.

The most gifted of the French composers of light opera at the end of the eighteenth century, and in the part of the nineteenth, was François Adrien Boieldieu (1775-1834). This talented musician was born at Rouen, where his father was secretary to the archbishop. The boy was educated in the ecclesiastical schools, having begun as a choir boy in the cathedral. His first little work for the stage was performed at Rouen when he was about seventeen, "*La Fille Coupable*," with such success that the author was encouraged to go and seek his fortune in Paris. Here for a long time he met with little encouragement, and was obliged to make a living at first as a piano tuner; later he was fortunate enough to have certain romances of his sung by popular singers, and thus his name became somewhat known. For these songs he received the munificent compensation of two dollars and a half each. Presently he secured a libretto, "*La Dot de Suzette*," which was composed and performed at the Opéra Comique, with so much encouragement, that he soon after produced his one-act opera, "*La Famille Suisse*." His popularity was not fully established, however, until "*Zoraime et Zulnare*" in 1798. This work possesses a vein of tenderness, a refined orchestration, and singularly clear and pleasing forms. In 1800 his world-wide favorite, "*Le Caliph de Bagdad*," was produced, and its taking overture was played from one end of Europe to the other, upon all possible instruments and combinations of them. His other two successful operas were "*Jean de Paris*" (1812), and "*La Dame Blanche*" (1825). Both these made as much reputation outside of France as in it, and are still produced in Germany. In 1803 Boieldieu received an appointment in St. Petersburg and lived there six years, but he returned to Paris later, and in 1817 became Méhul's successor as teacher of composition at the Conservatory.

Of the French stage during this epoch it is to be observed that nothing of a large and serious character was produced upon it, except the operas of Gluck, which of course were not indigenous to France. What progress was made by the composers before mentioned, and others of less importance, consisted in acquiring fluency, ease and effective construction. The ground had been prepared from which the century following would reap a harvest.

III.

In Italy during the eighteenth century, opera continued to be cultivated by a succession of gifted and prolific composers. At the beginning of the century, the great Alexander Scarlatti was at the height of his career, as also were Lotti and the younger masters mentioned in the former chapter. All these composers followed in the style established by Scarlatti and Porpora. The most talented of the Italians of this period was Giovanni Batista Pergolesi (1710-1737). This gifted genius was born at Jesin, in the Roman states, but when a mere child, was admitted to the conservatory "Of the Poor in Jesus Christ" at Naples, where his education was completed. He commenced as a violin player, and attracted attention while a mere child by his original passages, chromatics, new harmonies and modulations. A report of his performances of this kind being made to his teacher Matteis, he desired to hear them for himself, which he did with much surprise, and asked the boy whether he could write them down. The next day the youngster presented himself with a sonata for the violin, as a specimen of his power; this led to his receiving regular instruction in counterpoint. The first composition of his was a sacred drama called "*La Conversione di St. Guglielmo*," written while he was still a student. It was performed with comic intermezzi (*sic!*) in the summer of 1731, at the cloister of St. Agnello. The dramatic element in this work is very pronounced, and the violin is treated with considerable feeling. His first opera, "*La Salustia*," was produced in 1731. It is notable for improvement in the orchestration. In the winter of this same year he wrote his comic intermezzo, "*La Serva Padrona*," a sprightly operetta, which had a moderate success at the time, but afterward for nearly a hundred years was played in all parts of Europe. He wrote several other operas, which had but moderate success, although many of them were performed with considerable applause after his death. By general consent the most beautiful work of Pergolesi was his "*Stabat Mater*," which was written to order for a religious confraternity, for use on Good Friday, in place of a "*Stabat*" by Scarlatti, the price paid being ten ducats—about nine dollars. It is for two voices, a soprano and contralto, and is excellently written. No sooner was he dead than his music immediately became the object of admiration, his operas and lighter pieces being played in all parts of Italy. He died at the age of twenty-six, being the youngest master who has ever left a permanent impression in musical history.

One of the most prolific composers of this period was Nicolo Jomelli (1714-1774). Jomelli represents the Neapolitan school, having been educated first at the conservatory of San Onofrio, and later at that of "*La*

Pieta de' Turchini." His earlier inclination was church music, and in order to perfect himself in it he went to Rome. This was in 1740, and two of his operas were there produced. He afterward visited Vienna, where he produced several operas, and in 1749 he was appointed assistant musical director at St. Peter's in Rome, a position which he held for five years, after which he went to Stuttgart, as musical director. While in Germany he had a very great reputation as an opera composer. In 1770 Mozart wrote from Naples, "The opera here is by Jomelli; it is beautiful, but the style is too elevated as well as too antique for the theater." His later life was spent in Naples. Besides many operas he wrote a number of compositions for the church. It perhaps gives a good idea of the estimation in which he was held while living, that a critic highly esteemed in his day said that it would be a sorry day for the world when the operas of Jomelli were forgotten, at the same time pronouncing them superior to those of Mozart. Not a single line of Jomelli is performed at the present time, nor is likely ever to be; but the works of Mozart still retain their popularity.

Another prolific composer of the Neapolitan school was Antonio Maria Gasparo Sacchini (1724-1786). This clever composer was very successful in his lifetime, his operas being produced in all parts of Europe. Nevertheless they are monotonous in character, and have little depth. He has very little importance for the history of music. Still another, also from the Neapolitan school, was Piccini (1728-1800). His first operas were produced in 1754, and from that time on for about forty years he was a very popular composer, his works being produced in every theater, and in 1778 he was set up as an idol by his admirers, in opposition to Gluck. He was highly honored by Napoleon, who took pleasure in distinguishing him for the sake of humbling several much more deserving musicians. The complete list of his works in Fétis contains eighty operas. His biographer credits him with one hundred and thirty-three. Yet another composer of the Neapolitan school was Giovanni Paisiello (1741-1815). From the time of his first operas to his death, he was highly esteemed as a composer. In 1776 he was invited by the Empress Catharine to St. Petersburg, where he lived for eight years, and among other operas which he composed while there was "*Il Barbiere di Siviglia.*" In 1799 he was called to Paris, where Napoleon very greatly distinguished him. Upon leaving Paris, in 1803, Napoleon desired him to name his successor, when he performed the creditable act of nominating Lesueur, who was at that time unknown. The list of his works embraces ninety-four operas and 103 masses. His music was melodious and pleasing, but rather feeble; he is regarded, however, as the inventor of the concerted finale, which has since been so largely developed in opera. Perhaps the best of all the Neapolitan composers of this half century was Zingarelli (1752-1827). Zingarelli was not only a good musician and a good composer, but a man of ability and principle. He was an associate pupil with Cimarosa. After leaving the conservatory he took lessons upon the violin, and in 1779 produced a cantata at the San Carlo theater. Two years later his first opera was produced at the same theater with great applause, "*Montezuma.*" He then went to Milan, where most of his later works were produced. He was an extremely rapid worker, his librettist stating it as a fact that all the music of his successful opera of "*Alsinda*" was composed in seven days, although the composer was in ill health at the time. Another of his best works, his "*Giulietta e Romeo,*" was composed in about eight days. It is said that this astonishing facility was acquired through the discipline of his teacher Speranza, who obliged his pupils to write the same composition many times over, with change of time and signature, but without any change in the fundamental ideas. While busily engaged as a popular opera composer, Zingarelli found time to compose much church music, his most important works being masses and cantatas. Of the former there still exist a very large number; of the latter about twenty. He made a trip to France in 1789, where he brought out a new opera, "*L'Antigone*"; he was appointed musical director at the cathedral at Milan in 1792, and two years later at Loretto, Naples. Thence he was transferred to the Sistine chapel at Rome, and finally in 1813 he was appointed director of the Royal College of Music at Naples, in which position he spent the remainder of his long and active life.

He produced about thirty-two operas, twenty-one oratorios and cantatas, and there are about 500 manuscripts of his in the "*Annuale di Loreto.*" As a composer of comic operas Zingarelli became popular all over Europe, but he was nevertheless a serious, even a devout composer. He was extremely abstemious, rose early, worked hard all day, and, after a piece of bread and a glass of wine for supper, retired early to rest. He was never married, but found his satisfaction in the successes of his musical children, among whom were Bellini, Mercadante, Ricci, Sir Michael Costa, Florimo, etc.

IV.

In this, as in the preceding century, there was very little activity in England in the realm of opera music, beyond that of foreign composers imported for special engagements. In the last part of the seventeenth century, however, there was a real genius in English music, who, if he had lived longer, would in all probability have made a mark distinguishable even across the channel, and upon the chart of the world's activity in music. That composer was Henry Purcell (1658-1695), born in London, of a musical family. His father having died while the boy was a mere infant, he was presently admitted as a choir boy in the Chapel Royal, the musical director being Captain Cook, and later Pelham Humpfrey. In 1675, when yet only seventeen years of age, Purcell composed an opera, "Dido and Æneas," which is grand opera in all respects, there being no spoken dialogue but recitative—the first work of the kind in English. It contains some very spirited numbers. After this he composed music to a large number of dramatic pieces, many anthems, held the position of master of the Chapel Royal, and in many ways occupied an honored and distinguished position. He was one of the earliest composers to furnish music to some of Shakespeare's plays, and his "Full Fathom Five" and "Come unto These Yellow Sands," from the "Tempest," have held the stage until the present time. He was in all respects the most vigorous and original of English composers. He died in the fullness of his powers and was buried in Westminster Abbey. The portrait here given was painted by John Closterman, and originally engraved for his *"Orpheus Britannicus."* It is impossible not to wonder whether the future of English music might not have been better if the powerful figure of the great master Händel had not dwarfed all native effort in Britain after Purcell.

Fig. 63.

HENRY PURCELL.

In the eighteenth century the most notable English composer was Dr. Thomas Arne (1710-1778), who enjoyed a well deserved reputation as an excellent dramatic composer, the author of many songs still reckoned among English classics, and the composer of the national hymn "Rule Britannia," which occurred as an incident in his masque of "Alfred," 1740. Dr. Arne has all the characteristics of a genuine national composer. His music was immediately popular, and held the stage for many years. His first piece was Fielding's "Opera of Operas," produced in 1733. The full list of his pieces reached upwards of forty-one operas and plays to which he furnished the music, two oratorios, "Abel" and "Judith," and a variety of occasional music. His style is somewhat like that of Händel, a remark which was true of all English composers for more than a hundred years after Händel's death; but it is forcible, melodious and direct. His music was not known outside of England.

CHAPTER XXX.
PIANO PLAYING AND VIRTUOSI; THE VIOLIN;
TARTINI AND SPOHR.
I.

IT was during the eighteenth century that the pianoforte definitely established itself in the estimation of musicians, artists and the common people, as the handiest and most useful of domestic and solo instruments. The progress was very slow at first, the musicians such as Bach, Händel, Scarlatti and Rameau, the four great virtuosi of the beginning of this century, generally preferred the older forms of the instrument, the clavier or the harpsichord, both on account of their more agreeable touch and the sweetness of their tones. Nevertheless the style of playing and of writing for these instruments underwent a gradual change at the hands of these very masters, of such a character that when the pianoforte became generally recognized as superior to its predecessors, about the middle of the century, the compositions of Bach and Scarlatti were found well adapted to the newer and more powerful instrument. The pianoforte itself underwent several modifications from the primitive forms of action devised by Cristofori in 1711, rendering it more responsive to the touch. All this, relating to the mechanical perfection of the instrument, although appropriate in part to the present moment of the narrative, is deferred until a later chapter, when the entire history of this instrument will be considered in detail. From that it will be seen, by comparing dates, that every important mechanical step in advance was followed by immediate modifications of the style of writing and playing, whereby the progress toward fullness and manifold suggestiveness of music for this instrument has been steady and great.

The first of the great virtuosi was Domenico Scarlatti (1683-1757), son of the great Alessandro Scarlatti, and a pupil of his father, and of other masters whose names are now uncertain. He was a moderately successful composer of operas and works for the Church, but his distinguishing merit was that of a virtuoso upon the harpsichord—the pianoforte of that time. He was the first of the writers upon the harpsichord who introduced difficulties for the pleasure of overcoming them, and who, in his own country, was without peer as performer until Händel came there and surpassed him, in 1708. Scarlatti was also a performer upon the organ, but upon this instrument he unhesitatingly confessed Händel to be his superior.

In 1715 Scarlatti succeeded Baj as chapel master at St. Peter's in Rome, where he composed much church music. His operas were successful in their own day, but were soon forgotten. His pianoforte compositions still remain as a necessary part of the education of the modern virtuoso. They are free in form, brilliant in execution, and melodious after the Italian manner. Many of them are still excessively difficult to play, in spite of the progress in technique which has been made since.

There were many other composers in the early part of this century who exercised a local and temporary influence in the direction of popularizing the pianoforte and its music, through the attractiveness of their own playing, as well as by the compositions they produced. Among these must not be forgotten Mattheson, the Hamburgh composer of operas (p. 242), who published many works for piano, including suites, sonatas and other pieces in the free style. Johann Kuhnau (1667-1722), predecessor of Bach as cantor at Leipsic, published a variety of sonatas and other compositions in free style, about the beginning of the eighteenth century. Of still greater importance than the last named, was Rameau, the French theorist and operatic composer (p. 336). His compositions were attractive and very original, and in addition to the charm of his own playing, and that of his works, he placed later musicians under lasting obligations by his treatise upon the art of accompanying upon the clavecin and organ, in which his theories of chords were applied to valuable practical use.

The work of all these and of many others who might be mentioned, not forgetting several English writers, such as Dr. Blow, Dr. John Bull and the gifted artist Purcell (see p. 350), must be regarded as merely preparatory for the advance made during the last part of the eighteenth century. It was Haydn who began to demand of the pianoforte more of breadth, and a certain coloration of touch, which he must have needed in his elaborative passages in the middle of the sonata piece. This kind of free fantasia upon the leading motives of the work, was planned after the style of thematic discussion of leading motives by the orchestra, and the obvious cue of the player is to impart to the different sequences and changes of the motives as characteristic tone-colors as possible, for the sake of rendering them more interesting to the hearers, and possibly of affording them more expression. Haydn's work was followed by that of Mozart, who gave the world the *adagio* upon the piano. Then in the fullness of time came Beethoven, who after all must be regarded as the great improver of piano playing of this century, as well as that of the next following. Beethoven improved the piano style in the surest and most influential manner possible. In his own playing he was far in advance of the virtuosi of the eighteenth century, and in his foresight of farther possibilities in the direction of tone sustaining and coloration he went still farther. This is seen in all his concertos, especially in the fourth and fifth, in the piano trios, and the quartette; but still more in the later pianoforte sonatas. Here the piano is treated with a boldness, and at the same time a delicacy and poetic quality, which taxes the greatest players of the present time to accomplish. The most advanced virtuoso works of Chopin, Schumann and Liszt, the three great masters of the pianoforte in the nineteenth century, are but slightly beyond the demands of these later sonatas of the great Vienna master.

In the later part of the eighteenth century there were a number of pianoforte virtuosi whose merits claim our attention at this point. At the head, in point of time, was the great Italian master, Muzio Clementi (1752-1832). Born at about the same time as Mozart, he outlived Beethoven. His early studies were pursued at Rome with so much enthusiasm that at the age of fourteen he had produced several important compositions of a contrapuntal character. These being successfully performed, attracted the attention of an English amateur living in Rome, who offered to take charge of the boy, carry him to England and see that his career was opened under favorable auspices. Until 1770, therefore (the year of Beethoven's birth), Clementi pursued his studies near London. Then, in the full force of his remarkable virtuosity, he burst upon the town. He carried everything before him, and had a most unprecedented success. His command of the instrument surpassed everything previously seen. After three years as cembalist and conductor at the Italian opera in London, he set out upon a tour as virtuoso. In 1781 he appeared in Paris, and so on toward Munich, Strassburg, and at length Vienna, where he met Haydn, and where, at the instigation of the Emperor Joseph II, he had a sort of musical contest with the young Mozart. Clementi, after a short prelude, introduced his sonata in B flat, the opening motive of which was afterward employed by Mozart in the introduction to the overture to the "Magic Flute"; and followed it up with a toccata abounding in runs in diatonic thirds and other doublestops for the right hand, at that time esteemed very difficult. The victory was regarded as doubtful, Mozart compensating for his less brilliant execution by his beautiful singing touch, of which Clementi ever afterward spoke with admiration. Moreover, from this meeting he himself endeavored to put more music and less show into his own compositions. Clementi was soon back in England, where he remained until 1802, when he took his promising pupil, John Field, inventor of the nocturne, upon a tour of Europe, as far as St. Petersburg, where they were received with unbounded enthusiasm. In 1810 he returned to London and gave up concert playing in public. He wrote symphonies for the London Philharmonic Society, published very many sonatas for piano (about 100 in all), and in 1817 published his master work, a set of 100 studies for the piano, in all styles, the "*Gradus ad Parnassum*," upon which to a considerable extent the entire modern art of piano playing depends. Clementi's idea in the work was to provide for the entire training of the pupil by means of it; not alone upon the technical, but upon the artistic side as well, and the majority of the pieces have artistic purpose no less than technical. The wide range taken by piano literature since Clementi's day, however, reduces the teacher to the alternative of confining the pupil to the works of one writer, in case the entire work is used, or of employing only the purely technical part of the "*Gradus*," accomplishing the other side of the development by means of compositions of more poetic and older masters. The latter is the course now generally pursued by the great teachers, and this was the reason influencing the selection of studies from the "*Gradus*" made by the virtuoso, Tausig. Clementi's compositions exercised considerable influence upon Beethoven, who esteemed his sonatas better than those of Mozart. The opinion was undoubtedly based upon the freedom with which Clementi treated the piano, as distinguished from the gentle and somewhat tame manner of Mozart. The element of manly strength was that which attracted Beethoven, himself a virtuoso.

Fig. 64.

J.L. DUSSEK.

Another of the first virtuosi to gain distinction upon the pianoforte, in the latter part of this century and the first part of the nineteenth, was J.L.

Dussek (1761-1812). This highly gifted musician was born in Czaslau, in Bohemia, and his early musical studies were made upon the organ, upon which he early attained distinction, holding one prominent position after another, his last being at Berg-op-Zoom. He next went to Amsterdam, and presently after to the Hague, still later, in 1788, to London, where he lived twelve years. It was there that Haydn met him, and wrote to Dussek's father in high terms of his son's talents and good qualities. Afterward he was back again upon the continent, living for some years with Prince Louis Ferdinand, and having right good times with him, both musically and festively. He died in France. He made many concert tours in different periods of his life, and his playing was highly esteemed from one end of Europe to the other. A contemporary writer says of him: "As a virtuoso he is unanimously placed in the very first rank. In rapidity and sureness of execution, in a mastery of the greatest difficulties, it would be hard to find a pianist who surpasses him; in neatness and precision of execution, possibly *one* (John Cramer, of London); in soul, expression and delicacy, certainly *none*." The brilliant pianist and teacher Tomaschek said of him: "There was, in fact, something magical in the manner in which Dussek, with all his charming grace of manner, through his wonderful touch, extorted from the instrument delicious and at the same time emphatic tones. His fingers were like a company of ten singers, endowed with equal executive powers, and able to produce with the utmost perfection whatever their director could require. I never saw the Prague public so enchanted as they were on this occasion by Dussek's splendid playing. His fine declamatory style, especially in *cantabile* phrases, stands as the ideal for every artistic performance— something which no other pianist since has reached. He was the first of the virtuosi who placed the piano sideways upon the platform, although the later ones may not have had an interesting profile to exhibit."

The published works of this fine musician and creditable composer number nearly 100, and the sonata cuts a leading figure among them. He treated the piano with much more freedom and breadth than Mozart, though this is not so much to his credit as if he had not lived many years after Mozart died, his earliest compositions falling very near the last years of that great genius. He was distinctly a virtuoso, loving his instrument and its tonal powers. He was the first of all the players whose public performances called attention to the *quality* of tone, and its *singing* power. This also points not alone to the fact of his career falling in with the increased powers of the pianoforte, as a result of the inventions of Érard, Collard and Broadwood, but is to his personal credit, since it was genius in him enabling him to recognize these possibilities, at a time when most players were still in ignorance of them. As a composer he wrote many things of more than average excellence, and some of his lighter compositions still have vitality. It is altogether likely that Beethoven was influenced by Dussek's playing, in the direction of tone-color. Indeed, the third sonata of Beethoven can hardly be accounted for without recognizing Dussek as the composer upon some one of whose works its general style and form were modeled.

Another pianist of considerable importance, a disciple of Mozart, yet with originality of his own, was J.B. Cramer (1771-1858). This talented and deserving musician was the son of a musician living at Mannheim, who removed to London when the young Cramer was but one year old. There the boy grew up, receiving his education from several reputable masters, Clementi being among them. His taste was formed by the diligent study of the works of Emanuel Bach, Haydn and Mozart. In spirit Cramer was a disciple of the last named, but from living to a good old age, he naturally surpassed his ideal in the treatment of the pianoforte. In the latter part of the eighteenth century there were few musical compositions sold over the music counters in Vienna and the musical world generally, but those of Dussek, Cramer and Pleyel, while those of Beethoven were comparatively neglected. Cramer's compositions were slight in real merit, his fame resting upon his studies for the piano, of which about thirty out of the entire 100 are very good music. The second, and last, book of these were published in 1810. They do not form a necessary part of the training of a virtuoso, but they have decided merits, and are generally included to this day in the list of pianistic indispensables. Cramer's style of playing was quiet and elegant. Moscheles gives an idea of it in his diary, and regrets that he should allow the snuff, which he took incessantly, to get upon the keys. Cramer's studies preceded those of Clementi, and very likely may have inspired them through a desire of illustrating a bolder and more masterly style of pianism.

Among the many talented pupils of Clementi was Ludwig Berger (1777-1838), of Berlin, whose unmistakable gifts for the piano attracted the master's attention when he was in Berlin in 1802, and he took him along with him to St. Petersburg. After living some years in that city, and later in London, he returned to Berlin, where he was held in the highest esteem as teacher until his death. Among the distinguished who studied with him were Mendelssohn, Taubert, Henselt, Fanny Hensel, Herzsberg, and others. He was an indefatigable composer of decided originality. But few of his works were published. A set of his studies is highly esteemed by many.

In further illustration of the Mozart principles of piano playing, and with a reputation as composer, which in his lifetime was curiously beyond his merits, was J.M. Hummel (1778-1837). He was born at Presburg, and had the good luck to attract the favorable notice of Mozart. He was received into the house of the master, and was regarded as the best representative of Mozart's ideas. He made his early appearances as a child pianist under the care of his father, in most parts of Germany and Holland. In 1804 he succeeded Haydn as musical director to the Esterhazy establishment. He afterward held several other appointments of credit, and played much in all parts of Europe. He was a pleasant player, with a light, smooth touch, suited to the Viennese pianofortes of the time.

Fig. 65.

HUMMEL.

The latest of the virtuosi representing the classical traditions of the pianoforte, uninfluenced by the new methods which came in with Thalberg and Liszt, was Ignaz Moscheles (1794-1870). He was born at Prague, his father being a cloth merchant and Israelite.

Fig. 66.

MOSCHELES.

He had the usual childhood of promising musicians, playing everything he could lay his hands upon, including Beethoven's "*Sonata Pathetique*," and at the age of seven he was taken to Dionys Weber, whose verdict is worth remembering. He said: "Candidly speaking, the boy is on the wrong road, for he makes hash of great works which he does not understand, and to which he is entirely unequal. But he has talent, and I could make something of him if you were to hand him over to me for three years, and follow out my plan to the letter. The first year he must play nothing but Mozart, the second Clementi, the third Bach; but only that—not a note as yet of Beethoven, and if he persists in using the circulating musical libraries, I have done with him forever." Having completed his studies after this severe *régime*, Moscheles began his concert appearances, which were everywhere successful.

He continued his studies in Vienna with Salieri, and Beethoven thought so well of him that he engaged him to make the pianoforte arrangement of "*Fidelio*." This was in 1814.

In 1815 he produced his famous variations upon the Alexander march, Opus 32, from which his reputation as virtuoso dates. His active concert service began about 1820, and extended throughout Europe. In 1826 he settled in London, where he was held in the highest esteem, both as man and musician. He became a fast friend of Mendelssohn, who had been his pupil in Berlin, and in 1846 joined him at Leipsic, where he continued until his death. Moscheles was originally a solid and brilliant player. Later he became famous as one of the best living representatives of the true style and interpretation of the Beethoven sonatas. He never advanced beyond the Clementi principles of piano playing, the works of Chopin and Liszt remaining sealed books to his fingers, to the very last. As a teacher he was painstaking and patient, and he was honored by all who knew him. All his life he kept a diary, from which a very readable volume has been compiled, with many glimpses of other eminent musicians. It is called "Recent Music and Musicians."

II.

The art of violin playing also made great progress during this century, its most eminent representative being Giuseppe Tartini (1692-1770). He was born in Pirano, in Istria, and was intended for the church, but upon coming of age he fell in love with a lady somewhat above him in rank, and was secretly married to her. When this fact was discovered by her relatives he was obliged to fly, and having taken refuge in a monastery he remained there two years, during which he diligently devoted himself to music, being his own instructor upon the violin, but a pupil of the college organist in counterpoint and composition. Later, being united to his wife, he made still further studies on the violin, and by 1721 had returned to Padua, where he evermore resided, his reputation bringing him a sufficient number of pupils to assist his rather meager salary as solo violinist of the cathedral. He was a virtuoso violinist greater than any one before him. Besides employing the higher positions more freely than had previously been the case, he appears to have made great improvements in the art of bowing, and his playing was characterized by great purity and depth of sentiment, and at times with most astonishing passion. He was a composer of extraordinary merit, several of his pieces for the violin still forming part of the concert repertory of artists. His famous "*Trillo del Diavolo*," is well known. He dreamed that he had sold his soul to the devil, and on the whole was well pleased with the behavior of that gentlemanly personage. But it occurred to him to ask his strange associate to play something for him on the violin. Cheerfully Satan took the instrument, and immediately improvised a sonata of astonishing force and wild passion, concluding it with a great passage of trills, of superhuman power and beauty; Tartini awoke in an ecstasy of admiration. Whereupon he sought after every manner to reduce to paper the wonderful composition of his dream. Fine as was the work thus produced, Tartini always maintained that it fell far short of the glorious virtuoso piece which he had heard.

Tartini was in some sort a forerunner of the modern romantic school. He was accustomed to take a poem as the basis of an instrumental piece. He wrote the words along the score and conducted the music wherever the spirit of the words took it. He was also in the habit of affixing to his published works mottoes, indicative of their poetic intention. With this general characterization his music well agrees, for in dreamy moods it has a mystical beauty till then unknown in music. He is also entitled to lasting memory on account of his having first discovered the phenomenon of "combination tones," the under resultant which is produced when two tones are sounded together upon the violin, especially in the higher parts of the compass. These tones are the roots of the consonances sounding, and Tartini directed the attention of his pupils to them as a guide to correct intonation in double stops, since they do not occur unless the intonation is pure. He made this important discovery about 1714, and in 1754 he published a treatise on harmony embodying the combination tones as a basis of a system of harmony. This having been violently attacked, his second work of this kind, "On the Principles of Musical Harmony Contained in the Diatonic Genus," was published in 1767. Tartini, therefore, must be reckoned among the great masters who have contributed to a true doctrine of the tonal system. Copies of his theoretical writings are in the Newberry Library at Chicago.

In the latter part of the eighteenth century and the first of the next following the art of violin playing was best illustrated by the German artist, Louis Spohr (1784-1859), who was almost or quite as great as a composer, as in his early career of a virtuoso. In his own specialty he was one of the most eminent masters who has ever appeared. His technique was founded upon that of his predecessors of the school of Viotti and Rode, but his own individuality was so decided that he soon found out a style original with himself. Its distinguishing quality was the singing tone. He never reconciled himself to the light bow introduced by Paganini, and all his work is distinguished by sweetness, singing quality and a flowing melodiousness. He was fond of chromatic harmonies and double stops, which imparted great sonority to his playing. He was born at Brunswick, and early commenced to study music. At the age of fifteen he played in the orchestra of the duke of Brunswick, at a yearly salary of about $100. Later he studied and traveled with Eck, a great player of the day, and upon his return to Brunswick he became leader of the orchestra. His virtuoso career commenced about 1803. Two years later he became musical director at Gotha, where he married a charming harp player, Dorette Scheidler, who invariably afterward appeared with him in all their concerts. They traveled in their own carriage, having suitable boxes for the harp and the violin. In 1813 he was musical director at the theater, "*An der Wein*," at Vienna, where among his violinists was Moritz Hauptmann, afterward so celebrated as theorist.

Soon after his arrival in Vienna, Spohr received a singular proposition from one Herr von Tost, to the effect "that for a proportionate pecuniary consideration I would assign over to him all I might compose, or had already written, in Vienna, for the term of three years, to be his sole property during that time; to give him the original scores, and to keep myself even no copy of them. After the lapse of three years he would return the manuscript to me, and I should then be at liberty either to publish or sell them. After I had pondered a moment over this strange and enigmatical proposition, I asked him whether the compositions were not to be played during those three years? Whereupon Herr von Tost replied: 'Oh, yes! As often as possible, but each time upon my lending them for that purpose, and only in my presence.'" He desired such pieces as could be produced in private circles, and would therefore prefer quartettes and quintettes for stringed instruments, and sextettes, octettes and nonettes for stringed and wind instruments. Spohr was to consider the proposition and fix upon the sum to be paid for the different kinds of compositions. Finding on inquiry that Herr von Tost was a wealthy man, very fond of music, Spohr fixed the price at thirty ducats for a quartette, thirty-five for a quintette, and so on, progressively higher for the different kinds of composition. On being questioned as to his object, Von Tost replied: "I have two objects in view: First, I desire to be invited to the musical parties where you will execute your compositions, and for that I must have them in my keeping. Secondly, possessing such treasures of art, I hope upon my business journeys to make extensive acquaintance among the lovers of music, which may then serve me also in my manufacturing interests." This singular bargain was duly consummated and faithfully carried out, and the wealthy patron proved of great service to the Spohrs in procuring their housekeeping outfit from various tradesmen with whom he had dealings, and he would not suffer Spohr to pay for anything, saying only, "Give yourself no uneasiness; you will soon square everything with your compositions."

The most important of Spohr's works is his great school for the violin, published in 1831. He left also a vast amount of chamber music, fifteen concertos for violin and orchestra, nine symphonies, four oratorios, of which "The Last Judgment" is perhaps the best, ten operas, many concert overtures, etc.—in all more than 200 works, many of them of large dimensions. His best operas are "*Jessonda*" (1823), "Faust" (1818), "The Alchemist" (1832) and "The Crusaders" (1845). His orchestral works are richly instrumented, and the coloring is sweet and mellow, yet at times extremely sonorous.

During his residence in Vienna, Spohr met Beethoven many times. He was one of the first to introduce the earlier quartettes, in his concerts throughout Germany, and valued them properly. But in regard to the Beethoven symphonies he placed himself on record in a highly entertaining manner. He says of the melody of the famous "Hymn to Joy," in Beethoven's ninth symphony, that it is so "monstrous and tasteless, and its grasp of Schiller's ode so trivial, that I cannot even now understand how a genius like Beethoven could have written it."

Book Fifth.

THE

Period of the Romantic.

WEBER, PAGANINI, SCHUBERT, BERLIOZ, MEYERBEER, MENDELSSOHN, SCHUMANN, CHOPIN, LISZT, WAGNER; THE VIRTUOSI; MUSIC OF THE FUTURE.

CHAPTER XXXI.
THE NINETEENTH CENTURY, THE ROMANTIC;
MUSIC OF THE FUTURE.

IN ordinary speech a distinction is made between the musical productions of the eighteenth century and those of the next following; the former being called *Classic*, the latter *Romantic*. The terms are used rather indefinitely. According to Hegel, whose teaching coincided with the last years of Beethoven's life, the classic in art embraces those productions in which the *general* is aimed at, rather than the *particular*; the *reposeful* and *completely satisfactory*, rather than the *forced*, or the *sensational*; and the *beautiful* rather than the *exciting*. The philosopher Hegel, who was one of the first to employ this distinction in art criticism, took his departure from the famous group of Laocoön and his sons in the embrace of the destroying serpents. This group, so full of agony and irrepressible horror, belongs, he said, to a totally different concept of art from that of the gods and goddesses of Greece, in the beauty and freshness of their eternal youth. These qualities are those of the general and the eternal; the Laocoön, in its nature painful, was not nor could be permanently satisfactory in and of itself, but only through allowance being made by reason of interest in the story told by it. According to more recent philosophers, the romantic movement in literature and art (for they are parts of the same general movement of the latter part of the eighteenth century) has its essential characteristic in the doctrine that what is to be sought in art is not the pleasing and the satisfactory, so much as the true. *Everything*, they say, belonging to life and experience, is fit subject of art; to the end that thereby the soul may learn to understand itself, and come to complete self-consciousness. The entire movement of the romantic writers had for its moving principle the maxim, *Nihil humanum alienum a me puto* ("I will consider nothing human to be foreign to me"). Yet other writers make the romantic element to consist of the striking, the strongly contrasted, the exciting, and so at length the sensational. Whichever construction we may put upon this much used and seldom determined term, its general meaning is that of a distinction from the more moderate writings and compositions of the eighteenth century. *Individualism*, as opposed to the general, is the key to the romantic, and in music this principle has acquired great dominance throughout the century in which we are still living. Moreover, if the principle of individualism had not been discovered in its application to the other arts, it must necessarily have found its way into music, for music is the most subjective of all the arts; having indeed its general principles of form and proportion, but coming to the composer (if he be a genius) as the immediate expression of his own feelings and moods, or as the interplay of his environment and the inner faculties of musical phantasy.

In this sense there is a difference between the music of Bach and Mozart, on the one hand, and that of Beethoven and Schubert, on the other. Beethoven was essentially a romantic composer, especially after he had passed middle life, and the period of the "Moonlight" sonata. From that time on, his works are more and more free in form, and their moods are more strongly marked and individual. This is true of Beethoven, in spite of his having been born, as we might say, under the star of the classic. He writes freely and fantastically, in spite of his early training. The mood in the man dominated everything, and it is always this which finds its expression in the music.

The romantic, therefore, represents an enlargement of the domain of music, by the acquisition of provinces outside its boundaries, and belonging originally to the domains of poetry and painting. And so by romantic is meant the general idea of representing in music something outside, of telling a story or painting a picture by means of music. The principle was already old, being involved in the very conception of opera, which in the nature of the case is an attempt to make music do duty as describer of the inner feelings and experiences of the *dramatis personæ*. Nevertheless, while leading continually to innovations in musical discourse for almost two centuries, it was prevented from having more than momentary entrances into instrumental music until the beginning of the nineteenth century, when the general movement of mind known as the romantic was at its height. In France the writers of this group carried on war against classic tradition— the idea that every literary work should be modeled after one of those of the ancient writers; subjects of tragedy should be taken from Greek mythology or history; and the characters should think like the classics, and speak in the formal and stilted phraseology of the vernacular translations out of the ancient works. These writers, also, were those who upheld the rights of man, and produced declarations of independence. In short, it was the principle of individualism, as opposed to the merely general and conventional, for we may remember that the conventional had a large place in ancient art. Plato says (see p. 38) that the Egyptians had patterns of the good in all forms of art, framed and displayed in their temples. And new productions were to be judged by comparing them with these, and when they contained different principles, they were upon that account to be condemned and prohibited.

In farther evidence of the correspondence between the musical activity in this direction, and the general movement of mind at this period, including the shaking up of the dry bones in every part of the social order, (the French revolution being the most extreme and drastic illustration), we may observe that the composer through whom this element entered into the art of music in its first free development was Franz Schubert, who was born during the years when this disturbance was at its height, namely, in 1797. Moreover, the manner in which his inspiration to musical creation was received corresponded exactly to the definition of the romantic given above; for it was always through reading a poem or a story that these strange and beautiful musical combinations occurred to him, many instances of which are given in the sketch later. It is curious, furthermore, that the general method of Schubert's musical thought is classical in its repose, save where directly associated with a text of a picture-building character, or of decided emotion. Thus, while it is not possible to separate one part of the works of this composer from another, and to say of the one that it belongs to an older dispensation, while the other part represents a different principle of art (both parts alike having the same general treatment of melody, and the same refined and poetic atmosphere), it is, nevertheless, true that if we had only the sonatas, chamber pieces, and the symphonies of Schubert, no one would think of classing his works differently from those of Mozart, as to their operative principles. But when we have the songs, the five or six hundred of them, the operas and other vocal works, in which music is so lovely in and of itself, yet at the same time so descriptive, so loyal to the changing moods of the text, we necessarily interpret the instrumental music in the same light, especially when we know that there are no distinct periods in the short life of this composer concerning which different principles can be predicated.

Almost immediately after Schubert there come composers in whom the new tendency is more marked. Mendelssohn entered the domain of the romantic in 1826, with his overture to the "Midsummer Night's Dream," and directly after him came Schumann, with a luxuriant succession of deeply moved, imaginative, *quasi*-descriptive, or at any rate *representative*, pianoforte pieces. Schumann, indeed, did not need to read a poem in order to find musical ideas flowing in unaccustomed channels. The ideas took these forms and channels of their own accord, as we see in his very first pieces, his "*Papillons*," "*Intermezzi*," "*Davidsbundlertänze*" and the like. So, too, with Chopin. There is very little of the descriptive and the picture-making element in his works. Nevertheless, they chimed in so well with the unrest, the somewhat Byronic sentiment, the vague yearning of the period, that they found a public without loss of time, and established themselves in the popular taste without having had to find a propaganda movement for explaining them as the foretokens of a "music of the future."

This representative work in music has been very much helped by the astonishing development of virtuosity upon the violin, the pianoforte and other instruments, which distinguishes this century. Beginning with Paganini, whose astonishing violin playing was first heard during the last years of the eighteenth century, we have Thalberg, Chopin, Liszt, Rubinstein, Joachim, Tausig, Leonard, and a multitude of others, through whose efforts the general appreciation of instrumental music has been wonderfully stimulated, and the appetite for overcoming difficulties and realizing great effects so much increased as to have permanently elevated the standard of complication in musical discourse, and the popular average of performance.

Nor has virtuosity been confined to single instruments. There have been two great virtuosi in orchestration, during this century, who have exercised as great an influence in this complicated and elaborate department, as the others mentioned have upon their own solo instruments. The first of these was Hector Berlioz, the great French master, whose earlier compositions were produced in 1835, when the instruments of the orchestra were combined in vast masses, and with descriptive intention, far beyond anything by previous writers. In his later works, such as the "Damnation of Faust," and the mighty Requiem, Berlioz far surpassed these efforts, every one of his effects afterward proving to have been well calculated. Directly after his early works came the first of that much discussed genius, Richard Wagner, who besides being one of the most profound and acute intelligences ever distinguished in music, and a great master of the province of opera (in which he accomplished stupendous creations), was also an orchestral virtuoso, coloring when he chose, with true instinct, for the mere sake of color; and massing and contrasting instruments in endless variety and beauty.

The activity in musical production during the nineteenth century has been so extraordinary in amount and in the number of composers concerned in it, and so ample in the range of musical effects brought to realization, as fully to illustrate the truth of the principle enunciated at the outset of this narrative, namely: That the course of musical progress has been toward greater complication of tonal effects in every direction; implying upon the part of composers the possession of more inclusive principles of tonal unity; and upon the part of the hearers, to whom these vast works have been addressed, the possession of corresponding powers of tonal perception, and the persistence of impressions for a sufficient length of time in each instance for the underlying unity to be realized.

As an incident in the rapidity of the progress on the part of composers, we have had what is called "the music of the future"; namely, productions of one generation intelligible to the finer intelligences of that generation, yet "music of the future" to all the others; but in the generation following, these compositions have gone into the common stock, through the progress of the faculties of hearing and of deeper perceptions of tonal relations. Meanwhile there has been created another stratum of music of the future, which may be expected to occupy the attention of the generation next ensuing, to whom in turn it will become the music of the present.

In the nature of the case, there is not, nor can there be, a stopping place, unless we conceive the possibility of a return to the conservatism of Plato and the ancient Egyptians, and the passage of statute laws permitting the employment of chords and rhythms up to a certain specified degree of complexity, beyond which their use would constitute a grave statutory offense. It is possible that the ideal of art might again be "reformed" in the direction of restriction from the uncomely, the forced and the sensational, and in favor of the beautiful, the becoming and the divine. Nevertheless, it is the inevitable consequence of a prescription of this kind to run into mere prettiness and tuneful emptiness. Protection is a failure in art. The spirit must have freedom, or it will never take its grandest flights. And it is altogether possible that the needed corrective will presently be discovered of itself, through the progress of spirit into a clearer vision, a higher aspiration and a nobler sense of beauty. This we may hope will be one of the distinctions of the coming ages, which poets have foretold and seers have imagined, when truth and love will prevail and find their illustration in a civilization conformed of its own accord to the unrestricted outflowing of these deep, eternal, divine principles.

CHAPTER XXXII.
SCHUBERT AND THE ROMANTIC.

THE first two great figures of the nineteenth century were those of Carl Maria von Weber, whose work will be considered later, and the great song writer, Franz Peter Schubert (1797-1828). This remarkable man was born of poor parents in Vienna, or near it, his father being a schoolmaster, earning the proverbially meager stipend of the profession in Germany at that time, amounting to no more than $100 or $200 a year. The family was musical, and the Sundays were devoted to quartette playing and other forms of music. The boy Franz early showed a fine ear. He was soon put to the study of the violin and the piano—while still a mere child being furnished with a small violin, upon which he went through the motions of his father's part. He had a fine voice, and this attracted the attention of the director of the choir in the great Cathedral of St. Stephen's, as it had in Haydn's case, and he was presently enrolled as chorister and a member of what was called the "Convict," a school connected with the church, where the boys had schooling as well as musical instruction. Early he began to write, among his first works being certain pieces for the piano and violin, composed when he was a little more than eleven. In the "Convict" school there was an orchestra where they practiced symphonies and overtures of Haydn, Mozart, Kotzeluch, Cherubini, Méhul, Krommer, and occasionally Beethoven. Here his playing immediately put him on a level with the older boys. One of them turned around one day to see who it was playing so cleverly, and found it "a little boy in spectacles," named Franz Schubert. The two boys became intimate, and one day the little fellow, blushing deeply, admitted to the older one that he had composed much, and would do so still more if he could get the music paper. Spaun saw the state of affairs, and took care thereafter that the music paper should be forthcoming. In time Franz became first violin, and when the conductor was absent, took his place. The orchestral music delighted him greatly, and of the Mozart adagio, in the G minor symphony, he said that "you could hear the angels singing." Among other works which particularly delighted him were the overtures to the "Magic Flute" and "Figaro." The particular object of his reverence was Beethoven, who was then at the height of his fame, but he never met the great master more than once or twice. Once when a few boyish songs had been sung to words by Klopstock, Schubert asked his friend whether *he* could ever do anything after Beethoven. His friend answered, perhaps he could do a great deal. To which the boy responded: "Perhaps; I sometimes have dreams of that sort; but who can do anything after Beethoven?" The boy made but small reputation for scholarship in the school, after the thirst for composition had taken possession of him, which it did when he had been there but one year. One of his earliest compositions was a fantasia for four hands, having about thirteen movements of different character, occupying about thirty-two pages of fine writing. His brother remarks that not one ends in the key in which it began. He seems to have had a passion for uncanny subjects, for the next work of his is a "Lament of Hagar," of thirteen movements in different keys, unconnected. After this again, a "Corpse Fantasia" to words of Schiller. This has seventeen movements, and is positively erratic in its changes of key. It is full of reminiscences of Haydn's "Creation" and other works. The musical stimulation of this boy was meager indeed. Not until he was thirteen years of age did he hear an opera; and not until he was fifteen a really first-class work, Spontini's "Vestal," in 1812. Three years later he probably heard Gluck's "*Iphigenie en Tauride*," a work which in his estimation eclipsed them all. During the same year there were the sixth and seventh symphonies, the choral fantasia and portions of the mass in C, and the overture to "Coriolanus," of Beethoven. He was a great admirer of Mozart, and in his diary, under date of June 13, 1816, he speaks of a quintette: "Gently, as if out of a distance, did the magic tones of Mozart's music strike my ears. With what inconceivable alternate force and tenderness did Schlesinger's magic playing impress it deep into my heart! Such lovely impressions remain on my soul, there to work for good, past all power of time and circumstance. In the darkness of this life they reveal a bright, beautiful prospect, inspiring confidence and hope. Oh Mozart, Mozart, what countless consolatory images of a bright, better world hast thou stamped on our souls!"

Presently Schubert entered his father's school, in order to avoid the rigorous conscription, and remained a teacher of the elementary branches for three years. His first important composition was a mass, which was produced honorably October 16, 1814, and many good judges pronounced it equal to any similar work of the kind, excepting possibly Beethoven's mass in C. By 1815 the rage of composition had fully taken possession of the soul of Schubert, and thenceforth poured out from this receptacle of inspiration a steady succession of works of all dimensions and characters, very few of which were performed in his lifetime. Among these works in the year 1815, there are 137 songs, of which only sixty-seven are printed as yet. And in August alone twenty-nine, of which eight are dated the 15th, and seven the 19th. Among these 137 songs some are of such enormous length that this feature alone would have prevented their publication. Of those published, "*Die Burgschaft*" fills twenty-two pages of the Litolff edition. It was the length of these compositions which caused Beethoven's exclamation upon his death bed: "Such long poems, many of them containing ten others." And this mass of music was produced in the interim of school drudgery. Among these songs of his boyhood years are "*Gretchen am Spinnrade,*" "*Der Erl König,*" "Hedge Roses," "Restless Love," the "*Schaefer's Klaglied,*" the "Ossian" songs, and many others, all falling within the production of this year. It is said that when the "Erl King" was tried in the evening, the listeners at the convict thought it of questionable success. The music of the boy at the words "My father, my father" seemed to be inexcusable, for overwhelmed with fright, he sings a half a tone sharp of the accompaniment.

At length, after about three years, Schubert's services as a schoolmaster becoming less and less valuable, an opening was made for him by Schober, who proposed that Schubert should live with him. He was now free to devote himself to composition, and so thoroughly did he do this that in the year following, 1816, he experienced the novelty of having composed for money, a cantata of his having not only been performed upon the occasion of Salieri's fiftieth anniversary of life in Vienna, but money was sent him for it, 100 florins, Vienna money, about $20 American. He was already composing operas, and in 1816 there was one, "*Die Burgschaft,*" in three acts. In the same year there were two symphonies, the fourth in C minor, called "The Tragic," and the fifth for small orchestra. The songs of this year, however, were of more value. Among them were the "Wanderer's Night Song," the "Fisher," the "Wanderer" and many others now known wherever melody and dramatic quality are appreciated.

The rapidity with which he composed songs was incredible. October, 1815, he finds the poems of Rosegarten, and between the 15th and 19th sets seven of them. "Everything that he touched," says Schumann, "turned into music." At a later date, calling upon one of his friends, he found certain poems by Wilhelm Müller, and carried them off with him. A few days later, his friend desiring the book, called on Schubert for it, and found that he had already set a number of them to music. They were the songs of the "*Schöne Müllerin.*" A year or so after, returning from a day in the country, they stopped at a tavern, where he found a friend with a volume of Shakespeare open before him. Schubert took up the volume, turned a few pages, became interested in one of the pieces, took up some waste paper, and scribbling the lines proceeded to write a melody. This was the so-called "Shakespeare Serenade," "Hark, Hark, the Lark." The "Serenade," in D minor, is said to have been conceived in a similarly impromptu manner. In 1816 the great tenor, Vogl, made Schubert's acquaintance, having been brought by one of Schubert's admirers. At first the songs did not make much impression upon him; later they grew upon him, and he introduced them among the best circles of the Vienna aristocracy. Vogl appreciated the value of these songs. "Nothing," said he, "so shows the want of a good school of singing as Schubert's songs. Otherwise, what an enormous and universal effect must have been produced throughout the world, wherever the German language is understood, by these truly divine inspirations, these utterances of musical clairvoyance. How many would have comprehended for the first time the meaning of such terms as speech and poetry in music; words in harmony, ideas clothed in music, and would have learned that the finest poems of our greatest poets may be enhanced and even transcended when translated into musical language. Numberless examples might be named, but I will only mention the 'Erl King,' 'Gretchen,' '*Schwager Kronos*,' 'The Mignon's and Harper's Songs,' 'Schiller's Pilgrim,' the '*Burgschaft*' and the '*Sehnsucht*.'"

We are told that within the next two or three years Schubert made a number of friends, and the circle of his admirers was considerably extended. The same remarkable productivity continued. In the summer of 1818 he went to the country seat of Count Esterhazy, where he remained several months. This was in Hungary, and the Hungarian pieces are supposed to date from his residence there. It was not until 1819 that the first song of Schubert was sung in public. This was the "Shepherd's Lament," of which the Leipsic correspondent of the *Allgemeine Musikalische Zeitung* says: "The touching and feeling composition of this talented young man was sung by Herr Jaeger in a similar spirit." The following year, among other compositions, was the oratorio of "Lazarus," which was composed in three parts—first, the sickness and death, then the burial and elegy, and, finally, the resurrection. The last part, unfortunately, if ever written, has been lost. He made attempts at operatic composition, producing a vast amount of beautiful music, but always to indifferent librettos, so that none of his music was publicly performed. It was not until 1827 and 1828 that his continual practice in orchestral writing resulted in the production of real master works. In this year the unfinished symphony in B minor was produced, in which the two movements that we have are among the most beautiful and poetic that the treasury of orchestral music possesses. The other was the great symphony in C, which was first performed in Leipsic ten years after Schubert's death, through the intervention of Schumann. During all these years since leaving his father's school, Schubert had been living in a very modest manner, with an income which must have been very small and irregular. He was very industrious, usually rising soon after five in the morning, and, after a light breakfast of coffee and rolls, writing steadily about seven hours. The amount of work which he got through in this way was something incredible. Whole acts of operas were composed and beautifully written out in score within a few days. Upon the same morning from three to six songs might be written, if the poems chanced to attract him. He scarcely ever altered or erased, and rarely curtailed. All his music has the character of improvisation. The melody, harmony, the thematic treatment, and the accompaniment with the instrumental coloring, all seem to have occurred to him at the same time. It is only a question of writing it down. Very little of his music was performed during his lifetime—of the songs, first and last, many of them in private circles, and the last two or three years of his life, perhaps twenty or twenty-five in public. A few of his smaller orchestral numbers were played by amateur players, where he may have heard them himself, but his larger works he never heard. All that schooling of ear which Beethoven had, as an orchestral director in youth, Schubert lacked. His studies in counterpoint had never been pursued beyond the rudiments, and the last engagement he made before his death was for lessons with Sechter, the contrapuntal authority in Vienna at that time.

In spontaneity of genius Schubert resembles Mozart more than any other master who ever lived. His early education and training were different from those of Mozart, and musical ideas take different form with him. While Mozart was distinctly a melodist, counterpoint and fugue were at his fingers' ends, and his thematic treatment had all the freedom which comes from a thorough training in the use of musical material. Schubert had not this kind of training. He never wrote a good fugue, and his counterpoint was indifferent; but on the other hand he had several qualities which Mozart had not, and in particular a very curious and interesting mental phenomenon, which we might call psychical resonance or clairvoyance. Whatever poem or story he read immediately called up musical images in his mind. Under the excitement of the sentiment of a poem, or of dramatic incidents narrated, strange harmonies spontaneously suggested themselves, and melodies exquisitely appropriate to the sentiment he desired to convey. He was a musical painter, whose colors were not imitated from something without himself, but were inspired from within.

Schubert was a great admirer of Beethoven, and upon one occasion called upon him with a set of works which he had dedicated to the great master. Beethoven had been prepared for the visit by some admirer of Schubert's, and received him very kindly, but when he began to compliment the works the bashful Schubert rushed out of doors. Upon another occasion during his last illness Beethoven desired something to read, and a selection of about sixty of Schubert's songs, partly in print and partly in manuscript, were put in his hands. His astonishment was extreme, especially when he heard that there existed about 500 of the same kind. He pored over them for days, and asked to see Schubert's operas and piano pieces, but the illness returned, and it was too late. He said "Truly Schubert has the divine fire in him." Schubert was one of the torch bearers at Beethoven's funeral. In March 1828, he gave an evening concert of his own works in the hall of the Musikverein. The hall was crowded, the concert very successful, and the receipts more than $150, which was a very large sum for Schubert in those days. For several months before his death Schubert's health was delicate. Poverty and hard work, a certain want of encouragement and ease had done their office for him. He died November 19, 1828. He left no will. His personal property was sold at auction, the whole amounting to about $12. Among the assets was a lot of old music valued at ten florins. It is uncertain whether this included the unpublished manuscript or not. In personal appearance Schubert was somewhat insignificant. He was about five feet one inch high, his figure stout and clumsy, with a round back and shoulders, perhaps due to incessant writing, fleshy arms, thick, short fingers. His cheeks were full, his eyebrows bushy and his nose insignificant. His hair was black, and remarkably thick and vigorous, and his eyes were so bright that even through the spectacles, which he constantly wore, they at once attracted attention. His glasses were inseparable from his face. In the convict he was the "little boy in spectacles." He habitually slept in them. He was very simple in his tastes, timid and never really at ease but in the society of his intimates and people of his own station. His attitude toward the aristocracy was entirely different from the domineering, self-assertive pose of Beethoven, but he was very amiable, and dearly beloved.

Fig. 67.

FRANZ SCHUBERT.

His place in the history of music, aside from the general fact of his possessing genius of the first order, is that of the creator of the artistic song. While his pianoforte sonatas are extremely beautiful and very difficult, and anticipate many modern effects; his string quartettes, and other chamber music, worthy to be ranked with those of any other master; and his symphonies exquisitely beautiful in their ideas, orchestral coloring and the entire atmosphere which they carry—his habitual attitude was that of the writer of songs. Some of these are of remarkable length and range. One of them extends to sixty-six pages of manuscript. Another occupies forty-five pages of close print. A work of this kind is a cantata, and not merely a song. Many of the others are six or eight pages long, and in all the music freely and spontaneously follows the poem, with a delicate correspondence between the poetic idea and the melody, with its harmony and treatment, such as we look for in vain in any other writer, unless it be Schumann, who, however, did not possess Schubert's instinct of the vocally suitable. For with all the range which these songs cover, their vocal quality is as noticeable as that of Italian cantilenas.

CHAPTER XXXIII.
THE STORY OF THE PIANOFORTE.

THE popular instrument of the nineteenth century has been the pianoforte, the result of an evolution having its beginning more than six centuries back. It is impossible in the present state of knowledge to trace all the steps through which this remarkable instrument has reached its present form. In the Assyrian sculptures discovered by Layard, there are instruments apparently composed of metal rods or plates, touched by hammers, upon the same general principle as the toy instrument with glass plates, or the xylophone composed of wooden rods resting upon bands of straw. In these the use of the hammer for producing the tone is obvious. In the Middle Ages there was an instrument called the psaltery, apparently some sort of a four-sided harp strung with metal strings. The evidence upon this point is rather indistinct. Still later there is the Arab santir (p. 114). This was a trapeze-shaped instrument, composed of a solid frame, sounding board and metal wires struck with hammers. This instrument still exists in Germany under the name of *Hackbrett*, or the dulcimer. As now made, each string consists of three wires tuned in unison. It is played by means of leather hammers held in the hand. The difficulty of adapting this instrument to the keyboard consisted in the fact that if the hammers were connected with the keys, they would be under the strings instead of above them, and this difficulty for a long time proved insurmountable.

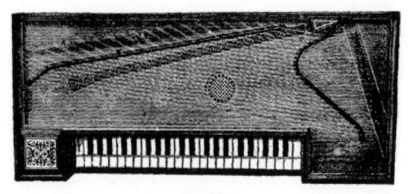

Fig. 68.

SPINET.

Two forms of instruments were at length developed, composed of a wire-strung psaltery, played from a chromatic keyboard like that of the organ. The first of these was the one called in England Spinet, or in Italy *Espinnetto*, and in Germany the *Clavier*. The essential characteristic of this instrument was the manner of producing tones. Upon the ends of the keys were brass pieces called "tangents," of a triangular shape, of such form that when the key was pressed, the tangent pushed the wire and so produced the tone. As it remained in contact with the wire as long as the key was held down, there was nothing like what we now call a singing tone. The instruments were very small, in shape like a square piano, but of three or four octaves compass; the wires were of brass, and quite small. In several representations which have come down to us from the seventeenth century, the number of strings shown is smaller than the number of keys, from which some writers have inferred that it might have been possible to obtain more than one tone from the same string, through a process of stopping it with one tangent and striking it with another. This, however, is highly improbable; the discrepancies referred to are undoubtedly due to carelessness of the engraver. The clavier, or spinet, was a better instrument than the lute, which at length it superseded, having more tones and a greater harmonic capacity. Besides which it was a step toward something much better still. In England they made them with pieces of cloth drawn through between the wires, to deaden the already small tone still further. These were sometimes called virginals, and seem to have been used as practice pianos, where the noise of the full tone might have been objectionable. The oldest form of the clavier known to the writer was that shown in Fig. 69, which was so small that it might be carried under the arm, and when used was placed upon the table. They were sometimes ornamented in a very elaborate manner.

Fig. 69.

KEYBOARD AND FRET WORK OF SPINET SHOWN IN FIG. 68.

Fig. 70.

RICHLY ORNAMENTED SPINET.

[Made for the Princess Anna, of Saxony, about 1550.]

Contemporaneously with the spinet, and of almost equal antiquity, was an instrument in the form of a grand piano, called in Italy the clavicembalo, and in England the harpsichord. In Germany it was called the *flugel* or wing, from its being shaped like the wings of a bird. These also, in the earlier times, were made very small, and were rested upon the table. The essential distinction between the cembalo and the spinet was in the manner of tone production. In the cembalo there was a wooden jack resting upon the end of the keys, and upon this jack a little plectrum made of raven's quill, which had to be frequently renewed. When the key was pressed, the jack rose and the plectrum snapped the wire. The tone was thin and delicate, but as the plectrum did not remain in contact with the string, the vibration continued longer than in the clavier. The cembalo was the favorite instrument in Italy during the seventeenth century, and in England it had a great currency under the name of harpsichord. Many attempts were made at increasing the resources of this instrument, one of the most curious being that of combining two harpsichords in one, having two actions, two sounding boards and sets of strings, and two keyboards related like those of the organ. This form seems to have been exclusively English. The form of the harpsichord is shown in Fig. 71.

Fig. 71.

MOZART'S CONCERT GRAND PIANO.

[Now in the Mozart Museum at Salzburg. Its compass is five octaves.]

Far back in the sixteenth century an attempt was made at a hammer mechanism to strike down upon the strings. For this purpose the strings were placed in a vertical position, the same as in our upright pianos of the present day. Mr. B.J. Lang, of Boston, has an upright spinet of this kind, which he bought in Nuremburg. It is a small and rude affair, having about four octaves compass and a very small scale.

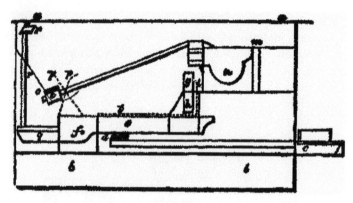

Fig. 72.

CRISTOFORI'S ACTION.

[According to his original diagram.]

A is the string; *b* the bottom; *c* the first lever, or key; there is a pad, *d*, upon the key to raise a second lever, *e*, which is pivoted upon *f*; *g* is the hopper—Cristofori's *linguetta mobile*—which, controlled by the springs *i* and *l*, effects the escape, or immediate drop, of the hammer from the strings after the blow has been struck, although the key is still kept down by the finger. The hopper is centered at *h*. *M* is a rack or comb on the beam, *s*, where, *h*, the butt, *n*, of the hammer, *o*, is centered. In a state of rest the hammer is supported by a cross or fork of silk thread, *p*. On the depression of the key, *c*, the tail, *q*, of the second lever, *e*, draws away the damper, *r*, from the strings, leaving them free to vibrate. (Hipkins.)

The pianoforte proper was not invented until 1711, when a Florentine mechanic, named Cristofori, invented what he called a Fortepiano, from its capacity of being played loud or soft. The essential feature of the pianoforte mechanism is in the use of the hammer to produce the tone, and the necessary provision for doing this successfully is to secure an instantaneous escapement of the hammer from contact with the wire, as soon as the blow has been delivered, while at the same time the key remains pressed in order to hold the damper away from the strings and allow the tone to go on. These features were all contained in Cristofori's invention. The above diagram, Fig. 72, illustrates the mechanism employed. It is from Cristofori's published account of his invention, dated 1711; but there is in Florence a pianoforte of his manufacture still existing, dated 1726, in which the action is more perfect, as shown in Fig. 73.

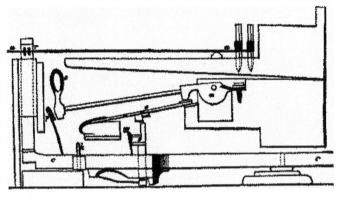

Fig. 73.

ACTION OF CRISTOFORI'S FORTEPIANO. DATE 1726.

[Besides several minor improvements over his first idea, the later instrument has a hammer check, *p*, and the hammer is more developed.]

The invention of Cristofori was taken up in Germany almost immediately, and a Dresden piano maker, Silbermann, became very celebrated. It was the pianofortes of his manufacture in the palace at Potsdam, which Frederick the Great made Bach try, one after another. The form of these instruments was the same as that of Mozart's piano, shown in Fig. 71. The square-formed piano began to be made about 1750, but the instrument involved no application of new principles, being merely a clavier with pianoforte mechanism. The new form, so much more compact and inexpensive, began to be popular, and was soon the standard form for private families, as that of the clavier had been before, and as the square piano, remained until as late as about 1870, when the inherent mechanical difficulties of the upright were for the first time satisfactorily overcome. Pepys, in his diary, tells of having purchased a virginal which pleased him very much. It cost five guineas—about $26.

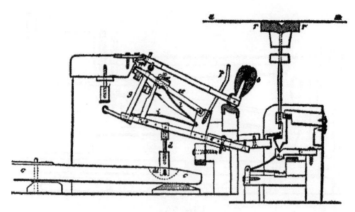

Fig. 74.

IMPROVED ACTION OF THE ÉRARD CONCERT GRAND.
(1821.)

C is the key; *d* is a pilot, centered at *dd* to give the blow, by means of a carrier, *e*, holding the hopper, *g*, which delivers the blow to the hammer, *o*, by the thrust of the hopper, which escapes by forward movement after contact with a projection from the hammer covered with leather, answering to the notch of the English action. This escapement is controlled at *x*; a double spring *il*, pushes up a hinged lever, *ee*, the rise of which is checked at *pp*, and causes the second or double escapement; a little stirrup at the shoulder of the hammer, known as the "repetition" pressing down *ee* at the point, and by this depression permitting *g* to go back to its place, and be ready for a second blow before the key has been materially raised. The check *p* in this action is not behind the hammer, but before it, fixed into the carrier, *e*, which also, as the key is put down, brings down the under damper. (Hipkins.)]

The instruments were still small, and strung with small wires; nevertheless, there was a tendency toward increased compass, which, by the beginning of the nineteenth century, led the Broadwoods, of London, to attempt a grand piano with six octaves' compass. But they found that the wrest plank (in which the tuning strings are placed), was so weakened by the extension that the treble would not stand in tune. In order to strengthen the instrument, he introduced the iron tension bar. This, like nearly all of the English improvements of the piano during the first quarter of the nineteenth century, was in the direction of greater solidity, and better resisting power to the pull of the strings.

Upon the artistic side, Sebastian Érard in 1808 patented his grand action, which, with very slight improvements, still remains the model of what a piano action should be. Fig. 74 shows this action and its parts.

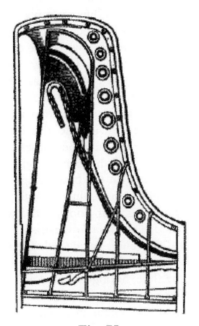

Fig. 75.

THE STEINWAY IRON FRAME.

[Showing the disposition of the sounding board, bridges, etc.]

Between 1808, when the Érard action was perfected, and 1832 or 1834, when Thalberg and Liszt began to revolutionize the art of piano playing, the instrument was the subject of a great number of improvements in every direction. The damper mechanism was perfected between 1821 and 1827; the stringing had been made heavier, the hammers proportionately stronger, and the power of tone had become greater. Thus the instrument had become ready for the great pianists—Liszt having made his first appearance in Vienna in 1823, and within seven years after having become generally recognized as a phenomenal appearance in art. Meanwhile, great improvements were continually carried on for the purpose of rendering the instrument impervious to the forcible attacks made upon its stability by these new virtuosi. In the early appearances of Liszt it was necessary to have several pianos in reserve upon the stage, so that when a hammer or string broke, which very often happened, another instrument could be moved forward for the next piece.

The most important improvement in the solidity of the piano came from the iron frame, which was introduced tentatively, somewhere about 1821, in the form of what is now called a "hitch-pin plate," or half iron frame. About 1825 an American, Alpheus Babcock, of Philadelphia, patented a full iron frame, but it was imperfect, and nothing came of it. Conrad Meyer, of Philadelphia, in 1833, patented an iron frame and manufactured pianos with it, which are still in existence. In 1837, Jonas Chickering, of Boston, perfected the iron frame by including in the single casting the pin bridge and damper socket rail. This improvement still remains at the foundation of the piano making of the world. Previous to this invention some of the American piano makers had constructed their cases upon a solid wooden bottom plank *five inches thick*. In 1855 the firm of Steinway & Sons exhibited their first overstrung scale, in which the bass strings were spread out and carried over a part of the treble strings, thus affording them more latitude for vibration, without interfering, and bringing the bridges nearer to the center of the sounding board. The idea of overstringing was not new at this time, Lichtenberg, of St. Petersburg, having exhibited a grand piano with overstringing at the London exposition in 1851, and Theodore Boehm, the celebrated improver of the flute, having invented an overstrung system for square pianos as early as 1835. In 1853, also, Jonas Chickering combined an iron frame with an overstrung system in square pianos, the instrument having been completed and exhibited after his death. The Steinway system of overstringing, however, was more extended, and solved the acoustical difficulties of cross-vibrations more successfully by spreading the long strings, and this, therefore, is the system now generally followed. The superiority of this principle was immediately acknowledged, and it has since been applied to grands and uprights, and few makers in the world but follow it in their work. Many minor improvements have been introduced in America by Steinway & Sons and others, whereby the artistic qualities and the durability of the best American pianos are now generally acknowledged throughout the world. The solidity of construction is such that with a compass of seven and one-third octaves the tension of the strings amounts to about 50,000 pounds avoirdupois. The hammers are larger and heavier, the action more responsive, and the singing quality and sustaining power has reached remarkable perfection. Perhaps the most curious and important of all American improvements in this direction is the so-called "duplex scale" of Steinway & Sons, patented in 1872, in which a fraction of the string is made to vibrate sympathetically, thereby strengthening the super-octave harmonic, and imparting to the tone a brightness and sweetness not so well secured in any other way at present known.

If space permitted it would be interesting to follow the course by which the difficulties of the upright piano have at length been surmounted, and the tone of this form of instrument rendered nearly equal to that of the grand. This was first accomplished by Steinway & Sons between 1862 and 1878, by a succession of improvements having for their object, first, the solidity of the instrument, then its prompt action, together with as much of the tone quality of the grand as possible. Many other American builders have taken part in this development, whereby the American pianoforte to-day is the strongest, the fullest-toned and the most expensively constructed of any in the world. Still later, quite a number of more or less successful attempts have been made to increase the stability of the tuning of the pianoforte by a different system of stringing, the tension of the strings being regulated by means of a tuning pin of "set-screw" pattern, working through a collar of steel, instead of being thrust into a wooden wrest-plank, where it holds fast by friction alone, as has been the universal way previous to these inventions.

CHAPTER XXXIV.
GERMAN OPERA; WEBER, MEYERBEER AND WAGNER.
I.

GERMAN opera reached an extraordinary development during the nineteenth century, the distinguishing characteristics being an extremely full and dramatically conceived treatment of the orchestra, and a mode of delivering the text partaking of the character of melody and recitative in about equal proportions, the entire object being to present the action to the inner consciousness of the beholder in the most impressive manner possible. In Italian opera, as we have seen, there was a large development of arias and vocal pieces, whose value lay in their beauty as melodies and as concerted effect, the action of the drama being meanwhile delayed sometimes for an entire half hour, while these pieces were going on. In Germany the effort to improve the delivery of the text and to bring it into closer union with the orchestra, and to develop the music from a dramatic standpoint exclusively, led to the vocal form known as *arioso*, or, to use Wagner's term, "endless melody," in which the successive periods follow each other to the end of the paragraph, or the end of the piece, without a full stop at any point until the end of the sense is reached. The great master of this form of composition was Richard Wagner, who may be regarded as the exponent of the extreme development yet reached by German opera. Wagner's endless melody proposed to itself the same ideal as that of Gluck, but it is only at rare moments that one will find in the music of the later master the symmetrical periods of the Gluck and Mozart epoch. Italian opera, as we have already seen, carried forward the dialogue mostly in *recitativo-secco*, that is to say, in a recitative following more or less successfully the modulations of speech, and accompanied only by detached chords marking the emphatic moments. This form of vocal delivery has the slightest possible musical interest, and the Germans almost immediately endeavored to improve it, as also did some of the Italian masters, the first result being *recitativo-stromentato*, or instrumented recitative, viz., recitative in which the text is accompanied by a flowing and more or less descriptive orchestral accompaniment. This differs essentially from the descriptive recitative in the works of the Mozart or Gluck period, or even in those of Haydn's later time. In the "Creation," for example, the descriptive recitative consists of vocal phrases with instrumental phrases interspersed, in dialogue form. The voice announces a certain fact and the orchestra immediately answers with a musical phrase corresponding to it, as, for example, in the recitative describing the creation of the world, where the phrase relating to the horse is immediately answered by an orchestral gallop; that of the tiger by certain slides and leaps in the melody remotely answering it; while the roar of the lion is immediately answered by a vigorous snort of the bass trombone. This is by no means of the same nature as the dramatic *arioso* of German opera during the nineteenth century. Händel came nearer to this type of musical formation, for example, in the "Messiah," at the recitative describing the appearance of the angels to the shepherds, where, after a phrase of unaccompanied recitative, the appearance of the angels is signified by an accompanied and measured strain, "And lo, the angel of the Lord came upon them."

This development of opera in the nineteenth century has been carried forward by the successive efforts of a considerable number of masters, among whom the three most important are Weber, Meyerbeer and Wagner, each of whom created a type of opera peculiar to himself, and left something as an addition to the permanent stock of musical dramatic ideas.

Fig. 76.

CARL MARIA VON WEBER.

II.

Carl Maria von Weber (1786-1826) was the son of a very musical family. He was born at Eutin, and fulfilled his father's desire, which had always been to have a child who should correspond to the youthful promise of Mozart. The father was an actor, and the director of a traveling troupe, largely composed of his own children by a former marriage. This mode of life continued for a number of years, while the future master was quite small. In 1794 Carl Maria's mother was engaged as a singer at the theater at Weimar, under Goethe's direction. Presently, however, the boy became a pupil of Heuschkel, an eminent oboeist, a solid pianist and organist, and a good composer. Under his careful direction Weber developed a technique which very soon passed far beyond anything that had previously been seen. Still later he became a pupil of Michael Haydn, a brother of Joseph. As early as 1800 the boy gave concerts in Leipsic and other towns in central Germany. At this time an opera book was given him, "*Das Wald Mädchen*," and the opera was composed and produced in November. Five years later it was highly appreciated at Vienna, and was performed also at Prague and St. Petersburg. Young Weber was of a most active mind, and interested himself in all questions of art. In 1803 he made the acquaintance of the famous Abbé Vogler, and became his pupil. Vogler commissioned him to prepare the piano score of a new opera of his. He still continued his practice as pianist, but when he lacked some months of being eighteen years of age he was made director of the music of the theater at Breslau. This was his first acquaintance with practical life as a musician. He showed great talent for direction and organization, and here he composed his first serious opera "*Rubezahl*" (1806). His next position was at Stuttgart, where he became musical director in 1807. After composing several short pieces, he led a somewhat irregular life for several years, concerting as a pianist, writing articles for the papers, at which he was very talented, beginning a musical novel, and at length, in 1810, producing his opera "*Abou Hassan.*" Then followed about three years of roving life as a concert player and occasionally as composer, until 1813, when he was appointed musical director at Prague. The opera here was in very bad condition, and the company incapable, but Weber engaged new singers in Vienna, and entirely reorganized the affair, and conducted himself so prudently that he gained the good will of nearly every one. As an example of his quickness it may be mentioned that upon discovering that certain musicians in the orchestra, who were not disposed to yield to his strict ideas of discipline, were conversing with each other in Bohemian, while the music was going on, he learned the language himself sufficiently to rebuke them in their own tongue. His next position was at Dresden in 1816, and here he remained nine years until his death. His position at first was somewhat ambiguous. There were two troupes of singers in the opera—an Italian and the German. The grand operas were given in Italian by the Italian company, and the light operas in German by the German company. It was Weber's task to change this, by producing new works of a distinctly higher character than the foreign works of the Italian company. The second year he was able to produce a few good operas of other schools in German versions, but it was not until 1821, when his "*Preciosa*" was produced at Berlin, and 1822, when "*Der Freischütz*" was produced in the same theater, that the reputation of the young master was established beyond question. It is impossible at the present time to describe the enthusiasm which the latter work created. It was a new departure in opera. It united two strains very dear to the German heart—the simple peasant life and the people's song are represented in the choruses, and in the arias of the less important people. Agatha, the heroine, has a prayer of exquisite beauty, which still is often heard as a church tune. And in contrast with these elements was the weird and uncanny music of Zamiel, the Satanic spirit of the wood, and the strange incantation scene in the Wolf's Glen at midnight, where the magic balls are cast. The story was thoroughly German, and the music not only German and well suited to the story, but distinctly original and charming of itself. In this work, perhaps first of any opera, Weber made use of what has since been known as "leading motives"—characteristic melodic phrases appropriate to Zamiel and Agatha. The instrumentation was very graphic, and as Weber had been brought up upon the stage, there were many novelties of a scenic kind. In fact, the work marked as distinct an epoch as Wagner's "Nibelungen Ring," and what is more to the point, it was one of the operative influences affecting the young Wagner, as he tells with considerable care in his autobiography. His next effort was a comic opera, the "Three Pintos," which was never finished. Then came "*Euryanthe*" performed at Vienna in 1823 with the most extraordinary success. This work is said to have been the model upon which Wagner created his "*Lohengrin.*" When it was produced in Berlin in 1825, the enthusiasm was yet greater and more remarkable than in Vienna. In 1825 he composed "*Oberon,*" the first of the operas in which the fairy principle has prominent exemplification. This was produced in London early in 1826. But by this time Weber's health had become completely broken, and he died there of overwork and fatigue. He was laid to his rest, to the music of Mozart's Requiem, in the chapel at Moorsfields in London.

Weber was the first of the romantic composers—the first, at least, to gain the ear of the public. These operas, with their beautifully descriptive music, in which voices and orchestra co-operate with the action and scene as one, were composed at the same time that the young Franz Schubert was improving his beautiful songs in Vienna. From one end of Germany to the other, and in all Europe, these operas made their way. "*Der Freischütz*" has lasted fifty years, and is still presented with success. More than that, as already noticed, Weber furnished the model, or point of departure, for a multitude of smaller composers, who developed the opera in various side directions; and last, but not least, for Richard Wagner himself.

Moreover, in the department of piano playing Weber was no less epoch-marking than in that of opera. In 1812 his sonata in C, Opus 24, was produced, a work which is distinctly in advance of those of Clementi or any other writer before that time. The finale of this work is the well known rondo "Perpetual Motion," which, indeed, contains no new principle of piano playing, but is an elegant example of melodiousness and real musicianly qualities displayed at the highest possible speed. His next sonata, Opus 39, in A flat (1816), is still more remarkable. The piano playing here is of an extremely brilliant and picturesque description. Here also, in the *Andante* we have the tricks which he afterward made so effective in the *Concertstück*, of the legato melody accompanied by chords *pizzicati*. Equally significant in this way is the sonata in D minor, Opus 49, published in the same year as the preceding. Here we have very strong contrast and an enormous fire and vigor. The romantic impulse, however, had been displayed yet earlier in his "*Momento Capriccioso*," Opus 12, in B flat (1808). This extremely rapid piece of changing chords *pianissimo* is like a reminiscence from fairy land, and the second subject contrasts with it to a degree which would have satisfied Schumann. It is a choral-like movement with intervening interludes in the bass, upon which Rubinstein must have modeled his "*Kamennoi Ostrow*," No. 22. But the most decided token of the romantic movement is seen in the "Invitation to the Dance," and the "*Polacca Brilliant*," both of which were published in 1819. Two years later came the concert piece, which for seventy years has remained a standard selection for brilliant pianists, and for fifteen years was Liszt's great concert solo. It marks a transition from Moscheles, Dussek and Clementi to Thalberg and Liszt. The "Invitation to the Dance," moreover, was the first *salon* piece idealized from a popular dance form.

III.

Yet another distinguished name might well have been enrolled among those of the great virtuosi of the first part of the nineteenth century. Jacob Liebmann Beer, better known as Giacomo Meyerbeer (1791-1864), was born at Berlin, the son of a rich Jewish banker. The name Meyer was prefixed to his own later, as a condition of inheriting certain property from a distant relative. As the boy showed talent for music at a very early age, he was put to the study of the pianoforte, and it was his ambition to distinguish himself as a virtuoso, which his talent undoubtedly permitted, if he had not been diverted from it by the success of his early attempts at opera. He was taught by a pupil of Clementi, and for a while by Clementi himself, as well as by other distinguished teachers, and if reports are to be believed concerning his playing, he must have become by the time he was twenty years old one of the very first virtuosi in Europe. His studies in theory were carried on under Abbé Vogler, at Darmstadt, where he was a schoolmate with C.M. von Weber and Gansbacher, and later with Salieri at Vienna. At Darmstadt he wrote an oratorio "God and Nature," which was performed by the *Singakademie*, of Berlin, in 1811; and an opera, "*Alimelek*" ("The Two Caliphs"), which also was successfully given at Munich in the Grand Opera House in the same year, 1811. Both works were anonymous. The opera made considerable reputation, and was played in several other cities. Upon Salieri's direction he went to Venice, where he arrived in 1815, to find Rossini's star in the ascendant, and all Venice, and Italy as well, wild over the bewitching melodies of "*Tancredi*." Meyerbeer, having that vein of cleverness and adaptability so characteristic of his race, immediately became a composer of Italian operas, and produced in Venice, "*Romilda e Constanza*" (Padua, 1815), "*Semiramide Riconosciuta*" (Turin, 1819), "*Emma di Resburgo*" (Venice, 1820), the latter also making a certain amount of reputation in Germany as "*Emma von Leicester*." Then followed "*Margherita d'Anjou*" (Milan, *La Scala*, 1820), "*L'Esule di Granata*" (Milan, 1822) and "*Il Crociato in Egitto*" (Venice, 1824). All of these were Italian operas, with melody in quite the Rossini vein, with the same attention as Rossini to the light, the pleasing and the vocal, but with a certain added element of German cleverness of harmony and thematic treatment.

Fig. 77.

GIACOMO MEYERBEER.

He now returned to Berlin, but his opera, "*Das Brandenburger Thor*," which he had written for Berlin, was not performed, owing to opposing intrigues. Nevertheless, for about six years Meyerbeer remained in his native city, married, and presently lost two infant children. In 1830 he took up his abode in Paris, where already his "*Il Crociato*" had been performed, in 1826, and in that city, as the leading composer for grand opera, he lived six years, and finally died there. For the Paris stage he produced a succession of large and sensational operas, following to some extent the footsteps of Spontini, in respect to the heroic, the spectacular and the theatrical. Up to the time of his going to Paris, Meyerbeer had figured as an Italian composer in grace of melody, German in his harmony, and now he became a French composer in refinements of rhythm. His first work in Paris was "*Robert le Diable*," 1831, and it made his reputation, and at the same time made an epoch in operatic construction. It was followed by "*Les Huguenots*," 1838, which when played in Berlin, in 1842, so pleased the king, Friedrich Wilhelm IV, that he created Meyerbeer "General Musical Director" for Prussia, and Meyerbeer came to Berlin to reside. Here in 1842 he wrote his "*Das Feldlager in Schlesien*" in which Jenny Lind made a great success. Later, however, he made over a great part of this music for his opera of "*L'Étoile du Nord*," 1854, for the Opéra Comique in Paris. His remaining works were "*L'Africaine*," performed after his death, in 1865; "*Le Prophète*," 1843, and "*Dinorah*," 1859. He died in Paris while superintending the production of his "*L'Africaine*." In his will he left a fund of 10,000 thalers, the interest of which to be used as a prize for the support of a young German composer during eighteen months' study in Italy, Germany and France, six months in each. Besides the operas above mentioned Meyerbeer wrote a quantity of other music for orchestra, cantatas, and occasional pieces for festival purposes, of which the "Schiller March" is an example.

The music of Meyerbeer is extremely sensational. His instrumentation is rich, at times *bizarre*, and strongly contrasted. His knowledge of stage effect, such that he knew by intuition what would do, and what not. He was to some extent created by circumstances, a striking instance of which is told in connection with the opera of the "Huguenots," where the parting with Valentine at the end of the fourth act was originally without important music. But the tenor declined to take the part unless suitable music could be furnished him at this point. Whereupon Meyerbeer wrote the impassioned duet, since so celebrated, and which in fact is generally recognized as one of the most suitable, not to say most effective, incidents of the whole opera. Meyerbeer's operas follow the lead of Spontini in their fondness for military glory and spectacle. They partake of the virtuoso spirit of the other great geniuses mentioned in a later chapter—all of whom wrote for the sake of an effect to be arrived at, rather than from any inner necessity of carrying out their tone-poems in such and such a way. Meyerbeer's influence, about 1830 to 1840, was supreme upon the stage. It was to consult him that young Wagner undertook his journey to Paris, bringing with him his splendid spectacular opera "Rienzi," quite in the Meyerbeer vein. This feature in the work, most likely, was the one chiefly concerned in preventing its acceptance at Paris under Meyerbeer's direction. Wagner was very much influenced by Meyerbeer in all his earlier works, particularly in the matter of splendid appointments for the stage. With all the splendid brilliancy of Meyerbeer's music, there is something insincere about it. It rarely touches the deeper springs of feeling. This is true of the greatest of his pieces, no less than of the smaller numbers.

IV.

The most interesting story in the history of opera, and one so resplendent that it is impossible not to regard the others as merely in some degree preparatory to it, is that of Richard Wagner (1813-1883). This remarkable man was born in Leipsic in 1813, the son of a superintendent of police. His mother was a woman of refined and spiritual nature. After the death of his father, his mother married again—an actor named Geyer—a circumstance having an important bearing on the future of the composer. His brother Albert and his sister Rosalie became actors, and Wagner himself was familiar with the stage from earliest childhood. He studied music while a boy, but his ambition was to become a poet. He translated the twelve books of the Odyssey. He made the acquaintance of Shakespeare's plays, first in German, afterward in English. He made a translation of Romeo's soliloquy, and began to compose music for it. At the age of eighteen he copied Beethoven's ninth symphony in score, for the purpose of knowing it more thoroughly. His musical progress was such that at the age of twenty-one he was able to accept a position as the conductor of the opera at Magdeburg. In 1836 this failed, and he accepted a place at Königsberg. He had then written one opera, called "The Love Veto." In 1837 he was much interested in Bulwer's "Rienzi," and immediately made a libretto from it. He was now musical director at Riga, and his wife had leading feminine rôles in opera. His favorite composer in opera just then was Meyerbeer. For some reason he lost his place at Riga, and resolved to visit London, taking ship across the Black sea. It was a sailing vessel of small burden, and they encountered a very violent storm. He heard the legend of the Flying Dutchman, and the next year made a poem of it and commenced to write the opera. He spent some time in Paris, where he hoped to get his "Rienzi" accepted at the Grand Opera. This opera he had written on a large scale in the hope of pleasing Meyerbeer, whose influence at Paris was very strong at this time. This, however, he failed to do, very possibly because his opera was too good. He was reduced to great straits, and had to write *potpourri* for the cornet and piano at a beggarly price, in order to gain a living. In 1843 his "Rienzi" was accepted at Dresden, through the influence of Meyerbeer. It was performed with great success, and Wagner was called there as conductor. Here he had an important position, having to produce the best operas of all schools. He brought out his own "Flying Dutchman" and had already finished "*Tannhäuser.*" He read the Arthur legends, and conceived the idea of an opera upon a subject connected with the Holy Grail. This was "*Lohengrin,*" completed in March, 1848. It was in a fair way to have been produced under his own direction if he had had the good sense to let politics alone; but in some way he mixed himself up in the revolutionary attempt of that year, and was obliged to flee the country. He went to Zurich, where he lived in great poverty at first, but afterward with a certain moderate income, for nearly ten years. This circumstance was evidently providential, as will appear in the sequel.

Fig. 78.

RICHARD WAGNER.

Franz Liszt was now conductor at Weimar, and he brought out "*Lohengrin*" in 1850. From this moment a friendship was established between these two remarkable men. Liszt sent Wagner a handsome *honorarium*, and from this time on was his financial guardian. By this time Wagner's art theories had become pretty well defined. From his standpoint the three great arts of music, poetry and drama had been independently explored to their limit— music by Beethoven, poetry and the drama by Shakespeare and Goethe—

and the only remaining thing of importance to do was to unite them all in one homogeneous mass, and by their combined operation accomplish a more profound and overwhelming effect than had been made before, or indeed would have been possible to them separately. In his autobiography, speaking of his early experiences as conductor, he says:

"The peculiar, gnawing feeling that oppressed me in conducting our ordinary opera, was often interrupted by an indescribable enthusiastic feeling of happiness, when here and there, in the performance of nobler works, I became thoroughly conscious, in the midst of the representation, of the incomparable influence of dramatic-musical combinations—an influence of such depth, fervor and life, as no other art is capable of producing.

"That such impressions, which, with the rapidity of lightning, made clear to me undreamed-of possibilities, could constantly renew themselves for me—this was the thing which bound me to the theater, much as the typical spirit of our operatic performances filled me with disgust. Among especially strong impressions of this character, I remember the hearing of an opera, by Spontini, in Berlin, under that master's own direction; and I felt myself, too, thoroughly elevated and ennobled for a time, when I was teaching a small opera company Méhul's noble 'Joseph.' And when, twenty years ago, I spent some time in Paris, the performances at the Grand Opera could not fail by the perfection of their musical and dramatic *mise en scène* to exercise a most dazzling and exciting influence upon me. But greatest of all was the effect produced upon me in early youth by the artistic efforts of a dramatic singer of (in my eyes) entirely unsurpassed merit—Schröder-Devrient. The incomparable dramatic talent of this woman, the inimitable harmony and strong individuality of her representations, which I studied with eyes and ears, filled me with a fascination that had a decisive influence on my whole artistic career. The possibilities of such a performance were revealed to me, and with her in view, there grew up in my mind a legitimate demand, not for musical-dramatic representation alone, but for the *poetic-musical conception* of a work of art, to which I could hardly continue to give the name of 'opera.'"

Fig. 79.

MME. SCHRÖDER-DEVRIENT (1804-1860).

Soon after his removal to Zurich, he commenced to compose the libretto of the "Nibelung's Ring." This work was founded on the famous old German poem, "*Die Nibelungen Lied*," but with very important modifications of Wagner's own. It is divided into four works. In the first, "*Das Rheingold*," the gold of the Rhine, is stolen, and a curse is laid upon it. The second opera of the series is "*Die Walküre*." In this work the remarkable character of Brunhilde is the central figure. She is one of the Wish-maidens of Odin, whose duty it was to conduct the souls of slain heroes to Walhalla, the dwelling place of the gods. The entire conception of this character is unique, and still more unique in the musical way in which it is worked out. We find in this work also the mother and father of Siegfried, and the opera closes when Brunhilde is thrown into the magic slumber with the fire around her. The third opera of the series is that of Siegfried, the half-divine, half-human hero, who knows no fear—who slays the dragon that captures the gold of the Rhine—awakens Brunhilde from her magic sleep, etc. The fourth opera is called "The Twilight of the Gods," or "The Death of Siegfried." I will not consume space by describing this poem in detail, since this material is easily accessible in every encyclopedia. I have already treated it at considerable length in the second volume of my "How to Understand Music." These works are especially remarkable upon a musical side. The opera of the "Rhinegold" is a little monotonous, but the orchestral score contains many points of beauty, and "The Valkyrie" is beautiful throughout, conceived in a very masterly and poetic vein; the instrumentation, also, is extremely noble and beautiful. In the whole of these two works there is scarcely a single piece which can be played apart from the rest as a concert number. The drama moves straight on from one thing to another. There are no melodies of the conventional type, and the music is closely woven together, like the effects of an April day, with storms, sunshine and shadows following each other without any perceptible break. So great has been the advance in musical taste since these were first composed, that "The Ride of the Valkyries," a famous descriptive piece for orchestra, forming the prelude of the second act, has been played in all parts of the world, as also the "Magic Fire Scene," which closes the opera. These are given over and over again by Thomas, and arrangements of them are often played at the piano. Directly he had finished "*Die Walküre,*" Wagner sent it to Liszt, and a letter with it, in which he modestly admitted that he thought it was very fine, or words to that effect. Liszt, on his part, was delighted with it. He wrote a most beautiful and noble letter to Wagner about it, and a little later he speaks of Hans von Bülow having been with him, when he could not refrain from giving him "a sight of Walhalla." So he brought out the score, and he said that Hans pounded at the piano, and he himself hummed and howled as well as he could, and they had a great time over it.

Wagner then set to work on the opera of "*Siegfried,*" which interested him very much indeed. This character also is a genuine conception of Wagner's. The wild forest boy who knows no fear, who has the most marvelous strength, is described in music as wild and powerful as himself. When Sieglinde, Siegfried's mother, was married, an old man appeared at the wedding with an ashen staff, his hat brim drooping over one eye, and in the midst of the festivities he drew a mighty sword and with a great blow thrust it into the stem of the ash tree which grew in the center of the house, saying that it was the sword of a hero, and that whoever was strong enough to draw it should wield it in the service of gods. All the strong men tugged at this weapon, but none were able to draw it. When Siegmund, Siegfried's father, comes there, he draws the weapon amid a splendid burst of music. This sword is broken on Wotan's spear, but the pieces are saved for Siegfried, and one of the great scenes in the opera of "*Siegfried*" is where he welds anew the broken sword, and at the end cleaves the anvil with one mighty stroke. The opera of "*Siegfried*" closes with the awakening of Brunhilde, and a splendid duet with Siegfried.

The composition of this work was interrupted at the end of the second act, and here we come to one of the most curious circumstances in Wagner's career. He says that he felt it necessary to stop now and write a practical opera for the stage as it then was, in order to re-establish his connection with the German theater, for he did not believe that these works would be performed in his own time. Accordingly he wrote "*Die Meistersinger*," and the opera of "Tristan and Isolde." They were finished in 1865, and Hans von Bülow, who was then director of the opera at Munich, took them both for rehearsal; they had there about 160 rehearsals of "Tristan and Isolde"— but gave it up as impossible, the singers forgetting from one day to another the music they had learned the previous day. The other work, "*Die Meistersinger*," fared better. They had sixty-six rehearsals, and finally brought it to a dress rehearsal, which was as far as they got toward performing it. Nothing shows the increased growth that Wagner had made, as well as his unconsciousness of this growth, like this experience of his operas at Munich, under so enterprising and able a director as Hans von Bülow— who was undoubtedly the most competent man in Germany, as well as the most courageous, for the task of producing this kind of work. Although these operas were not successful at the time, "*Die Meistersinger*" has since become highly appreciated upon large stages, and it is in my opinion the most beautiful opera that has ever been written. The music throughout is in a noble and dignified strain, with melodies beautiful and highly finished, almost suitable for church music, yet comedy in the best sense of the term. The famous prize song in this work is sufficiently well known. There is a most delightful finale in the third act, where Beckmesser's serenade occurs as one of the incidents. The other work, "Tristan and Isolde," is the most difficult opera that has ever been written, and will have to wait a generation yet, most likely, before its beauties are fully appreciated.

After composing these two enormous works, Wagner went on to finish "*Siegfried*," and then completed the work by writing "*Die Götterdämmerung*" ("The Twilight of the Gods"), or, "The Death of Siegfried," as he had originally intended to call it. This work contains one number which is stupendous in its pathos, "The Funeral March of Siegfried." Nothing like it exists elsewhere. These four operas have a very remarkable peculiarity, that throughout the four there are certain leading motives, which repeatedly occur. There is the motive of "the magic fire," which cuts a great figure in the first opera of the series, where Loki, the fire god, appears and is ushered in by this motive. It occurs again in the magic fire scene, at the close of "*Die Walküre*," where Wotan surrounds Brunhilde with shrieking flames, in order that their terrors may deter cowards from waking her. There is the "sword motive," which is heard in the first opera, when this sword is first spoken of; it is finely developed where the sword is drawn, and again in the opera of "*Siegfried*," where it is freshly welded. There is the "Walhalla motive," the "Siegfried motive," the "Valkyrie motive," and many others, to the number of nearly one hundred. These are woven together, especially in the last opera of the series, in a most astonishing and wonderful way, yet without impairing the musical flow of the work. The scores are also extremely elaborate, from an orchestral point of view, requiring a large number of instruments, most of them having a great deal to do. This great trilogy, as Wagner called it, which was at first supposed to be beyond the ability of the public to appreciate, has now been given in all parts of Germany with great success, and it is no longer beyond the ability of an audience to enjoy.

By the time he had completed this work, Wagner had conceived the idea of a national theater, to be completed regardless of cost, and with appointments permitting it to produce great works in a faultless manner. At first he thought of building it at Munich, but the Munich public proving fickle, he resolved to build it in an inland town, where all his audience would be in the attitude of pilgrims, who would have come from a distance to hear a great work with proper surroundings. The sum required to complete this was about $500,000. It is sufficient compliment to Wagner's ability to say that he secured it, King Louis, of Bavaria, having contributed more than $100,000. Large sums also were sent in by Wagner societies all over the world. The house was completed at Bayreuth. It was a little theater holding about 1,500 people, with a magnificent stage, which at that time was far in advance of any other, but has since been surpassed by many, notably by that of the Auditorium, in Chicago. Here he proposed to have what he called a stage festival—the singers to contribute their services gratuitously, the honor of being selected for this place, and the advantage of the experience, being regarded as ample compensation. The orchestra, likewise, in great part was to be composed of virtuosi—also to play without pay. All these expectations were realized. Leading the violins for several years was the famous virtuoso, Wilhelmj, and the singers of the Bayreuth festival were the best that the German stage possessed. The festival is now carried out upon a more rational basis, the singers receiving something for their services. Wagner completed his achievements by the opera of "*Parsifal*"—a work nearly related to "*Lohengrin*"—in some respects more beautiful. This is entirely like church music, and the whole effect of the performance at Bayreuth,—for it has never been given elsewhere—is noble and beautiful. It leaves an impression like a church service.

The peculiarities of Wagner's operas are many. The plays, from a poetic side, are in the vein of magic; irresistible causes work together for irresistible ends. They are somber and primeval, like the voice of the forest. The music fits the poem exactly, without making any attempt at being beautiful on its own account. It is extremely elaborate, and richly scored for orchestra, and full of beautiful science—not intended to be recognized as such by the average hearer. From a dramatic point of view the works are very consistent, and the stage effects are of a remarkable kind. Wagner was fortunate enough to make the acquaintance of a mechanic able to carry out some of his most impracticable suggestions.

Wagner left a large number of pamphlets and treatises, which are likely to remain among the classics of musical literature. The most important is his "Opera and Drama," written in 1851. This is a full discussion, in singularly vigorous and clear language, of the entire nature of opera as poetically conceived and as practically carried out by the previous masters, and as proposed to be carried out by Wagner himself. Many of Wagner's writings have now been translated into English. His opera texts are highly esteemed by his admirers, and respected by all. As a poet the general opinion seems to be that he was given to magnificent phraseology rather than to delicacy of fancy or humor. He is most at home with the grand, the gigantic, the superhuman; and in nearly all that he writes the primeval undertone of the minor makes itself felt.

It is entirely uncertain whether opera will continue to follow the lines he laid down, with the same severity, but there can be no question that his influence upon the course of art will be very great. In musical discourse, especially in the harmonic side of it, Wagner has made very great variations from the practices of his predecessors, even the most free of the instrumental writers—Schumann. His modulations are carried into more remote keys, and the tempered scale is taken as a finality of our tonal system. All the keys are brought near, as he treats them, and in any key any chord whatever can be introduced without effecting a modulation, provided it be so managed that the sense of tonality is not unsettled.

Personally Wagner was rather small, very fastidious in his attire and surroundings. In 1869 Mme. Cosima, daughter of Liszt, and wife of Von Bülow, left him and became the wife of Wagner. During the last ten years of his life they had an elegant residence at Bayreuth, where Mme. Wagner still has her home. Wagner died in Venice, whither he had gone for the mild climate. No musician in the entire history of art has occupied the attention of the whole contemporaneous world to anything like the same degree as did Richard Wagner, from the performance of "*Lohengrin*," in 1850, until his death in 1883.

CHAPTER XXXV.
VIRTUOSITY IN THE NINETEENTH CENTURY;
PAGANINI; BERLIOZ; CHOPIN; LISZT.

I.

STRICTLY speaking, there was no break in the continuity of art development represented in the virtuoso appearances recorded in Chapter XXX, and those with which we have presently to deal. In point of chronology, many of those recorded in the present chapter were contemporaneous with some of those in the former. Nevertheless, the artists with whom we are now concerned represent principles more decidedly belonging to the romantic, and hence to the nineteenth century, than did those whose operations have already been discussed as part of the record of the eighteenth. This is seen in the quality and the novelty of their playing, and still more in the influence which they exercised upon the musicians who came after.

Fig. 80.

Earliest of these in point of time, and most influential in other departments than his own, was the famous Italian violinist, Nicolo Paganini (1784-1840), perhaps the most remarkable executant upon the violin who has ever appeared. His father, a clever amateur, had him taught music at an early age, and when only nine years of age he played in a concert at Genoa with triumphant success. He had already practiced diligently and, with the intuition of genius, had found out his own ways of accomplishing things, so that when, at the age of eleven, he was taken to Parma to the teacher Rolla, he was told that there was nothing to teach him. Returning home, he continued his practice, applying himself as much as eight or ten hours a day, and producing a number of compositions so difficult that he alone could play them. His first European tour took place in 1805, and astonished the world. The most marvelous stories were told of him. It was popularly supposed that he could play upon anything, provided only the catgut and the horsehair were furnished him. His first appearance in France was in 1831, and in the same year he played in London. The height of his fame was reached in 1834, at which time Berlioz, the French composer, presented him with a beautiful symphony, *"Harold en Italie."* Notwithstanding the fact that Paganini lost money in Paris, he presented Berlioz with 20,000 francs, in order to enable him to pursue his career as a composer unhampered by financial distress. This act was greatly to Paganini's credit, and entirely contrary to the prevalent opinion concerning him, which was that he was very miserly. Among the works which Paganini produced was a set of caprices for the violin which were essentially novelties for the instrument. He enlarged the resources of the violin in every direction, employing double stopping, harmonics, and the high positions with a freedom previously unknown. Notwithstanding Spohr's modest remark that upon a certain evening when playing for some amateurs he delighted them "with all the Paganini juggles," it is certain that he did nothing of the kind.

Fig. 81.

PAGANINI AS HE APPEARED.

[From a drawing by Sir Edwin Landseer. (Grove.)]

It is impossible after this lapse of time to realize the sensation which Paganini's appearances made. His tall, emaciated figure and haggard face, his piercing black eyes and the furor of passion which characterized his playing, made him seem like one possessed, and many hearers were prepared to assert of their own knowledge that they had seen him assisted by the Evil Spirit. His caprices remain the sheet anchor of the would-be virtuoso. The entire art of violin playing rests upon two works—the Bach sonatas for violin solo, and the great Paganini caprices. Everything of which the violin is capable, or which any virtuoso has been able to find in it, is contained in these works.

Upon two composers of this century Paganini's influence was extremely powerful. Schumann took his departure from the Paganini caprices, seeking to perform upon the piano the same kind of effect which Paganini had obtained from the violin, or to discover others equivalent to them. And Liszt set himself to do upon the piano the same kind of impossibilities which Paganini had performed upon the violin. Both these masters accomplished more than they planned for. Schumann enriched the current of musical discourse by his experiments having their departure from

Paganini, thereby accomplishing something which Paganini did not; for while the great violinist's works are of astonishing value for the violin, they are not particularly significant as tone-poetry. They are pleasing and sensational, and at times passionate, show pieces for the virtuoso.

II.

Hector Berlioz (1803-1869), for whose genius Paganini had such admiration, was perhaps the most remarkable French personality in music during the nineteenth century, and one of the most commanding in the whole world of music. He was born at Grenoble, in the south of France. His father, a physician, intended that the son should follow his own profession, but when the young Berlioz was sent to Paris to study medicine, at the age of eighteen, music proved too strong for him, and he entered the Conservatory as a pupil of Lesueur. His parents were so incensed by this course that the paternal supplies were cut off, and the young enthusiast was driven to the expedient of earning a scanty living by singing in the opera chorus at an obscure theater, *La Gymnase Dramatique.* The daring originality of the young musician, and his habit of regarding every rule as open to question, rendered him anything but a favorite with Cherubini, the director of the Conservatory, and it was only after several trials that he carried off the prize for composition. The second instance of this kind occurred in 1830, the piece being a dramatic cantata "*Sardanapole,*" which gained him the prize of Rome, carrying with it a pension sufficient to maintain the winner during three years in Italy.

On his return to Paris, he found it extremely difficult to secure a living by his compositions, their originality and the scale upon which he carried them out, placing them outside the conventional markets for new musical works designed for public performance. In this strait he took to writing for the press, in the *Journal des Débats,* for which his talent was little, if any, less marked than for musical production upon the largest scale. As a writer, he was keen, sarcastic, bright and sympathetic. A man of the world, and at the same time an artist, he touched everything with the characteristic lightness and raciness of the born *feuilletonist.* Very soon (in 1834), he produced his symphony "*Harold en Italie,*" which Paganini so much admired that he presented Berlioz with the very liberal, even princely *douceur* of 20,000 francs ($4,000). Meanwhile Berlioz was unable to secure recognition in Paris. His compositions were regarded as extravagant and fantastic, and Parisians were curiously surprised at the reception the composer met with in Germany, when he traveled there in 1842 and 1843, and again in 1852, bringing out his works. The Germans were by no means unanimous regarding his merits. Mendelssohn, who found Berlioz most interesting as a man, had no admiration for his music. To him it appeared crazy and unbeautiful. The sole recognition which Berlioz had in France was the librarianship of the *Conservatoire*, with a modest salary, and the Cross of the

Legion of Honor. In spite of the small esteem in which this clever master was held by his countrymen during his life, he produced a succession of remarkable works, without which the art of music would have missed some of its brightest pages. Among these we may mention his dramatic legend of "The Damnation of Faust," for solos, chorus and orchestra, which marks one of the highest points reached by program music. This great work is now generally accepted as one of the best of the romantic productions, and the orchestral pieces in it have become part of the standard repertory of orchestras everywhere.

Berlioz was above all the composer of the grandiose, the magnificent. This appears in his earliest works. In 1837 he composed his Requiem, for the funeral obsequies of General Damremont. This work is of unprecedented proportions. It is scored for chorus, solos and orchestra, the latter occasionally of extraordinary appointment. In the "*Tuba Mirum*," for example, he desires full chorus of strings, and four choirs of wood-wind and brass. The wood-wind consists of twelve horns, eight oboes, and four clarinets, two piccolos and four flutes. The brass is disposed in four choirs as follows, each at one of the corners of the stage; the first consists of four trumpets, four tenor trombones and two tubas; the second of four trumpets and four tenor trombones; the third the same; the fourth of four trumpets, four tenor trombones and four ophicleides. The bewildering answers of these four choirs of brass give place at the words "Hear the awful trumpet sounding," to a single bass voice, accompanied by sixteen kettle drums, tuned to a chord. A movement of similar sonority is the "*Rex Tremendæ Majestatis*." At other times the work is very melodious. It is indeed singular that a young composer should commence his career with a piece so daring. But to Berlioz's credit it must be said he never makes a mistake in his calculations of effect. When he desires contrast and blending effect of different masses, these results always follow whenever his work is performed according to his directions.

All the music of Berlioz belongs to the category of "program music," that is to say, everywhere there is an attempt at painting a scene or representing something by means of music, that something being habitually suggested and explained by the text, if the work be vocal, or by explanatory notes, if the work be instrumental. This is as true of his symphonies, "Romeo and Juliet," and "Harold in Italy," as in the vocal works themselves. The list of these contains an oratorio, "The Childhood of Christ" (1854), "The Damnation of Faust" (1846), the operas "*Benvenuto Cellini*," produced at the *Académie*, 1838, "The Trojans" (1856), "*Beatrice et Benedict*" (1863). The first was performed under the direction of Liszt at Weimar, about 1850, but with indifferent success. Berlioz instrumented several pianoforte compositions for orchestra, the best known of them being Weber's

"Invitation to the Dance," and "Polonaise in E flat." His treatise upon instrumentation, published in 1864, remained standard until since the appearance of the elaborate and more systematic work upon this subject by F.A. Gevaert. The greatest of Berlioz's works is his splendid "*Te Deum*," written during the years 1854 and 1855, for some kind of festival performance. He planned this composition as part of a great trilogy of an epic-dramatic character in honor of Napoleon, the first consul. At the moment of his return from his Italian campaigns, he was to have been represented as entering Notre Dame, where this "*Te Deum*" is sung by an appointment of musical forces consisting of a double chorus of 200 voices, a third choir of 600 children, an orchestra of 134, an organ, and solo voices. The entire work was never completed, and the "*Te Deum*" had its first and only representation in Berlioz's lifetime at the opening of the Palace of Industry, April 30, 1855. The work is full of splendid conceptions, and is freer from eccentricities than any other of the author. It is extremely sonorous, and is destined to be better known as festival occasions upon a larger scale become more numerous.

The whole effect of Berlioz's activity was that of a virtuoso in the department of dramatic and descriptive music, and in the art of wielding large orchestral masses. It is curious that between him and Wagner the relations should never have been cordial, although the ends proposed by both were substantially identical, and the genius of both incontestable. Berlioz had no confidence in Wagner's "endless melody," and when he writes about music he does so in the attitude of a humble follower of the old masters.

III.

The progress in piano playing, in the course of the nineteenth century has been most extraordinary. The music of Beethoven and Schubert, composed during the first quarter of this century, and the influence of the virtuosi prominent during that time, whose activity has been told in connection with those of the century previous (the operative principles of which were the ones mainly influencing them); and the continual strife of the piano makers to increase the resonance, singing quality and artistic susceptibility of the tone and the strength and elasticity of the action, as recounted in the chapter devoted to the history of this, the greatest of modern instruments—were concentrating influences having the effect of calling attention to the new instrument in a very remarkable manner. Add to these causes the meteor-like appearance of Paganini, with his stupendous execution upon the violin, and its novel possibilities. All these together seem to have led four gifted geniuses at about the same time to make independent investigations into the tonal possibilities of the piano, and the mode of producing effects upon it, in the hope of creating a new art, and of rivaling the weird successes of the highly gifted Italian, who apparently had exhausted the possibilities of the violin. The artists thus occupied in developing the art of piano playing were Chopin, Liszt, Thalberg and Schumann, and it is far from easy to determine exactly which one it was who first brought his influence to bear upon the public; or which one it was who first arrived at the successful application of the principles of the new technique, whose essential divergences from the old consisted in a more flexible use of the fingers, hand and arm, and the co-operation of the foot for the promotion of blending, and of bringing into simultaneous use the tonal resources from all parts of the instrument. In this case, as in so many others of remarkable invention, the improvements seem to have been made by several independent investigators acting simultaneously, each one ignorant of the work of the others. The impulse in the direction of greater freedom had already found expression in the pianoforte pieces of the great master, Von Weber, whose sonatas and caprices had been published between 1810 and 1820. (See pp. 410 and 411.) These contain several novelties, which I have found it more convenient to discuss in connection with the personal history of the composer. Liszt has generally been held as a little the earliest of the four in point of time, his arrangement of Berlioz's "Harold" symphony having been published, according to the dates in Weitzmann's history, in 1827, but according to more accurate information, in 1835, while he had published his arrangement of the Paganini caprices in 1832, one year after hearing Paganini. In these works Liszt makes demands upon the hands which were not recognized as among the possibilities of the old technique. But for all this, it is apparently certain that the honor of having developed a style distinctly original, and with peculiarities easily recognizable by the average listener, belongs to the great virtuoso Thalberg. Sigismund Thalberg (1812-1871) was the illegitimate son of Prince Dietrichstein, a diplomat then living at Geneva. His mother was the Baroness von Wetzlar. Thalberg was carefully educated, and accustomed to high-bred society from childhood. His father intended him for a diplomatic career, but the boy's talent for the piano was irresistible, and, so well had his education been advanced by his teacher, the first bassoonist of the Vienna opera, that by the time he was fifteen he made a brilliant success at a concert in Vienna. His first composition in the style which he afterward made so famous was the fantasia on themes from "*Euryanthe*," which was published in 1828. Later, in 1835, he entered upon his public career as virtuoso with concert tours to all parts of the world, everywhere greeted with admiration and astonishment. He appeared in Paris late in 1834 or early in 1835, finding Liszt there in the plenitude of his powers. Then there was a rivalry between them, and opposing camps were instituted of their respective admirers. The dispute as to their relative excellence ran high, and, as usually happens in personal questions of this sort, victory did not belong entirely to either party. Nevertheless, at this distance it is not easy to see why the question should have been raised, since in the light of modern piano playing Liszt's art had in it the promise of everything which has come since; while Thalberg's had in it only one side of the modern art. Thalberg had a wonderful technique, in which scales of marvelous fluency, lightness, clearness and equality, intervened between chord passages of great breadth and sonority, so that all the resources of the piano were open to him. But his specialty was that of carrying a melody in the middle of the piano, playing it by means of the two thumbs alternately, the other hand being occupied in runs and passages covering the whole compass of the piano, crossing the melody from below, or descending upon it from the highest regions of the treble, and continuing down the keyboard with perfect equality and lightness, without in the slightest degree disturbing the singing of the melody. This, of its own accord, went on in the most artistic manner, as if the pianist had nothing at all else to do than to *sing* it. The perfection of Thalberg's melody playing was something wonderful, as well it might be; for in order to master the art of it, he studied singing for five years with one of the best teachers of the Italian school, the eminent Garcia. This, however, was later, after he had located in Paris.

This trick of treating the melody was not new with Thalberg. It had previously been done upon the harp by the great Welsh virtuoso, Parish Alvars (1808-1849), whose European reputation had been acquired by a succession of great concert tours, and who at length closed his days in

Vienna, where Thalberg lived. There was also an Italian master, Giuseppe Francesco Pollini (1763-1846), who in 1809 became professor of the piano in the Conservatory of Milan. Pollini had been a pupil of Mozart, and dedicated to that great master his first work. Early after being appointed professor he published a great school for the pianoforte (1811), in which the art is fully discussed in all its bearings, and minute directions given for touch and all the rest appertaining to a concert treatment of the instrument. He was the first to write piano pieces upon three staves, the middle one being devoted to the melody; a proceeding afterward followed in some cases by Liszt and Thalberg. Pollini surrounded his melodies, thus placed in the middle of the instrument, where at that time the sonority and singing quality of the pianoforte exclusively lay, with runs and passages of a brilliant and highly ingenious kind. This was done in his "*Una de 32 Esercizi in Forma di Toccata,*" but he had already, in 1801, published several brilliant pieces in Paris, in which novelties occur. I have never seen a copy of these works of Pollini, nor any other account of them than those in Riemann's dictionary and in Weitzmann's history of the pianoforte, but it is altogether likely that when they are examined we shall find in this case, as in many others of progressive development, that the final result was reached by a succession of steps, each one short, and apparently not so very important. The chain of technical development for the piano extended from Bach in unbroken progress, and the discovery of Pollini, who was less known in western lands than others of the great names in the list, enables us to fill in between Moscheles and Thalberg. Pollini's work anticipates the Clementi *Gradus* by about six years.

To return to Thalberg.—In 1856 he visited America, where his success was the same as in all other parts of the world. Having accumulated a fortune, he retired from active life, and bought an estate near Naples, where he spent the remainder of his life. There were reasons of a purely external and conventional kind why the playing of Thalberg should have attracted more attention, or at least been more admired, than that of Liszt, in Paris and in aristocratic circles everywhere. His manner was the perfection of quiet. Whatever the difficulty of the passages upon which he was engaged, he remained perfectly quiet, sitting upright, modestly, without a single unnecessary motion. Moreover, the general character of his passages, which progressed fluently upward or downward by degrees, instead of taking violent leaps from one part of the keyboard to another, permitted him to maintain this elegant quiet with less restriction than would have been possible in such works, for instance, as the great concert fantasias of Liszt. It is to be noticed, further, that the peculiar sonority of Thalberg's playing depended upon the improvements in the pianoforte, made just before his appearance and during his career. His method of playing the melody, moreover, while perhaps not distinctly so recognized by him, employed a noticeable element of the arm touch, while his passage work was a ringer movement of the lightest and most facile description. His chords, also, were often struck with a finger touch, and he was perhaps the originator of the peculiar effect produced by touching a chord with the fingers only, but rebounding from the keys with the whole arm to the elbow. A chord thus played has the delicacy peculiar to finger work, but in the removal from the keys the muscles of the arm are called into action in such a way that the finger stroke is intensified to a degree somewhat depending upon the height to which the rebound is carried.

IV.

François Frédéric Chopin (1809-1849) was one of the most remarkable composers of this epoch, and in some respects one of the most precocious musical geniuses of whom we have any record. He was born at Zela-Zowa Wola, a village six miles from Warsaw, in Poland, the son of a French merchant living there, who had married a Polish lady. Later, in consequence of financial reverses, his father became a teacher in the university. The boy, François, was brought up amid refined and pleasant surroundings, and his education was carefully looked to. Although rather delicate in appearance, he was healthy and full of spirits. His precocity upon the piano was such that at the age of nine he played a concerto in public with great success, from which time forward he made many appearances in his native city. He early began to compose, and by the time he was thirteen or fourteen, had undertaken a number of works of considerable magnitude. After having received the best instruction which his native city afforded, he started out, at the age of nineteen, for a visit to Vienna, where he appeared in two concerts, and to his own surprise was pronounced one of the greatest virtuosi of the day. This, however, is not the point of his precocity. When he started upon his tour to Vienna, he had with him certain manuscripts, which he had composed. His Opus 2 consisted of variations upon Mozart's air, "*La ci Darem la Mano*," of which later Schumann wrote such a glowing account in his paper at Leipsic. These variations were enormously difficult, and in a wholly novel style. There were several mazurkas, the three nocturnes, Opus 9, of which the extremely popular one in E flat stands second; the twelve studies, Opus 10, dedicated to Franz Liszt, and a concerto in F minor, and all or nearly all of that in E minor. These were the work of a boy then only nineteen, the pupil of a comparatively unknown provincial teacher. When we examine these works more minutely, our astonishment increases, for they represent an entirely new school of piano playing. New effects, new management of the hands, new passages, beautiful melody, exquisitely modulated harmonies—in short, a new world in piano playing was here opened. So difficult and so strange were these works, that for nearly a generation the more difficult ones of them were a sealed book to amateur pianists, and even virtuosi like Moscheles declare that they could never get their fingers reliably through them.

Fig. 82.

FRÉDÉRIC CHOPIN.

Much pleased with his success in Vienna, Chopin returned to Warsaw, and after some months, set out for London, by way of Paris. Here his fortune varied somewhat. At first he found it impossible to secure a hearing, his only acquaintances being a few of his exiled fellow-countrymen, who were there. At length one evening a friend took him to a reception at the Rothschild's, and in this cultivated society he found appreciative listeners to his marvelous playing. From that time on he remained in Paris, only leaving it when his health made it necessary to visit the south of France. He very seldom appeared in public. His touch was not sufficiently strong to render his playing effective in a large hall.

The whole of the Chopin genius is summed up in his early works, which he took with him on his visit to Vienna. All his later works are in some sense repetitions. The ideas and the treatment are new, but the principles underlying are the same, and rarely, if ever, does he reach a higher flight than in some of these earlier works. His most celebrated innovation was that of the Nocturne, a sentimental cantilena for the pianoforte, in which a somewhat Byronic sentiment is expressed in a high-bred and elegant style. The name "nocturne" was not original with Chopin—the Dublin pianist, John Field, having published his first nocturnes in 1816. Field himself derived the name from the prayers of the Roman Church which are made between midnight and morning. The name, therefore, implies something belonging to the night—mysterious, dreamy, poetic. In Field's there is little of this, aside from the name; the melodies are plain and the sentiments commonplace. With Chopin, however, it is entirely different. In some instances the treatment for the piano is very simple, as in the popular nocturne in E flat, already mentioned; but in other cases he exercises the utmost freedom, and very carefully trained fingers are needed to perform them successfully. This is the case, for example, in the beautiful nocturne in G, Opus 37, No. 2, where the passages in thirds and sixths are extremely trying; also in the very dramatic nocturne in C minor, Opus 48.

Chopin's place in the Pantheon of the romantic school is that of the popularizer of pianoforte sentiment. His compositions, by whatever name they may be called, are essentially lyric pieces, songs, ballads and fanciful stories in rhyme. The subjects are frequently tender or sad, sometimes morbid—in short, Byronic. The treatment is always graceful and high-bred, and the contrasts strong. The melodies are embroidered with a peculiar kind of *fioratura*, which he invented himself, founded upon the Italian embellishment of that kind—a delicate efflorescence of melody, which, when perfectly done, is extremely pleasing. The names applied to the different compositions such as Ballade, Scherzo, Prelude, Rondo, Sonata, Impromptu, have only a remote reference to the nature of the piece. Occasionally the entire composition is morbid and unsatisfactory to a degree. These belong to the later period of his life, when he was in poor health. He is a woman's composer. In his strongest moments there is always an effeminate element. In this respect he is exactly opposite to Schumann and Beethoven, whose works, however delicate and refined, have always a manly strength. Chopin made the most important modifications in the current way of treating the piano. In this part of his activity he seemed to realize the possibilities of the instrument, in the same way that Paganini had recognized those of the violin. His passages, while based upon those of Hummel, nevertheless produced effects of which Hummel was totally incapable. Chopin is the originator of the extended *arpeggio* chord, of the chromatic sequences of the diminished sevenths with passing notes, and cadenza forms derived from them. He is thoroughly French in his views of "changing notes," as, for instance, in the accompaniment to the impromptu in A flat, Opus 29. His influence upon the general progress of musical development is to be traced in the works of Liszt, especially in the later pianoforte works, and in a large number of less gifted imitators, like Doehler.

V.

Aside from Wagner, the most remarkable figure of this century is that of Franz Liszt, who was born at Raiding, in Hungary, 1811, and died at Bayreuth, 1886. His father, Adam Liszt, was an official in the imperial service, and a musical amateur, capable of instructing his son in piano playing. At the age of nine he made his first public appearance, with so much success that several noblemen guaranteed the money to enable him to pursue his studies for six years in Vienna. Here he became a pupil of Czerny, Salieri and Randhartinger. He made the acquaintance of Schubert, and upon one occasion played before Beethoven, who kissed him, with the prophecy that he would make his mark. His first appearance as a composer was in a set of variations on a waltz by Diabelli, the same for which Beethoven wrote the thirty-three variations, Opus 120. Liszt's variation was the twenty-fourth in the set to which Beethoven did not contribute. It was published in 1823, when he was twelve years old. The same year he went to Paris, his father hoping to enter him at the Conservatory, in spite of his foreign origin; but Cherubini refused to receive him, so he studied with other composers. His operetta of "*Don Sanché*" was performed at the *Académie Royale* in 1825, and was well received. At this time he was in the height of his youthful success in Paris, tall, slender, with long hair and a most free and engaging countenance, with ready wit and unbounded tact. He performed marvels upon the piano, such as no one else could attempt. His repertory at this time seems to have consisted of pieces of the old school. In 1827 he lost his father, and being thrown upon his own resources, he began his concert tour. He appeared in London in 1827, his piece being the Hummel concerto. Three years later he played in London again, his number being the Weber *Concertstück*.

There was something weird and magnetic about his playing. He was very tall, about six feet two inches, slender, with piercing eyes, very long arms, but small hands; he played without notes, and amid the most frightful difficulties of execution kept his eyes fixed upon this, that or the other person in the audience. He moved about at the piano very much in the exciting passages, not, apparently, on account of the difficulty of overcoming technical obstacles, but simply from innate fire and excitement. As for technical difficulties, they did not exist. Everything that the piano contained seemed to be at his service, and the only regret was that the instrument was not better able to respond to his demand. In the *fortissimo* passages his tone was immense, and his *pianissimos* were the most delicate whispers. In these his fingers glided over the keys with inconceivable lightness and speed, and the tone fell upon the ear with a delicate tracery with which no particular was lost by reason of speed or lightness. This wonderful control of the instrument stood him in equal stead with his own compositions, especially adapted to his own style of playing; or with the works of the old school, which he transfigured as they had never been played before; or the last sonatas of Beethoven, which at that time were a sealed book to most musicians. These, indeed, he did not play in public, but in private. The essential novelties of the Liszt technique were the *bravura* cadenzas. The other sensational features, such as carrying the melody in the middle range of the piano with surrounding embroidery, the rapid runs and the extravagant climaxes, were all more or less common to the three representative virtuoso piano writers of this epoch—Liszt, Chopin and Thalberg.

A careful study of all the circumstances and influences surrounding Liszt at the time, leads to the conclusion that his ideas of the possibilities of the pianoforte were matured very gradually, not reaching their complete expression in the operatic fantasias before about 1834 or 1835. His early appearances were in pieces of the old school, and there is nothing more to be found in contemporary accounts of his playing than admiration for its superior fire and delicacy. Upon the appearance of Paganini, however, this was changed. The temporary eclipse, which this brilliant apparition made of the rising Liszt, led him to new studies in original directions. Thus arose the transcriptions of the Paganini caprices in 1832, and the composition of his own "Studies for Transcendent Execution," in the same or the following year. Farther sensational improvements were probably the result of the Thalberg contest in Paris during 1835.

Liszt's influence may be inferred from such incidents as the following: In 1839 there was a movement on foot to erect a monument to Beethoven at Bonn, but after some months' solicitation the committee found it impossible to realize the desired sum, or anything approaching it. Whereupon Liszt wrote them to give themselves no further uneasiness, for he himself would be responsible for the entire amount, about $10,000. This large sum he raised by his own exertions, and paid over, and a monument was unveiled with brilliant ceremonies in 1845. One of the performances upon that occasion was that of the Beethoven fifth concerto, which Liszt himself played. Concerning this memorable performance Berlioz himself writes: "The piano concerto in E flat is generally known for one of the better productions of Beethoven. The first movement and the *Adagio*, above all, are of incomparable beauty. To say that Liszt played it, and that he played it in a fashion grand, fine, poetic, yet always faithful, is to make a veritable pleonasm, and there was a tumult of applause, a sound of trumpets, and *fanfares* of the orchestra, which must have been heard far beyond the limits of the hall. Liszt immediately afterward mounted the desk of the conductor to direct the performance of the symphony in C minor, which he made us hear as Beethoven wrote it, including the entire *scherzo*, without the abridgment, as we have so long been accustomed to hear at the Conservatory at Paris; and the finale, with the repeat indicated by Beethoven. I have always had such confidence in the taste of the correctors of the great masters that I was very much surprised to find the symphony in C minor still more beautiful when executed entirely than when corrected. It was necessary to go to Bonn to make this discovery."

In 1849 a new epoch was opened in the history of this remarkable man. The grand duke of Weimar invited him to assume the direction of his musical establishment, including the opera. The salary was absurdly small— $800 or $1,000 a year. This, however, cut no figure in Liszt's mind, for he had always been singularly open-handed, yet at same time prudent. From his successful concert tours he had put by funds, 20,000 francs for his aged mother, and 20,000 francs for each of the three children he had by the Countess D'Agoult (known in literature as Daniel Stern), and he considered that the position would afford him an opportunity of developing his own talent for composition, and at the same time of affording a hearing for important new works, which, on account of their novelty and originality, were impossible of performance in the theaters of large cities. The repertory of the Weimar opera, from this time on, was most extraordinary. Here were produced for the first time Wagner's "Flying Dutchman," "*Tannhäuser*," and "*Lohengrin*," "*Benvenuto Cellini*," of Berlioz, Schumann's "*Genoveva*" and "*Mannfred*," and Schubert's "Alfonso and Estrella." Here were produced, also, the best of the operas of previous generations. Every master work of this sort Liszt revised with the greatest care, giving endless patience to every detail, and supplementing the resources of the theater, when insufficient, by "guests" from the great operas in the capital. Thus the musical establishment at Weimar became a sort of Mecca, to which all the musicians of the world gathered, especially the young and energetic in the pursuit of knowledge, and creative artists seeking a hearing or fresh inspiration. From an artistic standpoint, nothing more beautiful than the life of Liszt at Weimar could be desired. Besides these operatic performances and his symphony concerts, he gathered about him a succession of young virtuosi pianists. These had lessons, more or less formally, some of them for many years. Liszt never received money for lessons, and took no pupils but those whom he regarded as promising, or who were personally attractive to himself. About 1850 the American, Dr. William Mason, was there, and for two years following. The class at this time contained the well known names of Rubinstein, Carl Klindworth, Pruckner, Tausig, Joachim Raff, and Hans von Bülow. From this time on there is scarcely a concert pianist in the world who did not spend a few months or longer with Liszt at Weimar. Nor did his influence stop here. He produced a constant succession of important works, and conducted concerts and festivals in Hungary, and in different parts of Germany and France. Everywhere his inspiring presence and his keen insight were prized above all ordinary resources.

There is not space here to sketch in detail his singular and trying relations to that self-conscious genius, Wagner, who, when absconding to Zurich, sent the score of "*Lohengrin*" to Liszt. It can be imagined with what force the elevated and noble beauty of this epoch-marking work appealed to a genius so sensitive as Liszt. He not only produced the opera with great care, but prepared the public for it by means of extended articles in important journals in Leipsic, Berlin and Paris. From this time on, Liszt became the good angel of Wagner. There are few records in the annals of music more creditable than the letters of Liszt to Wagner. He took charge of his business in Germany, exercised his wholly unique and commanding influence to secure performances of Wagner's operas, sent him money out of his own purse, and secured some from his friends. More than this, he greeted every new work of Wagner's with an appreciation as generous and noble as it was intelligent and fine.

About 1852 Liszt commenced his symphonic poems. In these he avails himself of two of Wagner's suggestions. Much is made of the leading motive, and the orchestration is handled in a sonorous and brilliant manner, which Berlioz and Wagner first introduced. The works are very effective and original. Certain ones of them have become almost classic, like "The Preludes" and "*Tasso.*" He also wrote a number of large choral works, among them his "Legend of the Holy Elizabeth," the "Graner Mass," etc.

Fig. 83.

LISZT AS ABBÉ.

[Grove.]

There is hardly a province of musical composition in which Liszt did not distinguish himself. The orchestral compositions number about twenty. There are several important arrangements, such as Schubert marches, Schubert's songs, "Rakoczy March," and a variety of arrangements for pianoforte and orchestra, including two concertos, the Weber Polacca in E, and the Schubert fantasia. The pianoforte compositions are extremely numerous. Of the original pieces there are perhaps one hundred. Of important arrangements, such as the *études* from Paganini, the organ preludes and fugues from Bach, Schubert marches, etc., there are thirty or forty. Of the operatic fantasias there are perhaps a hundred or more. There are fifteen Hungarian Rhapsodies, and a large number of transcriptions of vocal pieces (of songs alone there are upwards of a hundred). Of masses and psalms about twenty. Two oratorios, several cantatas, about sixty original songs for single voice and piano, and very many other writings of a literary and musical kind. In 1865 Liszt left Weimar for several years, and resided in Rome, where he began to take holy orders.

Fig. 84.

FRANZ LISZT.

In the closing years of Wagner's life, after the Bayreuth festival theater had been inaugurated, Liszt was a central figure, and there are few large cities in Europe which he did not visit for the sake of encouraging important productions of the Wagnerian works. Thus, taken as a composer, a performer, a conductor, and an appreciative friend of art, his name is one which deserves to be revered as long as the history of music in the nineteenth century is remembered.

Fig. 84 represents him as he appeared in the last years of his life. The portrait of Liszt as abbé is taken from Grove's Dictionary. Neither of these last pictures gives an adequate idea of the sweetness of his expression. While the profile in middle life was sharp and clearly cut, as we see it in the abbé picture, and while in old age the mouth assumed a stern and set expression in repose, his smile was extremely winning, and the habitual expression of his face in conversation one of amiability and kindness.

CHAPTER XXXVI.
MENDELSSOHN AND SCHUMANN.
I.

ONE of the most fortunate personalities among modern composers was Felix Mendelssohn Bartholdy (1809-1847), who was born in Berlin, the grandson of Moses Mendelssohn, the famous Jewish philosopher. The father of Felix was a banker, and his mother a woman of a very sweet and amiable disposition. The children of Abraham Mendelssohn were baptized in the Christian faith in order to escape in some degree the prejudice against the Jewish race. Felix, having a strong inclination to music, at an early age made great progress in it. His first concert appearance was made at the age of ten, in which he played the piano part in a trio by Woelfl, and was very much applauded. As early as his twelfth year he began systematically to compose, and being naturally of methodical habits, which were still further encouraged by his father and mother, he kept an accurate record of his works, which at the last filled forty-four folio volumes, the most of the pieces being dated, and the place given where they were written. In the year 1820 he composed between fifty and sixty movements, of almost every sort, songs, part songs, pieces for organ, piano, strings and orchestra, as well as a cantata, and a little comedy for voices and a piano. In the summer of 1820, the whole family made a tour of Switzerland, and a very large number of pieces were composed at this time. In this same year he made a more important concert appearance with Aloys Schmitt, in which he played with Schmitt a duet for two pianos. This continued exercise in composition was not entirely of an abstract nature, for the Mendelssohn family were accustomed to have reunions on Sunday evenings, when these pieces were played. For occasions like this he wrote several small operas, and his talent was encouraged in every way by his parents, and by his very judicious teacher, the celebrated Zelter. When he was scarcely more than twelve years old, Zelter had him play before Goethe, and a trio of the boy's was also played, after which he was sent to play in the garden while his seniors discussed his prospects. Thus the boy grew up under the most favorable circumstances possible, his father being a wise and careful man, who, although not a musician, thoroughly sympathized with the artistic aims of his son; and his mother also encouraged him to more serious efforts. Even at this early age he was a prolific composer of orchestral music, the year 1824 being that of the composition of the symphony in C minor, now known as No. 1, but in Mendelssohn's catalogue marked the thirteenth of his compositions. In this year Moscheles passed through Berlin on his way to London, and made the acquaintance of Mendelssohn. At the Sunday morning music in the Mendelssohn house, Moscheles recalls the performance of Felix's C minor quartette, D major symphony, a concerto by Bach, played by Fanny, and a duet for two pianos. In the same year Spohr came to Berlin, and a little later Hiller, both of whom speak of Mendelssohn's playing as something very remarkable. His celebrated octette for strings, Opus 20, was composed in 1825. This was the first of his works which has retained its popularity. The year following he composed the overture to "The Midsummer Night's Dream," one of the most remarkable pieces of the early romantic school. In this the fairy-like music of Titania and her elves is charmingly contrasted with the folk songs and the absurd bray of the transformed Bottom. He had already written an opera "*Camacho*," which had been submitted to Spontini, the musical director of Berlin, but it was never performed. He entered at the University and attended the lectures of Hegel and Carl Ritter, the geographer, but for mathematics he had no talent. Two folio volumes of notes of the lectures of Hegel and Ritter are preserved from the years 1827 and 1828. His overture to "The Calm Sea and Prosperous Voyage" was written in 1828. In the year following he started on a long journey of three years, carefully planned by his father, in which all the countries of Europe were to have been visited successively, and observations made on civilization and society. His first appearance before an English audience was at a Philharmonic concert, May 25, 1828, when he conducted his symphony in C minor and improvised on the piano. He was received with the utmost applause. Five days later he played the *Concertstück* of Von Weber, and, which was a great innovation at that time, with no music before him. His letters from London are very charming indeed. At a concert later, his overture to "The Midsummer Night's Dream" was performed with great success; this was the beginning of his English popularity, lasting all the rest of his life.

The first of his "Songs without Words" was published in 1830, having been originally composed for his sister Fanny. In this simple act he opened a new chapter of the literature for the piano. The form of the song without words had already been given in Field's nocturnes, the first of which were published in 1816; but Mendelssohn, by giving it the title, "*Song*, without Words," put the hearer in a different relation to the composition—that of seeking to find in the work a poetic suggestion in addition to pleasing melody and finely modulated harmony. This, also, is extremely characteristic of the romantic epoch, in which music has its origin in poetry. He had already written a number of those charming *capriccios*, in which the piano is treated with light staccato changing chords, such as Von Weber had suggested nearly twenty years earlier in his "*Moment Capriccio*," but which no writer brought to such perfection as Mendelssohn. These two styles of pianoforte writing—the fairy-like *scherzo*, and the "Song without Words," are Mendelssohn's specialties, in which no other writer can be compared with him. He also wrote a number of concertos for piano and orchestra, and one for violin, in which these two elements are very strong features. Without having the effective passage work of Thalberg, Liszt or Chopin, or the bold originality of Schumann, Mendelssohn was an extremely original and pleasing pianoforte writer. During his life, especially in the later part of it, he was somewhat over-estimated; but at the present time, through the emergence of Schumann from the obscurity into which Mendelssohn's reputation cast him, the works of Mendelssohn are often underestimated. He opened a new chapter in tone-poetry, popularizing pianoforte sentiment.

The famous G minor concerto for the piano was first produced in Munich in 1831. In the same year he went to Paris, where many of his works were performed and others were composed. The next year he was in London again, when the Hebrides overture was produced and the first book of "Songs without Words" was published. He also played the organ at several of the churches, and excited general admiration by his vigorous style. He is said to have been the first to play a Bach pedal fugue in England, certainly the first to play any of the important ones. In 1833 he was settled at Düsseldorf, as musical director of the church and two associations. There he immediately instituted a reform in the music of the church, and in the character of the selections for concert. In the church there were masses by Beethoven and Cherubini, motettes by Palestrina, and cantatas by Bach. The next year his oratorio of "St. Paul" was begun. In 1837 he was married to a very charming lady—Miss Cecilia Jeanrenaud, daughter of a clergyman of the Reformed Church at Frankfort. Very soon after the wedding he was in London and Birmingham, where he conducted "St. Paul" and commenced to prepare the libretto for his oratorio of "Elijah." Among the Bach fugues which he played in London on the organ at this time were the D major, the G minor, the E major, the C minor and the short E minor. His pedal playing was very highly esteemed.

Fig. 85.

MORITZ HAUPTMANN.

In 1835 he commenced to conduct the *Gewandhaus* concerts at Leipsic, and the celebrated conservatory there was founded in 1843. The first professors were Hauptmann, David, Schumann, Pohlenz and C.F. Becker. Ferdinand David (1810-1873) was the greatest master of the violin during the third quarter of the century. Moritz Hauptmann (1792-1868), originally a violinist, was one of the most original theorists of this century. His greatest work, "Harmony and Meter," was published in 1853. Soon afterward Moscheles became associated with them. The city of Leipsic remained his home during the remainder of his life. The founding of the conservatory may have been hastened by certain plans which Mendelssohn had endeavored three years before to get adopted in Berlin, where there was a project for founding a royal music school upon a different basis from any at that time existing. From some change in the ministry, or temporary political disturbance, the plan fell through, but in Leipsic it was carried out. This famous school from that time forward, for nearly fifty years, exercised an influence greater than that of any other music school in the world. Among its graduates are a very large number of the most successful teachers and celebrated professional musicians. They had been drawn to Leipsic by the reputation given the conservatory by the possession of such masters as Mendelssohn, Schumann, Hauptmann, Moscheles, Plaidy, Dr. Paul, Becker, Brendel, Reinecke and others. After Mendelssohn's death, indeed, the tradition of his ideas hampered the efficiency of the school to some extent, but very thorough work has always been done there. During his four years' connection with the conservatory Mendelssohn conducted the *Gewandhaus* concerts and superintended the entire educational operations of the school. In addition to this he conducted a succession of important festivals in all parts of Europe, producing new works of his own, and the greatest works of the masters before him. He made a great reputation as concert pianist, playing his own concertos and those of Beethoven, as well as the *Concertstück* of Von Weber. Everywhere he improvised upon the organ or the piano, and through all the admiration which he received remained the same simple, unaffected, sincere artist that he was when a boy. His home life was very happy. In Ferdinand Hiller's reminiscences many charming pictures of it are given.

The greatest of Mendelssohn's works was "Elijah," which was produced at Birmingham, August 26, 1846. Staudigl, the famous baritone of Vienna, was Elijah. The work went extremely well at the first performance—better, Mendelssohn says, than any former work of his. The continual anxiety of producing the new work, the travel and the many responsibilities belonging to his position finally undermined his health, and at length, November 4, 1847, he died at Leipsic. It is doubtful whether any musician ever left a warmer or a more distinguished circle of friends than Mendelssohn. In all parts of the musical world his death was regarded as a calamity.

Fig. 86.

FELIX MENDELSSOHN BARTHOLDY.

In "Elijah" and in the first part of "St. Paul" Mendelssohn made an addition to the world's stock of oratorios scarcely second to any other works, excepting Händel's "Messiah." "Elijah," in particular, had the advantage of an extremely dramatic and picturesque story, and a text well selected from the Scriptures. There are many moments in this work of rare and exquisite beauty. The choruses when contrapuntally developed, have themes somewhat too short, whereby the effect of the words is lost in the intermingling of voices coming in at later moments, but there are other parts of the work which are extremely beautiful. There is a lovely chorus, "He Watching over Israel," in which the gentle Mendelssohnian melody is accompanied by soft triplets in the strings, whereby a most delightfully light and *spirituelle* effect is produced. Near the end of the work there is a very graphic recitative to the words, "And One Cherub Cried to Another"; then a soprano voice with grand phrase sings "Holy, Holy Is God, the Lord," three other soprano voices joining in the last words. These are very lightly accompanied. Immediately thereupon, the entire chorus, orchestra and organ, with the utmost power, come in with the same melody, "Holy, Holy Is God, the Lord." This antiphon between the full chorus and the female quartette continues in varying style throughout the chorus, and the result is thrilling in the extreme. Extremely dramatic, also, is the great chorus "Thanks Be to God, for He Laveth the Thirsty Land." There are many solo numbers in the work, all of them remarkable for the care with which the text is treated, and the clearness with which the musical utterance expresses the words. The famous tenor song, "If with All Your Hearts Ye Truly Seek Him," the alto song, "Oh Rest in the Lord," the angel trio, "Lift Thine Eyes," the great soprano song, "Hear Ye Israel," and the bass aria, "It Is Enough," and especially the prayer of Elijah, "Lord God of Abraham, Isaac and Israel," are scarcely surpassed in the entire range of oratorio music. There is very remarkable instrumentation, also in the scenes on Mt. Carmel, and especially at the series of choruses where "God, the Lord, Passed By."

During his life, Mendelssohn was very highly esteemed as a composer of orchestral music, symphonies and overtures. While his works in this department contain many beauties, and are carried out with elegant clearness of form, and with that refinement and taste which characterized everything which Mendelssohn did, they have not maintained their reputation at the high level where it formerly stood. It was Mendelssohn's fortune to be one of the masters instrumental in introducing the romantic school; but upon principle and education he was classical in his taste and instincts, and while his works had a very important use in cultivating an appetite for novelty, whereby the other masters of the romantic school profited later, he went so short a distance in the new path that the march of events has since left him somewhat behind.

II.

If it were asked to name the two masters most representative of the nineteenth century, one could scarcely go amiss, the names of Robert Schumann and Richard Wagner immediately occurring. Robert Schumann (1810-1856), the son of a very intelligent book seller, was born at Zwickau, in Saxony, and was intended for the law. He received lessons in music at an early age, and his talent was unmistakable. When he was about eleven he accompanied a performance of Frederick Schneider's "*Weltgericht.*" At home, with the aid of some musical companions he got up performances of musical compositions, and had a small orchestra. He entered at the Leipsic University as a student of law, but devoted the most of his time to playing the piano, and to reading Jean Paul, for whom he had a great fondness. He immediately attached himself to the musical circles, entering himself as a pupil with Wieck, the father of his future wife. A year later he transferred his attendance to the University of Heidelberg, attracted thither by the lectures of the famous teacher Thibaut, the same whose work upon the "Purity of Musical Art," had only recently been published. Here, as in Leipsic, his principal occupation was practicing upon the piano, which he did to the extent of six or seven hours a day. Notwithstanding his fondness for music, his mother was violently opposed to his entering the musical profession, and as his father was now dead, her wishes naturally had much weight. He had already commenced to write songs, quite a number of which belong to the year 1830, when he was living in Heidelberg.

He made a tour to the north of Italy, and heard the Italian musician Paganini, which fired him with so much ardor, that he immediately set himself to transcribe his Caprices for the piano, and to accomplish upon this instrument similar effects to those which Paganini produced upon the violin. At length, after much difficulty with his guardian and his mother, it was agreed that he might fit himself for a musician, so in 1830 he was back again in Leipsic studying diligently with Master Wieck. In his ardor for great results in a short time, he undertook some kind of mechanical discipline for the fourth finger of his right hand, the effect of which was that the tendons became overstrained, the finger crippled, and for a long time he was utterly unable to use it in piano playing. In composition he now entered upon regular instruction with Heinrich Dorn, at that time conductor of the opera in Leipsic. Dorn recognized the greatness of Schumann's genius, and devoted himself with much interest to his improvement. In 1832 a symphony of his was produced in Zwickau, but apparently with little success, for the work was never heard of afterward. At this same concert

Wieck's daughter, Clara, who was then thirteen years of age, appeared as a pianist, and Zwickau, Schumann says, "was fired with enthusiasm for the first time in its life." Already he was very much interested in the promising girl, and expresses himself concerning her with much ardor. He seems to have been singularly slow in composition. At this time, 1833, he had written the first and third movements of the G minor sonata, had commenced the F minor sonata and completed the "Toccata," which had been begun four years before. He also arranged the second set of Paganini's caprices, Opus 10. He found a faithful friend in Frau Voigt, a pianist of sense and ability. Schumann usually passed his evenings in a restaurant in company with his friends, after the German fashion, but while the others talked he usually remained silent. Frau Voigt told W. Taubert that one lovely summer evening after making music with Schumann, they both felt inclined to go upon the water. They sat side by side in the boat for an hour in silence. At parting Schumann pressed her hand and said, "Good day, we have perfectly understood one another."

The immediate result of the musical associations of Schumann, in Leipsic, was the project for a musical journal, devoted to progress and sincerity. In opera Rossini was then the ruling force. At the piano Herz and Hünten; and musical journalism was represented by *Allgemeine Musikalische Zeitung*, published by Breitkopf & Härtel, which praised almost everything, upon general principles. In 1834, the first number of the *Neue Zeitschrift für Musik* saw the light. The editors were Robert Schumann, Friedrich Wieck, Ludwig Schunke and Julius Knorr. Schumann was the ruling power, and he proceeded to develop his literary faculty in a variety of forms. He writes under many pseudonyms, and has much to say about the "David league against the Philistines," a society existing in his imagination only. One of the famous early articles in this paper was that upon Chopin's variation "*La ci Darem*," greeting the work of the talented young Pole as a production of rare genius. Schumann himself thought so well of this article that he placed it at the beginning of his collected writings. It will be impossible within available limits to define the influence of this journal. During the ten years when Schumann was editor, many of the most important productions of the modern school first saw the light, and all come in for discussion, from a point of view at the same time sympathetic and intelligent.

As an example of the musical life at Leipsic in this time, Moscheles mentions an evening in 1835, when Mendelssohn conducted his first concert in the *Gewandhaus*; the day before this there had been a musical gathering at Wieck's, at which both Mendelssohn and Schumann were present, perhaps the first time that these two great geniuses were brought together. The next day Mendelssohn, Schumann, Moscheles and Banck dined together, and the next day there was music at Wieck's house—

Moscheles, Clara Wieck and L. Rakemann from Bremen, playing Bach's D minor concerto for three pianos, Mendelssohn putting in the orchestral accompaniments on the fourth piano. With Mendelssohn he contracted quite an intimacy. In 1836 he found himself very much devoted to Clara Wieck, and in order to secure a more favorable opening for his career, resolved to transfer himself and the paper to Vienna, but after a year he returned again to Leipsic, and then the course of true love became more difficult, for Papa Wieck was resolutely opposed to the match; but after some months his consent was given, and they were married in 1840. During this year he had an extraordinary activity as a song writer. The "Woman's Love and Life," the "Poet's Love," and various other cycles of song, were all produced under the stress of his happy prospects with Clara. It is not easy to ascertain the order of his compositions, since, as we have already seen, the sonatas and some of the other works appearing late in the list of opus numbers were composed very early.

The romantic tendency is the most marked of all of Schumann's characteristics as a composer. He is above all others the composer of moods. His long pieces are invariably aggregates of shorter ones. The typical forms of Schumann's thought are two, and two only, the Song and the Fantasia. He made diligent efforts to master counterpoint and fugue, and manly attempts in these provinces can be found among his writings; but counterpoint and fugue remained to him a foreign language. The smoothness of Mendelssohn, the readiness of Bach, of Beethoven, or even Mozart, are impossible to him. On the other hand, when he follows his own inclination, he creates forms that are clear, concise and original. One scarcely knows which to admire more—the graphic correspondence of the music with the suggestive title placed at the head, or the original style of the music itself, which is entirely unlike anything by any former composer. His Opus 2 is a set called *Papillons,* "Butterflies," or "Scenes at a Ball," consisting of twelve short movements in different style, without explanatory titles. Some are fantastic, others are sentimental, all original and striking. The eleventh number of this is a short but magnificent polonaise in D major, an extremely spirited and beautiful movement which has since been very popular. The transcriptions of the Paganini caprices were undertaken as studies for the composer himself in the direction of unexplored pianoforte effects, but Schumann had also the intention of providing in music new discipline for piano students. In my opinion the technical value of these works has not yet been realized, and it is quite possible that a later generation may esteem them more highly than the present. However this may be, the practice of writing gave Schumann a greater freedom, the effect of which is seen upon the next set of pieces, the six *Intermezzi*. These, however, are vague and mystical, rather than clear. With the "David's League Dances" the Schumann nature appears more plainly. The style is freer, and these new combinations are very charming, although they must undoubtedly have been fatal stumbling blocks to the fingers of a pianist trained in Dussek and Hünten. "The Carnival," a series of fanciful scenes, belongs to an earlier period, having been composed in 1834 and 1835. The different numbers, of which there are twenty-one, are provided with explanatory titles, such as "Pierrot," "Harlequin," "Valse Noble," "Eusebius," "Chopin," etc. Of all the earlier works the Fantasy-Pieces, Opus 12, are the most successful. These eight pictures, "In the Evening," "Soaring," "Why," "Whims," "In the Night," "Fable," "Dreams," and "The End of the Song," or peroration, are extremely characteristic and beautiful, and it is not easy to assign the pre-eminence of one number over the others. Of the same general class, only upon a smaller scale, are the "Scenes from Childhood," Opus 15, of which there are thirteen little pieces, each with an explanatory title, such as "Playing Tag," "Happy Enough," "Dreams" (*Traumerei*). In this direction Schumann often composed at a later period of his life. There is the "Album for the Young," Opus 68, containing forty-three short pieces, all with titles; the twenty "Album Leaves," Opus 124, and the "Forest Scenes," with titles like "The Entrance," "The Hunter on the Lookout," "Solitary Flowers," "Prophetic Bird," "Hunting Song," etc.

Schumann's greatness as a composer for the pianoforte, both from a technical and poetic standpoint, is shown in such works as the "*Études Symphoniques*," the "*Kreisleriana*," and the concerto in A minor. The first of these works is regarded by many as the most satisfactory of any of this author's works. It consists of an air, nine variations and a finale which is in rondo form. The variations, however, are fantasies rather than variations, the theme itself appearing very little in any of them, and in some of them not at all. It would be impossible to find within the same compass a similar number of pages covering so wide a range of beautiful pianoforte effects, and highly suggestive and poetic music. In the fantasia in C, Schumann's fancy takes on a more serious mood. He treats the piano with great freedom, requiring of the player a powerful touch and much refinement of tone-color, as well as a style of technique which he himself has largely created. The second movement of this, the march tempo, represents Schumann's imagination in a forcible light in two directions—its bold, strong moods, and its deeply subjective, meditative activity. The "*Kreisleriana*" consists of eight fantasies named after an old schoolmaster near Leipsic, noted for his eccentricities. This work was coldly received when first produced, but later has become very popular. The best movements are the first and second, but the entire work is strong. The concerto in A minor is by no means a show piece for the piano, but an extremely vigorous and poetic improvisation, in which the solo and orchestral instruments answer each other, and work together in a furor of inspiration.

The entire art of modern piano playing is indebted to Schumann for some of its most impressive elements. He was fond of playing with the dampers raised, and might well contest the honor with Liszt of having originated the modern style of pedal legato as distinguished from the finger legato of Chopin and all the early writers. He seems to have discovered the touch which Mason called elastic; that made by shutting the hand and at the same allowing the wrist to remain flexible. In quite a number of his pieces this effect is very marked, as the first number of "*Kreisleriana*," the first of the "Night Pieces," and especially the fourth of these, where the chords are purposely spread beyond the octave, in order to necessitate their being struck with the finger and arm touch combined, in the same manner as that illustrated on a larger scale in the eleventh study of Chopin's, Opus 10. Indeed, if one were to attempt to characterize the Schumann technique by some one of its more prominent features, the free use of the arm would be, perhaps, the one best representing the depth and sonority of tone required for these effects. But while Schumann demands broad, deep, elastic tone color for the stronger moments in his work, there is no other writer so desirous as he of the soft, full, mysterious tone representing what he was fond of calling *Innigkeit* ("inwardness"). There are many minor mannerisms which have been diligently cultivated by later composers, the most prominent among them being perhaps what might be called the accompaniment upon the off beat. In many of his works Schumann occupies the middle ground of the piano with soft chords which are felt rather than heard, and which always come in upon the half beat or the quarter beat, and rarely or never upon the full accented part of a measure. The differentiation of the melody from its harmonic and rhythmic background is accomplished by this great master in a beautiful manner. Take for instance, the romanze in F sharp, Opus 28, No. 2. The melody of the first strophe of this exquisite music might have been written for Church. It is a duet for baritones, the voices being represented by the thumbs of the player. Against this melody in quarter notes and eighths, there is an accompaniment in sixteenths, covering two octaves and a third, the entire effect being soft and distant. In the second strophe the soprano voice takes the melody, which is supported by rare harmonies and a lovely figuration in the alto. The third strophe brings back again the principal subject, and a splendid climax is made, after which an elaborate coda concludes the work. It is impossible to play this lovely piece with good effect without the Schumann technique. Played with the Mozart technique it would be simply insipid, and with a Beethoven technique it would still be dry and harsh. It is only by the combination of the arm touch for the melody, the very obscure, unobtrusive finger touch for the accompaniment, and the constant use of the pedal for promoting blending of tones, that the vague and poetic atmosphere of this piece can be realized.

Schumann might also be credited with the invention of a new style of composition, or of music thinking. The element of canonic imitation occurs in his works in wholly new form. A single phrase or motive is repeated through nearly an entire movement, in a thousand different forms and transformations, so that the whole movement is made up from this single germ; and yet with such mastery of rhythm and of harmony as to conduct the thought to a powerful climax, without any impression of monotony interfering with it. One can hardly go amiss in the large works of Schumann for illustrations of this style of composition. Take, for example, the Novelette in B minor, Opus 99; the Novelette in E major, Opus 21, No. 7; the first of the "*Kreisleriana,*" and many other parts of the same work. This style I have elsewhere called the "Thematic," as distinguished from the "Lyric," in which a flowing melody is a distinctive trait. Beethoven, in a number of cases, employs a style of thought development somewhat similar, but the results accomplished are tamer than with Schumann. One of the most striking examples is found in the finale of the sonata in D minor, Opus 31, No. 2, and in the first movement of the sonata in C minor, Opus 111. In this point of view Schumann appears as the predecessor of Wagner, who almost certainly took his departure for thematic work from Schumann.

If it were not for these numerous, highly poetic and masterly compositions for pianoforte solo, and for the chamber pieces, the symphonies and other large works, Schumann would have been entitled to a very eminent place among composers by his songs alone. These are as different as possible from those of previous writers, excepting Schubert, and the voice itself is not always well considered in them; but there are no other works in this department in which the poetic sentiment is so thoroughly reproduced in the music as Schumann has done it in his "Woman's Love and Life," and in "Poet's Love," and in many single songs of other sets, "The Spring Night" being a very marked example. If the future should chance to produce a race of poetic and intelligent singers, these songs will be found among the most effective which the whole literature of music can show. Some of them are already well and favorably known in all parts of the world.

The excellencies of Schumann as a song writer are only in part reproduced in his larger works in the form of cantatas, and in the opera of "*Genoveva.*" He was without the technique of chorus construction, and writes injudiciously for voices in mass. His instrumentation, although graphically conceived, is not cleverly worked out, in consequence of which we find in such works as the "Pilgrimage of the Rose," "Paradise and the Peri," the "Faust" music, and the opera of "*Genoveva,*" some extremely brilliant suggestions and contrasts, and occasionally fine moments, intermingled with many others which fail for want of technical skill in the use of the performing material.

The same restriction may be applied to the orchestral and chamber works, in spite of the inherent force and beauty of the ideas they contain. In the symphony, for example, he writes badly for the violins, the very soul of the orchestra. The phrases are short, staccato notes abound, and scarcely in an entire score have the violinists the long sustained phrases, where the singing power of this beautiful instrument appears. The best of the chamber pieces are those in which the piano is the principal instrument, especially the great quintette. This is a master work of a very high order, and while the strings do not have the consideration that belongs to them, the pianoforte is treated with so much freedom and power as in a great measure to compensate for this lack.

Of the Schumann works as a whole the most striking characteristic is the spontaneous, improvistic effect. Every Schumann piece—that is to say, every *successful* Schumann piece—has the character of an improvisation, in which the power and fancy of the composer are as marked as his deep tenderness and sentiment, fine instinct for poetic effect and a delicate ear for tone-color. For this reason the popular appreciation of the Schumann works upon a large scale is only a question of an educated generation. There are many indications of progress in this direction on the part of musical amateurs the world over. In Schumann's lifetime, and immediately after his death, the neglect of his compositions was extreme. Dr. Wm. Mason narrates that when he visited Leipsic in 1850, one of the first symphonies he heard was Schumann's in B flat, the first composition of this writer he had ever heard. The beauty and force of the work took complete possession of him. A new world of tone was opened to him. He dreamed of the Schumann symphony all night, and at early morning went down to Breitkopf & Härtel's to inquire whether this man Schumann had written anything for the piano. The salesman laid before him a few dusty compositions off the shelves. The young American asked, "Is that all?" More were produced. "Is that all?" he asked again, whereupon the salesman, discovering that he had a Schumann enthusiast to deal with, took advantage of the moment and in the cellar showed him whole editions of Schumann pianoforte pieces tied up in bundles, exactly as they had come from the printers. Liszt in some of his earlier concerts attempted to patronize the Schumann compositions. Their style, however, was so different from the sensationalism of his own pieces or the sentiment of Chopin, that the public failed to appreciate them, and the pianist dropped them. Nevertheless, there were reasons why Liszt ought to have played these works. The Schumann technique is not sensational, like that of Liszt, but it has with it one element in common, already referred to—the pedal legato—and no pianist of that time was so well prepared to recognize and interpret this element as Liszt if he had realized his opportunity.

Fig. 87.

ROBERT SCHUMANN.

In person Schumann was of medium height, inclining to corpulency, with a very soft and gentle walk and a most invincible habit of silence. Old residents of Leipsic remember his visits to the rehearsals at the *Gewandhaus*, where for a whole evening he would sit with his handkerchief held over his mouth, never speaking a word to any one from the beginning to the end, and going away as silently as he came. Nevertheless, it was universally recognized that upon these occasions Schumann heartily enjoyed himself, and to use his own words again, he and the music "perfectly understood one another." His mind was intensely active and fanciful. This is seen in all his pieces. The rapidity of the musical thought, the strong contrasts of mood, the proximity of remote chords and modulations, are all indications of this mental trait. It was this, also, which finally destroyed him. His mind became unbalanced, and after intermittent attacks of melancholy his life ended with two years' almost entire oblivion of reason. In spite of his comparative unpopularity in his own day, no one of the romantic masters has left so strong an impression upon the composers who came after him. In my opinion, the four great names which have been most operative in establishing forms of musical thought and in creating wholly original and highly poetic and masterly tone-poems by means of those forms, are Bach, Beethoven, Schumann and Wagner, and each one of the earlier masters has in his work the prophecy of most of the qualities of those who come after, while each of the later reflects the characteristic traits of his predecessors.

CHAPTER XXXVII.
ITALIAN OPERA DURING THE
NINETEENTH
CENTURY.

THE strongest personality of the Italian composers (though by no means the loveliest), at the beginning of the nineteenth century, was that of Gasparo Spontini (1774-1851). He was born of peasant stock in the Roman states and educated at Naples, where his boyish successes were made. In 1803 he went to Paris, where he composed several operas with very poor success. Nevertheless, having full confidence in his own powers, he was not discouraged, and in 1804 his one-act opera of "Milton" was performed successfully at the *Théatre Feydeau*. He had already begun his "*La Vestale*," which was brought out in 1807, and immediately achieved a remarkable success. Spontini was appointed "*Compositeur Particulaire*" to the Empress Josephine, in spite of which an oratorio of his was hissed from the stage in Holy Week of the same year that his "*Vestale*" had been so favorably received. The popularity of "The Vestal" continued to grow, so that it had been performed more than 200 times in Paris before 1824. In Italy and Germany, where its career began, in 1811, its popularity was similar. His next opera was "*Fernand Cortez,*" (1809), afterward materially improved. These two works mark the highest point reached by Spontini. They are brilliant, martial, vigorous and spectacular, and the legitimate predecessors of the Meyerbeer grand operas. Spontini's smaller works failed, and in 1819 negotiations were concluded with King William III, who had been impressed with "*La Vestale*" when he had visited Paris, whereby for twenty years Spontini was made "director general" of the opera in Berlin. In this position he produced a number of other works, the best being "*Nurmahal*" (1822), "*Alcidor*" (1825) and "*Agnes von Hohenstaufen*" (1829). Spontini was a vigorous director, but unprincipled, vain and narrow. Nevertheless, at his concerts he produced the fifth and seventh symphonies of Beethoven for the first time in Berlin, as well as parts of the great Bach mass in B minor, and much other great music. Opposition to his tyranny culminated in 1842 by his dismission from the directorship, Meyerbeer being his successor. His popularity paled from the production of Weber's "*Der Freischütz*" in 1821. Spontini died in his native town of Majolitat.

Fig. 88.

ROSSINI.

The Italian composer most famous in the earlier part of the century was Gioacchino Antonio Rossini (1792-1868), a native of Pesaro, a small town on the Adriatic. After a short course at the Conservatory of Verona, the boy commenced to compose, and no less than thirteen short pieces preceded his first really popular opera, "*Tancredi,*" which was produced at *La Fenice*, in Venice, in 1813. The success of this work led to many others, among which the best known are "The Italian in Algiers," "The Turk in Italy," and (in 1816) no less than five operas in one year—"*Torvaldo e Dorliska,*" "The Barber of Seville," "*La Gazetta*" and "*Otello,*" his first serious opera. He composed with the utmost facility. "The Barber," one of the most successful operas ever performed, and the one of Rossini's works which bids fair to outlast the rest, was composed and mounted within a month. For this work he received eighty pounds sterling. It was not at first successful. In 1823 he brought out "*Semiramide,*" which was only moderately successful at first. The next turn in Rossini's fortune found him in London, where he had accepted an engagement with the manager of King's Theater, and here he produced a number of his former works with moderate success. Rossini himself appeared upon the stage and sang the solos in a cantata which he had composed in honor of the King, George IV. He turned many honest pennies during his London engagement by acting as accompanist at private *soirées* for a fee of £50. At the end of five months he found himself in possession of £7,000, with which he made a graceful retreat to Paris, where he accepted the musical direction of the *Théatre Italienne*, at the salary of £800 per year. This was in 1826. After the expiration of his engagement at this theater several of his works were produced at the Grand Opera, among which were the "Siege of Corinth" and "*Moise*" (March 27, 1827). This work, which is given in England as an oratorio, was a revised edition of his opera of "Mose," which he had written for Naples five years before. The most taking number in it is the famous prayer, which has been played and sung in every form possible for a popular melody. The operatic career of Rossini ended in 1829 with the production of his opera of "William Tell," at the Paris *Académie*, with a brilliant cast. In this work he forswears florid writing, and makes a serious effort at dramatic characterization. The opera is extremely melodious, and a very great advance over any of his former productions. Having now accumulated a fortune, he retired from the stage and lived the remainder of his life near Paris in elegant leisure, composing a solemn mass and a few other sacred works, but no other operas.

In reviewing the career of this singularly gifted Italian melodist, it is impossible to resist the conclusion that his talents were worthy of a nobler development. Among his sacred works the "*Stabat Mater*" is the most popular. It contains some very beautiful chromatic writing, and is really an art work of distinguished merit. His latest work was the "*Messe Solennelle*" (1864). Rossini was fond of good living, very witty in conversation, and his house was frequented by the most brilliant wits and the best artists of the thirty years between "William Tell" and his death.

Upon the whole, the most brilliant master of Italian opera during this period was Gaetano Donizetti (1797-1848), who was born at Bergamo and educated at Naples. His first opera was produced in Vienna in 1818, but his first complete success was "*Anna Bolena*," which was written for Milan in 1830, the principal parts having been taken by Pasta and Rubini. Soon after this followed "*L'Elisir d'Amore*" (1832), "*Lucia di Lammermoor*" (Naples, 1835), "*Lucrezia Borgia*" (1834), "*Belisario*" (1836), "*Poliuto*" (1838), "*La Fille du Régiment*" (1840), "*La Favorita*," "*Linda di Chamounix*" (1842), "*Don Pasquale*" (1843). Besides these well known works there were many others, the total number reaching sixty-three, brought out in various Italian theaters and in Paris. Donizetti's traits as a composer are pleasant melody, effective concerted pieces (as, for instance, the sextette in "*Lucia*," which is perhaps the best concerted piece in Italian opera), and a good constructive ability. Like Rossini he was a writer of florid music, and "*Lucia*" remains one of the favorite numbers of *coloratura* singers to the present day, which, considering that more than fifty years have intervened since it was composed, is a great compliment.

Vincenzo Bellini (1802-1835) was born at Catania, in Switzerland, the son of an organist. He was educated at Naples under Zingarelli, his first opera having been composed in 1826, while he was still a member of the Conservatory. It was "*Bianca e Fernando*," produced at San Carlos. His next work, "*Il Pirata*," was written for *La Scala* in Milan, the tenor part having been especially designed for the celebrated Rubini. Among the other successful operas of this composer were "*I Capuletti e i Montecchi*" (in 1830), "*La Sonnambula*" (1831, at *La Scala*), "*Norma*" and "*I Puritani*." It was this latter work which contains a brilliant duet for two basses, "*Suona la Tromba*," of which Rossini wrote from Paris to a friend at Milan, "It is unnecessary for me to write of the duet for two basses. You must have heard it." Bellini was essentially a melodist, a lyric composer of ideallic *naiveté*. Of dramatic power he had very little. His orchestration is simple, although frequently very sonorous. If he had lived to the age of Donizetti or of Rossini it is not impossible that much greater works would have emanated from his pen, for in his next great successor we have an example of such a growth under conditions less favorable than those promised in Bellini's case.

Fig. 89.

GIUSEPPE VERDI.

The most vigorous of all the Italian composers of this epoch is Giuseppe Verdi, who was born at Roncole, October 9, 1813, his father having been a small inn keeper. The boy was of a quiet, melancholy character, with one passion—music; and when he was seven years of age his father purchased a spinet for his practice. When he was ten years old he was appointed organist of the Church in his native town. At this time his necessary expenditures amounted to about $22 per year, and his salary as organist $7.20, which after many urgent appeals was increased to $8. In addition he had certain perquisites from weddings and funerals, amounting to about $10 per year. In this way he continued until he was sixteen, having by this time become conductor of a philharmonic society, and the composer of quite a number of works, at the little town of Dusseto. He went to Milan, where he was refused admission to the Conservatory on the ground of his showing no special aptitude for music. Nevertheless, he persevered in his chosen vocation, receiving lessons of Rolla, the conductor of *La Scala*. He studied diligently for two years, Mozart's "*Don Giovanni*" being a part of his daily exercise. After this he returned for five years to his country life, and by the time he was twenty-five he was back again in Milan, in the hope of securing the performance of his opera, "*Oberto.*" This for quite a long time he was unable to do, but at length in 1839 it was performed at *La Scala*. The moderate success of this work secured him an engagement to produce an opera every eight months for Milan or Vienna. But his first work, a comic opera which the managers demanded, "*Un Giorno di Regno,*" was a dead failure, and disgusted the composer to such a point that he declared that he would never write again. At this time Verdi was the victim of most severe affliction. In addition to poverty, within the space of about two months he experienced the loss of his two children and of his wife, to whom he was devotedly attached. After living some time in Milan, he received a copy of the libretto, "*Il Proscritto,*" and in 1842 it was performed. It was well staged, and achieved an unqualified success. Then followed "*I Lombardi*" (1843), "*Ernani*" (1844), "*I Due Foscari*" (1844), "*Attila*" (1846), "Macbeth" (1847), "*Rigoletto*" (1851), "*Il Trovatore*" (1853), "*La Traviata*" (1853), "*Les Vepres Siciliennes*" (1855), "*Un Ballo in Maschera*" (1859), "*La Forza del Destino*" (1862), "*Don Carlos*" (1867), "*Aida*" (1871), "*Otello*" (1887). In addition to these works he has written a great "Requiem Mass," and many smaller works. Besides the operas above mentioned there were several others now mostly forgotten, the total number being twenty-nine; and there is not one of them that does not contain more or less of striking melody, with effective concerted pieces and choruses. Verdi's melody was much more vigorous than that of either of his predecessors. In "*Trovatore*" there are ten or twelve numbers which have become famous in the barrel-organ repertory. His instrumentation was very full and sonorous, and his dramatic instinct excellent. We do not find the long roulades and ornamental passages according to the taste of his predecessors, but instead of them, clear, sharp, concise, manly melodies—unfortunately, however, they are so near the line of the vulgar that only a refined treatment on the part of the singer can save them for poetry and beauty.

Beginning with "*Aida*," a very important change can be seen in Verdi's style. By the time this work was undertaken the Wagnerian theories were attracting general attention, and it was impossible that a man of Verdi's intellectual force should have failed to be affected by them. "*Aida*" is much more refined and dramatically truthful than any of those before it. As the composer was now an old man nothing farther was expected from his pen. Nevertheless, in "*Otello*," he has given the world a masterpiece of a still higher order, the music throughout being subservient to the story, while the dramatic handling of the work is masterly in the extreme. For this he was in part indebted to his librettist, the distinguished poet and composer, Signor Arrigo Boito. The strangest thing in regard to Verdi is that at the present writing (1891) he is engaged upon a comic opera, "Falstaff," a subject which he says has interested him for about forty years, but which until now he has never had time to undertake. As a man and a patriot Verdi is held in the highest possible honor in Italy; and for his own original genius, as displayed in his works, and especially in his aptitude for progress, no less than for his dignified and simple private life, he deserves to be admired as the foremost Italian master of the present century.

One of the most earnest among Italian composers and musicians is Arrigo Boito (1842), who, from an origin which is German from his mother's side, possesses an earnestness and force in music not usual in southern lands. After composing two cantatas, which had a good success, his grand opera of "*Mefistofele*" was produced at Milan in 1868, and later in other leading cities. Two more operas "Hero and Leander" and "Nero" are not yet published. M. Boito is equally celebrated in his own country as musician and as poet. In the latter capacity he prepared his own librettos, besides furnishing that of "*Otello*" to Verdi and "*La Gioconda*" to Ponchielli. He has published several books of poems, and other operatic books. As composer he partakes much of the spirit of Wagner. He has yet another opera nearly completed, but in 1891 little is known of it. It is called "*Orestiade.*"

Amilcare Ponchielli (1834-1866) is generally regarded in Italy as having been the most distinguished Italian composer after Verdi. He was educated at Milan, but his early triumphs were made elsewhere, his famous "*I Promessi Sposi*" having been performed there only in 1872. His principal works are the preceding, which was composed in 1856, "*La Savojarda*" (1861), "*Roderico*" (1864), "*La Stella del Monte*" (1867), "*La Gioconda*," his master work, produced at *La Scala*, 1876, and "*Marion Delorme*" (1885). His music occupies a middle ground between the melodiousness of the Italian composers of the early part of the century and the seriousness of later German opera.

In spite of the few examples reaching foreign countries, there is a continuous and rather abundant production of light and serious operas in Italy, every principal theater making it a point to bring out one or more new works every season. The best of these, after a long interval, become known abroad. It is a great mistake to suppose that the few Italian operas of recent date performed in England and America adequately represent the present state of Italian art.

CHAPTER XXXVIII.
FRENCH OPERATIC COMPOSERS OF THE NINETEENTH CENTURY.

IN the earlier part of the nineteenth century the operatic stage of Paris shared with those of Berlin and Dresden the honor of producing brilliant novelties by the best composers. In France there had been a persistent cultivation of this province of musical creation, and many talented composers have appeared upon the scene of the Grand Opera and that of the *Opéra Comique*. French opera has developed into a genre of its own, rhythmically well regulated, instrumented in a pleasing and attractive manner, and staged with considerable reference to spectacular display.

Fig. 90.

AUBER.

The oldest of these masters to achieve distinction, and the one most successful in gaining the ear of other countries than France, was Daniel

François Esprit Auber (1782-1870). He was born in Caen, in Normandy, of a family highly gifted and artistic in temperament. Nevertheless, his father intended him for a merchant, and sent him to England in 1804, in the hope that the study of commercial success there might wean him from his love of music. But the boy came back more musical than ever. After composing several pieces, a little opera, a mass, etc., his first opera to be publicly performed was "*Le Séjour Militaire.*" During the fifteen years next following he wrote a succession of light operas for the smaller theaters of Paris, most of them with librettos by Scribe. No one of these works had more than a temporary success, and the names are not sufficiently important to be given here. At length, in 1828, he produced his master work, "*La Muette di Portici,*" otherwise known as "*Masaniello,*" which at once placed its author upon the pinnacle of fame. This was an opera upon the largest scale, and was the first in order of the three great master works which adorned the Paris stage during this and the three years following. The others were Rossini's "Tell" in 1829, and Meyerbeer's "Robert" in 1831. The subject was fortunately related to the spirit of the times, Masaniello having been leader of the insurgents in Naples. The work well deserved its success, since for melody and pleasing effects it has rarely been surpassed. The overture is still much played as a concert number, but the opera itself has nearly left the stage, excepting in Germany, where it still has a distinguished place. All his later works were lighter than "*Masaniello.*" They were "*La Fiancée*" (1829), the extremely melodious and popular "*Fra Diavolo*" (1830) and many others, for more than twenty years still. Among them were "The Bronze Horse" (in 1835), "*Le Domino Noir*" (in 1837), and "The Crown Diamonds" (1831). Auber was elected member of the Institute in 1829, and in 1842 succeeded Cherubini as director of the Conservatory. He was an extremely witty and charming man, beloved by all.

Contemporaneous with Auber, but more allied to the genius of Boieldieu, was Louis Joseph Ferdinand Hérold, (1791-1833). After studying at the Conservatory and composing a number of operas which failed, or had but moderate success, he brought out "*Zampa,*" in 1831. This work had an extraordinary success, and its overture is still often heard. Another work "*Le Pré aux Clercs,*" (1832), is generally esteemed in France more highly than "*Zampa,*" but outside of his native country public opinion universally regards the latter as his best work. Hérold's operas are extremely well conceived from a dramatic point of view, and his melody has much of the sweet and flowing quality of the best Italian. His concerted numbers also are well made, and in all respects he is to be regarded as a master of high rank within the province of light opera, verging indeed upon the confines of the romantic type, like that of Weber.

The true successor of Boieldieu, with perhaps somewhat less of originality, was Adolphe Charles Adam, (1803-1856), son of a piano teacher in the Conservatory at Paris. His most lasting work was "*Le Postillon de Lonjumeau*" (1836), in which the German tenor Wachtel made himself so famous. Most of the other productions of this clever, but not deep, composer, are now forgotten. In their day they pleased.

The most important work of the last half century of French opera was the "*Faust*" of Charles François Gounod (1818-), produced in 1859. Gounod was born and educated at Paris, took the prize of Rome in 1837, after composing quite a number of works of a semi-religious character, in which direction he has always had a strong bias. His first opera was produced in 1854, "*La Nonne Sanglante.*" In 1852 he was made director of the Orpheonists, the male part singers of Paris, numbering many thousands, somewhat answering to the organization of the Tonic Sol-fa in England. "*Faust*" made an epoch in French opera. Its rich and sensuous music, its love melodies of melting tenderness, and the cleverness of the instrumentation, as well as its pleasing character, combine to place it in a category by itself. This was the beginning and the end of Gounod, for in his other works, while there is much cleverness and melodiousness, there is also much reminder of "*Faust.*" Perhaps the best of his later operas are "*Romeo et Juliette*" (1867), and "*Mireille*" (1864). Among the others were "*Cinq-Mars,*" "*Polyeucte,*" "*Le Tribute de Zamora.*" He has also written an oratorio, "The Redemption," produced at Birmingham in 1882, many numbers in which are truly imposing. As a whole the work is mystical and sensuous, rather than strong or inspired. A continuation of this work "*Mors et Vita*" was given at Birmingham in 1885, and the following year several times in America, under the direction of Mr. Theodore Thomas. In this work, a part of the text of which consists of the Latin hymn "*Dies Iræ,*" Gounod contrives to repeat certain of the sensational effects of Berlioz's work. Both these oratorios belong to an intermediate category in oratorio, sensational effects possible only in the concert room intervening with others planned entirely in a devotional and mystic spirit. As a composer, Gounod has two elements of strength.

He is first of all a lyrical composer of unusual merit, as can be seen in his "Oh that We Two were Maying," "Nazareth," "There Is a Green Hill Far Away," etc. His second element of greatness is his talent for well sounding and deliciously blending instrumentation, in which respect he is one of the best representatives of the French school. This quality is happily shown upon a small scale, in connection with the other already mentioned, in his famous "*Ave Maria,*" with violin and organ obligato, superimposed upon the first prelude in Bach's "Well Tempered Clavier." Unfortunately his structural ability is not equal to the strain of elaborate dramatic works, in which the interest greatly depends upon the music following the complications of the drama. In "Faust," and in all his other operas, the songs are the main attractions—the songs and the choruses. The finales are poorly constructed, with little invention and less progress of dramatic intensity.

Among the better composers of the later French school was Felix Marie Victor Massé (1822-1884), who experienced the usual fortunes of the better class of French composers, having taken the prize of Rome in 1844 and produced his first opera, "*La Chanteuse Voilée*," in 1850, which was followed by his "*Galathéa*" in 1852 and the "Marriage of Jeanette" in 1853. Encouraged by these successes he produced a large number of operas in Italy, of which the best were "*La Reine Topaze*" (1856) and "*Les Saisons*" (1855). In 1860 he became chorus master at the Academy of Music, and in 1866 professor of composition at the Conservatory. In 1872 he was elected to the Institute as successor of Auber. In addition to the works already mentioned he produced "Paul and Virginia" (1866), and several others, besides a number of songs. His last opera, "*Le Mort de Cleopatre*," was written during his long sickness, and on the whole was not a success.

Another pleasing French composer is Jules Émile Frédéric Massenet (1842-), who took the prize of Rome in 1863, and in 1867 produced his first opera, "*La Grande Tante*." In addition to this he composed a number of operas, "*Le Roi de Lahore*" (1877), "*Marie Madeleine*" (1873), an oratorio, and "Eve" in 1875. He has also written a number of orchestral suites which have been very popular in all countries. His latest work, "*Le Mage*," was produced at the Grand Opera, Paris, March, 1891.

One of the most brilliant and versatile of the French musicians of this generation is M. Camille Saint-Saëns (1835-), a virtuoso upon the piano and organ, and an orchestral tone-poet of very rare quality. Educated in the Conservatory, he composed his first symphony when he was sixteen, and was organist of the Church of St. Marri at the age of eighteen. In 1858 he became organist at the Madeleine. He has produced a number of operas, of which "*Le Timbre d'Argent*" (1887), "Samson and Delilah" (1877), and "*Etienne Marcel*" (1879), "Henry VIII" (1883) and "*Ascanio*," produced in 1890 at the Grand Opera. In addition to these, Saint-Saëns has produced a large number of orchestral pieces, including "*Le Mouet d'Omphale*," "*Le Dance Macabre*," and other symphonic poems of the programme character. He has also written several oratorios, of which "The Deluge" is the most important, and a large amount of chamber and pianoforte music. He is a brilliant writer about music, and is favorably known in Germany and all the rest of Europe as a virtuoso upon the piano and organ. His second concerto for piano is one of the best virtuoso pieces for that instrument. In his "*Melodie et Harmonie*," a collection of newspaper essays, he discusses many interesting questions. His fame with posterity is more likely to rest upon his orchestral pieces, which are extremely clever and interesting, than upon his operas. Personally he is said to be very witty and entertaining. He has been a member of the Institute since 1874.

Another French composer, versatile and well gifted in orchestral composition, is Clément Philibert Léo Délibes (1848-). After his education at the Conservatory, and his service as accompanist at the Grand Opera, he received, in 1866, a commission to compose a ballet, "*La Source*," in which he displayed such a wealth of melody and such fortunate rhythm that his talent was henceforth unmistakable. He has since composed a large number of ballets, many of which are known in all parts of the world, such as "Sylvia"; also a large number of songs. His principal opera was "Lakmé" (1883). He is a professor at the Conservatory, a member of the Legion of Honor, and the successor of Victor Massé at the Institute.

Still another very talented composer of orchestral music is Édouard Victor Antoine Lalo (1823-), who was originally a violinist in a favorite string quartette. He has composed a large amount of orchestral music, a violin concerto in F (1874), "*Symphonie Espagnole*" (1875), for violin and orchestra, a rhapsody "*Norvegienne*," and many other orchestral works, besides several operas, of which the "*Roi d'Ys*" (1888) is the most important. He received the Cross of the Legion of Honor in 1880, and is one of the best of the French composers. Many of his works have been played by Theodore Thomas.

Georges Bizet (1838-1875) is best known as the composer of "*Carmen*" (1875). He had previously produced a considerable number of smaller works, which had been but moderately successful. In "*Carmen*," however, he showed qualities of rhythmic and harmonic coloration which promised brilliant results in the future. His career was prematurely cut short by death. He was a fine pianist.

The Nestor of still living French composers is M. Charles Ambroise Thomas (1811-), born at Metz in the same year as Liszt, and only one and two years after Schumann and Chopin. This venerable and highly gifted master early succeeded in catching the ear of the French public, and between 1837, when his "*La Double Echelle*" was performed at the *Opéra Comique*, until 1848, he produced a succession of charming light pieces in the taste of the day. There was a sort of middle period in which he wrote several very witty works for the same stage, but the time of his greatest career dates from the production of "*Mignon*" (1866), "*Hamlet*" (1868), and "*Francesca da Rimini*" (1882). He was elected to the Institute in 1851, and at Auber's death in 1871 was made director of the *Conservatoire*, in which important position he has accomplished much toward systematizing and deepening musical education. M. Thomas is a highly cultivated man of the world; tall, slender, fond of physical exercise, he has retained the faculties of an active and very versatile mind to an old age. His opera of "*Mignon*" is probably the one of his productions which will last longest.

Of French opera as a whole during this century, the general characterization may be made that it has gained in cosmopolitan quality, nearly all the composers mentioned in the present chapter having gained a world-wide fame. The distinguishing feature of this class of opera is its sprightly rhythm, and the clearness of the melodic forms. The instrumentation, also, is generally clever. The music is pleasing rather than deep, and the popularity of French opera in Germany, for example, is mainly due to its value as a relief to the often undue elaboration of the original German article.

CHAPTER XXXIX.
LATER COMPOSERS AND PERFORMERS.

BEFORE summing up the remaining names of musical history, a brief retrospect over the present century may be in place. The first quarter of the nineteenth century was distinguished by two composers of the first order—Beethoven and Schubert; and by a large number of highly gifted lesser artists, some of whom, such as Spohr and Weber, bid fair to remain long enrolled in the list of immortals. The second quarter of the century was made memorable by the rise and blossoming into full glory of the romantic school, all the works of this school (excepting a few of the earlier of Mendelssohn) having been produced during this period. Mendelssohn, Schumann, Chopin and the young Wagner were the active spirits of this time, and their productions not only enriched the store of the world's tone poetry, but changed the general direction of musical ideals in many ways.

The great feature of the third quarter of the century was the conception and execution of the Wagnerian music-drama, with its wealth of sense incitation and its somber appeal to accumulated experiences of the race. The "Ring of the Nibelungen" was completed during this period and received its first performance at Bayreuth in 1876. During the same period Franz Liszt had conceived a modification of the symphony form, bringing its four movements into a single one, or uniting the different movements (if such there were) by means of motives common to all or several of them. In this way a certain novelty was attainable in the most important province of instrumental music; and while the new compositions generally acknowledged their indebtedness to external incitation by titles, such as: "What One Sees from a Mountain," the "Battle of the Huns," "Romeo and Juliette," and the like, there was nothing to prevent them being in the fullest sense musical works, having a musical life as such wholly independent of the suggestion given by the title. Berlioz had been the founder of programme music, and his leading works had been produced during the second quarter of the century, but their full force was not recognized until later. It was a follower of Liszt, the brilliant Frenchman, Camille Saint-Saëns, who stated the central thesis of the whole romantic school, when he said that a composer had the same right to affix a title to his work, in order to give a pleasing standpoint for judging it, as a painter had to name his picture. And in the case of music, he added, as in that of painting, the real question finally was not whether the suggestion of the title had been fully satisfied, but whether the picture were good painting and the composition good music. If it were good music, no flaw in the title and no disagreement between the title and the work could impair its value and lasting quality.

When carefully scrutinized, the progress of music during the present century has been governed by certain leading principles which are not contradictory, although at first glance they might appear so. Since the time of the Netherlandish contrapuntists, the primary impulse in musical creation has been the *musical* ideal—the creation of tonal fancies, novel, inspiring, musical, satisfactory. Out of this desire has arisen the entire fabric of fugue, sonata, symphony and the whole world of free music. And at every period there have been those also who sought to connect these tonal fancies with the inner life of the spirit—to awaken feeling, inspire imagination, deepen dramatic impression; in short, to give us in place of irresponsible tonal crystallizations a poetically conceived discourse, operative upon the feelings and stimulative to the entire mind. This was the ideal of the new movement in Italy at the beginning of the seventeenth century, and opera has steadily worked along this ideal. Sebastian Bach had moments when he himself attempted the programme music; and Beethoven made many attempts of the same kind, some of which are significant and lasting. Hence the romantic impulse was not something new in the history of music, but the blossoming of buds from seeds planted long before. The programme music of Berlioz was simply larger and more flamboyant than the little exercises of Bach in the same direction. Wagner's idea of bringing together the entire resources of musical, dramatic and scenic art into a single highly complex work was merely the idea of the unity of all the arts, upon which Æschylus worked two thousand years earlier, and upon which Jacopo Peri and Claudio Monteverde worked at the beginning of the seventeenth century. In short, the art of music, while in this century being enriched by a multitude of new creations representing a variety of subordinate ideals, is nevertheless still a unity, constantly becoming more elaborate and masterly upon the tonal side, and continually more and more in touch with the deeper springs of duration in art, the intuitively realized correspondence between certain art forms and modes of expression and human feeling.

The composers of the last quarter of the century are very numerous; indeed, so numerous that a catalogue even of their names would occupy too much space. Moreover, their proximity to our own times brings them too near for successfully estimating their places in the pantheon of art, or even for the much simpler task of deciding upon certain names which undoubtedly should occupy places in the list. For present purposes it will be more convenient to notice them by nationalities, since every racial stock has certain individualities and ideals which the national composers eventually bring into art, as we see brilliantly illustrated in the case of the Russians, both in music and in painting.

There are, however, certain names which stand out above all others and at the present writing appear destined for place among or very near the immortals of the first order. These great names are those of Johannes Brahms, Camille Saint-Saëns, Peter Ilitsch Tschaikowsky, Antonin Dvorak and Edvard Grieg.

I. Music in Germany.

In Germany, very naturally, the activity in the higher departments of music remains more intense than in any other country, and the seat of musical empire may be said to still abide in southern Germany, where it was established by Haydn, Mozart and Beethoven. The most eminent living composer in the higher department of the art, Johannes Brahms, resides at Vienna since these many years; there also Max Bruch long resided, and there the greatest of the light opera composers, the Strauss family and Von Suppé, have lived and worked. It is in the provinces of the Austro-Hungarian empire, moreover, that the Bohemian composer, Dvorak, has his home.

In Johannes Brahms (1833-) we have still living a musical master of the first order, whose quality as master is shown in his marvelous technique, in which respect no recent composer is to be mentioned as his superior, if any can be named since Bach his equal. This technique was at first personal, at the pianoforte, upon which he was a virtuoso of phenomenal rank; but this renown, great as it is in well informed circles, sinks into insignificance beside his marvelous ability at marshaling musical periods, elaborating together the most dissimilar and apparently incompatible subjects, and his powers of varying a given theme and of unfolding from it ever something new. These wonderful gifts, for such they were rather than laboriously acquired attainments, Brahms showed at the first moment when the light of musical history shines upon him. It was in 1853, when the Hungarian violinist, Edouard Remenyi, found him at Hamburgh and engaged him as accompanist and having ascertained his astonishing talents, brought him, a young man of twenty, to Liszt at Weimar, with his first trio and certain other compositions in manuscript. The new talent made a prodigious effect upon Liszt, who needed not that any one should certify to him whether a composer had genius or merely talent. The Liszt circle took up the Brahms cult in earnest, played the trio at the chamber concerts, and the members when they departed to their homes generally carried with them their admiration of this new personality which had appeared in music.

Johannes Brahms was born at Hamburgh, May 7, 1833, the son of a fine musician who was player upon the double bass in the orchestra there. The boy was always intended for a musician, and his instruction was taken in hand with so much success that at the age of fourteen he played in public pieces by Bach and Beethoven, and a set of original variations. At the age of twenty he was a master, and it was in this year that he accompanied Remenyi, made the acquaintance of Joachim and Liszt, and had a rarely appreciative notice from a master no less than Robert Schumann himself, who in his *New Journal of Music* said:

"He has come, a youth at whose cradle graces and heroes kept watch. Sitting at the piano he began to unveil wonderful regions. We were drawn into more and more magical circles by his playing, full of genius, which made of the piano an orchestra of lamenting and jubilant voices. There were sonatas, or rather veiled symphonies; songs whose poetry might be understood without words; piano pieces both of a demoniac nature and of the most graceful form; sonatas for piano and violin; string quartettes, each so different from every other that they seemed to flow from many different springs. Whenever he bends his magic wand, there, when the powers of the orchestra and chorus lend him their aid, further glimpses of the magic world will be revealed to us. May the highest genius strengthen him! Meanwhile the spirit of modesty dwells within him. His comrades greet him at his first entrance into the world of art, where wounds may perhaps await him, but bay and laurel also; we welcome him as a valiant warrior."

The next few years were spent by Brahms in directing orchestra and chorus at Detmold and elsewhere, and in Switzerland, which has always had great attraction for him. In 1859 he played in Leipsic his first great pianoforte concerto; most of the criticisms thereon were, however, such as now excite mirth. Lately he has played in Leipsic again, conducted several of his works, and was greeted with the reverence and enthusiasm due the greatest living representative of the art of music. In 1862 Brahms located in Vienna, where he has almost ever since resided. Mr. Louis Kestelborn, in "Famous Composers and Their Works," says: "About thirty years ago the writer first saw Brahms in his Swiss home; at that time he was of a rather delicate, slim-looking figure, with a beardless face of ideal expression. Since then he has changed in appearance, until now he looks the very image of health, being stout and muscular, the noble manly face surrounded by a full gray beard. The writer well remembers singing under his direction, watching him conduct orchestra rehearsals, hearing him play alone or with orchestra, listening to an after-dinner speech or private conversation, observing him when attentively listening to other works, and seeing the modest smile with which he accepted, or rather declined, expressions of admiration."

The most important works of Brahms, aside from his "German Requiem," are four symphonies for orchestra, two concertos for pianoforte, a concerto for violin and 'cello with orchestra, a violin concerto, many songs, a variety of compositions for chamber, embracing a number for unusual combinations of instruments (such as clarinet and horn with piano), sonatas for piano solo, etc. In the songs he attains a simple and direct expression, not surpassed in musical quality since Schubert and Schumann; in the concertos he is more for music than for display, which is merely to say that in conceiving the display of his solo instrument, he has sought rather to display it at its best in a musical sense than to exhibit its peculiar tricks of dexterity. As a symphonist he follows classic form, and is more successful than any other writer in the slow movements, a department in which most of the later writers are distinctly weak, since in an idealized folk song (which is the essential ideal of the symphonic slow movement) poverty of imagination cannot be concealed by dexterity of thematic treatment and modulation. As a writer for the pianoforte he has made important enlargements of the technique, not alone in his arrangement of easier compositions by earlier writers, but still more by original demands upon the fingers, as illustrated in his great sets of variations.

Distinguished among German composers is Max Bruch (1838-) who was born at Cologne, and educated there and almost everywhere else in Germany. Bruch is best known by his works for chorus with orchestra, of which "Frithjof," "A Roman Song of Triumph," "The Song of the Three Kings," "Odysseus," "Arminius" are best known. His concerto for violin is also played in all parts of the world, but his opera of "Hermione" made but a moderate success at Berlin in 1872. Riemann considers his greatest works for mixed chorus to be "Odysseus," "Arminius," "The Song of the Bell," and for male chorus "Frithjof," "Salamis" and "The Normans." His style is closely wrought, musical, full of deep and natural musical expression, and well colored instrumentation.

Anton Bruckner (1824-) a highly gifted organist and composer, has written seven symphonies, in which the style is very modern, and shows the influence of the theatrical style of Wagner. He is a composer of considerable vigor.

II. Music in Russia.

The awakening of musical art has been remarkable in all parts of the civilized world, and in many countries not previously distinguished in music composers have arisen who have embodied the rhythms and spirit of the national songs in their works, composed dramatic works upon national subjects, and so have created a national school of music. In some cases the works of these men have proven of world-wide acceptance; in others they have set in operation musical life in their own country, and have been followed quickly by younger composers working in a more cosmopolitan vein, who have created works which have been taken into the current of the world's music and bid fair to hold an honorable position in the pantheon.

MICHAIL IVANOVITCH GLINKA.

One of the most brilliant cases of this kind is Russia, that country so vast, so powerful, so mysterious. The first composer in Russia to distinguish himself and to create a national opera was Michail Ivanovitch Glinka (1803-1877), born near Selna. His first schooling was at the Adelsinstitute in St.

Petersburg, where he distinguished himself in languages. But presently, under the teaching of Bohme upon the violin and Carl Mayer in pianoforte and theory, he showed the musical stuff which was in him. Leaving Russia for his health, he resided four years in Italy, constantly studying and incessantly composing. On his way back to Russia he placed himself for a time under the teaching of the distinguished S. Dehn in Berlin, in theory. Dehn recognized his originality and encouraged him to write "Russian" music. His first opera, "A Life for the Czar" (December 9, 1836), was a great triumph. The subject was national, the contrast between Polish and Russian subjects in the music was brilliant, and actual or simulated folk songs gave a local coloring highly grateful to the Russian audience. The work received innumerable repetitions and still remains one of the most popular operatic works upon the Russian stage. His next work, "Ruslan and Ludmilla," was also successful, and Liszt, who happened to be in Russia at the moment of its production, accorded the young composer distinguished praise. Berlioz took up the pen in honor of Glinka and of his new Russian school of music, and so the composer's powers were widely celebrated. During the remainder of his life Glinka made long residences in the south, especially in Spain, and several orchestral works, with Spanish coloring, represent this portion of his creative career. His last years were spent in rural life near St. Petersburgh, busy with new opera projects, and especially seeking some rational manner of harmonizing the Russian popular songs. Riemann calls Glinka "the Berlioz of Russia," in the originality of his invention and his clever technique; and something more, namely, that he created a national school of music for his country. The list of his works is very long, embracing compositions in almost every province. There are two symphonies, both unfinished, several dances for orchestra, a number of chamber compositions of various combinations of instruments, a tarantella for orchestra, with song and dance ("*La Kamarinskaia*"), etc. His operas, however, are his lasting monument.

ANTON VON RUBINSTEIN.

The next great name in the roll of Russian music is that of the pianist, Anton von Rubinstein (1830-1895), who was born at Wechwotynez, in Bessarabia. His father presently removed to Moscow, where he carried on a manufactory of lead pencils. The boy Anton showed such talent for music under the skillful and affectionate teaching of his mother, that at the age of ten he was brought before various musical authorities in Paris for opinions concerning his talent. His concert life began almost immediately from this period. His mother went with him, and wherever there were pauses of a few days the studies were resumed, exactly as had been the case with Mozart, long before. In 1848 he found a friend and appreciative companion in the Princess Helene, and then he wrote several operas upon Russian subjects, of which two were published—"Dimitri Donskoi" and "Toms der Narr." The success of these works was such that in 1854 the composer was given a subvention for further foreign study by the Princess Helene and Count Wielhorski, upon which followed four brilliant years of incessant activity as virtuoso pianist and composer, extending as far as London and Paris. Rubinstein had already lived some years in Berlin, where he was as well known as at home. Returning to Russia in 1859, he received important appointments as musical director, founded the St. Petersburg musical conservatory, of which he remained the director until 1867, when ensued a new series of concert journeys covering Europe, and in 1872-1873 extending to America, where he had a wonderful success, carrying back to

Russia as proceeds of the American tour the at that time unprecedented sum of $54,000.

As pianist, Rubinstein was distinguished for his grand style, broad and noble mastery of the instrument, and his consummate sympathy and innate musical quality. He was a player of moods, at times playing like a god, at other times his work disfigured by many errors, but always interesting, commanding and noble. He played best the compositions of Beethoven and Schumann, their innate depth and intense musical expression appealing to his richly gifted musical nature irresistibly. His personality was commanding and attractive. Saint-Saëns relates how Rubinstein played in Paris the concertos of Beethoven and of Rubinstein, while Saint-Saëns conducted the orchestra. At the close of the concerts Rubinstein desired to give yet another in which he himself would direct the orchestra, while Saint-Saëns should play. It was for this occasion that the Saint-Saëns second concerto was written. In his later life Rubinstein lived like a prince in a beautiful estate near St. Petersburgh. The list of his works is something enormous. Of operas and dramatic works there are twelve, several of which, such as "The Tower of Babel," "Paradise Lost" and "Moses," are biblical operas, a type of dramatico mystical work created by Rubinstein. It contains the gravity and depth of oratorio combined with the intense realism of the stage. There are six symphonies, of which the famous and several times enlarged "Ocean" symphony is perhaps best known, a "Heroic Fantasia" for orchestra, three character pieces for orchestra, "Faust," "Don Quixote" and "Ivan"; three concert overtures, a quantity of chamber music, compositions for piano, songs, and the like. In everything of Rubinstein beautiful melodies are found; his weakness lies in the development, which occasionally is carried too far, and with insufficient vitality of thematic work.

PETER ILITSCH TSCHAIKOWSKY.

Even greater than Rubinstein as composer was the brilliant Peter Ilitsch Tschaikowsky (1840-1893). Tschaikowsky was intended for the profession of the law, in which he took his degree. But his love for music asserted itself, and after a short career as pupil in the St. Petersburgh conservatory, he was appointed teacher of harmony in that institution, and entered upon his career as composer. Here he remained but a short time, resigning in 1877, after which he lived by turns at St. Petersburgh, in Italy and in Switzerland. Tschaikowsky was of a lyric musical nature, and in his early life his taste was entirely for Italian music. This shows to a remarkable degree in all his earlier productions, even if he had not himself published the fact so often and unmistakably. In 1869 he produced his first Russian opera, "Der Woiwode" which was followed by eight others, of which the best known are "Eugene Onegin" and "Makula, the Smith." Several of these are now played throughout Europe. It was in his orchestral compositions, however, that Tschaikowsky most illustrated his unexampled powers. Besides a number of brilliant and highly sensational overtures, he composed six symphonies, of unexampled sonority, rich coloring and strange musical expression. The fifth symphony of Tschaikowsky met with almost universal recognition at the hands of the leading orchestral conductors of the world; and the last, the so-called "Tragic," only deepened the impression of the composer's powers. Several points are unusual. The themes themselves are original, forceful and lend themselves easily to elaboration. The harmonic treatment is highly original, as if the author had found, as Bülow said, "new harmonic paths." The instrumentation is richly colored and the climaxes are of vast power and effect. The whole is a grandly composed tone poem which even if regarded as surpassing the proper reserve of symphonic form must nevertheless be counted as one of the most valuable enrichments of the world's orchestral repertory. In several places in his works Tschaikowsky introduces peculiarities of Russian folk music, as for example in the movement in 5-4 measure in the fifth measure symphony. Nevertheless, the works belong to the world's music, being in no sense provincial, narrow or limited. Æsthetically considered, they illustrate the quick technique and over-mastering energy of the race to which the composer belonged.

III. Music in Bohemia.

Another country in which a notable musical revival has taken place during the latter part of the present century is Bohemia, where two names are to be mentioned. Bedrich Smetana (1824-1884), is to be remembered as the creator, or at least the awakener, of Bohemian music. After a short education at the Prague university Smetana entered diligently upon the study of music, becoming a brilliant pianist, and as such forming one of the circle of enthusiastic and advancing souls surrounding Liszt at Weimar, between 1850 and 1860. His first position as musical director was at Gothenberg, 1856. Here he lost his wife, the brilliant pianist Katharina Kolar. In 1861 he made a long concert tour to Sweden. In 1866 he was appointed director of the music at the national theater in Prague, a position which he held until obliged to give it up on account of loss of hearing in 1874. Smetana wrote eight operas upon Bohemian subjects, with music in the Bohemian spirit; one best known is "The Bartered Bride," which was the last composed. He also wrote about ten symphonies or symphonic poems, and a great variety of chamber music. Of his symphonic poems those most often played are: "In Wallenstein's Camp," "Moldau," "Sarka" and "Visegrad." In all these the titles are mainly suggestive, although in "Sarka" a programme is quite closely followed. Smetana was a brilliant composer, but his value lies in his awakening of the Bohemians to musical creation.

BEDRICH SMETANA.

ANTON DVORAK.

The most brilliant name in Bohemian music, and the one most valued by the world in general, is that of Anton Dvorak (1841-), who was the son of a butcher at Mulhausen. The boy early applied himself to the violin, and after some years' playing in small orchestras, found a place as violinist in the orchestra of the National theater at Prague. This was at the age of nineteen. About ten years later he first attracted attention as composer, by means of a hymn for mixed chorus and orchestra. The attention of his countrymen, thus gained, Dvorak fastened still more by a succession of compositions of varied scope, ranging from the Slavic dances and Slavic rhapsodies to symphonies, chamber music and choral works of great brilliancy. In 1892 Dr. Dvorak was called to New York as director of the so-called National Conservatory of Music. In 1895 he returned to Bohemia. The choral works of Dvorak were generally first written for English musical festivals. "The Specter's Bride," "Stabat Mater," "Saint Ludmilla." The list of his works includes five symphonies for full orchestra, several concert overtures, a very beautiful air and variations for orchestra, and seven operas upon Bohemian subjects. Dvorak is one of the most gifted composers of the present time, especially in the matter of technique. His thematic treatment is always clever, his orchestral coloring rich and varied, and his style elegant. If deficiency is to be recorded concerning him it is in invention or innate weight of ideas. During his residence in America he promulgated the idea that an American school of music was to be created by developing the themes and rhythms of the negro melodies, and he wrote a symphony, "From the New World," in order to illustrate his meaning. The second or slow movement of this work attained a distinguished success almost everywhere; but the themes of the first and last movement are not sufficient for the treatment they receive. This work has been more successful in Europe than in this country. Perhaps the most notable quality of Dr. Dvorak's personality is his naiveté, which shows well in his music. He is quite like a modern Haydn, who has learned and remembered everything of musical coloration which has been discovered, but who applies his knowledge in a simple and direct manner without straining after effect.

IV. Music in Scandinavia.

EDVARD HAGERUP GRIEG.

Foremost of Scandinavian composers is Edvard Hagerup Grieg (1843-), who was born at Bergen, Norway, and received his early musical education from his mother, who was an excellent pianist, and very musical. By the advice of the celebrated violinist, Ole Bull, Grieg was sent in 1858 to Leipsic for further instruction, where he became a pupil of Moscheles, Hauptmann, Reinecke, Richter and Wenzel. In 1863 he pursued further studies under Gade at Copenhagen. In companionship with a talented young composer, Ricard Nordraak, Grieg set himself, as he says, "against the faded Scandinavianism of Gade and Mendelssohn intermingled, and undertook to put into tones the real beauty, strength and inner spirit of the northern folks-life." He composed in many varieties of work, and in 1879 attained German recognition by playing his own piano concerto at the Gewandhaus in Leipsic. Grieg's works are full of poetry, easy and natural expression, and are pervaded by northern coloring, so decided as in some cases to approach what in speech is called dialect. Nevertheless, it is indubitable that his music has distinctly enriched the world's stream of tone-poetry, and introduced a new accent and voice. He has distinguished himself in almost every department, in songs, choral work, chamber music, symphonies, sonatas for piano and piano and violin, and orchestral suites, of which perhaps his two "Peer Gynt" are the most celebrated. In person Grieg is slight, fair-haired, with lovely deep blue eyes and a charming manner. He is subject to pulmonary weakness, and is compelled to reside much of his time in warmer climates than those of his native land.

Niels W. Gade

An older composer than Grieg is Niels Wilhelm Gade (1817-1890), of Copenhagen, who after a thorough musical education received in his native city, attracted wider attention in 1841 by taking the prize for his concert overture, "Night Sounds from Ossian," the judges being Fr. Schneider and Spohr, the violinist. This gave Gade a royal stipendium, with which he immediately betook himself to study at Leipsic, where he came under the personal influence of Mendelssohn, an influence which he never outgrew. At the death of Mendelssohn he was appointed director of the

Gewandhaus, but not proving in all respects satisfactory he held the position only a part of one season. After the death of Gläser in 1861, Gade was made royal music director at Copenhagen, a position which he filled many years. He was active as composer in every direction, his published works embracing eight symphonies, five overtures, two concertos for violin and orchestra, three violin sonatas, several cantatas for mixed voices, soli and orchestra, and many other works. The ultimate judgment of Gade as a tone-poet is likely to be that while distinctly talented, he never attained imagination of the first order.

Among the younger composers Christian Sinding (1856-) is to be mentioned. Besides many works for chamber, he has written one symphony, which while not very original gives promise of better productions later.

V. MUSIC IN ENGLAND.

The relation of England to the higher art of music has been peculiar. In the sixteenth century and earlier it was one of the most musical countries in Europe; but from the appearance of Händel, about 1720, German music and German composers absorbed public attention to the exclusion of the natives—no one of whom, it may be added, evinced creative powers of any high order. England was a liberal patron of all the leading German masters, from Haydn, who wrote twelve symphonies for the London Philharmonic, to Beethoven, whose ninth symphony was written for the same society; Mendelssohn, whose "Elijah," was written for the Birmingham festival, and Wagner, who received handsome compensation for conducting a series of concerts in London. A little past the middle of the present century, however, more creative activity began to show itself among English composers, until at the present time there are excellent English composers in all the leading departments of musical production. The more celebrated names follow.

One of the most graceful and talented of English composers was Sir William Sterndale Bennett (1816-1875), who came of a musical stock, and was duly trained as a choir boy in King's Chapel, and at the Royal Academy of Music. In 1836 he went to Leipsic, in order to profit by the Gewandhaus concerts there and the friendship of Mendelssohn. Here he produced a number of orchestral compositions which were so highly esteemed that in 1853 the directorship of the Gewandhaus concerts was offered him. After a short sojourn at Leipsic he returned to London, where he ever after lived, highly honored as composer, pianist, teacher and man. In 1856 he became the conductor of the London Philharmonic concerts, and in 1866 principal of the Royal Academy of Music. He was knighted in 1871, having previously been honored by degrees from Cambridge and Oxford. He was professor of music in Cambridge University from 1856 until his death. As a composer Bennett was influenced by Mendelssohn, but he had much delicacy of fancy and a certain originality of his own. His compositions embrace four concertos for piano and orchestra, several concert overtures for orchestra, one symphony, much chamber music, a cantata, "The May Queen" (1858), "The Woman of Samaria" (1867), and a number of occasional odes, anthems and part songs.

The successor of Sterndale Bennett as principal of the Royal Academy of Music was Sir George A. Macfarren (1813-1887), who although totally blind for many years before his death, produced a greater number of important compositions than any other English composer of the century.

He was educated in London, and in 1834 became one of the professors in the Royal Academy of Music. His first opera was produced in 1838, "Devil's Opera," "Don Quixote" (1836), "Jessy Lea" (1863) and "Helvellyn" (1864). He wrote a number of cantatas for chorus and orchestra, oratorios, "St. John the Baptist" (1873), "The Resurrection" (1876), "Joseph" (1877), and other works of less importance. There are also many anthems, several overtures and other pieces for chamber. Personally he was kind-hearted, intelligent, helpful and public spirited. The amount of work that he accomplished under the greatest of disadvantages is wonderful, as well as its generally superior quality. As a lecturer and teacher he was the foremost musical Englishman of his time. His compositions are strong and respectable, but not especially inspired.

The successor of Sir Geo. Macfarren in the principalship of the Royal Academy of Music was Alexander Campbell Mackenzie (1847-), the youngest eminent English composer, but also the most successful and promising. He was educated as a violinist, and resided at Edinburgh as a teacher of the pianoforte and violin until his compositions attracted the attention of his countrymen and induced his being called to London. The most important compositions of Dr. Mackenzie up to the present time are the operas "Colomba" (1883), "The Troubadour" (1886) and the oratorio "The Rose of Sharon" (1884). There are several cantatas, "Jason," "The Bride," "The Story of Sayid" (1886) and a considerable number of orchestral pieces, of which two Scotch rhapsodies and the overture to "Twelfth Night" are the best known. He has also produced a violin concerto (played by Mr. Sarasate), and much chamber music and songs. On the whole, Dr. Mackenzie seems the most gifted English composer who has yet appeared.